The Lawrence Watt-Evans Fantasy MEGAPACK®

The Lawrence Watt-Evans Fantasy MEGAPACK®

LAWRENCE WATT-EVANS

WILDSIDE PRESS

CONTENTS

AUTHOR'S INTRODUCTION

One of the problems in writing short stories is that they wind up scattered across a variety of venues, which makes it hard for readers to find them. The stories here were published in an assortment of anthologies and magazines and chapbooks over a period of more than thirty years; up until now I doubt anyone outside my immediate family has read all of them.

Oh, some have been reprinted multiple times, but most haven't seen the light of day in decades. It's nice to have them collected in one place, where readers can *find* them!

They're all fantasy, from old-fashioned sword-and-sorcery to a Christmas story; you'll find werewolves, elves, dragons, and wizards.

All of these are stories that have not appeared in any of my previous collections. That's a large part of why this is specifically a *fantasy* collection. You won't find any science fiction, horror, vampire stories, or tales of Ethshar—those have already been published in previous collections. (Well, mostly; there are a few more science fiction stories that haven't been collected yet.) You won't see any collaborations or licensed properties; it wasn't worth the legal hassles. I also kept out a couple of stories about the monster-hunting librarian George Pinkerton because I hope to eventually collect that whole series in its own volume. And there's one story called "Sit!" that doesn't seem to fit anywhere, including here, so it will probably never be reprinted.

But what you *do* have here is all the rest of the short fantasy I've had published. And some of it, if I do say so myself, is pretty darn good.

When I was going through my files to assemble this volume I discovered that I had several of these stories in multiple versions; in those cases I tried to use whichever version had been published originally. I may have gotten that wrong once or twice.

Whatever their history, I hope you like them.

—Lawrence Watt-Evans
Takoma Park, 2017

THE TEMPLE OF LIFE

Few ships came to Avitaine any more and the docks at which the *Broken Stone* made its mooring were deserted and rotting. This was one reason for choosing them, as Elihaniku had no particular desire to attract attention. One could never be sure how far away his enemies would look before giving up the chase, and the distance put behind him so far was not as great as he might have wished.

And as Merek, his captain, reminded him, there are no mooring fees at abandoned piers.

In keeping with Elihaniku's policy of caution, no one left the ship until nightfall; even then, half the crew was kept on board in case a hasty departure became advisable. The others, including Elihaniku and his mysterious companion the Pad, but not Merek, dispersed quickly into the dark, empty streets in search of congenial company.

To Merek's astonishment, within the hour many had returned, and each in his turn told the same tale. Not a single tavern, inn, or brothel was to be found open; all were unlit, windows shuttered and doors barred. No one had seen so much as a single person on the streets. Some ventured to guess that the city was haunted, or cursed, or that a plague was loose; all were eager to depart as soon as possible.

These stories made Merek himself most uneasy, but he knew that an immediate departure was out of the question. This stop was no mere pleasure visit; the ship's stores were dangerously low, her water nearly exhausted. Both had to be replenished before she could sail again. This was of the most especial importance since the next voyage planned would be a very, very long one; Elihaniku had decreed that the *Broken Stone* was to sail for the legendary Land of the Sun, in the Ultimate East, and Elihaniku owned the ship. Merek suspected that the noble love of adventure that the old man boasted of to the crew was so much nonsense, and that the ancient coward simply wanted to reach someplace so distant that none of his pursuers, not even the Dark King of Nathmar, would follow. Not that the captain didn't sympathize; he hoped that when – and if! – he ever reached Elihaniku's age he would not have one-tenth the enemies that the Chronan did. There were times when it seemed that all the world save Merek and the Pad was allied against the old thief, and Merek's loyalty was a direct result of the fact that he somehow always had ready gold with which to pay his captain.

Merek mulled over the situation as the night wore on; as dawn approached, he realized that all his crew had been back for a hour or more, but that no word had come from his employer or the Pad.

He began to worry with the first greying of the eastern sky, and by full daylight he was equipping a landing party to scour the city.

These preparations ceased suddenly, however, when the Pad strolled out of an alleyway as though nothing out of the ordinary had happened. Merek knew better than to talk to the Pad; in fact, most of the crew thought the odd little man was mute. Only in complete privacy would he speak, and then only to a chosen few. Merek had just recently become one of those few. Still, the captain was of by the Pad's nonchalance, and beckoned him to his cabin. With a casual nod, he complied.

The instant the door swung to behind them, the Pad's manner changed completely. He spun on his heel, and locked and barred the door. He peered out the stern window, and seeing no one, drew tight the curtains. Merek was astonished to see him sweating, his hands trembling, for the Pad rarely displayed any emotion other than suspicion; yet now he was frightened, and that simple fact seemed somehow much more ominous than any number of scared sailors or shuttered taverns.

The two men seated themselves at the captain's rough oaken table, and the Pad spoke in his customary harsh whisper. "The old man's a prisoner. A wizard, Garl, runs the place, and don't like visitors."

"Why did he take Elihaniku and no one else?"

"We went near his palace, others didn't. Didn't see me."

Merek knew quite well that when the Pad chose not to be seen, he wasn't. When the captain first met his employers they were the most successful thieves in Feltharucesh, largely because of the Pad's stealth. The little man could move in almost complete silence, and vanish with startling speed.

"How did Garl capture him?"

"Bats."

There the conversation ended; the Pad had said his piece, and no coaxing from Merek could get more out of him. Merek knew better than to try very hard; he knew everything he needed to know, except what to do next.

After due consideration he decided upon a fairly direct course of action; he would find a talkative native, find out what he could, and try to get into the palace to free the old Chronan.

Thus it was that two strangers settled in the Crimson Peacock for dinner; the taverns were open from sunrise to sunset, but not a moment longer.

The big man talked and sang, and in general made himself congenial company, while the other said not a word and kept his hand always near the hilt of his dagger. It was not long before someone told them the tale of the young king of Avitaine's unhappy wedding day two years earlier, when their rightful ruler and his new bride, during their nuptial ceremony, entered the Temple of Life never to be seen again; the wizard Garl had sealed the building up, and made himself master of the island during the consequent confusion.

This story was followed by countless anecdotes of the cruelty of their new overlord.

Upon hearing these tales, Merek grew less and less cheerful; how could they hope to free Elihaniku from such a fiend? And how were they to resupply the ship, when Garl kept close watch on all commerce and had forbidden foreign trade? The longer Merek listened, the more convinced he became that it was little short of miraculous that most of the ship's company still remained unharmed and apparently undetected.

As if summoned by these dreary thoughts, a man burst into the tavern, crying, "Garl has found a strange ship in the harbor, and even now he is freezing it!"

Merek joined the crowd that rushed out into the street and down toward the docks where the *Broken Stone* lay at anchor; to his horror, he saw that despite the mild spring weather ice clung to his ship's sails, and grew visibly as he watched. The sailors on the decks were utterly still, as if instantly frozen, and stood in grotesque postures on the whitening planking. As the tavern crowd stood helplessly by, the ice grew and spread until at last the entire vessel was sealed in a vast block of crystal, glittering diamondlike in the sun.

Severely shaken, Merek returned to the Crimson Peacock, where the Pad still sat. He described what he had just seen, but of course received no reply. The Pad sat in total silence, and seemed to be thinking intently. Abruptly he rose, and made as if to leave. Merek rose to follow, but was motioned back to his seat. He complied, and the Pad vanished through the door.

Perhaps an hour later Merek sat staring at his fifteenth beer, wishing the alcohol would affect him, when the Pad slipped in as silently as he had left. He motioned to Merek, and the two strolled casually out into the street.

At the mouth of an alleyway nearby, the Pad vanished, and Merek was jerked roughly back into the shadows. When his eyes had adjusted to the gloom he found himself again facing his companion, who whispered quickly, "Spoke to the old man through the window; you get Garl to the temple by sunset."

Before Merek could reply the Pad had disappeared again, and this time he did not return.

The Pad moved easily through the alleys and byways of Avitaine, and came without incident to the end of an alley which opened onto the great square in front of the Temple of Life. Here he paused to inspect the building. Hewn of solid marble, it gleamed in the afternoon sun. The Pad could see gargoyles with Gail's face perched, leering evilly, upon door, frame, and eaves, where the wizard's magic had installed them two years earlier.

Seeing no means of entry he slipped back into the shadows, and stole silently around the north side of the temple, which proved to be completely blank and featureless; the south side was likewise unadorned. The east end, however, was joined to the house where the temple priests dwelt; the Pad decided that this deserved a closer look.

The windows of the priests' house were unbarred, and within a very few minutes the Pad stood silently in an upstairs room, every sense alert. When he detected no movement nor any indication that his presence had been noticed, he crept with the utmost stealth to the back of the house, and began a systematic search of the unoccupied rooms for any entrance to the temple proper. After considerable exploration, he was forced to admit to himself that there was only one door linking the house to the temple, and that was in the main hallway, where three solemn robed figures stood talking quietly. It was clearly beyond even his consummate skill to slip by this trio unnoticed.

Desperate now, for the plan, if it was to be successful, must be carried out by sundown, the Pad picked up a nearby candelabrum and hurled it across the hall to a chamber opposite, where it struck the floor with an alarming crash and clatter.

The three priests abruptly ceased their conversation and turned toward the noise; as they hurried into the empty room to investigate, the Pad slipped by and hurried to the door. Breathing a silent sigh of relief he grasped the handle and pulled.

It was locked.

After the Pad left, Merek wasted no time in returning to the tavern, where he finished his fifteenth beer and three more as well, to strengthen his nerve. Thus fortified, he set out boldly for the palace; as the drinks at last began to make themselves felt, he began swaggering. By the time he reached the palace gate, he was boasting and singing, and the appearance of two cloaked guards failed to disturb him until they grabbed him by the arms and proceeded to drag him through the entrance to the royal courtyard.

He was led unceremoniously to the Great Hall, and tossed on his face before the throne. He scrambled to his knees, lifting his gaze slowly to the bedizened figure of Garl, who sat brooding over him. The wizard shone with an unearthly dark fire, towering from his throne; he was inhumanly tall with a gaunt, drawn visage, and glared down at the besotted seafarer as a pagan idol might regard an insect that had had the effrontery to walk across his altar. His voice rolled forth like the boom of a great drum, resounding from the tapestried walls.

"Who are you, and what do you mean brawling about my city?"

"I am Mcrek sen Ermi, merchant and mercenary of Feltharucash in the Sealands, and captain of the caravel *Broken Stone*. How is it your mightiness need ask? Are you not a great wizard, with all knowledge at your fingertips?"

"You speak insolently, Merek sen Ermi; are you perhaps weary of life? I am in truth a mighty wizard, and it is dangerous to doubt it; but I have better uses for my art than to waste my time keeping track of such scum as you."

"Indeed? What else has such a piddling overlord to do? You rule nothing but a small island, and a city, by your words, of scum; does this befit a mighty wizard?"

"You talk boldly indeed, and I suspect it is mostly liquor speaking, and not your better judgment. Know that I am master of all the arcane arts, and in my mastery choose to devote but a tiny portion of my time to statecraft."

"Ah, so you have mastered all arts! Then tell me, O great Garl, why do you bother with such trash as myself? Why do you argue with me, when here in your own city is a much greater foe? Why, I venture that even I could best you at the art of swordcraft, and there can be no doubt that there is in your city one who you concede to be your superior in many things."

"Who is this foe you speak of, then? Why has he not challenged my rule?"

"Because you have imprisoned him by trickery, of course, being afraid to face him openly. I speak of Avitaine's rightful king, and the Spirit of Life that anoints him King." Merek had no idea if the King was really in any way Garl's better, or even if he still lived, but the Pad had said to bring the wizard to the temple, and Merek, in his drunken bravado, thought this the moat expedient way.

He was quite correct. Unfortunately, he had also spoken a boast that could well bring his own death.

"Perhaps, fool, there is some sense in what you say. It is time that I made plain my mastery over this absurd Spirit, and completed the task I began two years ago. First, though, I would answer a challenge you have made. You ventured that you could best me at swordplay; would you then be so good as to support your claim?"

Merek's alcoholic courage abruptly vanished. He was a fair swordsman, but surely no match for a wizard. He sought to delay. "Very well, but as the challenged, I claim the right to choose time and place."

"Granted, if they be in the city and ere dawn."

That demolished any hope of significant delay, and Merek, placing his faith in the Pad's mysterious plan, said, "Then I choose the temple steps at sunset."

"Done. My men shall assist you."

Merek found himself escorted roughly from the room. As he was led to a cell to await evening, he consoled himself with the thought that he had obeyed the Pad's instructions – and it rather appeared that it would cost him his life.

Meanwhile, the Pad had found no means of escape, and confronted the three priests in a fighter's stance, dagger in hand.

"Who are you that enter here unbidden? Do you come from Garl?"

The Pad made no answer, but straightened a bit. Had he perhaps assumed too quickly that these holy men were his enemies? The priest's tone held no love for his sorcerous overlord.

"Answer us, man. We shall not harm you. We are not armed."

Still slightly suspicious, the Pad sheathed his dagger.

"Why do you not speak? Have you no tongue?"

The Pad made a motion with his head which the priests took as confirmation. They looked at one another.

"Surely Garl would not send a mute!"

"Are you from Garl?"

The Pad shook his head vigorously.

"Are you perhaps a thief, then?"

Again, no.

"Then what do you here?"

The Pad motioned toward the temple door.

"What would you in the temple?"

"Do you not know that Garl has sealed it?"

"Even we are no longer admitted; it is Garl's punishment to us that we live ever near the temple unable to enter."

The Pad looked at them quizzically. Then he drew his dagger again and stepped to the door.

The priests crowded around him and watched in amazement as he drew an assortment of curious implements from a pouch on his belt. First, he wedged the dagger into the crack as far as it would go, so that the door would spring open when the lock released, and also so that the cold iron would interfere with the magical seal. Next he produced a succession of lockpicks, and tried each in turn until a deep, satisfying click was heard. Thus encouraged, he tried the door, which still refused to budge. He reached again into his pouch, and when his hand emerged it held a gleaming silver talisman in the shape of a key that bore the stamp of the Thieves' Guild of Thalasme. This was one of his most prized possessions, and had brought him many a rare treasure from magically-sealed vaults – which had cost many a magician his job. It glittered brightly in his hand and he gazed at it silently for a moment. Then, with carefully-learned gestures taught him by his father, he directed it at the door and to the astonishment of the priests intoned a slow, deep chant.

He concluded the chant with no visible effect, but now the priests were praying, a chant of their own, calling for the omnipotent Spirit to aid this little house-breaker. The Pad did not interrupt; who could better assist him in entering the Spirit's own temple?

The prayer droned on, and just as the Pad's hopes began to fade, a shiver ran through the heavy door. With a sudden snap it sprang open, and his dagger clattered to the floor. He snatched up his weapon and sped through the opening; the priests, with a cry of joy, followed him.

Inside, a spiral staircase led up to a balcony; from there, the Pad could see the entire interior of the temple. It was a single great room, stretching out a hundred yards before him, dim and grey with incense, which hung in curiously motionless clouds about him. Candles burned with an oddly steady flame along the walls, and bright carpets lined the floor.

On one of these carpets knelt a handsome young couple, completely motionless, apparently praying.

The Pad stopped abruptly; how could there be living people in here? The temple had been sealed since Garl's usurpation two years earlier; no one could have entered, and surely the King and his bride must have starved to death long ago!

Or had they? Perhaps one could not starve in the Temple of Life; the Pad had heard that said, but always took it to refer to the famous munificence of the priests toward the poor. Could it be that the saying had a more literal significance?

Carefully, he stepped down from the balcony, and moved toward the worshippers. They were richly dressed and wore coronets, and they took no note of his approach. The Pad began to suspect that the temple was as frozen as the *Broken Stone*, save only that no ice and cold were manifest here.

The deathly silence was broken abruptly from behind, and the Pad whirled to see the priests on the balcony beginning a solemn chant. Ignoring them, he turned back to the west, and moved swiftly past the kneeling pair to the great golden doors. As he neared them, he fancied he could hear the sounds of an excited crowd outside, and he remembered his instructions to the captain.

M erek stood terrified on the steps of the Temple of Life, sword in hand, as the wizard took a few practice swings at the air. The crowd muttered about him, and the catcalls were heard directed at both sides.

Merek suddenly found himself propelled forward, his sword-arm raised, and heard the wizard speak.

"Well, captain, you seem less eager for combat now. Come, cheer up! I'll even let you have the first blow. Go ahead; let the battle begin!"

Summoning his nerve, Merek swung powerfully, and to his amazement saw his blade strike home – and glance off the sorcerer's bare neck.

The necromancer laughed. "Fool! Now you see part of my mastery! Where other men suffer and die, I cannot! I am immortal!" Then there was no time for words, as swords met and clashed.

The battle raged, Merek taking only defensive measures; what profit lay in striking at impervious flesh? He chose instead to simply try and prolong the battle, and therefore his life, as long as possible. Small wounds soon appeared on his arms and forehead, and as blood obscured his vision he gave ground and silently began his death-prayer.

I nside the temple, the Pad tugged at the golden portals; they had neither handle not lock, and seemed free to move, yet utterly refused to do so. The priests' chant droned on until all the temple seemed to ring with it. It echoed and throbbed and became impossibly loud, making the Pad's head swim. Then one candle seemed to flicker; then another, and the clouds of incense swirled sluggishly. The king stirred slightly, and now, untouched, the doors that had yielded not at all to the Pad's strength began to inch inward.

* * * *

Merek was trapped; there was nowhere he could run, for the crowd encircled the steps. He backed against the wall of the shrine, his blade desperately parrying the wizard's blows.

A movement at the corner of his eye caught his attention, while his body automatically continued to fight. Yes, it was true! The temple doors were opening! The instant he saw a gap in the web of steel that his opponent wove about him he dove through it, and through the widening space between the great gold valves.

With a cry, the wizard followed, and though none saw the blow, all saw the robed figure falter, then collapse forward, to lie motionless with the hilt of the Pad's dagger protruding from his back.

Merek dropped his unbloodied sword and staggered out again into the fading dusk, and immediately behind him came a wondering young king and his beautiful bride. A stunned silence fell upon the crowd, quickly broken by a shout that grew into a roar of acclamation.

As the royal couple were borne away by the cheering crowd, Merek and the Pad remained standing over the strangely unimpressive corpse of the dead necromancer. With a grimace, the smaller man bent and pulled his dagger free, muttering, "sixteen." He wiped his blade and sheathed it, as a priest joined them.

"I don't understand," declared Merek, puzzling over the wizard's body. "He was invulnerable."

"No," said the priest softly. "He had reversed nature, so that he was invulnerable where other men are not; but here in the Temple of Life, no ordinary man can suffer or die. Thus it was here alone that he could be slain. That is why his first action was to seal it; he knew it held the power to destroy him."

Merek gazed at the priest for several minutes, but made no answer.

Four days later the *Broken Stone* set sail, a good wind to her back and her holds full with supplies that were the gift of a grateful monarch. The ice had melted quickly in the sun and had left the crew unharmed; Elihaniku was free once more, at his accustomed place on the poop.

Merek was pleased to be at sea again, and almost completely recovered from his fight, but one question remained to trouble him. When he was sure that the sails were properly set and the helmsman sure of his course, he asked Elihaniku, "Old man, you were imprisoned from the first; how did you know what the Pad and I should do?"

Elihaniku paused before answering, then said, "Does it not seem to you that such a vast temple must have more than three priests?"

"I had not thought of it."

"Ah! You should think of everything."

"Forgive me, old man, but I cannot. How does a lack of priests account for your knowledge?"

"Have you no wit at all? There was a priest imprisoned in the next cell who told me all. And better company than I have here, he was!"

Leaning on the rail beside them, the Pad grinned.

MEHITABEL GOODWIN

In the Year of Grace 1689, in the town of Berwick, in the County of York, in the Province of Maine, in the Colony of Massachusetts, Thomas and Mehitabel Goodwin were fully four years wed, and yet their first child was still an infant. God had not hurried to bless their union.

That made the babe all the more precious to them, of course. That which is easiest in the getting is esteemed least.

And by that standard, Mehitabel believed that surely every good thing in her life was dear beyond reckoning, for life in the New World was not easy.

Her father and elder brother had been slain by the Indians in King Philip's War when she was a girl, and she and her mother and her surviving brother Ichabod had all lived for years in fear of the Indians' return—but the Indians had not troubled the town since. Mehitabel had grown strong and comely, and ten years after her father's death she had gone happily to Thomas Goodwin's home, her fears forgotten.

The soil was poor and rocky, hard to plow and yielding its fruits reluctantly—but Mehitabel and Thomas worked the land patiently, and in time the crops came, augmented by the game Thomas took in his hunting.

The winters were long and cold, but Thomas had built their home sound and snug, and Mehitabel kept the fire well.

And because she had lost her father and brother, Mehitabel loved Thomas the more; because the land was hard, the fruits were sweet; because the winters were harsh, the warmth of the hearth was all the more welcome.

And because he had been so long in arrival, Mehitabel thought all the world revolved about her blessed Roger, that in all the history of the world only holy Mary herself had had a finer babe.

It was for that reason that she would not leave him in the house while she worked in the field, scraping weeds and stones from the soil, inspecting the vines for any sign of blight or rot. Instead, she kept him on her arm, placing him carefully on the ground when the task to be performed called for both hands.

He was not yet crawling, though he would be soon, so she had no fear that he might wander off while she worked. He would stare up at her, or at the sky or the surrounding plants, with oh, such a serious expression, and then he would smile and gurgle and wave his arms about in the delight of being alive.

And she would smile back at him, set her hoe aside and tickle his chin.

She had just done that, kneeling beside him and asking, "Whose little blessing are you?" when a shadow fell across his face.

She looked up, startled. She had heard tales of eagles carrying off infants, and though she did not fully believe such tales, and had not seen an eagle in years, her first thought was to look to the sky.

The sky above was blue and almost cloudless, without a bird in sight—but a man stood before her, and it was his shadow that had darkened her baby's face.

He was clad in soft undyed deerskin from neck to toe, decorated with beads and bits of shell; his head was bare, with no decent hat to shield him from the sun, and his face was brown. His hair was black and coarse, not the soft brown or blond of an Englishman. His nose was crooked.

The Indians had returned.

Any thought she might have had that this might be a party come to parley, or to trade, vanished in an instant when she saw the man's face. His cheeks were daubed with paint, and his expression fierce beyond anything Mehitabel had ever imagined on a human visage.

"Oh, dear Lord, protect me," Mehitabel said.

Then the man, the Indian, reached down and grabbed her by the arm, hauling her to her feet, and she saw that he was not alone.

Thomas was out hunting; Mehitabel had been hoping for venison for that night's supper. Their home was at the northernmost end of the village of Berwick, and she was a hundred yards north of the house; there was no one she could call to for help as the Indian dragged her from the field.

A second Indian snatched up her baby, and brought him along as well. Roger, startled and unhappy that this stranger was handling him, began wailing, but his captors paid no attention.

Mehitabel called out, "My baby!"

Her captors ignored that, as well.

In the distance, Mehitabel heard a woman scream. She turned, and saw more Indians, dragging someone. The two parties were converging, and heading north, into the wilderness.

A moment later Mehitabel recognized the other captive—Mary Plaisted, wife to Mehitabel's brother Ichabod. She was struggling, thrashing about, cursing her captors in a way that shocked and amazed Mehitabel.

"Mary!" Mehitabel called.

Mary turned and saw her.

"They threw my daughter in the river!" she called back, still struggling. "Mehitabel, help me, they threw Margaret in the river!"

Mehitabel stared at her sister-in-law for a moment, then wrenched free of the hands that held her and snatched at her own child.

They would not throw *Roger* in the river, not while there was breath in her body!

The Indian holding Roger lifted him up, out of Mehitabel's reach; Roger squalled anew, and two men grabbed Mehitabel and dragged her back.

"Give me my baby!" she cried.

The Indians paid no attention—but one of them said something in his own tongue, and pointed.

Mehitabel turned, and saw the great oak that marked the northern boundary of the Goodwin lands, and of Berwick. A man was standing under it—an Indian, but one dressed differently from the warriors. The man under the tree was smaller and older than the others, and instead of buckskin he wore a bearskin robe. Bones and feathers were woven into his hair and hung on cords around his neck, and his black hair was streaked with gray. A small drum was slung on one hip, and a good-sized black bird perched on one shoulder.

For a moment Mehitabel thought the bird was dead, but then it turned its head to look at her, and she blinked in astonishment. It was a crow, and very much alive.

A live crow, standing on a man's shoulder?

It was not large for a crow—Mehitabel had taken it for some lesser bird at first—but it was a crow.

This, she realized, must be a wizard—every Indian tribe had its own wizard, she knew, who served as priest and doctor to his people. Some of the townsfolk mockingly called them "medicine men," since the Indians seemed to make no distinction between the medicines that God had provided and the magic that was a snare of Satan.

The wizard called out something to the warriors, and a moment later Mary and Mehitabel stood side by side beneath the oak, facing the old man.

He stank; the bear hide still carried the thick reek of bear, and the wizard had rubbed himself with some sort of grease that added a stench of its own.

"You will come with us," the wizard said. "You will walk on your own feet."

"Give me my baby!" Mehitabel demanded.

"A baby will slow you," the wizard replied. "And we would have no more Englishmen growing up in this land—your men should all go back to England, whence they came."

"Roger was born here," Mehitabel protested. "His father was born here, *I* was born here, *my* father was born here! This is our home!"

"This was Penobscot land before your fathers were born, English-woman, and before *their* fathers came across the sea," the wizard replied. "Further, the babe's cries are unpleasant to my ears." He said a word in his own tongue to the warrior who held Roger.

Mehitabel screamed and struggled, but she could not free herself in time; the Indian shifted his grip, lifted Roger up by his feet, then swung the screaming infant so that his head smashed against the thick trunk of the oak.

The screams stopped abruptly; a horrible silence fell.

The warrior holding the dead child looked questioningly at the wizard; he, in turn, glanced thoughtfully up at the oak branches above him. He said something in his own language, then addressed Mehitabel in English.

"Your babe shall serve as a reminder that the English are not welcome here," he said. "You and your man shall have the pleasure of seeing it whenever you walk this road."

As he spoke, the warrior was climbing the oak and clambering out on one of the larger limbs. There, he wedged the dead child into a fork, leaving it dangling limply.

Mehitabel screamed, and pulled free at last of the arms that held her. She ran forward, then fell to her knees and stared up at Roger.

Then she bent her head in prayer, asking God to make this all a nightmare, begging God to give her back her child, her son. She prayed in a half-spoken mutter.

"Your babe is dead, woman," the wizard said. "Now, stand and walk, or you will join him."

Mehitabel ignored him, and prayed, "Oh, God, I beseech thee, give my Roger back."

Annoyed, the wizard said, "Your babe is *dead*, woman! Look, if you doubt me!"

He turned his head and whispered something to the crow on his shoulder, and with a flutter of black wings the bird arose, and landed on the branch a few inches from Roger's remains, where it turned its head from side to side.

Mehitabel looked up, and anger flooded through her. She called aloud, "God, do not let them do any more!"

"Your babe is dead," the wizard repeated, "and if you would not see the eyes plucked from his head, then stand and come!"

"God will not allow it," Mehitabel shouted, with a sudden feeling of absolute certainty, a strange sensation of knowledge and power that she had never experienced before. "God cannot be so cruel!"

The wizard shrugged, and waved to the crow; the bird stepped forward…

And a hawk plunged from the sky, and swept the crow from the tree.

Stunned, all present watched as the hawk carried its prey to a clear patch of ground, where it snapped the crow's neck and began to feast.

Mehitabel felt the thing within her, the sensation of power, subside. Even beneath the shock and grief of Roger's death, however, some tiny part of her watched with satisfaction as the hawk ate.

The wizard was particularly upset by the crow's death. He gave up any further argument with Mehitabel; instead he snapped an order to the other men, and began walking northward.

The warriors dragged the two women; after a few steps Mary was willing to walk under her own power, but Mehitabel continued to resist, and at last was bound, gagged, and slung over a man's shoulder, still struggling.

They travelled all that day, Mary walking and Mehitabel carried, then made camp for the night, and continued on in the morning; their course was north by east. Still, Mehitabel had to be carried.

Late in the afternoon of the second day they arrived at their destination, an Indian village comprised of a single long structure surrounded by campfires, drying racks, woodpiles, and the like. There they were dragged inside and brought before two men seated on red blankets; both women were forced to kneel.

One of the men was another Indian, older than the warriors and wearing a more ornate headdress; the other was a white man—at least technically. He was almost as sun-browned as the Indians, but his hair was brown and wavy, and he wore a decent broadcloth coat and breeches buckled at the knee, a clump of lace at his throat and more lace at his cuffs.

The Indian spoke first, in clear but slow English.

"I am Madockawando, chief of the Penobscot," he said. "I have had you brought here as a warning to all English, and as a favor to my brother." He gestured at the white man. Then he spoke to the women's captors in their own tongue.

The warriors replied briefly, one by one; the wizard held forth for some time.

Mehitabel, however, paid little attention; she was staring at the white man in his foppish clothes.

The chief had said she had been brought here as a favor to this man; did that mean that it was he who had ordered her son's death?

"Did you tell them to kill my baby?" she said, while the wizard was still speaking.

One of the warriors clouted her on the back of the head, sending her sprawling at the edge of the red blanket.

"Women do not speak unless spoken to," Madockawando told her. "Most certainly, they do not interrupt the speaking of men."

Mehitabel glared up at him, but held her tongue.

Mary glanced back and forth between Madockawando and the white man, but said nothing.

"Tell them, brother," Madockawando said.

The white man nodded.

"Ladies," he said, "I am the Baron de Sainte Castine, in the service of His Most Christian Majesty, Louis XIV." He spoke with a definite French accent—in fact, the supposed savage, Madockawando, pronounced English more correctly. "I regret to inform you that due to the folly of your parliament, our two nations are at war. Your foolish lords have deposed their rightful king, James II, and placed a Dutch usurper on the throne; naturally, my lord Louis wishes to see his fellow sovereign restored to his proper position, and to that purpose has declared this war."

"King James was a bloody papist!" Mary protested.

"Exactly," Ste. Castine agreed. "A good Catholic, as are all Frenchmen."

"What does that have to do with *us*?" Mary asked.

"Ah, well, when my friend Madockawando calls me 'brother,' he is not speaking figuratively. I am married to his sister. Thus, when I am at war with the English, so must he be, by the blood bond between us. When word of the war reached us, he acted immediately to strike against the English—and what better way to drive your men from this land than to take you ladies from them, to be returned only when they depart forever from America?"

"And your King Louis makes war against infants?" Mehitabel demanded. "Was it he who ordered my baby be slain?"

Ste. Castine glanced sideways at Madockawando, who sat impassively listening.

"I fear that is the custom among my brother's people," Ste. Castine said. "Babies are too much trouble on the trail, and can grow up to be warriors."

"My medicine man tells me you are a witch," Madockawando interjected. "You could not save your child?"

"I am…" Mehitabel stopped in mid-sentence and stared at him.

"You called down a hawk to slay Pessatawbo's crow brother, yet you let your child die."

"I…it was so fast," Mehitabel said.

She was trying to think. Since little Roger had died she had been so lost in grief that thought had seemed impossible, but now it was necessary—here before her were the men who would control her destiny, the men who had sent their warriors to kill Roger and drive her people from their home. She wanted them dead, wanted them in Hell—but she was just one woman, surrounded by enemies. If she flung herself on Madockawando she would die, to no purpose, with Roger unavenged.

She was too caught up in the need for revenge to think about the accusation of witchcraft. Of course she was no witch.

But she remembered the odd feeling of power she had felt when the hawk dove.

That was nothing like witchcraft, though; that had surely been righteous anger and faith in God.

"Ah," Madockawando said. "You had no time for your magic."

Mehitabel said nothing.

"Listen to me, woman," the chieftain said. "A magic that is stronger than Pessatawbo's, that can slay his creatures—this is something we want. Tell me how you called the hawk."

Mehitabel decided to tell the truth—perhaps God would send more aid, as he had sent the hawk.

"I am no witch," she said. "I prayed, and God sent the hawk."

Madockawando sat back, obviously dissatisfied with this answer.

"I have seen and heard many white men pray," he said. "I have never seen their prayers answered this way. I say there is magic here, not just prayer."

Mehitabel said nothing.

"We will keep you here until you speak, then. When you tell Pessatawbo how you called the hawk, perhaps we will release you." He gestured in dismissal, and said something in the Penobscot tongue.

Mary and Mehitabel were hauled away, separately.

Mehitabel did not see where Mary was taken, but she herself was dragged out of the longhouse to a hut built of treebark over a wooden frame, a hut no more than ten feet across and hardly high enough for a man to stand upright in.

The two warriors threw her inside and then departed, dropping the blanket back across the entrance and leaving her in semi-darkness. She lay there, still bound hand and foot, and waited.

In time the Indian wizard, Pessatawbo, came.

"This is my home," he told her, "and you will remain here until you tell me how you called the hawk."

Mehitabel stared up at him with hatred, and said nothing.

He kept her bound for all that first evening and night. On the second day he cut the thongs that bound her ankles, so that she could walk, but he tied one end of a strong rope to her wrists, the other end to a sturdy post, staking her out as if she were an animal. This, she realized, was so she would not be forced to further befoul the wizard's hut.

As if anything could further despoil the home of such a creature!

That evening the wizard noticed that her lips were dry and her breathing shallow, and gave her water, holding the dipper for her.

She drank. If she were to die, who would avenge Roger's murder? And suicide was a sin.

She said nothing during any of this. She endured it all in silence, watching with implacable hatred the man who had ordered her son's death.

On the fourth day, the wizard gave her the first food she had eaten since the morning of her capture—the morning her baby had died.

The wizard did not watch her constantly; rather, he went about his ordinary business, and when he had a free moment he would find her and demand that she tell him how she had brought the hawk down from the sky.

"A charm? A word?" he demanded. "A token of power?"

She said nothing.

She endured.

When she was alone, she prayed—for her freedom, for Pessatawbo's destruction, for the safety of her countrymen and the defeat of the French and the Penobscot.

She often dreamed at night that Roger was still alive and well, and woke from her dreams smiling—only to weep when she realized they were only dreams, and not reality. She kept her sobs as quiet as she could, and thought she had hid them from Pessatawbo.

She did not see Mary again; she had no way of knowing whether the other woman was alive or dead.

She often wondered what Thomas was doing, and the other men of Berwick—did they know she was still alive, and a captive? Would they come to her rescue?

Or had the Indians returned to Berwick and slaughtered everyone there, all her family, her friends?

She had no way of knowing.

On the evening of the tenth day, Pessatawbo seated himself facing her.

"Englishwoman," he said, "I am tired of you. I have not harmed you because I do not know the limits of your witchcraft, but I grow tired of waiting. If you tell me what I want to know, I will let you go free, I will let you return to your people. If you do not tell me, I will beat you until you do tell me."

Mehitabel looked him in the eye. "If you strike me, God will strike you dead," she said, and as she said it she felt a certainty that she was speaking the literal truth.

Pessatawbo saw her certainty. He hesitated, then got to his feet and walked away.

He did not beat her, then or ever.

Mehitabel wondered how she could feel so utterly certain of what God would do; was that not blasphemy? Yet she *was* certain. It was almost as if there were some power within her, some power she had never before known.

The days passed, and then the weeks, and then months. Mehitabel wore through or cut any number of thongs and ropes, and several times fled the Indian camp, but each time she was tracked down, overtaken, and recaptured.

When the winter was well advanced she abandoned any thought of escaping before spring; the snow would make it impossible to hide her tracks. She concentrated on simply staying alive and not losing any fingers to frostbite.

On occasion Pessatawbo, in an attempt to pry her secret from her, would keep her tied outside in the cold—but he always relented and brought her in by the fire before any permanent damage was done.

At times, during this torture, she wished she really *did* know some magical secret, so that she could have the pleasure of knowing that she really *was* withholding something from her captors.

She even explained once to Madockawando, when he happened to stop by, that any power she had was that of a good Christian, whom God favored, but these savages were so sunk in their heathenism that Pessatawbo merely mocked her for spouting such arrant foolishness.

"Power comes from nature around us, or from spirits within ourselves," he said, "not from some ghost in the sky."

The snow was melting, the air warming, and Mehitabel was beginning to contemplate escape, one evening when Pessatawbo squatted in front of her.

"You still have not told me how you called the hawk," he said.

"I have nothing to tell you," Mehitabel snapped in reply.

"Then I will tell *you* something. I think you have only a little power,

Englishwoman. I think you know a trick or two, but you have not gotten any great power. Perhaps all you know is how to call a hawk; perhaps you learned this to keep the crows from your fields. Still, I would have uses for this knowledge. I want it. And if you do not give it to me, I will not hurt you, as I once threatened—I have seen during the winter that you do not fear pain or even death. You said your god would strike me dead if I harmed you; I do not believe this, but I think perhaps your own spirit might strike at me. So I will not harm *you*." He smiled coldly. "Instead, Madockawando and I will lead our warriors to your home camp, and slay everyone there. Madockawando's French brother asks us to do this, and we will. But if you teach me your trick, Englishwoman, I will spare your man—or whichever one man you choose, if you would have another woman's instead of your own. Tell us how you called the hawk, and tell us how we may know which man you want spared—or else *all* will die."

"You think I will betray all my people for Thomas' life?"

Pessatawbo didn't answer that directly; instead he said, "We go to the English town at sunrise."

Mehitabel did not speak again for the brief remainder that day, but that night, as she lay wrapped in the blanket Pessatawbo allowed her, she prayed endlessly that God would preserve Berwick, and most especially her beloved Thomas.

She dozed off at last, and dreamt that she was back home, standing by Thomas as he lay alone in their bed. She called to him, trying to warn him that the Indians were coming—and at last he rolled over and looked up at her. She gave her warning again, and he sprang from the bed, reaching for his gun.

Then the dream was over, and it was morning.

She called out to Pessatawbo, "God will protect them!"

He ignored her.

She was left under the guard of the Indian women, none of whom spoke any English. They fed her, but otherwise ignored her.

Four days later the warriors returned—and Mehitabel took a savage, sinful joy in seeing that there were fewer of them, and that some of those were bandaged, or limping.

The men held a meeting in the longhouse, but afterward Pessatawbo returned to his hut and confronted Mehitabel.

"Did you send a bird, perhaps, to warn your people?" he asked.

"God warned them," Mehitabel replied, smiling at the memory of the dream God had sent her.

"Something did," Pessatawbo said bitterly. "We slew but two, and they struck down five of our warriors, my own sister's son among them."

He added fiercely, "I hope your man was one of the two."

"God protects his own, and always shall," Mehitabel retorted.

"The French say this God of yours is on *their* side, as well."

"The French are wrong."

"I still do not believe in this god of yours. I say *you* warned the English."

"And if I did, I am proud of it and will do it again," Mehitabel said.

Pessatawbo had no reply to that—but no further attacks were made on Berwick. Elsewhere, the various tribes allied with the French continued their raids, but Berwick was not troubled again.

Pessatawbo seemed once more determined to wait Mehitabel out; after all, she was merely a woman, and would surely tire of her captivity in time.

The remainder of 1690 passed. Mehitabel grew accustomed to her harsh, limited existence, and retained her faith that in time, God would liberate her.

That summer Pessatawbo captured a crow, and began training it to act as his familiar—his "spirit brother," as the Indians called them. Mehitabel watched silently. One day, as she sat before Pessatawbo's hut and he fed the crow tidbits, she looked up and saw a hawk circling above.

She smiled with the memory of how Pessatawbo's previous familiar had died, and hoped the miracle would be repeated—but the hawk flew away.

Mehitabel's smile vanished, and anger grew within her. She looked at the crow.

The bird looked back at her, then suddenly took off and fluttered into the trees.

Pessatawbo looked up, startled, and gave the whistle that should have brought the bird back to him.

The bird did not come; instead it flew deeper into the surrounding forest.

Pessatawbo waited, calling, whistling, and shaking his little talismans of bone and feather, but the crow did not return, then or ever.

At last the wizard gave up. He glowered angrily at Mehitabel, but said nothing to her.

He caught no more crows, trained no more "spirit brothers."

And as the weather turned cold again and Mehitabel still would not yield, Pessatawbo grew increasingly more frustrated.

Early in 1691, he told her, "I will attack the English in ways your warnings cannot prevent. I and the other medicine men among the Penobscot have summoned the north winds, that the winter shall be cold and the snow deep. Our own people will suffer, but you English will suffer the worse. And we will send fevers and sickness among the English."

She stared at him, wondering whether he could actually carry out such threats. He was a witch, she knew, though God had forbidden him a witch's familiar, but surely no ordinary witch could do what he claimed. Had he made pact with the Devil, perhaps? His heathen gods, whatever they were, were not gods, but imps and demons; could they give him such power?

"Why do you tell me this?"

"Because I no longer care what the French want. If you will give me all your secrets, I will not call the wind, I will not send sickness. Let the French fight their own wars."

Mehitabel did not reply; she simply stared at him.

She had no secrets to give him. To yield to Satan's power would be wrong in any case.

That winter was, indeed, harsh—but Mehitabel wondered whether that was the wizards' doing, or simply God's plan.

In the spring, reports came of smallpox and other diseases spreading throughout New England—but even if Mehitabel believed the reports, was it surprising that disease should follow such a winter?

And what could she do? She had no secrets to give.

She endured.

When winter came again, and an early, hard winter, as Pessatawbo had promised, one day Pessatawbo came and sat before her, staring at her, for an hour or more.

"Perhaps," he said at last, "you do not believe that I called the wind, and sent the sickness."

Mehitabel didn't answer.

"Perhaps you do not fear the cold, the wind, the fever."

She sat silently.

"What *do* you fear, Englishwoman? Do you fear madness, perhaps?"

Mehitabel tried not to react to that, but Pessatawbo must have seen some response; he leaned back with a satisfied smile.

"You *do* fear madness. Good!" Then he frowned. "But you are too strong; I cannot make you mad without losing the secrets I want."

Mehitabel relaxed imperceptibly.

"I do not know if you love your man. Perhaps he beat you and was cruel to you. I know you love children, though—English children. Give me your secrets, Englishwoman, or English children will run mad."

"I have no children. You killed my baby."

"Not *your* children, no—not even the children of your own town, not yet. Instead I will send mad some English children somewhere else, and the madness will spread to young and old alike until you give me what I want. In time, if you do not yield, all the English in this land will go mad and slay one another in their madness. That is what I promise you, Englishwoman. The madness will only stop when you tell me your secrets."

Mehitabel did not answer.

Pessatawbo stared at her for a moment longer, then rose and marched away.

He did not speak to her again, nor she to him, for some months. Mehitabel judged it to be the first week in February of 1692 when Pessatawbo told her, "The madness has begun."

She looked up.

"Two girls have gone mad," he said, "in a place to the south, called Salem. Now they shall spread their madness to those around them."

"What girls?" Mehitabel asked. She had never been to Salem, had no way of verifying anything that Pessatawbo might say of what happened there; she suspected the old wizard of lying. If he could truly send people mad, why would he choose some place as far away as Salem? That was fifty or sixty miles from Berwick.

"El...Elizabeth Parris," Pessatawbo said, "and Abigail Williams." He shook his head. "You English with your names."

Mehitabel knew no one named Parris or Williams, but the names sounded genuine. She felt a chill.

Then she shook it off. He was lying, she was sure. He had simply learned a couple of names, perhaps from the Baron de Ste. Castine. She closed her mouth and said nothing further.

Throughout the following months, Pessatawbo would come to her every so often with some new tale of madness in Salem, some new name of a supposed victim. Pessatawbo claimed that the people of Salem were blaspheming their God, imprisoning one another, seeing devils and visions. Mehitabel believed none of it.

In June he told her, quite seriously, "They have hanged a woman because madwomen shouted at her."

Mehitabel did not deign to reply to such an absurd lie.

A little over a month later she was told, "They have hanged five more women. The madness is spreading. Two were from a place called Topsfield and one from Amesbury—it is not just Salem Village that runs mad."

The reports continued. In late September, when Pessatawbo reported eight more hangings, Mehitabel burst out, "I believe not a word of it!"

"You do not?" Pessatawbo said, taken aback.

"Of course not! 'Tis absurd!"

He nodded thoughtfully. "I must show you I do not lie," he said.

It was almost Christmas, Mehitabel felt sure, when Pessatawbo stepped into the hut one evening with a document in his hand.

Mehitabel stared. The Indians did not use paper.

He handed it to her without any comment beyond, "You can read?"

She nodded, and took the document.

It proved to be a pamphlet entitled *Some Miscellany Observations*, by one Reverend Samuel Willard, of Boston. She read slowly, hampered by the poor light in the hut.

At first she could not understand why Pessatawbo had given it to her; it was a learned discussion of various matters, such as what forms devils might take, and the rules to be observed in locating and convicting witches and sorcerers.

But then she read some of the examples Rev. Willard gave of cases where accusations were accepted at face value, against all reason. Mehitabel's face went pale, and her hand trembled.

Trials had been held at Salem Village, on the accusation of a group of girls and young women. Men and women had been hanged—nineteen in all, with a twentieth dying under torture during questioning, crushed to death.

"This is madness," Mehitabel gasped.

A broad smirk spread across Pessatawbo's face, clearly visible in the firelight.

"*Now* you know I did not lie!" he said. He nodded proudly. "Madness, as I said! Madness that will spread as long as I live and will it!"

A wave of fury swept over Mehitabel, emotion stronger than that she had felt when Pessatawbo and Madockawando led the attack on Berwick, stronger than anything she had felt since she saw her tiny Roger murdered.

"You do the Devil's work!" she shouted, flinging the pamphlet in Pessatawbo's grinning face, "and may God damn your soul for it!"

Something stirred within her, something she did not recognize at first—and the smile vanished from Pessatawbo's face, to be replaced first with a look of astonishment, then with agony. His left arm seemed to stiffen, and his right clutched at his chest. He staggered, turned, pushed his way past the blanket and out of the hut, out of Mehitabel's sight.

Then she remembered when she had felt that thing within her before. That had been what she felt when the hawk took the crow to save poor Roger from desecration.

She dared not think it was the power of God, moving within her; she was merely a woman, hardly a worthy vessel for God's wrath. At any moment Pessatawbo would return, she was sure; whatever spasm had troubled him would have passed.

She sat alone, waiting, but no one came. In time she picked up the pamphlet, and read and re-read it until the fire had burned too low for her to see the printing.

Pessatawbo did not return, and at last she fell asleep.

In the morning she was awakened by a kick; she opened her eyes to find Madockawando and Ste. Castine standing over her. Bright sunlight spilled in through the door of the hut.

"Get up," Madockawando ordered.

Mehitabel obeyed, and was led out of the hut into the sunshine.

Pessatawbo lay on a blanket on the ground before her. He was quite obviously dead, his face fixed in a rictus of agony.

"His heart burst last night," Madockawando told her. "Before he died he said *you* did it."

"God struck him down for his sins," Mehitabel said, a trifle uncertainly.

"And if we kill you for it, your God will strike us down?"

Mehitabel blinked at him, unable to think how she should respond.

"My brother says it is accident," Madockawando said. "He says you have no magic. Pessatawbo said you do. Maybe my brother is right— but I will not take that chance. You go, out of my land. I will not fight the English more. To hell with King Louis and King James." He turned away.

Ste. Castine stayed a moment longer.

"You have been exceptionally fortunate, Madam," he said. "Perhaps you are indeed among God's chosen favorites—or perhaps you are a true witch, unlike those poor fools in Salem. I have done my best to serve my king, but if I am to have any peace in my own family, I must know when to let matters drop. Go, then, and my best wishes go with you."

Then he, too, turned away.

Mehitabel stood for a moment, too dazed to react.

She remembered what she had felt, that power she had felt deep within her when she had lashed out at Pessatawbo.

Was that some black magic? Or was it some unknown gift of God?

Was she the chosen vessel of God's wrath upon the unrighteous?

She didn't know—and didn't think it mattered. She would never need it again. She flexed her fingers, realizing that she was outside the hut but unbound, that no one was guarding her, no one would stop her.

Then she took a step, and another, and another, and in seconds she was running, down the trail away from the longhouse and the Indian village, southwest through the woods, toward Berwick and her Thomas.

Original Author's Note:

Mehitabel Goodwin reached home safely, and bore her husband Thomas a son, Ichabod Goodwin, in 1700. Ichabod Goodwin was my six-times-great grandfather.

The events in this story are as historically accurate as I could make them; only two names, Pessatawbo and the baby Roger, are invented. (The records do not mention the name or sex of Mehitabel's murdered child, and Pessatawbo is entirely my own creation.) The real Mehitabel Goodwin was indeed held captive by Indians for several years after seeing her baby's brains dashed out against a tree, as a result of the Anglo-French wars; she was a captive throughout the Salem witch trials.

And I've wondered how that madness could happen, could spread, and could then end so suddenly.

Additional Author's Note:

After I wrote the above story and note, one of my sisters turned up additional information. I had a few significant things wrong.

Mehetable Goodwin (she was surprisingly consistent in spelling it that way, and not how I had it in the story) was captured by the Abenaki, not the Penobscot, and not held captive, but sold to the French in Quebec. After she had spent five years as a Frenchman's slave/wife, Thomas Goodwin found out she was still alive, traveled to Quebec to ransom her, and took her back to Maine.

HEART OF STONE

When they came for the wizard and dragged him from his little house of carved stone and wood, carrying him away to the gallows, she was lost in dreams, unaware of the outside world. It was not until they began to smash equipment and furniture that she awoke and swam to the surface, where she looked out of the wall upon chaos.

None of them noticed her arrival, and she stared in horror at the frenzy of destruction. Jars of precious herbs brought thousands of miles across sea and mountain were shattered on the floor; pages were torn from ancient books of lore that had survived centuries of careful use, and flung upon the wind.

"Smash it all!" a man in a black robe shouted. "Unclean, all of it!"

She stared in silent shocked stillness as the villagers obeyed.

At last there was nothing more to smash, and the dozen men stood, panting heavily, their clothes damp with sweat, their booted feet awash in the wreckage of the wizard's life, and glanced at each other and around the room.

One of them caught sight of her and stared. He pointed.

"What's that on the wall?" he asked.

The others looked.

"It's just a shadow," someone said.

"I thought it moved."

"It doesn't look like a shadow to me."

"An image in charcoal, perhaps?"

She let herself sink back into the stone in terror until she could barely see the villagers, until they were just vague shapes seen dimly through the thick gray of the wall.

"…gone now," she heard, faintly. And then came the crackle of flame, and heat and light penetrated dimly into the stone.

She cowered, safe within her wall, for a long time. Then, when the stone was long cold, she cautiously drifted back up to the surface and looked over the ruins.

There was nothing left but bare stone and rubbish. The glass was gone from the room's one window, and harsh sunlight shone unfiltered on a layer of ash and debris.

She wondered what had become of the wizard, and why the men had come and destroyed everything. The wizard had told her that people feared him—it seemed plain they had not feared him as much as he thought, or they would never have had the courage to do this.

Or no—perhaps their fear had become unbearable, and they had resolved to destroy it the only way they could?

Whatever the exact truth might be, she did not think the wizard would be returning. Even if he yet lived, even if he had somehow escaped their fury, what was here that would be worth returning to? All his precious belongings were gone. The books were burned to ash. The bell jar that had held the homunculus was smashed, the creature itself gone. The scrying glass was shattered.

Only she remained—and she did not think the wizard would trouble himself about her. After all, he had created her in the first place, and if he were lonely wherever he might now be, he could always make another. It was not as if he could take her away with him to some new home; she was bound within the stone of the wall, an image brought to life.

But what was to become of her, then? She could not leave. She needed no food nor drink; the wizard's spell sustained her, so she would not starve, nor age. She would not die—would she?

She was unsure how long the wizard's magic would last without the wizard himself present, but clearly, since she was still alive, it had not faded yet. He had gone away for weeks at a time in the past, and she had not suffered from his absence...

Or rather, she had not suffered physically; she had been very lonely indeed during his travels.

And of course, she had always known he would return in time. He had been alive somewhere in the world. This time, she was fairly certain he was not.

No one to talk to, no one to watch as he went about his studies and experiments, ever again—perhaps in time she would die of loneliness.

She stared forlornly from the stone and wept at the thought, fine drops of moisture trickling down the cool stone. Then she could not bear to look at the chamber any longer, nor that fraction of the outside world she could see through the shattered window, and she let herself sink down into the wall, where she could neither see nor be seen, where the cool substance of the stone strengthened her and gave her rest. She sank down to the heart of the wall, where it rested upon the earth itself. And hours later, as she lay deep in the stone, she found herself wondering whether she could pass down beneath the wall, into the earth, and thus be free, to roam the world and find new companions.

For the next few days she spent most of her time deep in the stone, digging downward with fingers and toes and thoughts, trying to pierce the earth, to make an opening between the magical substance of the enchanted wall and the magical substance of the greater world. She made no perceptible headway, but she did not give up—after all, what other choice did she have?

And then she heard footsteps upon the flagstones. Joy burst into bloom in her heart, and she leaped upward—the wizard had returned after all! He still lived!

But when she reached the plaster surface, when her face appeared as a shadowy outline and she looked out at the dusty, wind-scoured ruin of the wizard's chamber, the two men she saw there were strangers.

"Look at this!" one of them said, as he stirred the ash with his foot. "They left nothing!"

Thieves, she realized—they were just thieves, come to steal the wizard's treasures, and disappointed to find none.

But of course, one of the wizard's treasures did still remain, and wanted to escape. These men might be worthless scavengers, but they were still men, someone she could talk to. They might be able to answer her questions, tell her what had become of the wizard, help her get free—or perhaps, if they couldn't free her, they would stay to keep her company. She pressed up against the outside world and watched them for a moment, gathering her courage before speaking.

But the shorter one looked up just then and saw her image sharpening into detailed clarity. He slapped the other on the arm and shouted, "Look!"

"What?" the taller man asked, looking first at his companion, then at the wall. He saw her face, and his jaw sagged.

"That wasn't there before," he said.

She hesitated, unsure what to say.

"It's magic," the shorter man said. "The wizard must have left it."

She smiled at him, and started to open her mouth.

"It's moving!" the taller man barked, cutting her off.

She blinked in surprise, and her mouth closed again as she tried to find the right words. Of course she was moving.

"A guardian spell," the shorter man said. "Let's get out of here!"

The taller man nodded and took a step backward. "I think you're right," he said.

Then both men whirled and hurried toward the door, as she finally found her voice.

"Wait!" she cried softly—her voice had never been as loud as a real person's, for the wizard had liked peace and quiet.

If the thieves heard her, they paid no attention—unless it was to hasten even more. She stared helplessly after them.

"Wait," she whispered, but they were gone.

She stayed at the surface for hours, staring out at the stone walls and the darkening evening sky outside the window, hoping they would return, but they did not, and at last she let herself sink back into the stone.

For a night and a day she sulked and mourned, but at last she gathered herself together, telling herself that she would do no one any good with such behavior. She debated whether to resume her attempts at digging out the bottom of her home—her home, which had become her prison—or whether she would do better to stay near the surface, where she might catch the attention of any further intruders.

Eventually she decided to do both, in alternation.

She was pressed up against the surface, her eye to the slight imperfections in the wall to get the sharpest angle, trying to see through the door to the narrow little entryway, when she heard voices. She swallowed—or rather, did her immaterial equivalent—to be better ready to speak, and listened closely, hoping the speakers would approach.

This time, she promised herself, she would not wait—she would call out as soon as she could to assure any visitor that she would not harm him. She strained to hear.

The voices had been approaching, but now she heard one say, "I'm not going any closer! Duin said there was a monster in there, guarding the old wizard's treasure!"

It was a high-pitched voice, plainly audible through the glassless window, though she could not see the speaker. She had never heard a child before, but she guessed that this was a child.

"Duin's a liar," the other voice, another child, replied. "If the wizard had a monster, would he have let the priest's men catch him and burn all his things?"

"Maybe the monster was sleeping," the first voice said. "I don't know. But Duin said he saw it—it had the face of a beautiful woman, but the body of a winged serpent, and it came right through a stone wall at him."

"And you believe him?"

"Maybe," the first said, a little less certain. "But believe him or no, I'm not going in there. Even if there's no monster, there could be traps."

"Or just snakes," the other said. "Maybe that's what Duin really saw, a snake in a hole, and he made up the woman's face so we wouldn't know he was scared of a mere snake."

"So are you going in to see if it's a snake?" the first speaker challenged the second.

For several long seconds there was no reply, and she held perfectly still, listening intently.

"No," the other said at last. "I guess not. It might be dangerous. I don't believe in snake-women, but I guess there could still be something in there."

And then they turned away, and spoke of other things, as she called desperately after them, too quietly to be heard, "I am no serpent! I'm just a woman, alone in here, trapped!"

They didn't hear her, and then they were gone.

She strained against the surface for several long minutes, but at last sank back into the stone, weeping in frustration.

She lost track of the days after that. The sun rose and set, rain came and went, and in time the cold winter winds blew in through the empty windowframe, bringing white flakes that danced briefly in the air before settling into pale streaks in the dark ash on the floor. She struggled fruitlessly against the limits of her home, but could not break free; sometimes she sank into silent depression for days or weeks at a time. She often called out, as loudly as she could, but received no answer.

And then one day, when the wind howled around the walls and snow was piling up on the sill, she heard a man's voice, cursing. It was barely audible over the storm, but it was growing louder. He was at the door of the house, she was certain.

Then he stopped cursing. "Hello!" he called. "Is anyone here? Am I intruding?"

She hesitated. Her voice could not be heard over the wind, she was certain. She waited, at the very surface of the wall, plainly visible should he come inside the house and up the two steps from the entryway to the room that had once been the wizard's home and study.

She wished she could go down into the entryway to greet him, but the walls there were not of stone. They were mud and wood and plaster, and she could not enter them.

"It would appear not," the man said, more quietly. She listened, struggling to hear over the wind's complaints.

And she held very still as the man came inside—she could not hear his boots on the stone floor, but she could hear the difference in the wind when he pushed shut the broken remains of the exterior door that had hung open for so long.

And then he stepped into the room, scuffing at the ash and snow, looking about curiously. He was a tall man, heavily built, with a thick black beard and curly black hair, clutching a sheepskin cloak tightly around himself.

"Hello," she said, and she smiled nervously, as broad and welcoming a smile as she could manage.

He stopped dead in his tracks and stared at her, thunderstruck.

"You're welcome to stay here, if you like," she said. "I'm sorry it's such a mess."

He looked around at the empty windowframe and the gray ash.

"It is, isn't it?" he said. Then he took a few cautious steps toward her, and stared at her intently. "What are you?" he asked.

She frowned helplessly, confused by the question. "I don't know," she said. "I'm me."

"Are you a woman, then? Or something else?"

She remembered conversations with the wizard, when he would reply to something she said with, "Of course you would say that, since you're a woman," or some similar remark.

"I'm a woman," she said.

"Where are you?"

Puzzled, she answered, "I'm right here, in the wall in front of you."

"You're in the wall? Inside it?"

"Yes."

"How did you get there? Is it magic?"

"The wizard put me here."

"The wizard?" He looked around, suddenly nervous. "What wizard?"

"The wizard who used to live here. The villagers came and took him away, and left me here alone."

He relaxed. "He's gone, then?"

"Yes."

"And you're trapped here?"

"Yes!" He understood!

He stroked his bearded chin. "Now, that's interesting!"

She hesitated, then asked, "Can you free me?"

She wasn't really sure what she would do if she were free; she didn't really understand how people lived, what they did with themselves, what would become of her if she were out of the wall and free to move about as other people did. Still, it seemed the best possibility—she was so very tired of being alone here, trapped in the tiny world inside the wall. She had some concept of hunger and cold and pain, though she had never experienced any of them, and she knew that if she were freed she would probably suffer all those and more, but she could see through the window, could see the wide world, the vast sky, the days and nights, the changing seasons, and it all seemed so open and glorious that she was sure it would be better to suffer betimes out there in the wide world than to endure her lonely and limited existence in the wall.

"I'm afraid not, my dear. I'm no wizard; I haven't the slightest notion of how to free you."

"Oh," she said sadly. "But will you stay here, then, and keep me company? At least for a little while?"

"Oh, I'll stay, have no fear," he said. He gestured at the window. "At the very least, I'll stay here until this storm ends."

"Of course," she said, embarrassed and grateful. "I'd offer to help make you comfortable if I could, but I can't do anything from in here."

"Well, you can talk," the man said. "Can you tell me where I might find firewood?" He gestured at the fireplace in the end wall. "I'd like to warm the place up a little."

"I'm sorry," she said. "I don't know. There may not be any left. The men who took the wizard away smashed or burned or stole just about everything."

"Just my luck," the man muttered, pulling the sheepskin cloak more tightly about himself. He looked around, then said, "I'll be right back."

She waited eagerly as he hurried down the two steps to the entryway, and out of her sight. She listened as he pried open the door, admitting the howling wind. A moment later she heard a distant crunching and crashing, then silence until he returned, stamping snow from his boots as he slammed the broken door.

He held up his prize, two lengths of damp wood, a streak of snow still clinging to one. "From the fence," he said. "Hope I can get it lit." He tossed it into the fireplace, then squatted on the hearth, pulled out a tinderbox and a wad of kindling from somewhere under his cloak, and began building a fire.

"It'll be good to have some heat," he said. "You must be freezing, in that light dress!"

"No," she said. "I can't feel the cold."

He looked up at her, startled. "You can't?" He turned his attention back to the fire. "Must be part of the spell. I suppose you don't need to eat, or drink, or breathe, while you're in there?"

"That's right."

He snorted. "Trust a wizard to find an easier way to keep a woman," he said. He leaned forward and blew gently at the smoldering tinder; when it was burning satisfactorily he glanced up at her. "What's your name?" he asked.

"I...I don't know," she said.

"You don't remember?"

"I don't know."

He considered her for a moment, then shrugged. "So be it, then." He turned back to the fire, tending it carefully.

She watched, fascinated. When the wizard had wanted a fire he had simply spoken a certain Word, and flame burst from wood laid in place by the homunculus. He hadn't had to worry himself with all this painstaking effort.

At last he sat back, gazing critically at the small, steady blaze he had achieved. He held out his hands, warming them before the flame.

"What's your name?" she asked.

He looked over his shoulder at her. "Reuel," he said.

"A pleasure to meet you, sir," she said, curtseying—the wizard had always been fond of that effect.

"By the good Lord," Reuel said. "That looks very odd! It's as if your body faded away, while your face bobs up and down."

"Oh," she said, flustered by this reminder that Reuel was not at all like the wizard.

He stared at her. "You can fade in and out, then? And appear anywhere on the wall?"

"Yes," she whispered.

He considered her silently for a moment, then said, "You asked if I could stay, to keep you company—you're lonely?"

"Very much so," she admitted.

"I think I might be persuaded to stay for a time, even after this storm has passed," he said. "And I think I may bring you some other people to talk to, as well, if you'll do as I say."

She blinked at him, unsure how to respond. Do as he said? She was trapped in the wall; what could she do?

"I'll try," she said.

He looked around. "I'll need to clean this place up," he said. "And a curtain would add to the effect..." He was talking to himself, not to her; she listened without replying, just enjoying the sound of a human voice.

The storm died away by mid-afternoon; by evening Reuel had swept the ash, dust, and debris from the chamber, leaving only bare stone. The fire burned cheerily on the hearth, warming the room somewhat and melting away the snow that had blown in, though the stone remained chill.

He stayed that night, and slept wrapped in his cloak on the bare stone floor in front of the fire. He talked to her before dozing off, telling her tales of lands he had seen, and listening to her own reminiscences about the wizard and his magic.

In the morning he arose shortly after dawn, washed his face with snow, then told her, "I'll be back soon," and departed. She listened longingly to the fading crunch of his footsteps in the crusted snow as he trudged away; when at last she admitted to herself that she could no longer hear him she sank back into the wall to think.

Would he really be back? He had said he would be, but she knew that men could lie.

At least they had spoken the day and night before; their talk had given her strength. He hadn't fled at the sight of her. Their conversation had been different from her conversations with the wizard, but in its way quite satisfactory. She was much reassured; even if he did not return as promised, she had hope for the future in the knowledge that others might yet take pleasure in her company.

Night was falling when she heard a distant scraping and rose to the surface. Something was approaching, but the sound was not exactly foot-steps; instead it sounded as if something large and heavy were being dragged through the snow.

And in fact, when Reuel finally appeared in the doorway, it appeared he was dragging something large and heavy—an immense bundle. He dropped it in the entryway and began unwrapping it.

She stared as he began hauling his treasures into the chamber.

Rugs, and draperies, and cushions, a bedroll, two folding chairs and a little table—in a matter of minutes the chamber was furnished once again.

It was nothing like the wizard's chamber of old; there were no bell jars, no crowded shelves, no books nor scrolls, no oaken bedstead, no elaborate workbench with its dozens of drawers and compartments. There was no homunculus nor mummified crocodile, no herbs nor alem-bics, no scrying glass.

Still, it was furnished.

"That's better," Reuel said, looking over his handiwork.

She clapped her hands silently. "It's lovely!" she called. "I'm so glad you're back!"

He smiled at her, and doffed the black cap she had not until then noticed, making a sweeping bow. "The pleasure is all mine, milady," he said. "I've spent every ducat I had, sold half my gear, and pledged my credit to the very limits of what the merchants would accept in order to equip this place appropriately, but I am quite certain that with your coop-eration I shall swiftly earn back every bit of it."

Her own happy smile vanished, and she studied him uncertainly. "My cooperation? But what can I do, here in the wall?"

"You, milady, can tell fortunes. I have spread the word in yonder vil-lage that I am a holy man, drawn here by my mystical knowledge, and that I have found the late unlamented wizard had confined spirits here, with whom I can speak. I propose to bring those interested in knowing the future here, where they, too, can be counseled by those trapped spirits—for a fee. You, milady, will of course play the part of the spirits." He clapped his hat back on his head. "It would be even better if in fact you actually can see the future, or judge a man's fate—can you?"

"Of course not!" she said. "Reuel, I am glad you're here, but I fear you've misjudged or misunderstood something. I am no wizard. I can't tell fortunes!"

"Certainly you can! It's easy; I'll teach you. You need merely speak in terms so vague they might mean anything, and then let the customer's own words lead you on to the specifics. They'll be so astounded by the wonder of speaking to an apparition such as yourself that they won't notice any errors."

She hesitated. She was not sure she understood him—though she feared she did. "But it would be lies and trickery," she said.

"In a way, in a way," he said, with a wave of dismissal.

"I can't do it," she said unhappily.

He frowned, then shrugged. "If you cannot, then you need merely appear on cue, speak nonsense or move your lips silently, and I will translate. That will be just as effective, I'm sure."

"But it's untrue!"

"Who does it harm? 'Twill bring us all we need, and do no one any hurt. You'll see, you'll see—we'll only be telling them what they want to hear."

"It's still wrong," she said, but with less certainty.

The argument continued for a time, but after that they both knew he had won, and that she would do as he asked.

That night he hung a curtain on the long wall, over the spot where she appeared most readily. She protested without effect. Her discomfort with his plans and with the presence of the curtain put a damper on their conversation.

In the morning he departed for a time, leaving the curtain open, but then he returned—and not alone. She heard his voice outside the window, telling someone, "Wait here while I prepare; I'll call you in when I'm ready."

"Reuel?" she called. Then she heard the door open—it creaked on its hinges now, in a way the wizard would never have permitted. Reuel's footsteps entered, and then he was there on the steps, a finger pressed to his lips.

She frowned at him, unhappy that he was determined to carry out his ruse.

"Listen," he said, "I want you to disappear, and then when I say, 'spirits, come forth!' you appear. Move your lips, but do not speak aloud. That's all you need do this time. Will you do it?"

"I don't want to," she said.

He growled deep in his throat. "Do this for me, and I'll stay, and we'll talk in the evenings. Refuse, and I'll go on my way and leave you here alone. It's your choice."

She hesitated, and he demanded, "Well?"

"I'll do it," she whispered.

"Good!" He smiled broadly, not just with his mouth but with his eyes and cheeks and beard. "Then get out of sight until I call you."

She sank down into the wall, watching the gray stone close over Reuel's face like gathering clouds—and she saw him close the curtain as well, shutting out the light.

This was not right. And Reuel, while he smiled often and spoke freely with her, while he told fine stories, was not the man the wizard had been. He had not even thanked her for agreeing to perform on cue; the wizard almost always thanked her when she was of service to him.

She ached at the realization that she was beginning to not really like Reuel.

But what choice did she have? Reuel was the one who had come to her.

She could no longer see anything but cool darkness, but she could hear, faintly, as Reuel called out to someone, inviting him in. The two of them spoke for a time, and then light filtered in—the curtain had been opened again. Reuel began chanting nonsense—not true incantations that made the stone hum and the air tingle, like those the wizard had used, but childish babbling.

"Arkazam noggle-torp wicko da wicko pung dorpander…"

Utter nonsense, she thought. She could do better herself. But then, she had spent years as a wizard's companion, while her conversations with Reuel led her to suspect that he had never met a true magician.

"By the Unholy Powers I command you! Spirits, come forth!"

Reluctantly, she rose to the surface and looked out at the chamber that had once been the wizard's.

Reuel knelt on the carpet before her, arms spread wide, head bowed; behind him stood a well-dressed young man, staring wide-eyed over Reuel's head at her.

She had seen the stranger's face before, she was certain. "I know you," she said, before she remembered Reuel's instructions. Then she lowered her gaze and recalled what she was supposed to do.

She raised her own arms high over her head, then spread them wide in what she hoped was a mystical gesture. Then she silently mouthed, "Reuel is deceiving you, young man."

Reuel looked up at her face.

"The spirit speaks!" he said.

"Why do I know your face?" she asked silently, lowering her hands. "Were you one of the thieves?"

"She knows your heart, knows your future," Reuel proclaimed.

She shook her head; she knew him now. "No, not the thieves," she mouthed. "You were here with the priest, when my master was taken from me and all his precious belongings destroyed."

"She tells me that you are destined for greatness, Alberch, son of Alberin—you are to be a leader of men, a wise counselor to a score of followers."

"You are a hypocrite, Alberch, son of Alberin," she said inaudibly. "You destroyed a wizard because the priest told you his magic was unholy, yet here you are, seeking counsel from unholy spirits."

"She says you must leave your home soon, to seek out the destiny that awaits you."

"Then I...my destiny isn't here?" Alberch asked.

Reuel shook his head, and looked up at her, but she merely looked back, meeting his gaze. She had no more to say.

"No," Reuel said. "Your destiny is too great for a town of this size; you must find it elsewhere, in richer lands than this, in greater towns than this."

"But..."

She looked directly at Alberch, met his gaze, then slowly shook her head, left to right to left. She meant him to understand that he was not to believe Reuel's lies, but she knew he would probably not interpret her gesture so.

"I will have no more to do with this," she mouthed. Reuel was a scoundrel, deceiving this man—but Alberch was no better, coming here seeking magic when he had aided in destroying the town's real magic months before. She wanted nothing more to do with either of them just now. She sank back into the wall, vanishing from their sight.

"The spirits depart!" Reuel announced, as if Alberch could not see that for himself.

She stayed down in the darkness for a long time, refusing to listen as Reuel and Alberch spoke for a time, then fell silent. At last, though, she grew bored and curious, and returned to the wall's surface.

Reuel was sitting cross-legged on his red-and-gold silk prayer rug, gnawing at a hambone. He looked up.

"There you are!" he said. "Have you had enough of sulking, then?"

"I did as you asked," she said.

"You disappeared before I commanded you to begone," he said.

"I am not yours to command," she said. "You are in my home."

He grinned at her. "It's my home now, as well. We can live together in peace and cooperate with one another, or you can be difficult; the choice is yours."

She stared at him for a moment, then asked, "Why did you tell Alberch to leave the village?"

He shrugged. "It does a man good to travel."

"And he shan't tell anyone you've lied to him, if he is not here."

"That, too. But he doesn't know I've lied to him; I confess, you played your part well."

She had no answer to that.

"Do the same a few more times, and I can make a tidy sum."

"As you will," she said resignedly.

He smiled broadly. "That's my girl!" he said. "And I'll do my part in return. Have I told you yet about the day I came to the banks of the River Oullen, and wished to cross?"

She listened as he told his tale, and much as she hated Reuel's deceptions, and what she was beginning to see as mistreatment of her, she enjoyed the flow of words, the images they conjured in her mind. The man could speak and speak well.

How odd, she thought, to take such pleasure in his talents while she was coming to despise him.

In the days that followed Reuel would leave each morning. Sometimes he would return by midday, accompanied by some trusting soul come to have his or her fortune told. Sometimes it would not be until late afternoon, and on those days Reuel was irritable and impatient. Whenever he brought a customer he would go through the ritual of calling upon the spirits, and she would appear, to mouth silent insults at him and his client that he interpreted as prophecies of happiness and good fortune.

And on some days he did not return until after dark, and he returned alone. On those days he staggered and shouted and fell asleep early, without his evening's full share of conversation. He was drunk, she knew, when he did this, and when he was drunk he boasted openly of his quick wit and his prowess at all the manly arts.

She came to see that even the tales told when he was sober held hidden boasts. In his accounts of his travels he was never bested by anyone; when he was wronged he always triumphed in the end, and he never wronged another unless it was plainly deserved and just.

Somehow, she doubted that he was such a paragon among men. Deceit came naturally to him.

A day came when he did not return until the next morning, and would not explain his absence.

"Were you lonely, then?" he demanded when she asked where he had been. "Well, so was I. Maybe it was a reminder of what you'll have to live with if I ever leave. I saw what you said the other day—I recognized the movement of your lips. You called me a liar in front of a customer. You do as you're told, and don't defy me, or I'll go."

She stared at him, but did not reply.

She had not been lonely that night, when he was gone; she had been relieved.

Still, she did not rebel openly. Instead, when he brought another customer, she simply recited over and over, silently, "I am no spirit. I am a woman. I am no spirit. I am a woman."

"That's better," he told her that night, when the two of them were once more alone.

For three more days he brought clients to have their fortunes told, and then on the fourth day he returned late, alone and drunk.

And on the fifth day he came back late in the afternoon, accompanied by a young woman. The wizard's creation sank down into the wall, awaiting Reuel's summons.

It never came; instead she heard sounds she did not recognize, whisperings and high-pitched giggling and animal gruntings, and at last she could resist her curiosity no longer. She emerged far enough to peer around the closed curtain and observe Reuel and the woman coupling on the hearth, lit only by the fire. The sight fascinated and repulsed her.

When they were done she heard Reuel say, "Now, wasn't that better than that boy Alberch?"

She did not wait for the woman's reply, but sank back into the stone.

There were no customers for several days after that, but the woman came and went frequently. The woman in the wall stayed out of sight much of the time.

And then one day the girl was gone, and Reuel was gone for a day, and then Reuel was back, without her. After that he returned to the old pattern.

And finally, one morning, she had had enough; as a plump old man stared goggle-eyed at her, instead of staying silent she said aloud, "I am no spirit summoned by this man; I am a woman, imprisoned here by the wizard who built this house. I do not prophesy; any words this man speaks to you are his own, not mine."

And with that she sank down out of sight, down into the stone, ignoring the old man's querulous demands and Reuel's desperate attempts at persuasion.

Then the old man was gone, and Reuel screamed at the blank wall, "Bitch! You worthless bitch! You think I'll stay here now? You think I'll forgive you? Never! May you rot in Hell, you faithless abomination!"

She let herself rest in the guarding darkness, drifting in and out of dreams, one part of her trying to forget that Reuel ever existed while another listened intently to the stamping of his angry footsteps as he stripped the chamber of everything of value and bundled it up, preparing to depart. And a third part, one surprisingly small and weak, screamed silently for Reuel to forgive her, to stay, not to leave her trapped and alone in the wall.

She stayed dreaming in the dark for a long time.

She was awakened at last by the sound of many voices, frightened and angry voices. She recognized one—the priest who had come for the wizard, so long ago.

"We should never have let this evil place stand!" he cried. "We do now what should have been done long ago. Let not one stone remain upon another!"

And then, before she could move from her resting place deep within the stones, she experienced something new, something she had never known before—a sensation, a pressure.

A pain.

And then another, and another, and she pressed toward the surface of the wall to look out and see what was happening, but the surface was already cracked and she could not see clearly, could not press herself too close.

Still, she could see the men with great hammers, the handles as long as a man's arm, the iron heads as big as a man's thigh, black against the late afternoon sunlight as they swung blow after blow against the carved stone walls of the wizard's house.

She screamed, and saw the men shiver and hesitate—but not stop. A hammerblow struck over her belly, and the pain was intense, overwhelming; defeated, she let herself fall back into the stony depths.

There was nothing she could do. The house would be destroyed, the wall would be destroyed—and surely, she would perish as well.

She did not want to die, but what was the use in struggling? She had never been able to touch the outside world, to affect it, and nothing she could do would change that.

Her tears slicked the stone, and splashed into nothingness as the hammers struck.

Death might not be so very terrible, she told herself, as she struggled to swallow her pain. No one knew what lay beyond death—the wizard had told her that, and she believed it, for the wizard had never lied to her. Death would mean an end to loneliness, an end to betrayal and neglect, and an end to pain.

She sank down into the stone and tried to return to her dreams, to die in peace, but the blows of the hammers rained down, breaking the wall down, and sending jabs of pain through her. She burrowed as deeply as she could, down to the very foundations of the wall, and crouched there, curled up within herself, waiting for it to all be over.

And at last it was over, her consciousness gone—but after a time she became aware again, slowly, as if awakening from her dreams, and wondered. Was she dead?

She tried to rise up through the stone, but nothing happened; her will did not propel her. Panicky, blind, she raised her head, uncurled, flung her arms wide.

Stone cracked and split like an eggshell, and tumbled away. She heard the sharp rattle and felt the wafer-thin shards fall from her, a sensation like nothing she could remember. She looked up—and saw stars.

She stared.

She had seen stars before—a few at a time, glimpsed through the window. Now she saw thousands upon thousands of them, a glittering river across all the world, and she realized that the roof was gone, that she was seeing the entire sky for the first time.

A cold wind blew across her back, and she shivered.

She could feel the air and the stone, and realized that the wall that had always surrounded and protected her was gone. She was crouched in a hollow in the earth where the foundation of the wall had been, but the wall was gone; the men had smashed it all, broken away all the stone until only she was left, hidden in a thin shell, so thin she was able to break out of it, like a chick being born.

She was not dead. She was not blind. She was alive, and gazing up at the night sky, and she was out of the wall.

Carefully, she uncurled further and stood up, slowly and cautiously, sending a cascade of rocks and dirt from her back. She stood tall and straight and looked around, feeling the wind on her arms and face. Her hair, which had always draped elegantly across her shoulders, now snapped and writhed in the breeze, whipping across her face.

The wizard's house was gone—and the wall was gone. She was free, standing amid the scattered stones that had been her prison. The world was dark and colorless, lit only by the stars, but she could see more of it than she ever had before.

She was free.

She was cold and aching and alone, standing amid ruins in a thin, dusty dress on a cold night in early spring—but she was free. She could go where she pleased; she needed no longer wait for the world to come to her, for Reuel or the wizard to call upon her.

Joy bubbled up within her.

She was, she supposed, merely human now, subject to all the usual mortal ills—hunger and thirst, pain and disease, aging and death. The spell was broken.

That was, she thought, a more than fair exchange.

She looked around, at hills and trees and fields, and westward at the dim grey outlines of the village houses in the distance. She could find food and warmth there, she supposed—but she would also find far too many familiar faces.

Reuel was a wanderer, and had told her how he had adventured across many lands. If he could do it, she thought, then so could she.

She turned, and without another look back began walking to the east, toward where the sun would rise.

THE FINAL CHALLENGE

The royal funerary rites were long since finished and the crowd along the high street was thinning rapidly, but the last of the auxiliary troops were still straggling past when the old soldier ducked into the tavern. He grabbed himself a tankard of ale from a passing tray, turned to face the crowded room, and hoisted it in salute.

"To the old king!" he cried. "We won't see a man like *him* again!"

Most of the tavern's patrons smiled and murmured agreement, lifting their own drinks in reply.

Not everyone did, though. "You old fool," someone called back, "the old king's dead, and now that he's properly buried, let's drink to his son, the *new* king!"

The soldier hesitated, startled; for an instant his teeth bared in an angry grimace, but then he turned it into a rather stiff smile. "Fair enough," he answered, "I'll drink the new king's health, for he's a good man, too—but I'll tell you, good as he is, he's not his father's equal." He swigged ale.

"And how is it you're so certain of that, then?" the other man called belligerently.

The soldier peered over his mug for the source of the voice, and spotted it—a strapping young man of twenty or so, wearing the livery of the crown prince's personal guard, a uniform that no longer had quite the meaning it had had three days before. He was sitting with three other young men, all three in the attire of other divisions of the royal service.

That explained the fellow's hostility. The soldier knew that this was a hard time for the prince's men, as they sought to prove themselves— the relative roles of the Prince's Guard and the King's Chosen Regiment were not yet settled. Such uncertainty could make anyone surly; there was no point in arguing with the fellow about it.

"Why, I've served with them both, boy," the soldier called back to the guardsman, "and I'll be glad to tell you all about it, if you'd like. I meant no disrespect to you, or to Prince...that is, King Philip."

"I don't need to hear any tall tales, old man," the guard answered.

"If by that you mean the sort of lies men usually swap in taverns," the soldier said, approaching the guard's table, "why, I don't mean to tell any—just a few memories about young King Philip, long may he reign, and old King Geoffrey, bless his memory, and every word the truth."

The guardsman hesitated; he glanced around at his companions, judging their reactions, then shrugged. "Talk if you want, old man," he said, "but I don't promise to listen."

"I'd never expected such a promise," the soldier said, sinking into an empty chair across from the guardsman and setting his tankard on the table. He gazed around, as if thinking, and asked, "Ah, where to begin?"

"You say King Philip's no match for his father," the guardsman said challengingly. "I say that's crap. His Majesty's a warrior and a match for any man."

"Oh, he knows how to wield a sword, I'll give you that," the older man agreed, "but a warrior? How's anyone to say, when he's never gone to war?"

The guard's eyes narrowed. "I've seen His Majesty fight, and to my eyes a finer swordsman never lived; certainly no bent old fossil like King Geoffrey could match him!"

"You've seen him *fence*," the soldier corrected. "And in all likelihood you've seen him wrestle and box and ride and shoot and throw the javelin. But you've never seen him fighting for his life, because he's never had to—he was born a prince, where his sire was a minor baron's second son who fought his way to the throne."

"What of it, then? All the more honorable, then, to fight for what's his by right!"

"You think so?"

"I know it!" The guardsman made as if to rise.

The soldier did not; he shrugged, lifted his mug and drank, then put the tankard down empty and wiped his mouth with the back of his hand. The guard hesitated, then settled back into his chair.

"King's son or not," the soldier said, "the old king was one hell of a man, and a warrior to the end, even when he was too old to use a blade."

The guard snorted.

"No, it's true!" the soldier insisted. "Listen, I was at Prince Philip's manhood feast—His Majesty was still the prince then, I mean no disrespect."

"Go on," the guard said. "I've heard the tale; let's hear your version. You say you were there?"

"That I was, lad, that I was. Not at the head table or anything—no, I was just one of the guards at the door, the old king had his own old regiment there as an honor, but whether for us or the boy I don't know." He looked down into his empty mug and sighed. "That was when old Geoffrey fought his last battle with the sword, that feast—you've heard the story, you said. Did you know that the king was more than sixty years of age at the time? Sixty-five, at least, I'd guess—not the typical thing for the father of a lad just coming of age, but what with the wars and the rest of it, he'd got a late start at siring sons. His hair had gone grey, and his belly sagged, but he was still a fine man, with his own teeth and his eye still bright."

"An old man," the guard said derisively. "Like you."

The soldier snorted. "If I should be half so formidable at that age, I'd thank God and sing His praises half the day!"

"Still an old man."

"Aye," the soldier admitted. "An old man—but the king, and still a warrior. He sat at the high table with his councillors and his old cronies, the Red Duke and Tom o' the Axe and the rest, shouting and drinking and carrying on…"

The guard muttered sarcastically, "Nothing like maintaining the royal dignity." His companions chuckled.

"The old king never worried overmuch about his dignity, true enough," the soldier agreed. "Certainly not then. He was having a fine time, he and his comrades taking turns telling stories. The boy—Prince Philip, that is—was seated at the second table, in accordance with protocol, until the stroke of midnight, when he'd be able to take his place with the men, and he had his own comrades about him. Some were men from your own company, some were courtiers and courtiers' sons, and his mother's friends, and his old playmates, all gathered about, making merry. If the truth be told, some were there because of their names and fathers, rather than because the prince actually liked them or wanted them there." He winked at the guard.

"I know the sort," the young man agreed.

"Whatever their excuses, there they all were, drinking and talking—but being young, few of them had any great tales to tell, and in large part they listened to the boasting of their elders."

"I know that sort, too," the guardsman muttered.

The soldier nodded. "Don't we all," he said. "At any rate, there was one lad there who had drunk perhaps more than was good for him, a brawny fellow of twenty-three years or thereabouts, standing six and a half feet when he was upright, and strong as an ox. Perhaps he was unused to strong drink, or perhaps the excitement overcame him, or perhaps he was just a fool, but when the festivities grew loud, he was loudest; when the boys at the second table became rowdy, he was the rowdiest; and at last, upon hearing Lord Ashleigh's account of the defense of the Crimson Gate, he stood up and announced that the tale was nonsense."

"Was it?" the guardsman asked.

The soldier shrugged. "I wasn't at the Crimson Gate," he said, "nor was this lad—yet he went farther, and pronounced *all* the stories being told at the high table as the self-serving lies and senile exaggerations of useless old men."

"Were they?"

The soldier shrugged again. "The ones I knew first-hand were more truth than not."

"Go on."

"Well, the lords at the high table spoke out angrily, and called the lad a young idiot, among other disparagements, but King Geoffrey called for calm, and for a moment it appeared that reason and good will would triumph. The lords ceased their protests, and the lad found himself standing alone and silent, looking rather foolish.

"All might have been well, had not one of the other boys tugged at the oaf's sleeve and urged him to sit. 'Let the old men remember their days of glory,' the fellow said. 'They're the king's good servants.'

"And at that, the drunkard shouted out, 'They're liars, the lot of them, and the king's the worst of them all!' "

"Hunh," the guardsman muttered.

"Indeed," the soldier agreed. "I can still remember the utter silence, that tension in the air—ever been in a real battle, friend? No? Well, if you had, you'd know that moment just before the first charge is made, before the first blow falls. It felt much like that—but in the king's own great hall, and with no armies at the ready, but only a hot-tempered young fool making trouble.

"I watched from my post at the door as the king rose to his feet and faced the youth. Of course, all the others made to rise, too, as protocol demands, but the king motioned them back in their seats.

"'Lad,' the king said quietly, 'Think well on what you've just said.'

"The young fool shouted back, 'I know what I said; I called you a liar. That's what you are—a liar, and a usurper, and a coward who'd never dare face me if he didn't sit on a stolen throne!'"

"The boy had courage, anyway," the guardsman remarked.

"But little wit," the soldier said.

"Go on with the story."

"Well, now, you'd expect the king to rant and rage, and order the young man thrown in the deepest dungeon, but in fact he sighed, and he looked the lad in the eye, and told him, 'I know the hot temper of youth, and the courage we all find in strong drink; I suggest you take a moment to reconsider, and perhaps you'll wish to retract what you have said.' "

"Fairly spoken."

"I thought so," the soldier agreed. "I told you, the old king was one hell of a man."

The guardsman gestured for the story to continue.

"Well, as I already said, the hall was silent, so still it seemed that no one even breathed, and every soul present heard the youth pause, and draw a deep breath—and then not recant, not at all, but instead say, 'I've nothing to retract—you're a scared old man, afraid to die in an honorable combat.'

"The king answered him, 'There is nothing honorable in such a duel,' but it was clear the youth was determined to have his duel, or else, should the king fall back upon the royal prerogatives and have him imprisoned or slain, to become a martyr to the king's tyranny. I suppose the boy's family or friends had some old grudge against the king that had inspired this; I doubt it could be purely drunken folly, though that was plainly to be the excuse."

The soldier paused long enough to signal for another ale, explaining, "Talking's thirsty work." Then he continued, "The king knew the boy wanted to fight, and he made no further attempt to avoid it. Instead he called for his sword, and ordered that the boy's own sword be found and brought, and then he marched down from the high table to the center of the hall, where there was room to fight.

"Everyone else just watched, the feast forgotten, as the two swords were delivered and the two men faced each other across a few yards of stone pavement.

"Whatever the lad had said, it seemed at that moment that no one could doubt the old king's courage. An old man, past sixty, against this young man in his prime.

"The sight—ah, I remember it well! What a contrast! That great hulking youth, glowing with health, took up a formal fighting stance as if he were performing for his fencing master. And the old king stood a head shorter, his face lined, the tendons standing out as he gripped the hilt, hands shaking, his gray hair partially obscuring his face. He fell from old habit into *his* preferred stance, which was a sort of wary crouch, crooked and graceless. He looked like a troll facing a god." The soldier shook his head at the memory, then swigged ale.

The young men at the table shifted restlessly, and one glanced behind, as if he feared someone might be waiting to arrest him for not objecting to such an unflattering description of the late monarch.

The soldier paid no attention; when he had wet his throat sufficiently he continued, "The youth attacked first, swinging the sword like an axe—he couldn't be troubled with fencing's fine points, not against a tired old man, not when they were both drunk. He swung with such strength that it would have gone clear through the king—had it struck him. The king stepped aside, though, and deflected the blow, sending it harmlessly aside with his sword.

"'It's not too late to apologize,' the king said.

"The boy bellowed a wordless challenge, and attacked again, this time showing some pretty skill—in fact, now that he knew a single blow would not serve, he put on a display of the finest fencing-school flutters and flourishes that ever I saw, the blade weaving about like a snake, fast as a cat's paw striking. The king gave ground, turning each attack with his own sword, or else contriving not to be in quite the spot where the blow fell, but it appeared that only by great effort and astonishing luck did he turn the attacks.

"At last, the lad had the king backed up against a pillar.

"'Your last chance,' the king said.

"The youth laughed, and roaring with confidence, he lunged forward in a simple thrust—and fell to the floor with a look of dumb amazement on his face, having been run through the heart once the king had his measure."

The soldier shook his head and smiled.

"Old Geoffrey knew it's not youth and strength that make a warrior, nor a king," he said. "He gave that boy his chance several times over. He never lost his temper, never did anything rash, never let his enemy know his strengths."

"You mean his weaknesses."

"No, no—I mean his *strengths*. So the boy ran right into them. The shaking hands, the seeming weakness—what better way to mislead a foe? And King Geoffrey was brave, but he was no fool; he'd not have fought had he not been certain he would win. Why risk his life when a word would have had the boy arrested and hanged? Oh, a martyrdom might be trouble, but better to face a later insurrection than to die in a stupid brawl. Dead kings do no one any good, most especially not themselves. Geoffrey knew that well." The soldier sighed. "He would never have fought if he didn't know his own strengths, and he knew them well, after all those years. Age and experience outweigh strength and bravado any day."

"So you old men would have us believe," the guardsman said.

"Oh, no," the old soldier said. "Better for us if you don't! Had that young idiot known it, he'd never have challenged the king so openly."

"Ha, a point!" one of the guard's companions shouted, and the four young men laughed.

The soldier did not join them.

"Finish your tale, old man," another said when the laughter had passed.

"Oh, that's all of it, really," the soldier said. "After the king had won, after the boy had died there on the floor, King Geoffrey called for the party to continue, apologized for the unpleasantness, and sent for servants to clean up the mess. And twenty minutes later, at midnight, young Philip came to take his seat at the high table.

"And that," said the old soldier, finishing his ale, "was twenty years ago next month."

BETH'S UNICORN

Beth had loved the unicorn once; she had thought it was the most beautiful, wonderful thing in the world.

That had been when she was just a little kid, though. Now that she was almost fifteen the whole idea of having her very own unicorn somehow seemed a little bit silly. None of her friends had unicorns—or at least, if they did, they didn't talk about them. And grown-ups, like her parents, didn't even *believe* in unicorns, so far she could tell.

Beth believed in unicorns—she had to, since one lived in the woods behind her house and followed her around every chance it got.

The unicorn had been living out there, and following her around, for as long as she could remember. It had definitely been an old friend by the time she had started the first grade, all those years ago—she could still remember the embarrassment when she told her first-grade teacher that she had her very own unicorn that lived out back. Beth had thought it was a perfectly reasonable thing to say.

The teacher hadn't believed a word of it. She had said that it was a very nice story, and then when Beth's mother came to school for conferences she had talked to Beth's mother about invisible playmates and how important it was not to stifle a child's imagination. Beth's mother had repeated this, in a tone of mild puzzlement, to Beth.

"Do you have an invisible playmate, Beth?" she had asked.

Beth had silently shaken her head. The unicorn wasn't invisible. And it wasn't really much of a playmate, either. It couldn't talk or anything. It didn't have hands, so it couldn't throw a ball or a Frisbee, or dress and undress Barbies, or play any good games. It was pretty good at tag—though Beth had to be careful when they played, because that horn was *sharp*; she had gone back inside with nasty little cuts once or twice. It was okay at races and things like that, though it could outrun a little girl so easily that it wasn't really fair, but it wasn't good for much else, so far as Beth could see.

It wasn't any fun playing hide-and-seek with the unicorn because it could just plain disappear; Beth *never* found it when it hid. Now that she was older she wasn't all that sure she'd have said it wasn't invisible. It wasn't *always* invisible, but sometimes she wasn't sure.

Whether it was invisibility or ordinary stealth at work, it never let anyone else see it—only Beth.

When Beth was little she had thought that was pretty neat, having a magical animal that wouldn't let anyone else near it, and she had given it names and pretended she was secretly a princess and the unicorn was the only one who knew it, and had played a lot of other silly baby games, but she had gotten tired of all that. None of the names had stuck, anyway; the unicorn never cared what she called it.

Now she just called it "the unicorn," when she called it anything at all. It wasn't as if she'd ever seen any others.

And she wasn't sure she liked seeing the one. All in all, Beth preferred other kids as playmates.

She wondered whether any of the other girls in the neighborhood had unicorns that followed them around when they were alone. She knew the boys didn't; they'd always made fun of her when she talked about it. Sometimes that was almost as bad as the grown-ups not believing her.

But some of the other girls had said they had unicorns, too, and had described them and told Beth their names—but she was never sure if they were serious, or just pretending, going along with Beth's stories.

It didn't matter. She was too old for all that stuff now, anyway. Nobody else she knew still admitted to ever having even *seen* a real, live unicorn.

She was almost grown up now, Beth told herself as she looked at herself in the mirror. She was almost a woman. She didn't look like a kid playing dress-up any more when she put on make-up and wore heels.

And Josh, who was almost seventeen, didn't think she was a little kid. He'd agreed to drive her to the mall and shop with her—it was practically a date! Her first date!

Dates, boys…who wanted unicorns?

She glanced out the window of her bedroom, and there was the unicorn standing under the trees, looking up at her, its golden horn gleaming in the light of the setting sun.

"Screw you, unicorn!" Beth said. She thumbed her nose at it, and danced out the door of her room and down the stairs to wait for Josh.

It wasn't a long wait.

"You look pretty," he said, when she answered the door.

"Thanks," she answered, smiling foolishly. She knew she looked silly the way she was grinning, but she couldn't stop. She bounced down the steps toward the car waiting at the curb. Josh had borrowed his mother's car; Beth climbed in carefully, almost catching her high heels on the doorframe.

Beth had a fine time at the mall; Josh didn't even act bored when she looked at clothes she couldn't afford. They got giant cookies, and ate them while sitting by the fountain in the center of the mall, and talked about school and music and TV and stuff. And Josh held her hand.

Then he drove her home, and when he pulled up in front of the house he came around and opened the car door for her, like someone in an old movie, and when she got out he leaned over and kissed her.

She was scared and excited, and kissed him back, and put her hands on his shoulders.

His arms went around her and the kiss continued, and she felt his hand sliding down her back. She thought she was on the verge of trembling. This was thrilling and frightening at the same time, and she wasn't sure what she should do, whether she should stop or what.

She liked it, though—until the unicorn squealed.

Josh started and pulled away from her. He turned, and saw the unicorn standing a dozen feet away, pawing the ground with a cloven hoof, that golden horn lowered and pointed straight at his chest.

Beth turned, as well.

She had seen the unicorn do that before. It was getting ready to charge. She had seen it charge any number of times over the years.

Always before, though, it had charged at nothing. This time it looked ready to charge at Josh.

And that horn was *sharp*.

"Stop it!" she called angrily, her voice unsteady. "You stop that this minute!"

The unicorn raised its head and whinnied; the hoof stopped moving. It looked astonished.

"And just what do you think you're doing?" Beth demanded, facing the unicorn with her hands on her hips. "He wasn't hurting me!"

The unicorn stared at her for a moment, then lowered its head again.

Josh stepped away from her, his hands dropping away from her, and Beth felt as if she wanted to cry. "You just go away, unicorn!" she shouted.

The unicorn raised its head and looked at her, and a tear appeared in one eye. It didn't leave, though; it stood its ground.

Beth felt like crying herself, but she didn't know why. She didn't even *like* the unicorn any more. And why was it acting like this? She hadn't been doing anything to harm it.

It acted as if it were trying to protect her, but protect her from *what*? From Josh? Josh hadn't been hurting her; quite the contrary.

Maybe she was angry because her first real kiss had been ruined, but it was too late now—the kiss was ruined and there wasn't anything that could be done about it. And maybe the unicorn had meant well.

It was still staring at her unhappily.

"Oh, all right, you can stay," Beth said, "but don't you touch Josh!"

The unicorn nodded reluctantly, and Beth turned back to Josh.

He was too busy staring at the unicorn to notice at first. Then turned and stared at her instead.

"That's a *unicorn!*" he said breathily.

"Yeah, I know," Beth said. She grimaced. "It's mine, I guess."

Josh blinked in astonishment. "You have a *unicorn!*"

"Yeah." She stood, wanting him to hold her again but unsure how to make it happen. "Listen, Josh, I… I'm sorry it did that, I don't know what's wrong with it. It never threatened anyone before. I mean, it never even let anyone but me *see* it before."

"It was protecting you," Josh said, stepping back, away from Beth.

She wanted to cry. "But you weren't hurting me!" she said. "I don't *want* to be protected!"

"Yeah, but…" Josh stammered. "I… I mean, Beth, unicorns…you have to be a virgin to have a unicorn around."

She looked up at him, puzzled. "So?" she said. "You thought I wasn't?"

"Well, I…" He shook his head. "No, I mean, don't you have to be not just a virgin, but you know, a true innocent, or something?"

She shrugged. "I don't know; I never studied unicorns. I don't think I'm an innocent—I mean, not any more than anyone else. I know, you know, stuff." She laughed nervously.

"But you must be special. You have a unicorn!"

"I don't *want* a unicorn!"

"But I don't want to be responsible for driving it away—I mean, you must be really *special*."

Beth frowned. "I don't think I'm special," she said. "And I don't care if you drive it away." But she looked at the unicorn again, and with a bit more interest in it than she had of late.

Special? Because she had a unicorn?

Nobody else did, true, but she'd always just thought that made her *weird*, not special. It wasn't as if she'd ever *wanted* a unicorn.

It really *was* a beautiful animal, though—a little smaller than a horse, bigger than a pony, all of it shining white except the horn and hooves, which were golden. A little beard, like a goat's, hung from its chin; its tail was a swirling brush of gleaming white curls, not straight like a horse's tail.

It was still looking straight at her.

For the first time it occurred to her that the silly animal loved her.

If it really did leave for good, she realized, she would miss it.

"*It* would care if it had to leave you," Josh said, pointing at the tears that were dribbling slowly down the unicorn's face. "I couldn't do that to it."

"I guess not," Beth admitted.

"I never saw a unicorn before," Josh said. "I thought they were just in stories!"

Beth shrugged.

Josh looked from the unicorn to Beth, then back to the unicorn.

"You must be really special," he said again.

Beth didn't know what to say.

"I better go," Josh said. He backed away, around the car, watching the unicorn the entire time.

Beth stood there on the sidewalk and watched as Josh climbed into the car and drove slowly away, almost stalling the engine as he stared at the unicorn. She felt both sad and somehow relieved—the kiss had been exciting, but scary.

Then she looked around, and saw the neighbors staring at her from half a dozen windows and porches—no, not at her; at the unicorn. She turned, and saw her parents staring from the front window, as well.

Maybe having her own unicorn was something special, after all.

She walked up to the unicorn and brushed away its tears, then hugged it around the neck.

"Okay," she said, "you can stay for awhile. You're going to have to leave some day, because I really *am* growing up, and I can't keep a unicorn around forever—but you can stay for awhile."

Then she let it go.

She watched as the unicorn pranced off into the woods; then she turned and walked into the house, wondering how she could explain the unicorn's presence to her parents—surely, they'd want to know where it had come from, and when, and why. They'd want to know why she'd never told them about it before…

Wouldn't they?

Maybe not, she realized. Maybe she wouldn't have to explain anything at all. Maybe they'd just accept it, the way she always had.

Maybe, she thought, they already knew all that mattered.

THE BRIDE OF BIGFOOT

July, 1990:

Rodney MacWhirter had drunk a very pleasant little lunch back at the rest stop and was feeling the after-effects. He was of the opinion that the six-pack of Bud had not impaired his driving skills whatsoever, and would gladly argue the matter with any state cop who thought otherwise, but there was no denying the pressure in his bladder.

And the next rest stop, according to the sign, wasn't for fifteen miles.

Rodney blinked thoughtfully, then announced to no one, "Guess it's time to water the trees." He found the brake pedal on the second try, and managed to bring his battered Plymouth to a stop on the outer edge of the paved shoulder.

He was zipping his fly when someone tapped him on the shoulder.

He turned around, and the world seemed to vanish into a brown blur; startled, Rodney stepped back, tried to focus, and found himself staring at a broad expanse of shaggy brown hair. He blinked, decided it was a coat of some kind, then raised his eyes, looking for a face.

He had to go much farther than he expected, and when he arrived he wished he hadn't.

There was a face there, as he had expected, but the face was brown and furry, with deep-set brown eyes, a broad black-tipped nose, a wide, lipless mouth, and with stubby fangs protruding from the upper jaw. The heavy brow-ridges were a good eight feet from the ground.

"Whoa!" Rodney said. "Hi, there, fella! You're a big one, ain'cha?"

The creature smiled, revealing several dozen yellow teeth, and nodded. Then it held up a stack of mismatched sheets of rather used paper in one hand, and pointed to it with the other, which clutched a handful of battered crayons.

Rodney squinted at the top sheet of paper and read, in large, shaky, red letters, I NEED RIDE TO OREGON WOODS.

"Whoa!" Rodney said again. "That's a mighty long way, friend; I can't take you that far." From the corner of his eye he saw the thing's smile vanish, and he hastily added, "But I can get you partway, I guess."

The smile returned, and together, Rodney and the creature walked to the car.

"So, you got a name?" Rodney asked.

The creature shook its head, and hair scraped audibly against the car's roof lining. A Plymouth Duster might have more headroom than the typical modern car, but it was never intended for anything the size of Rodney's passenger.

"No?" Rodney said, mildly surprised; he turned to stare, then snapped his attention back to the road at the sound of a horn blaring. A car coming the other way roared past, the driver's fist waving in Rodney's direction.

For a moment Rodney concentrated on his driving; then he suggested, "How 'bout I call you Bubba? You remind me of a fellow I useta know went by Bubba."

The creature shrugged, as best it could while squeezed into the Plymouth.

"Bubba it is, then," Rodney said. For a minute or so he hummed quietly to himself.

"So where you going in Oregon, anyway?" he asked a moment later, still watching the highway unroll before him. He waited a few seconds, to give the creature time to write, then glanced over.

The beast didn't hold up a paper; instead it shrugged again.

"Just tired of Wisconsin, huh?" Rodney said, with a sympathetic smile. "I can understand that. You really need to go all the way to Oregon, though? You couldn't just check out Minneapolis?" He watched the highway, then added, "But I guess you're not the city type. Still, there's plenty of nice country in Minnesota. Or up in Maine; might be more traffic that way. Why's it got to be Oregon? Got family out there?"

The creature hesitated, then pulled a wrinkled piece of newsprint from its pile of scrap paper and held it up. Rodney glanced at it, and saw a battered fragment of tabloid—specifically, the *Midnight News* for October 1, 1987, featuring the headline, "THE BRIDE OF BIGFOOT! Scientists Report Sighting Female Creature In Oregon Woods!'"

There was no photo, but a drawing captioned, "Artist's Rendition of Creature, from Scientists' Description," accompanied the article, and depicted a stooped, furry, apelike figure with ragged, waist-length head hair and immense breasts.

Rodney slowed the car slightly and looked the clipping over again.

"Bride of Bigfoot," Rodney read aloud. "That your wife, then? Mrs. Bubba?"

The creature shook his head.

"But you'd like her to be, maybe? You looking for a date out there?"

Bubba hesitated, then nodded.

"You don't like the local girls?" Rodney asked.

Bubba found one of his crayons and scrawled quickly, then held up a paper saying, CAN'T FIND ANY.

"What, *none*?"

Bubba shrugged again.

"What about guys? You got friends around here, might want help?" Rodney thought he might have a money-making idea here—a dating service for bigfoots!

Or was it bigfeet?

While Rodney was trying to puzzle out the correct plural, Bubba wrote, ALL ALONE. NO OTHERS.

Well, Rodney thought, so much for *that* idea. "Wow, tough," he said. "No family? Nothing?"

Bubba held up the same paper after underlining *ALL ALONE*.

"Jeez, no wonder you want to get out there," Rodney said. He thought for a moment.

There ought to be some way to make money off this, he told himself. He couldn't make a career out of matchmaking if Bubba and the lady in the picture were the only ones out there, but there had to be *some* way to cash in on picking up a mythical creature as a hitchhiker.

He'd intended to just drop Bubba off, but as he sobered up the possibilities began to occur to him. As they crossed the Minnesota state line he said, "Look, I was only going as far as St. Paul, but maybe I can... I mean, I might be able to take you clear to Oregon, if you're not in a hurry." He glanced over.

Bubba nodded, smiling.

Smuggling something Bubba's size in and out of motel rooms was an art Rodney had never acquired; fortunately, despite his bulk, Bubba could be amazingly stealthy. He moved in utter silence, and could hold so still that a bored motel maid might pass within a yard of him without noticing his presence.

That at least explained something of why the scientists still didn't believe in Bigfoot, or sasquatches, or whatever Bubba was.

Feeding him turned out to be simple enough—fast-food salad bars provided everything Bubba needed. Cherry tomatoes seemed to delight him no end, and Rodney made a point of getting as many of those as he could, despite the dirty looks from restaurant staffs.

Bubba had no idea what a bed was for; he was perfectly happy curling up on the motel-room carpet. He didn't understand indoor plumbing, either, but finding a few out-of-the-way bushes was usually easy enough. Rodney gathered, from a conversation that was largely grunts or nods on Bubba's side, that the creature had learned English from spying on campers, and taught himself to read and write from studying the news-papers, labels, and other scraps they left behind—a project that had oc-cupied most of the past ten years, inspired by a discovery of a "bigfoot" photo in an old tabloid. Bubba, however, had never been inside a build-ing before, and was not much interested in human civilization—except for picking goodies from its trash, and using it to find himself a mate.

That first night Rodney, now thoroughly sobered up, was a trifle uneasy about sleeping in the same room as this immense beast—even though Bubba had made it clear that he preferred salads to burgers, Rod-ney still worried about all those teeth and claws.

When he awoke the next morning, completely intact, at first he thought he'd dreamed or imagined the whole thing; he came within inches of stepping on the still-sleeping Bubba, who had rolled over close to the bed.

By the second night they were both old hands at it.

And on the third night they made it as far as Walla Walla, Washing-ton, just across the Oregon state line—Rodney had decided the fastest route was to leave the Interstate and take U.S. 12.

He didn't tell Bubba how close they were, for fear he'd want to go on that same night—Rodney was *tired* of driving.

When morning rolled around, though, the two of them got rolling as well, and had gone just a few miles when Rodney pointed out the WEL-COME TO OREGON sign.

"We're in the right state," he said with a smile. "So where's this lady-friend you're looking for?"

Bubba handed him the clipping.

Rodney glanced at it, then pulled over to the shoulder atop the next ridge and read through the clipping carefully. As he read, his smile slow-ly faded, to be replaced with a worried frown. "Bubba, ol' buddy," he said, "It doesn't *say* where she was, anywhere in here. There's no date-line or anything, it just says 'somewhere in the Oregon woods,' and that doesn't tell us enough."

Bubba growled, and tapped a claw-tipped finger insistently on the word OREGON.

"Bubba," Rodney said, "hop out of the car for a minute, okay?"

The pair climbed out and stood by the road; Rodney waved an arm to take in the entire surrounding countryside, a broad vista of hills and forests extending seemingly forever.

"Bubba," he said, "*that's* the Oregon woods. Everything you see, and a lot more besides."

Bubba stared for a moment, then made a noise that Rodney could only liken to a strangled kitten. The huge creature turned and stared helplessly at Rodney.

Rodney thought for a moment the sasquatch was going to cry.

"Hey, don't worry, Bubba," he said. "We'll find her somehow. You just come with me."

"I tell you, Bubba, I felt really stupid buying this thing," Rodney said, as he thumbed through the latest issue of *Midnight News*. The two of them were seated in the Plymouth, parked in front of a drugstore in Milton-Freewater, Oregon. "Oh, here we go, page 6—*Midnight News*, editor, managing editor, yadda yadda yadda…telephone! Editorial, area code 407…" He lowered the paper. "Where the heck is area code 407?"

Bubba just stared silently at him.

Area code 407 turned out to be central Florida; the address was further down the block of tiny print on page 6.

"Figures," Rodney said in disgust, as he dialed the motel-room phone. "The damn opposite corner of the whole damn country, is all. This call is probably gonna cost more than the damn room."

Bubba didn't answer; he sat and stared.

The phone on the other end only rang once before a female voice said, "*Midnight News*."

"Hi," Rodney said. "Look, I need to know more about something you ran in your paper—it's very important to a friend of mine."

"What is it, exactly?" the voice asked warily.

"It's about this piece you ran in October '87, about seeing a female bigfoot in Oregon…"

Before he could finish, the voice cut him off. "'*87?!*" the woman exclaimed. "Mister, are you crazy? That was three years ago!"

"Yes, I know," Rodney said patiently.

"I'm sorry, but we don't keep…" She stopped, thought better of whatever she had been about to say, and instead asked cautiously, "What did you want to know?"

"I want to know where in Oregon this bigfoot sighting was," Rodney explained. "It just says 'Oregon woods.' Oregon's a big state."

"I suppose it is," she agreed.

"So where was this sighting?"

"Mister, is there a by-line on the article you've got there?"

Rodney blinked, and squinted at the yellowed clipping. "Uh…yeah," he said. "Special correspondent Maurice Betterman, it says."

"Moe Betterman?" The voice sighed. "Well, at least I know who that is; he's a freelancer, still writes for us sometimes. Lives in Eugene."

"Eugene, Oregon?"

"That's right."

"So, can I reach him…"

"Listen, Mister, that's all I can tell you. It's probably more than I *should* tell you."

"But…" Rodney began.

Then he realized he was talking to a dead phone; she had hung up.

"Eugene," he said. "That's the other end of the state." He hesitated, then dialed again.

"Directory assistance," said the voice. "What city, please?"

There was a listing for an M.C. Betterman; a few minutes and a dozen rings later Rodney finally heard someone pick up the phone—then drop it; Rodney winced at the clatter.

After assorted bumps and rattles, a bleary voice said, "'Lo?"

"Is this Maurice Betterman?" Rodney asked.

"Who wan'sa know?"

Rodney sighed. "I'm looking for the Maurice Betterman who writes for the *Midnight News*," he said.

"Why?"

"Are you him?"

"He," the voice corrected. "Are you *he*."

Rodney took that as a good sign; in his experience only teachers and writers corrected people like that. "Are you?" he asked.

"Migh' be; why?"

"We need a little more information about an article you wrote back in 1987," Rodney explained.

For a long moment there was no answer, and Rodney was beginning to wonder if he had been cut off, or if Betterman had fallen asleep, when the voice finally asked, "Who's 'we'?"

"Me'n Bubba," Rodney explained.

"Bubba."

"Well, that's what I call him."

Click. Betterman had hung up.

Rodney dialed again, and let the phone ring twenty-two times, hoping the motel operator wouldn't notice and cut him off before Betterman answered.

The motel operator didn't.

"Yeah?" his voice asked.

"It's me again," Rodney said. "Look, please don't hang up..."

"You'n Bubba?"

"That's right."

"Why should'n I hang up? You got three seconds to convince me."

"Money," Rodney said quickly. "Lots of money."

For another long moment the line was silent—but no one hung up. Then Betterman sighed.

"Okay," he said. "Tell me about it."

Rodney told him.

"You got a sasquatch there?" Betterman asked when Rodney had finished. "A real one?"

"That's what I said," Rodney replied. "And he wants to know where you saw that other one in '87."

"And suppose I tell you—then what?"

"Then we hang up and stop bothering you."

"Suppose I *don't* tell you?"

"Then we'll keep bothering you."

"You said there was money involved..."

"Well, sure—aren't pictures of a sasquatch worth money?"

"Depends how good they are."

"You can take all the pictures you want of this one."

Betterman was silent for a moment before asking, "So where are you? Where can I see this thing?"

Betterman stared at Bubba. "I didn't believe you," he said to Rodney. "I figured you'd just tell me it had got away or something."

The three of them had rendezvoused at a rest area on I-84, a few miles west of Hood River; Bubba had waited in the woods while Rodney met Betterman and escorted him over for a good long look.

"Then why'd you come?" Rodney asked.

"Oh, I figured I could get a story out of it anyway—and besides, it seemed like the quickest way to get rid of you," Betterman explained, never taking his eyes from Bubba.

The attention seemed to make the creature uneasy, but he didn't flee.

"I call him Bubba," Rodney explained. "He doesn't have a name, really—I guess his kind don't bother with them."

"Does it...does it talk?" Betterman asked hesitantly.

Bubba grunted.

"No," Rodney said. "But he writes notes. You brought your camera?"

"It's in the car," Betterman answered.

"Okay. Look, here's the deal—Bubba, here, is lonely, and he saw in that article that you saw a female bigfoot, so he wants to meet her. Now, *you* tell us where she is, and *we* let you take pictures and ask questions. Fair enough?"

Betterman looked at him, startled. "*I* never saw one before!" he said.

"Okay, okay," Rodney said. "You wrote that article, but I guess it somebody else that actually saw the critter?"

Betterman shrugged, then hesitated, then looked warily at Bubba. The creature looked nervous, and despite the size, fairly harmless.

"I made it up," he said.

Rodney and Bubba were thunderstruck. For a moment they just stared.

Then Bubba growled. Betterman, suddenly aware that he might have done something stupid, began desperately explaining, "Look, I'm being honest with you, I could've jerked you around until I got the pictures, I could've told you anything, but I figured I should be honest, I just made it all up, honest!"

"You did?" Rodney asked ominously.

"Sure!" Betterman babbled, "I make it *all* up! I mean, everything, the Elvis sightings, Hitler's clones, the UFO aliens, the three-headed babies, it's all made up! Just entertainment, just stories!"

"Nobody saw a female bigfoot?"

"Not… I don't… I don't know!" Betterman wailed, as Bubba's huge paw closed on the front of his shirt.

"You don't *know*?" Rodney demanded.

"No! I mean, I do research my stuff, I collect clippings and everything, and maybe somebody saw one and maybe that's what gave me the idea for my article, but I don't remember! It's been three years!"

Rodney looked at Bubba, and Bubba looked at Rodney. Bubba let go of Betterman's shirt and turned, reaching for his writing supplies.

"You want to go check this out?" Rodney asked. "See what he's got in his files?"

Bubba nodded. Then he scribbled quickly with a stub of purple crayon.

Betterman stared, amazed, at the sight of the huge hairy beast *writing*; when he saw what it had written, however, he let out a low moan of terror.

OR I RIP HIS HED OFF, Bubba said.

* * * *

The drawer marked MYTH. BEASTS was two feet deep and full to overflowing; yellowed clippings were spilling out the sides. Betterman carefully hauled out the two fattest folders, labeled BIGFOOT and BIGFOOT (CONT.).

Bubba stared as the clippings spilled out across the rickety table. His own collection was mostly tabloids, and these were not; instead, Betterman had restricted himself to relatively respectable sources. Where Bubba's stories were mostly front-page features with screaming headlines, Betterman's were mostly tiny items clipped from the back pages of obscure local weeklies, from columns with titles like "Unexplained" and "Briefly Noted."

Rodney was impressed—until he began looking over the material at hand.

"There's nothing on here to tell where it is!" he pointed out. "Or on this one, or this…" He picked up a larger scrap, stared, and said, "And *this* one's from 1964!"

"I've been at this a long time," Betterman muttered.

Rodney could believe that; Betterman had to be in his fifties, at least. "Why don't you note where they're *from*?" he asked.

"Who cares?" Betterman shrugged. "This is just for ideas, I'm not writing a book or anything."

Rodney frowned.

"Well, there might be *some* we can use," he said. "I guess we better start sorting." He sat down, and began reading.

August, 1992

"Look, Moe," the voice on the phone said, "They're *great* pictures, I don't know how you do it, they're better than the stuff our lab here does, but we're *tired* of bigfoot stories! Two years now you've been sending us bigfoot stories! People are sick of bigfoot, Moe; give us something on Elvis, or something."

"But they're *real*," Betterman insisted desperately. "I keep telling you that!"

"If they're real," his editor answered, "Why are you sending them to *us*, and not *Scientific American*?"

"Because *Scientific American* doesn't believe me!" Betterman shouted, "And Bubba draws the line at letting anyone else see him!"

"Bubba?"

"Never mind," Betterman mumbled. "Look, I'll do an Elvis sighting, okay? I'll have it in the mail tomorrow. How about he's in a drug rehab program?"

"Well, maybe," the editor said. "But remember, people want him to look like a good guy."

"Maybe he's been held hostage?"

"Yeah, I think we could go for that. And if you could get photos…"

"No photos," Betterman said. "You'll have to do that part."

"Okay, no photos. And no more bigfoot." He hung up before Betterman could answer.

Betterman sighed and turned to his ancient typewriter; by the time Rodney MacWhirter came in for dinner he had a complete draft of "Elvis Escapes Terrorists!" done.

When Rodney and Bubba had first shown up, two years before, he had never expected it to turn out this way—two years spent trying to convince *somebody* that Bubba was real, when Bubba had apparently hit his limit of how many people he would allow to see him—two, Moe and Rodney.

And Rodney had gone home to Milwaukee and packed up his belongings and moved out to Eugene, trying to find some way to cash in on his friendship with Bubba, all while tracking down bigfoot sightings and trying to find Bubba a mate.

And neither of them had anything to show for it except a bunch of by-lines in cheap tabloids—Moe writing the articles, Rodney providing the pictures.

And they hadn't found another sasquatch. Poor Bubba was getting depressed, frustrated, and angry.

"So how goes it?" Moe asked, when Rodney had thrown himself into the sagging armchair by the window.

"Lousy," Rodney said. "I checked out the last one of your clippings today."

"Nothing?" Moe asked sympathetically.

"Nothing," Rodney agreed.

"So now what?"

"So now we go tell Bubba the bad news. And maybe I see about finding an honest job again—my savings are just about gone."

"Ha!" Moe said. "I never *had* any savings! *Or* an honest job!"

They met at the back corner of a rest stop on I-84 again, but nowhere near Hood River this time; Bubba had been working his way eastward, searching the forests, and had gotten out past the Wallowa-Whitman National Forest, to somewhere in Baker County.

Rodney explained.

"We've tried 'em all, Bubba—everything we know to do. And we haven't found a thing." He shrugged, and turned up empty palms.

"There's nothing more we can do."

Bubba frowned, and wrote.

ASK LEADING PYSCHICS, he said. He held up one of his own clippings; he had been collecting them from campsides and trash cans all across Oregon. This one's banner headline read, "Psychic Locates Child Lost In Woods For Five Years!" The subhead explained, "Boy Lived on Roots and Berries!"

"Psychics are all fakes," Moe said. "We've told you that."

Bubba wrote, ASK ELVIS, and held up a clipping headlined, "Elvis' Ghost Leads Woman to Lost Jewelry!"

"Elvis is dead," Rodney said. "Fifteen years, now."

Bubba shook his head angrily and held up "Stunning New Proof the King Still Lives!"

"But even if he does," Moe said, "How do we find *him*? He's in hiding!"

Rodney turned to argue, then thought better of it; Bubba wrote again.

ASK UFO ALEINS, he said. His exhibit this time read, "Space Aliens Reveal Pyramid Secrets!"

"There *aren't* any UFO aliens!" Moe insisted. "I keep telling you, Bubba, it's all *made up!* All that stuff in the tabloids! It's all lies!"

ALL? Bubba asked, holding a clipping of "Bigfoot Prowling Central Park!" against his chest.

"All of it," Moe insisted. "*You're* real, but the rest of it is all fiction. They just made it all up. Elvis is dead. There aren't any aliens."

NO BIGFOOT? Bubba asked.

"None except you," Moe said.

WHERE'D I COME FROM?

"I don't know," Moe said helplessly, "but you're the only one."

Bubba stared at him for a moment, then turned, and before Moe or Rodney could protest, he had vanished into the woods.

"You sure about this?" Moe asked, as Rodney forced down the trunk lid on his ancient Plymouth.

"I'm sure, all right," Rodney said. "Back in Milwaukee I've got friends and contacts; around here, I've got you, and about a thousand people who think I'm a nut who believes in Bigfoot."

"You *are* a nut who believes in Bigfoot," Moe pointed out.

"Yeah, but it doesn't help my job prospects," Rodney said, as he headed for the driver's seat.

"Drive safely, then," Moe said.

"I will," Rodney said, hoping Moe couldn't see the cooler of Budweiser in the shotgun seat. Driving across all that empty country was bad enough under any circumstances; he didn't want to face it sober.

One of these days, he thought, he was probably going to get himself killed by misjudging how much he drank—but right now he didn't care.

"Say hello to poor Bubba if you see him."

"I will."

And then he was gone.

The gas station was utterly nondescript except for the guy behind the counter. Rodney blinked at him in surprise.

The fellow had thick, slicked-back black hair, a heavy and oddly familiar face; he wore studded white denim and very dark sunglasses, though the light in the little mini-grocery was hardly bright. He was also grossly overweight and obviously on the wrong side of fifty, which made the hair and studs and sunglasses look very odd. Rodney had the feeling that if he could see better, and hadn't had those last few beers, he might recognize the man.

But that was silly; who would he know at a gas station outside Missoula, Montana?

"Somethin' I can help you with?" the cashier asked.

"Wish you could," Rodney said, staring at the issue of the *Midnight News* on display beside the cash register. One of his last photos of Bubba was featured on the front page.

"How's that, friend?"

Rodney pointed. "Friend of mine," he said. "Can't get a date."

The man behind the counter made a wordless noise of surprise. "The hairy fella?" he asked.

Rodney nodded, then waited for the room to steady again. "Yup. Ol' Bigfoot himself, out there in Baker County, Oregon—he's been looking for a female for years, can't find a one."

"That so?"

Rodney decided against nodding again. "Yup."

"Seems to me someone could maybe do somethin' about that," the cashier said. His voice was familiar, too, Rodney thought.

"I tried," he said. "I spent the last two years asking people all over the northwest." It occurred to him that he must sound like a lunatic, and that he would never have been talking about it if he were sober, but the cashier didn't seem to think there was anything wrong.

"Mebbe you asked the wrong folks," the man said. His accent, Rodney realized, was from somewhere a lot farther south than Montana. "I been doin' some travelin' these past fifteen years," the cashier continued, "and I met some interestin' folks, some that was what you might call right out of this world. I'd guess that they might help us out here." He picked a copy of the *Midnight News* from the rack and studied the photo. "Seems like him and me, we got some things in common, you might say," he said, tapping the headlines.

Rodney struggled to focus on the newspaper. The photo was down at the foot of the page, captioned, "New Sightings of Mystery Beast!" Beside it, a box proclaimed, "Elvis in Iraq for Secret Negotiations!" The main headline, under the clerk's hand, read, "Space Aliens Save Sinking Ship! Bermuda Triangle Victims Rescued By UFO!"

"Poor Bubba," Rodney muttered.

"Don't you fret, son," the clerk said. "Things'll turn out jest fine. Now, you had the nachos and the bean dip; anythin' else?"

Twenty minutes later Rodney decided, as he sat in his car munching the last of the chips, that he was too tired—and, he admitted to himself, too drunk—to drive any more just then. He settled back for a quick nap.

He awoke to a loud buzzing and a bright light; blinking, trying to shield his eyes against the glare, he stared out at the gas station.

The light was coming from somewhere overhead; Rodney couldn't see its source. He *could* see the overweight clerk standing in the doorway, head tilted back, dark sunglasses protecting his eyes as he gazed upward.

He seemed to be signalling, making signs with his hands.

That was crazy, Rodney decided. He must be dreaming. He closed his eyes and went back to sleep.

When he awoke again he shook his head to clear it, blinked, and put the car into drive.

Weird dream, he thought. Some guy who looks like Elvis signalling the flying saucers—obviously, Rodney thought, I've been reading too many tabloids.

The following night UFO sightings were reported all over Baker County, Oregon. The most peculiar feature was the story, repeated by a dozen witnesses, that a big hairy man had been standing on a hill near a campground, waving sheets of paper at the UFOs. The deputy who investigated the next day found letters burned into the grass.

They were obviously the work of pranksters; after all, why would space aliens write WE'RE ALL IN THIS TOGETHER, BUBBA on a hillside, in plain English?

* * * *

As Moe Betterman read the report his eyes widened, and then a slow smile spread across his face.

Bigfoot sightings were common enough; he had been collecting them for thirty years. People reported lone creatures most of the time, but sometimes pairs, trios, whole families, entire herds; it didn't mean much.

But when half a dozen sightings in succession, all in eastern Oregon, *all* reported *two* sasquatches, one smaller and more delicate than the other…

"Congratulations, Bubba," he said quietly. "And my best to the little lady."

KEEPING UP APPEARANCES

Maribelle stared at the little black-iron cage in dismay. She had known when she returned from visiting her family and found the room deserted, with a note from Armus dated the day before yesterday directing her to look for him here if he wasn't home yet, that there was trouble.

But she hadn't expected *this*.

The hamster in the iron cage stared back at her. It was small and round and golden and looked totally harmless.

And rather stupid, but that didn't surprise Maribelle at all. "That's really Armus?" she asked.

"So the wizard's messenger said," Derdiamus Luc replied.

The hamster squeaked and nodded.

"Oh, dear," Maribelle sighed. "*What* will I tell his mother?"

"I'm sure I don't know," Luc said with an uneasy smile.

"Speaking of things you do or don't know," Maribelle said, "would you know how to turn him back? I mean, is this permanent? Is there some way to break the curse?"

"I'm afraid I have no idea," Luc said. "The messenger didn't tell me much of anything."

"Did the messenger tell you *why* the wizard Esotissimus turned Armus into this little furball?"

"Well..." Luc coughed.

Maribelle tore her gaze away from the hamster and looked at Luc. It wasn't hard to see that the merchant was hiding something.

And it wasn't hard to guess what it was, either. When she got Armus home she intended to have a few words with him, whether he was hamster or human at the time.

For now, though, she stared at Luc in wide-eyed innocence, pretending she hadn't a clue as to why the wizard would have been irked with Armus.

"I'm afraid it's partly my fault," Luc admitted. "Esotissimus has been telling my customers the most terrible lies about some of the goods I sell, and I hired the young man to deliver a strong complaint about this practice." He glanced at the hamster. "It appears the wizard didn't appreciate it. I *am* sorry."

Maribelle sighed again.

Actually, she supposed the wizard had been merciful, since the "strong complaint" Armus was supposed to deliver had almost certainly been a dagger between the ribs. And the "terrible lies" were probably accurate assessments of the value of some of the charms and potions Luc sold; Maribelle was fairly certain that Luc's so-called "irresistible love spells" were just civet and musk, and the "miraculous medicines" nothing but willow bark in distilled wine, with no magical content at all.

But what had Armus thought he was doing, going after a wizard alone?

"Well, I'm sure you meant well," she said, picking up the cage. She turned to go, then paused and turned back to Luc. "Um…while I can see that the response wasn't what you might have hoped, Armus apparently *did* deliver your message. Shall I send a bill, or would you like to pay now?"

Luc's jaw dropped, then snapped shut.

"Pay?" he said, sounding a bit strangled.

"Well, yes," Maribelle said. "I'm afraid that the Assassins' Guild would insist. Armus is a member, after all, so even though you merely hired him as a messenger, Guild rules would apply. Wouldn't they, Armus?"

The hamster made a noise that was clearly meant as agreement.

"Assassins' Guild? You mean there really *is*…" Luc stopped in mid-sentence. He looked at Maribelle's wide-eyed innocent gaze, and at the hamster's beady little eyes, both fixed on him.

"Of course," he said through clenched teeth. "I believe we had agreed upon a price of fifty royals…"

Armus cheebled angrily.

"How foolish of me," Luc said, forcing a laugh. "I mean *one hundred* and fifty. I'll just write you a chit…"

"Sire Luc, I'm afraid I may be traveling soon, on short notice," Maribelle said, her voice oozing regret. "I'll need to have cash."

"Well, I don't see how I…" Luc began.

Maribelle interrupted him, her tone still regretful but a little harder than before. "I wouldn't want to tell my friends in the Guild you were *uncooperative*, after you got the man I love turned into a *hamster*…"

Luc winced. "Of course," he said quickly.

Maribelle waited patiently as Luc counted out the coins. So far as she knew there *was* no Assassins' Guild, here in Verengard or anywhere else, but Luc wouldn't know that. Merchants heard all the rumors, and never knew which to believe. And Luc certainly knew what Armus did for a living. What's more, the amount of money involved confirmed that Luc hadn't hired Armus the Assassin just to deliver a message. He could have hired any urchin off the street for two royals—or maybe it would have taken as much as five, since a wizard was involved.

A hundred and fifty meant something more than a message, something a bit more pointed.

Twenty minutes later, back in the rented room two streets over, Maribelle opened the cage and pointed to the sheet of parchment and the little pan of ink she had set out.

"Now," she said, "would you mind telling me what you thought you were doing, contracting for an assassination without me? And agreeing to kill a *wizard*, without properly researching the job? I was only gone for eleven days! You couldn't wait that long?"

The hamster cheebled angrily at her.

"I can't understand anything you say," Maribelle told it. "Just dip a claw in the ink; I know you can't hold a pen."

The hamster glared at her for a moment, then scurried to the ink.

The result was smeared and messy, but legible.

I WAS BORED. LOOKED EASY. PAID WELL.

"A hundred and fifty royals?" Maribelle protested.

The hamster let out an offended squawk, and scrawled 600. 150 ADVANCE, 150 MORE EVEN IF WIZARD LIVED.

"And the rest if you actually pulled it off."

Armus nodded.

"And did you *really* think you could kill a wizard single-handed?"

The hamster shook his head, and reached for the ink.

SCOUTING, he wrote. THEN WAIT FOR YOU, FINISH THE JOB TOGETHER.

"But you got caught."

The hamster looked sheepish—which was an impressive accomplishment for a hamster, but Armus had always been a talented, charming individual.

Not all that *bright*, but talented and charming.

"All right," Maribelle said. "Tell me all about it, step by step. Then we'll see about getting you turned back."

She didn't say it aloud, but mentally added, if you *can* be turned back. She knew perfectly well that transformations were tricky stuff. Some could only be reversed by the wizard who initiated them. Others could only be ended by the wizard's death—she didn't think she would very much mind arranging that in this case.

And some transformations couldn't be undone at all.

She shivered at the thought as she watched the hamster scratching ink onto the parchment, leaving smudgy little footprints everywhere. She and Armus had been working together for a little over four years now, and she had hoped they would stay together for the rest of their lives. She'd put aside almost half the money they had earned as assassins, with the intention of someday retiring on it and settling down somewhere— after all, they couldn't keep killing people forever. She wouldn't always be sufficiently young and pretty and innocent-looking to use their preferred methods, where Armus would threaten the intended target, drawing all the attention while poor helpless-looking little Maribelle put a knife in the victim's back.

Settling down with a hamster, rather than a man, hadn't been at all what she had in mind.

The wizard Esotissimus was clearly a traditionalist. His establishment was built of wrought iron, smoke-blackened oak, and equally smoke-blackened granite, lavishly trimmed with spikes and gargoyles. Maribelle paused on the street and looked up at it before entering.

Maribelle usually liked traditionalists; they tended to be easy targets, never ready for the unexpected. They either ignored her completely or tried to seduce her, and both options provided plentiful opportunities for poison or a quick stroke of the blade.

She wasn't here to kill this particular wizard, though, but to coax a favor out of him, and traditionalism might work against her there. Wizards had a traditional dislike for reversing their
spells.

And Esotissimus was not merely a traditionalist, but a very powerful wizard. That was why Maribelle had chosen the direct approach. Armus swore he hadn't even seen the wizard's hands move when the transformation spell was cast. He hadn't even realized the wizard was really angry with him until he started shrinking and growing fur.

Armus had attempted a ruse; he had pretended to be a prospective customer, hoping to study the layout of the wizard's home and learn a bit of his capabilities. He still, he said, didn't know what had gone wrong, or how the wizard had known he was lying.

Maribelle lifted the immense iron knocker and let it fall; a muffled boom echoed, and with a creak of bending metal the two black iron gargoyle faces on either side of the door turned to look at her.

She looked back, quickly putting on her dumb-and-demure working expression and smiling at first one, then the other. Just because the iron faces could move that didn't mean they could see her, but there was no reason to take unnecessary chances.

And it was very obvious that this was *real* magic here, not the cheap imitations offered by Derdiamus Luc and his ilk.

The oaken door opened a crack, and a heart-shaped female face framed in lustrous black curls peered out at her.

"Hello there," Maribelle said. There was no point in turning the charm on full for a woman, but she smiled brightly. "I'd like to see Esotissimus, please."

"You don't have an appointment," the black-haired woman said accusingly.

"I didn't know how to make one," Maribelle explained. "Please, it's *very* important." She adjusted the strap of the bag slung over her shoulder.

"What's it about?" the woman demanded.

Maribelle looked at her, trying to judge whether to admit the truth or insist on seeing the wizard. The woman was short, shorter than Maribelle—she would scarcely have reached Armus' shoulder if Armus were still himself. She wore a low-cut, tight-fitting gown of black velvet that combined with her lush mop of hair to frame and accentuate her pale skin and fine features. She had made herself up expertly, but Maribelle could see that she was past the first bloom of youth—perhaps thirty, or even thirty-five. If she were a slave-girl kept entirely for her decorative appearance she could expect to be cast aside any day now, whenever her master might trouble himself to really look at her and see past the cosmetics.

If she had other talents, Maribelle couldn't see them.

She was likely to be balky, then—she would be insecure in her position, and reluctant to risk any disturbance should she admit the wrong person. Better, then, to tell her the truth.

"It's about my husband," Maribelle said.

The woman's eyes darkened. "Oh?"

"Yes," Maribelle said. "The wizard turned him into a hamster. I'd like him turned back."

Enlightenment struck; the woman's eyes widened with sudden understanding.

"Oh, the *hamster*!" she said. "I hadn't…well, come in; I'll tell the great Esotissimus you're here." She swung the door wide, and ushered Maribelle inside, down a corridor to a small, windowless, sparsely-furnished room lit by a dozen fat candles.

"Wait here," the attendant said.

Maribelle settled onto an oaken chair and waited. She opened the bag so that Armus could have a little light and air—though the air was sufficiently thick with candle-smoke that it probably wasn't much of an improvement over the inside of the pouch.

"Was that woman here before?" Maribelle asked.

Armus nodded and gave an affirmative cheeble—the two of them had worked out a few simple codes to aid communication.

"She let you in?"

Again, Armus nodded.

"Did you see any other servants?"

That drew a negative hiss. Of course, that didn't mean there *were* no other servants. The place might be full of spying apprentices, for all she or Armus knew, peering through invisible

eyeholes in every wall, or watching them with scrying spells.

Armus was looking up at her expectantly, as if he had more to say, but she couldn't think what it would be. They hadn't brought paper and ink; it hadn't seemed practical.

"Did Esotissimus keep you waiting…"

She didn't have a chance to finish the question, as the door opened just then. The dark-haired woman stood in the corridor, beckoning. Apparently Esotissimus did not keep visitors waiting long.

Maribelle gave Armus a second or two to settle securely back into the pouch, then rose and followed the woman down the passageway and through an imposing set of double doors.

The room beyond was large, dim, and mostly empty. At the far end a dais held a throne, and seated on the throne was a robed figure; all the light in the room came from some hidden source behind the throne, so that the figure's face was completely hidden in shadows.

Maribelle knew she was supposed to be impressed—in fact, she *was* impressed—so she dropped her jaw and said, "Ooooh!" in her best little-girl voice.

Behind her, the dark-haired woman slammed the great doors shut. Maribelle blinked foolishly, then turned to look—she always wanted to know whether anyone was in a position to stab her in the back.

The serving woman, or whoever she was, was leaning casually on the closed doors. Maribelle suppressed a frown. It was probably silly to worry about such things when she was facing a powerful wizard, but she really hated having anyone behind her during a negotiation.

At least she could put some distance between them. She put on a scared-but-attempting-bravery expression and marched forward, toward the throne.

"Greetings, mighty wizard!" she said, letting her voice squeak a bit.

The figure on the throne raised one hand and said, "Come no closer!" The wizard's voice was deep and rich and echoed from the stone walls.

Maribelle stopped and looked puzzled. "All right," she said. "I didn't want to shout, that's all."

"I will hear you well enough where you are," the seated shape announced. "What would you have of me?"

"Well," Maribelle said, holding up the pouch, "you turned my husband into a hamster. I'm sure you had your reasons—I know he can be *very* annoying at times—but could you please turn him back now? I promise he's learned his lesson, and we won't bother you again."

"You say that the assassin who intruded upon me was your husband?" the wizard boomed.

She hesitated before replying as she debated whether she should object to hearing Armus called an assassin. If she were truly the naive innocent she was pretending to be, she should at least express some surprise.

Generally speaking, though, arguing with wizards wasn't a good idea.

"Well, we never got around to a formal marriage ceremony, but we've been together for a few years," she said.

Then, abruptly, she turned—she wasn't consciously aware what had alerted her, whether she had heard breathing or felt the air moving, but she knew someone was coming up behind her, and she whirled to find the black-haired woman had come forward from the door and was now just a few feet away.

Maribelle let out a yip.

"You *startled* me!" she said, backing away—but carefully not even beginning to reach for any of her hidden weaponry.

"Pay no attention to my servant!" the wizard thundered.

"Oh, *excuse* me, sir!" Maribelle said, turning back toward the throne. She bowed, and then stepped aside, farther off the line between the woman and the throne, so that neither the woman nor the wizard would be directly behind her when she spoke to the other.

The woman frowned at her, and drummed her fingers on the black velvet covering her thigh. Maribelle noticed that the servant did not glance at the wizard for direction before retreating to one of the side walls. There she leaned back against the stone and stared at Maribelle.

"Does she have to be in here?" Maribelle asked the wizard, jerking a thumb at the woman. "She makes me nervous."

For a moment the wizard sat silently—Maribelle couldn't see his face, couldn't guess at his thoughts. Finally he spoke.

"*She* makes you nervous?"

"Well, I mean, of course *you* make me nervous, too, but you're *supposed* to. You're a wizard, after all."

"She makes you nervous."

"Yes, she does. Could you send her away?"

"No."

That didn't leave much room for argument. Maribelle shrugged. At least the woman was at the side now, rather than behind her, and Maribelle had had plenty of practice watching people out of the corner of her eye.

"Whatever you say," she said. "But could you please change Armus back to a man?" She held up the pouch, displaying the hamster.

"Why should I?" the wizard asked. "He came here to slay me. The two of you are fortunate that I permit him to live in *any* form!"

"Oh, absolutely," Maribelle agreed, "it was very kind of you to let him live. But you know, he didn't come to kill you at all, he *swore* to me that he didn't!"

"And you believe him?"

"Of course I do! He's my husband."

"And why did he come to me, then?"

Maribelle glanced at the servant, still leaning against the wall; she couldn't make out the wizard's expression at all, but the woman's face was interestingly blank.

The time had come, Maribelle thought, to surprise Esotissimus and tell the truth.

"Oh, he came to decide whether or not to take the job of killing you. But he hadn't agreed yet, and he wouldn't have, once he saw you."

Maribelle thought she saw the woman's mouth twitch, as if she were suppressing a smile.

"And you think I should forgive him for even *considering* an attempt to slay me?"

"Well, yes," Maribelle said. "It was stupid, and he should have known better, definitely—but everyone does stupid things once in awhile."

"And when they do, they must pay the price!" Esotissimus roared.

"But no harm was done," Maribelle insisted. "Won't you please forgive him? Isn't there *anything* I can offer you to change him back? We have money—we could pay you."

"What use do I have for earthly wealth?"

Maribelle blinked foolishly. "The same uses as anyone else," she said. "I know you charge people for the magic you do for them."

"If I did not, they would never cease to trouble me," the wizard said. "I need no gold."

"Maybe we have information you could use?" Maribelle suggested. "After all, Armus knows who hired him."

"Derdiamus Luc," Esotissimus said.

"Oh," Maribelle said, crestfallen. "You knew."

"Of course. My servant knew where to take the hamster, did she not?"

Maribelle glanced at the woman leaning against the wall—*she* was the messenger who had delivered Armus to Luc?

"Well, if you like, Armus could kill Luc for you," Maribelle said.

"I could dispose of him myself, should I choose to do so," the wizard replied.

That was probably true enough. Maribelle was running out of suggestions, but there was always one possibility. Her voice suddenly dropped the better part of an octave and turned husky. "Surely there must be *something* I can do for you?"

"Are you offering to betray your husband?"

"I'm trying to *save* my husband," Maribelle protested, holding up the pouch.

"I have no interest in you," the wizard said coldly. "I am above such worldly concerns.

"But you must be lonely..." Maribelle began. Then somewhere in her head something fell into place, and instead of finishing the sentence she turned to look at the dark-haired woman.

A mighty wizard who claimed to be above any sort of earthly matters, but who still had one servant—and *only* one—who he insisted must be present during this audience. A woman who was not quite the young beauty she tried to appear. Armus hadn't seen the wizard even move when he was transformed. And Armus tended to fiddle with weapons behind his back when he was nervous.

Maribelle looked down at the hamster. "She was behind you when it happened, wasn't she?" she asked.

Armus cheebled, and Maribelle looked up in time to see the dark-haired woman's hands raised, fingers arranged to cast a spell. Maribelle flung herself sideways, out of the line of fire, ignoring Armus' tiny shriek of terror as he flew out of his pouch; she landed rolling on the floor, and rose to her knees as she pulled one of the concealed daggers from her sleeve.

She didn't want to use the knife; for one thing, it probably wouldn't work. Even as she prepared to throw it she groped for alternatives, and one came to her.

If her guess was right, then the black-haired woman might well want something Maribelle was uniquely equipped to provide.

"Wait!" she shouted, as she readied the knife. "Please, wait!"

The black-haired woman turned, hands raised to enchant.

"*Aren't* you lonely?" Maribelle called.

The woman paused, fingers poised and ready but unmoving. Clearly she had expected Maribelle to beg for her life, or offer some sort of bribe, not repeat the question she had asked the wizard. "What?" she said.

"Aren't you lonely?" Maribelle repeated, lowering her dagger. "I mean, living here all alone with just him—is he even real? Wouldn't you like someone to, you know, just *talk* to?"

The woman looked at the dagger, and belated realization dawned—a realization very much like the one that had struck Maribelle. "You aren't just an assassin's *wife*, are you?" she asked.

Maribelle risked a faint smile. "And you aren't just a wizard's servant."

The woman lowered her hands. "Go on," she said. "What did you want to say?"

"Armus wasn't going to kill you," Maribelle said. "If we'd taken the job, I would have. Armus is a sweet boy, but he isn't much of an assassin—I'm the brains, he's the decoy. And you're the wizard, and that thing on the throne is just for show." She pointed to where the wizard sat, unmoving and completely uninvolved in the rather intense discussion going on a few yards away. "You're the brains, it's the decoy."

"So now I really *should* kill you," the woman said, raising her hands again. "Not only are you an admitted assassin, but you know my secret."

"And you know mine," Maribelle said. "You can kill me any time—but wouldn't you rather have someone you can talk to? Someone you can trust? Someone who's used to keeping secrets? Aren't there times it would be handy to have a trusted friend who's trained at theft, deception, and assassination? Someone you can talk shop with?"

"It *would* be nice," the wizard said hesitantly. "It *is* lonely. But can I really trust you? Both of you?"

"Why not?" Maribelle said. "I'll vouch for Armus—he can be foolish, but he can keep his mouth shut, and I'm sure he doesn't want to be a hamster. We've kept *our* secret well enough—why not yours?" She put the dagger on the floor and displayed her empty hands. "My name's Maribelle, by the way."

For a moment the dark-haired woman still hesitated, but then she gave in. "I'm Essi," she said, reaching out a hand to help Maribelle to her feet.

"I'm pleased to meet you," Maribelle said. "I've never met a female wizard before."

"I don't think there are any others," Essi said. "My father trained me in wizardry, but after he and my mother died no one would ever take me seriously—it's not just that I'm female, but I'm so short, and not ugly enough for a witch. Besides, I don't know witchcraft, just wizardry. I could have changed my appearance, but that's so uncomfortable and hard to maintain! So I made Esotissimus over there—he's a homunculus, sort of half-alive—and played the part of a servant."

"Nobody would hire a woman to fight openly," Maribelle said, dusting off her skirt. "So I tried to hire out as an assassin, but even that wasn't working until I teamed up with Armus." She looked around, and spotted the hamster trying to scramble up onto the dais. "Could you *please* change him back?"

"Of course," Essi said. A moment later Armus, restored to human form, sat on the corner of the dais, looking dazed.

"Mari?" he said.

"I'm fine," Maribelle answered. "Now shut up and let us talk."

Armus blinked. "All right," he said. He turned and began poking experimentally at the homunculus' unresponsive legs.

"You really *are* the brains, aren't you?" Essi asked, staring at Armus.

"Of course," Maribelle replied.

Essi smiled.

"Mari," she said, "this could be the start of a beautiful friendship."

DROPPING HINTS

The young duke glanced around uneasily as he waited for the wizard's door to open; he was uncomfortably aware of how very little he knew about magic in general, and the wizard Rasec in particular. Magicians were notoriously eccentric, and it was obvious from the bizarre and haphazard architecture of Rasec's home that he was no exception. Rasec had always been a cooperative neighbor, and had never given previous dukes any real trouble—but Lord Croy was not any of the previous dukes. He was the last duke's third son, acceding to the title only because of the recent plague that had taken his father and both his older brothers, as well as a good part of the local population.

As the new duke, it behooved Croy to pay a courtesy call on the wizard. It would not do to antagonize his realm's only real magician—especially when that magician might be able to assist in preventing any further outbreaks of plague.

Croy hoped he had not erred in choosing the size of his escort; he did not want to threaten the wizard, but it would not do for the duke to travel alone. A dozen had seemed about right back at the castle, but here on the stony hilltop, at the door of the wizard's home, the twelve guardsmen seemed like an entire mob.

The latch rattled, and Croy looked directly forward, composing his features. The door opened, and there was the wizard's inhuman servant.

Croy suppressed a shudder. The creature standing in the doorway stood between four and five feet tall, with gleaming gray hairless skin, naked and sexless. Its face was narrow and triangular, its eyes golden, its ears large and pointed.

"Please come in, my lords," it said, stepping aside. "My master awaits you in his chamber of art."

"Thank you," Croy replied, as he stepped across the threshold.

He hoped he had the protocols right; he had never been trained for any of this, had never accompanied his father here. His elder brothers had both been taught a duke's duties and privileges, but no one had seen any reason to include a *third* son, and now he was forced to improvise.

He led the way into the house, his soldiers marching behind him, two abreast.

The servant directed them down a broad corridor, and another, identical servant waited at the far end, its hand on the handle of a great oaken door. Croy, startled, glanced from one servant to the other, looking for some distinguishing marks, some way to tell them apart.

He could see no difference at all; the two were so alike that he wondered whether Rasec might have found a way to have his servant in two places at once.

But then the second servant opened the oaken door, and Croy was struck dumb by the wonders of the wizard's sanctum.

The circular chamber was vast but windowless, lit by a ring of crystal skylights; the bright midday sunlight gleamed and sparkled from a thousand strange devices arranged on shelves, mounted on iron rods, or suspended from the ceiling on wires. There were tangles of polished brass and gleaming ebony, layered constructions of silver and ivory, mummified beasts pierced by golden wires, and things that Croy could not even begin to describe.

And in the center of the room stood Rasec, dressed in flowing robes of red and yellow silk, holding a golden scepter. Behind him stood his servant...

A *third* servant, Croy realized, indistinguishable from the others.

Croy hesitated at the door for only a fraction of a second before striding into the great room. He walked directly toward the wizard, along a red carpet laid out for him, and stopped at a polite distance, perhaps seven feet away.

The wizard bowed deeply, and Croy felt an immense rush of relief; Rasec had acknowledged his authority.

"My lord Duke," the enchanter said. "Welcome to my home; you honor us with your presence."

Croy bowed in return, though only a small formal bob. "Thank you, Sir Wizard," he said.

"May I ask, your Grace, to what do I owe this honor?"

"Of course," Croy replied. "I have come to assure us both of the continued good will between our houses, and to discuss certain matters with you."

"I have only the best of intentions toward you, your Grace, as I did toward your late, lamented father. I extend my most heartfelt condolences on your recent losses."

"Thank you; I am reassured to hear this. As I'm sure you will understand, I have found myself thrust into a role for which I was not entirely prepared; I was not entirely certain just what arrangements might exist between my father and yourself."

"The arrangements are simplicity itself, your Grace—but forgive me, before we continue this, might I ask why you have brought these others with you?" He gestured over Croy's shoulder at the dozen guardsmen.

"Merely an honor guard, Sir Wizard. If they trouble you, perhaps you could find a place for them to wait?"

The wizard nodded, then beckoned. "You!" he called. "Is it Nampach? See these gentlemen to the rose garden."

One of the gray servant creatures responded from the doorway, "Yes, sir." Then it turned to the soldiers. "If you would follow me, please?"

"My lord?" Telza, the squad's captain, asked uncertainly.

"Go with it," Croy said. "Enjoy the flowers, find a bench and rest your feet. I'll send for you when I need you."

The captain saluted, wheeled on his heel, and barked an order.

As the party marched away, Croy said, "If you don't mind my asking, Sir Wizard, what *are* those gray creatures?"

"Homunculi," Rasec answered. "I made them some time ago; I find them more reliable than human servants. They eat little, never sleep, and require no clothing. I have five of them, and they attend my needs quite effectively."

"I confess, they appear so similar that I cannot tell one from another."

"Yes, I cast them all in the same mold; I can't tell them apart by appearance myself. I'm not sure *they* can distinguish one another. Their personalities vary, though. Nampach is the brightest of them; it will make sure your men are safe." He lowered the scepter he still held, and asked, "Shall we make ourselves comfortable?"

"That would be fine," Croy replied, glancing around for somewhere to sit.

As he turned his head, he heard the wizard say, "Here, take this," and from the corner of his eye he glimpsed the wizard handing the scepter to the servant behind him.

Then a loud metallic ringing startled him, and his head snapped back.

The servant had dropped the scepter, and it had bounced on the stone floor; as Croy watched it rolled under a nearby cabinet.

"Idiot!" Rasec bellowed. "Clumsy fool!"

The servant dove toward the cabinet, and in an instant knelt before it, groping for the scepter.

"Leave it for now," the wizard snapped. "Fetch two chairs from my study, and *then* get it out."

"Yes, sir," the servant muttered. It got to its feet, essayed an awkward bow, then tried to back out of the room, but bumped into a framework of wires and brass rods that jangled and wobbled.

"Watch where…oh, just get the chairs."

"Yes, master," the servant said, bowing quickly before turning to hurry out.

"As you can see," the wizard said, "they aren't perfect. Every so often one of them seems to lose its wits temporarily, and begin bumping into things, or dropping them. It's very aggravating; there must be a flaw in the design, but I have no idea where it lies."

The young duke nodded as he watched the homunculus vanish, then looked back at Rasec, and found the wizard staring at him expectantly.

"Ah," Croy said, gathering his wits. "Yes. Regarding any arrangements you might have had with my late father, uh…" He could think of no graceful way to complete the question, and after a moment's hesitation asked simply, "Were there any?"

Rasec smiled. "Our arrangement was quite simple, as I believe I started to say once before—he left me alone, and I left him alone. In exchange for being permitted to remain here untroubled and untaxed, I agreed to provide magical services when necessary, with the very clear understanding that such necessities could not be frequent."

"I see," Croy said. "It sounds straightforward, and I hope we can continue in the same fashion."

"Of course, your Grace."

A movement caught Croy's eye, and he glanced over the wizard's shoulder to see the servant returning, hauling two chairs, one under each arm.

Rasec noticed Croy's gaze, and turned in time to see the servant drop one of the chairs. It clattered on the stone floor, and the servant looked up, stricken.

"Imbecile!" the wizard raged, raising a fist—a fist, Croy saw with astonishment, that was *glowing*.

The servant cringed, then quickly set the undropped chair upright, positioned for the wizard's use, and hurried to retrieve the other.

The glow faded from Rasec's upraised hand.

"My apologies, your Grace," he said. "I don't know what's wrong with them tonight." He looked down at the chair, then sighed. "And the stupid thing has given me the wrong chair; this is by far the better of the two, and therefore yours." He pushed the chair across, and Croy accepted it.

"Thank you," he said, as he seated himself.

Then the servant had placed the other chair, and the wizard settled into it. He rubbed at one of the carved wooden arm.

"It's ruined the finish here, do you see?"

Croy nodded, and cast a look at the servant who had brought the chairs, who was once again on its knees, groping under the cabinet where the scepter had rolled.

"You have heard of the plague, Sir Wizard. Do you have any idea, then, what might have *caused* it?"

"Foul air, I would guess," Rasec said. He turned at the sound of the servant's approach.

The creature had finally managed to retrieve the scepter, somewhat the worse for wear; cobwebs had wrapped themselves around the shaft, and one of the ornamental protrusions on the head was visibly bent. The servant held it out for its master.

"I don't want it," Rasec snapped. "Put it somewhere!"

The creature blinked. "Where, master?"

"Somewhere even *you* can find it again!"

The servant looked down at the scepter, closing both hands on the heavy shaft; it looked at the wizard.

Then with horrifying suddenness it swung the scepter up in a swift arc, and brought it slamming down on the wizard's head.

Croy jumped from his chair with a wordless shout, and caught Rasec as he slumped sideways.

The servant flung the scepter aside, and ran; Croy, holding the wizard's crumpled body, was unable to pursue. Instead he shouted, "Stop! Help!"

The servant ignored him, and vanished through the nearest doorway.

"Help!" Croy bellowed. "We need help here!" He looked around the room, but saw only inanimate devices; then he looked down at Rasec.

What he saw did not look good; there was a visible dent in the old man's skull, and blood seeping from a hole made by one of the points on the scepter.

"Sir Wizard," he said, "can you hear me?" He lifted the wizard's shoulders, and the head flopped backward limply. Croy could not hear any breath, nor did the wizard's chest show any sign of a beating heart.

Rasec did not respond to his question; even if the wizard still lived, he was obviously not conscious.

"Help!" Croy shouted again.

This time he received an answer. "What appears to be..." a voice began.

Croy turned to see the servant re-entering the room through a different door—or so he thought at first, but then he realized that this was probably *not* the servant who had wielded the scepter, but one of the others.

The newcomer caught sight of the wizard, and did not complete its question.

"Fetch my men," Croy barked. "Bring them at once. Nampach took them to the rose garden."

"At once, my lord. And I'll send someone to tend to my master."

"Bring my men first," Croy barked. "I'll do what I can for your master, but I fear it's too late."

"Yes, sir…"

Then the servant was gone, and Croy was alone with the wizard.

He knelt and put an ear to the narrow chest, then felt a bony wrist; he could find neither heartbeat nor pulse, and the flesh already seemed to be cooling.

The wizard Rasec was dead.

An hour later Rasec had been laid out upon his bed, and Croy's men had the five servants under guard in a bare stone storeroom. That was where Croy confronted them.

The soldiers had found the five scattered about the house, and had brought them here. All five had vehemently denied killing the wizard, and had not admitted to any knowledge of which of their fellows might have committed this heinous act.

It was up to Croy to decide what to do with them all.

The simplest thing would be to have them all put to death, on the grounds of conspiracy to commit murder, and as Duke he certainly had the authority to do so—but these five were probably the only beings alive who knew anything about Rasec's magic, who knew their way around the household, who knew whether Rasec had any family.

And more importantly, four of them might be innocent of wrongdoing, and while they were not human, still they surely deserved whatever justice he could arrange.

He could have freed them all, pardoned the killer, perhaps let it be known that the wizard had died of the plague—but that would leave a murderer alive and loose on his lands, and furthermore, Rasec deserved better. That meant that Croy needed to determine which of the five had killed their master.

Looking at the five of them seated on the storeroom floor, however, he could see no way at all to distinguish one from another.

"Fetch me ribbons, or strips of cloth," he ordered one of his soldiers. "Tear them from draperies if you must. I need at least five different colors."

The man saluted, and hurried away, leaving Croy standing in the storeroom doorway, looking in at the homunculi. Their inhuman faces were hard to read, but none of them appeared any more agitated than the others.

"This is a serious matter," Croy said. "Your master has been killed, do you understand that? I must question you to determine who is responsible. Lying to me in such a circumstance is grounds for execution."

"We understand, my lord," said one of them. The others nodded agreement.

That said, Croy tried to think what to ask, but the words did not want to come. He was distracted by footsteps, and turned to see the soldier returning.

"I found the kitchen ragpile, your Grace," the man said, holding out several strips of cloth.

Croy selected five, red, white, green, blue, and brown, and tossed them to the homunculi. "Now," he said, "each of you will wear one of these tied around your right arm at all times, so that we can tell you apart."

The servants sorted out the tags, and secured them in place, as ordered, with varying degrees of reluctance.

"I wonder," Croy said, "that your master never saw fit to label you. Could he tell you apart by sight?"

"No," said the nearest, who now wore a green band around his arm.

"He knew our voices," said the creature wearing the white band.

"I don't think he *cared* which of us was which," said the brown-wearing servant.

"He called one of you by name," Croy said. "Nampach."

"He had heard me speak just a few moments before," said the one wearing white.

"You are Nampach?"

"Yes, your Grace."

Croy looked at the green-banded servant, and asked, "Can *you* tell your companions apart by their voices?"

"Usually, my lord."

"Close your eyes."

The one in green obeyed.

"Now, tell me each name as you hear each voice." Croy pointed to the brown-banded creature.

"What would you have me say, my lord?"

"That's either Suturb or Nahris," the green promptly announced.

"I'm Suturb."

Croy pointed to the white.

"I take it I should not say my own name." The voice was somehow a little richer than Suturb's.

"Nampach."

Croy nodded, and pointed again, choosing red this time.

"I'm Suturb," the indicated homunculus said.

"Is it Suturb again?" the green asked. "You sound more like Nahris."

"It's Nahris," Nampach said.

"It is," Nahris admitted. "I was just seeing if I could fool you."

That left one who had not spoken, wearing a blue band; Croy pointed.

The blue-banded creature did not respond immediately, but Nahris prodded it with a thumb, and it said, "I can't think of anything to say."

"Thoob," the green-wearer pronounced, as it opened its eyes. "And my name is Yar, my lord."

It occurred to Croy that perhaps he should be able to recognize the murderer's voice himself; after all, he had heard the creature speak. Unfortunately, he could not be certain; while there were subtle differences, the voices were fairly similar, and he had not been listening carefully when the killer replied to the wizard's commands.

He was fairly sure that it hadn't been Nampach—but then, he already knew that Nampach had been sent to escort his men to the rose garden.

"Which of you answered the door and admitted us?" he asked.

"I did, my lord," Yar replied.

None of the others spoke up, but Croy asked Nampach, "Is that right?"

"I believe so, your Grace."

That left three. "And which of you was assisting your master in the great chamber?"

The homunculi glanced at one another, but none spoke.

"Your Grace, we may not be as clever as true men," Nampach said after a moment's awkward silence, "and I can scarcely comprehend the thinking of one who would strike our master, but I do not believe you will catch the killer *that* easily! We all know that the one who was serving in the great chamber is the murderer."

"And does any of you know which it was? Nampach?"

"Alas, I do not, your Grace."

"Yar?"

"No, my lord."

"Thoob?"

The blue-marked creature shook its head.

"Suturb?"

"I know only that I was not there."

"Nahsir?"

"I say what Suturb said, my lord."

"One of you is lying."

"One of us is," Nahsir agreed, "but I assure you, it is not me."

Croy stared at the five of them for a moment, remembering puzzles he had heard as a boy about men who always lied but might, by clever questioning, be coerced into yielding useful information.

Unfortunately, these creatures were not so limited; they could speak lies or the truth as they pleased. And presumably only one of them knew who was guilty, so the others had no information to yield.

He had narrowed it down to three, in any case. That was a start. He could not spot the killer by appearance, nor by voice; what did that leave?

Actions, of course—actions, so it was said, spoke louder than words. The killer had been clumsy, constantly dropping things—but Rasec had said that all of them had spells of clumsiness.

Was there some *pattern* to those spells, some way to determine which of them was afflicted today?

"Yar," he said, "come with me." He gestured to the soldiers. "You two, with us. The rest of you wait here." Leaving the remaining servants under guard, he led Yar and his two chosen men down the corridor and into the scullery. There he posted the two soldiers at the door, then turned and looked at the servant's wary face.

"You need have no fear," Croy said. "You and Nampach are not suspected, and even if we find it necessary to hang all three of the others, you two will be free to go your own way. In fact, it may be that we will find a comfortable place for you."

"Thank you, my lord," Yar said, bowing—but its expression did not entirely relax.

"I sincerely hope that we will *not* find it necessary to hang two innocents, but the guilty party cannot be permitted to live; I hope you understand that."

"I believe I do, my lord."

"Good. Now, I noticed something about the killer's behavior. Your late master said that there was a flaw in your construction, and that sometimes you have spells in which you lose your wits and become quite clumsy. Are you familiar with this?"

"Of course, my lord; I have seen my companions drop fragile objects or trip over their own feet, on occasion."

Croy nodded. "And when did *you* last experience such a spell?"

Yar hesitated. "My lord, I do not remember *ever* experiencing one."

Croy frowned. "Speak honestly, now, or it will go ill with you."

"My lord, I *am* speaking honestly! I do not say I have never experienced such a spell, merely that I do not *remember* one. I have seen them affect the others, and perhaps one result of the unhappy event is that one does not remember it."

"Very well. But you have seen all the others afflicted?"

Yar hesitated again, then said, "I do not know, my lord."

Croy sighed. "Explain yourself," he said.

"I have certainly seen *someone* be clumsy, at least half a dozen times," Yar said, "but I don't know which of my fellows was involved in each instance. The clumsy one did not generally speak, and without a voice I cannot tell them apart any more than you can."

"Have you ever seen more than one be clumsy at a time?"

Yar thought that over carefully, then said, "No, my lord."

"Might it be that only one of you is *ever* afflicted?"

"Our master said there was a flaw in our design, my lord, and we were all made to the same design."

"But of your own knowledge, you cannot say how many have actually been affected?"

"No, my lord, I cannot."

"Have you ever seen one of your fellows lose his temper? It seemed to me that the blow was struck in a fit of rage, without planning or forethought; I cannot otherwise account for how anyone could be so foolish as to slay your master today, when my men and I were here, rather than on some private occasion when no witnesses were present."

"Indeed, my lord, I cannot imagine how it could be otherwise."

"Have you ever seen one of the others lose his temper?"

"Often, my lord. Nampach was furious at the mice in the pantry, and the other day Thoob went shouting across the yard about something. Someone threw a pot at me once, but I never determined who was responsible. I fear we are all as prone to anger as any human."

"Do you have any idea who slew your master?"

Yar looked down at the floor for a long moment before replying, "I have no knowledge of who did it, my lord. Sometimes I think it might have been Nahsir, as part of a joke gone wrong, but I have no evidence to support that suspicion."

"It appeared to be a fit of temper, not a joke gone wrong."

"And all of us are capable of fits of temper."

"Indeed. Thank you, Yar. You are free to go."

Nampach was the next to be questioned. His responses were much like Yar's, right down to acknowledging that fits of clumsiness were common, but denying any memory of ever having had one himself.

"Nor am I aware of any gaps in my memory, your Grace," he said. "But I suppose I might have lost the memory of such gaps, as well."

Croy had definite suspicions about the clumsiness now. "Can you say for certain which of your fellows *have* had these spells? I realize you cannot say with certainty who has *not*, but can you confirm any who *has*?"

Nampach had to think about that, and finally answered simply, "No."

Each of the others, in turn, denied any memory of experiencing bouts of awkwardness.

"I don't think I've ever seen Nampach drop anything," Suturb volunteered. "Nahsir is usually quite agile, but there have been incidents that might have been its doing."

Nahsir shrugged when asked who had been clumsy. "I'm afraid I just haven't paid attention, my lord."

"They always blame me," Thoob said, "but I never drop anything! I think it's mostly Yar, my lord."

Where Yar and Nampach had been released, the three still under suspicion were escorted back to the storeroom after questioning.

"Perhaps we could use the wizard's magic to determine the guilty party, your Grace," Captain Tilza suggested. "These creatures have been assisting him; surely, they must have learned some of the art! Ask the two you trust to work a spell that will compel the truth."

Croy shook his head. He did not like the idea of inviting the homunculi to practice the arcane arts; it seemed somehow unholy. And besides...

"I have a simpler idea," he said, picking three apples from a bin. "One I really should have thought of sooner."

Fruit in hand, he returned to the storeroom.

The three suspects were seated on the floor, simply waiting; they looked up at his arrival.

"Catch!" he said, tossing an apple.

The red-banded homunculus, Nahsir, caught the apple easily, and looked up questioningly.

Croy tossed another, and Suturb, banded with brown, snatched it from the air. The third was lobbed toward blue-marked Thoob.

It bounced from Thoob's fingers, ricocheted from Nahsir's shoulder, and was neatly captured by Suturb just short of the floor. Suturb handed it to Thoob.

"Now, toss them back," Croy ordered.

Suturb tossed its apple in a gentle overhand; Nahsir glanced at the others, then used a side-arm snap to send its fruit back to the duke's hand.

Thoob demanded, "Why? What's going on?"

"Suturb, Nahsir," Croy said, "please move back, away from Thoob."

"Why?" Thoob asked angrily, as the others obeyed.

"You dropped the scepter," Croy said. "You dropped a chair. You couldn't catch the apple."

"I didn't catch the apple, but I didn't drop any scepter! That was one of *them* having an attack, it wasn't me!"

"No one has any attacks, Thoob," Croy said. "You're just clumsy. There's no design flaw in anyone else; it's just *you*. You're *always* clumsy and awkward. But you've been blaming the others when you break things, saying it wasn't you, so everyone, even poor Rasec, believed you and thought that you *all* had moments of ineptitude."

"We all *do*!"

"I don't think so."

"The master *said* so!"

"Because you fooled him."

"I didn't fool him! He *knew* it was me all along!" Thoob leaned forward, hands on the floor, as it shouted. "He said it was the others so they wouldn't realize he was always yelling at *me*, never at anyone else. He made me clumsy on purpose, so he'd have someone to take out his bad temper on, and I put up with it for *years*, I played along, I let him mock me and abuse me in front of the others, but when he shouted at me in front of *you*, the new Duke…"

Thoob suddenly stopped, realizing what it had said. It looked around, at the shocked expressions on Nahsir and Suturb, the determined ferocity of the soldiers guarding the door, and the sadness on Duke Croy's face, and licked its lips.

"Kill it," Croy said, stepping aside to make room for the guardsmen.

The soldiers drew their swords and stepped forward to obey their lord's command.

THE BOGLE IN THE BASEMENT

Mary watched as the movers brought the trunks down the front hall, one by one, and with much grunting and muttering maneuvered them around the corner and down the basement stairs.

She could hear horns beeping out front as the lunch hour traffic tried to get past the double-parked van, and hoped the cops wouldn't be too quick to ticket it. That would mean an argument between the movers and her parents about who was to pay the fine.

"I can't believe you had all that stuff shipped all the way from Scotland!" she said.

"Well, what else was I going to do with it?" her mother asked. "Great-Aunt Margaret left it to me, and I couldn't just throw it all away, could I?"

"It must have cost a *fortune*," Mary said. "What if it's all just junk?"

"It's not just junk," her mother said. "I looked in enough of them to see *that* much."

"You want us to stack 'em?" the man holding the front of the latest trunk asked.

"Not if you can help it," Mary's mother replied.

"Okay," the mover said, and trudged onward.

"How many trunks *are* there?" Mary asked, as the movers dropped the latest and went back for the next.

"Thirteen," her mother replied. "They *should* all fit down there."

Mary tried to imagine how anyone could cram thirteen big old-fashioned steamer trunks into the little stone-walled cellar of their Boston townhouse without stacking them. The furnace and the water heater and the boxes of Christmas decorations and the like already half-filled it.

When the movers had collected her mother's signature on the necessary paperwork and departed, Mary made her way down the old bare wood steps to the basement.

The trunks filled almost all the previously-available floor space, leaving only two narrow aisles.

"Mind if I look in them?" Mary called upstairs.

"Go ahead," her mother called back.

Mary opened the heavy brass latches on the first one and lifted the lid; inside, neatly folded, were woolens—scarves, blankets, shawls. Mary stroked them, and burrowed down into the stacks, and found everything wonderfully soft; they were lovely, and would be welcome in cold weather, but they weren't very exciting.

The next trunk was full of linens and lace—again, pleasant, but nothing thrilling.

The third trunk was locked. Mary shrugged, and went on to the fourth.

By the time her father got home that evening Mary had rummaged through twelve of the trunks, and found a few treasures as well as mountains of boring household goods. She had begged her mother into giving her a carving of a cat, had played with an antique nutcracker, had polished up some old brass trivets and other knicknacks, and had marveled at a drawstring bag full of exotic old coins. She had glanced at the books and letters, but had not yet read any of them; that could wait.

That locked trunk fascinated her, though; why was just one out of thirteen trunks locked? What treasure was in there that Great-Aunt Margaret had thought deserved special treatment?

She brought it up at dinner, but her mother didn't know anything about it, and didn't have the key.

"We'll get it open eventually," she told Mary, "but there's no hurry."

Mary had to be content with that.

Over the next three weeks the contents of the trunks were largely absorbed into the everyday supplies of the family home—linens went into the sideboard cupboard in the dining room, scarves and mufflers in with the winter coats in the attic cedar closet, and so on. Some items went to the antique shops on Charles Street, or to various charities.

The locked trunk stayed locked.

Then one day Mary was rummaging through the trunk where Great-Aunt Margaret had stored books and old letters when she happened to pick up a bundle of envelopes and put it to one side.

The bundle had been stored upright, but she placed it on its side, without really looking.

She heard a little click.

She looked, and found that a small brass key had fallen out of one of the envelopes.

She stared at it for a moment, then grinned. She picked up the key and studied it.

It sparkled in the light of the two bare light bulbs that served as the basement's only illumination; being tucked away in an envelope had kept any hint of corrosion from dimming its luster. It was the right size and general shape to be a trunk key.

And there was no better time to try it, she decided. She closed up the trunk of books and letters and sidled along the aisle to the locked one. Half the trunks were empty, but none had been removed yet, so the basement was still crowded and hard to maneuver in.

She knelt and fitted the key in the lock.

It slid in easily, but didn't seem to want to turn, and she was beginning to wonder if maybe it went to one of the other trunks after all when the lock finally yielded and clicked open.

Holding her breath, Mary opened the latches and started to lift the lid.

Before she had it open more than a few inches, though, the lid sprang upward, out of her hands. She yelped and stepped back, colliding with the empty trunk behind her; she lost her balance, swayed, and abruptly sat down on the closed lid.

And there, before her eyes, the lid of the formerly-locked trunk was flung up, and a creature lifted itself up from the trunk and stared at her.

Mary shrieked in surprise.

It was black and leathery, with long, bony arms and long, bony fingers, with huge pointed ears on either side of a mostly-bald head. Tangled wisps of white hair clung to either side of its pate, while the center was bare and wrinkled.

Its nose was a great dark hook, its mouth broad and lipless, and its eyes a ghastly shade of yellow.

It grinned at Mary, showing a great many crooked yellow teeth.

Mary shrieked again.

"Mary?" her mother's voice called from the top of the stairs. "Are you okay?"

"*NO!*" Mary shouted.

Her mother clattered quickly down the stairs, but the thing in the trunk didn't vanish, didn't seem particularly disturbed by the noisy approach; it hoisted itself up out of the open trunk and clambered atop the closed one next to it, squatting with sharp, bony knees thrusting up above its head. It crouched there, blinking at Mary.

Its body was tiny, almost doll-like; its head was the size of a man's; and its arms and legs were impossibly long and spidery. Each limb was like muscles stretched taut over bone and wrapped in coarse black leather, utterly without fat or other padding, and each was, Mary estimated, more than a yard long. If the thing stood up it would be about her own height of five foot two—but more than two-thirds of that would be leg.

It wore a burlap rag wrapped loosely about itself, and she couldn't tell whether it was male or female.

She didn't particularly want to.

Then her mother saw the thing, and gasped.

"Oh, my God," she said.

The creature winced.

"It's a bogle!" Mary's mother said.

"A what?" Mary asked.

"A bogle," the creature said, sketching a bow. "An' I suppose ye'd hae me gie my name now, arter the fashion o' ye mortals, but I'd no' gie ye power o'er me."

"It talks!" Mary said.

It was undeniable that it spoke, but on the other hand, its Scottish accent was so thick she wasn't sure what it had said. Mary stared.

"What's a bogle?" she asked.

The creature glanced at Mary's mother. "Are ye tellin' me the lass knows nought o' bogles? Is she not a McTeague?"

"She's a Fiorelli," Mary's mother replied. "*I* was a McTeague, before I got married."

The thing eyed first Mrs. Fiorelli and then Mary suspiciously. "An' this man o' the outlandish name that ye've wed holds not wi' the old tales, then?"

"Neither of us does," Mary's mother said. "Besides, I couldn't remember most of the ones my parents told me. God, I can't believe I'm talking to you!"

"Mother, what's a bogle?" Mary demanded. She was over her initial fright, and beginning to be angry—her mother and the creature were speaking as if she wasn't even there!

"*That* is," her mother said, gesturing at the creature. "It's a sort of... of Scottish goblin. A nasty kind. They play tricks on people, and catch unwary travelers, and make noises in the

night. Except I thought they were just stories."

"We're nae just tales," the bogle agreed. "We're all o' that you've said, and more besides." It turned and leered at Mary, displaying an incredible number of large yellow teeth. "If you'd hae lied when you said ye'd no' heard o' bogles, me pretty lass, I'd hae ripped the tongue from your head, for a bogle can't abide a liar, nor any ither scoundrel or blackguard. That's another thing

that we are, it is!"

"Oh, my," Mrs. Fiorelli said, sitting down abruptly on the stairs.

Mary backed away suddenly when she realized that the creature meant its words literally, and that those long, strong arms and fingers probably *could* tear her tongue out. She swallowed.

"Oh, gross," she said. She turned to her mother, and said, "Get it out of here!"

"How?" her mother said. "I don't even know how it got in!"

"It was in Aunt Margaret's locked trunk!"

"You opened it? Oh, Mary!"

"I found the key in the other trunk," Mary said defensively. "How was *I* supposed to know there was a goblin in there? It's our trunk, I figured we had a right to open it!"

"Aye, you'd the right," the bogle agreed, "and I thank ye for the doin' of it, lass, for I've been locked inside for many a long year."

"Well, I'm glad you've had a nice time," Mary said, cautiously taking a step closer, "but now climb back in, would you, please?"

"What, and let you lock me in again?" The creature scuttled suddenly farther away from the open trunk. "I'm no' such a fool as that, lass! I'm out, and 'tis out I'll stay!"

"Mom?"

"I don't know, Mary," her mother said, but she rose and approached the bogle from the other side.

The thing saw that the two women intended to trap it, and let out a shriek of hysterical, grating laughter. Then it scampered wildly away on its long, long legs, springing from trunk-lid to trunk-lid, swinging from beams overhead, bouncing from the ductwork and plumbing as it darted and leapt about the little basement.

For a moment the two humans tried to catch it, but it quickly became obvious that they had no chance of catching the creature. It danced away, shouting and yelling, whenever they approached, and it was much faster than they were, able to dodge with superhuman speed and agility.

And it shrieked amd gibbered constantly.

"Stop that racket!" Mrs. Fiorelli ordered it.

"Ah, nay," it said. "I'm an eighth banshee on my mother's side, and blood will out!" Then it laughed again and jumped over Mary's head.

At last, as it clambered through the pipes above the furnace, at the far end of the basement, Mrs. Fiorelli beckoned to her daughter, and the two hurried up the stairs.

At the top they slammed the door, and Mrs. Fiorelli threw the bolt.

Then they looked at each other.

"Now what?" Mary asked.

"Now we wait for your father to get home," her mother replied.

"Why?" Mary asked.

"Because he's bigger and faster and stronger than we are, and with the three of us working together maybe we can catch that thing!"

"What do we do with it if we catch it?"

"I don't know," Mrs. Fiorelli admitted. "Stuff it back in the trunk, maybe?"

"Sounds good to me."

A gale of inhuman laughter came from the basement just then, followed by several loud thumps.

"What's it *doing* down there?" Mary asked.

"I don't want to know," her mother replied.

They tried to go on about their business, but it wasn't easy; the afternoon was punctuated with screams, giggles, and bumps from the basement. Whenever either of them was just getting settled down in front of the TV, or reading a magazine, after a lull, there would suddenly come a resounding crash or other loud noise. It was impossible to concentrate on anything.

At last, though, Mary's father walked in the back door.

Just then the bogle let out an ear-piercing shriek.

"What was *that*?" Mr. Fiorelli said, startled. "It sounded as if it came from the basement."

He turned, and before his wife or daughter could stop him, he slid back the bolt and opened the basement door.

The bogle, gibbering wildly, sprang up the stairs at him; he stepped back in surprise, and it vaulted neatly over his head, into the kitchen.

There, it snatched up a pair of saucepans and began clanging them together.

"Free!" it shrieked, as it danced around the breakfast table. "Free at last! And 'tis a fine home I've found here! I'll be staying here for long and long, my fine McTeagues! Oh, Margaret McTeague, ye thought you'd seen the last o' me, but your family shan't e'er hae done!"

"My good lord in heaven," Mr. Fiorelli said, backing away, "What's *that*?"

"A bogle," his wife said. She led him into the living room, where she and Mary tried to explain over the din of clashing cookware.

"They aren't generally so loud as this," Mrs. Fiorelli said, apologetically. "I think it's from being cooped up in that trunk for so long."

"I don't *care* why it's so loud," her husband replied, "I won't have it! I want it out of this house!"

Mary agreed enthusiastically, but her mother hesitated. "You want it loose on the streets of Boston?" she said. "Bogles are supposed to injure or even kill unwary travelers—it'd probably have a fine old time scaring drivers or jumping on people in dark alleys."

"Well, what's it going to do if we *don't* throw it out?" her husband demanded. "I don't want it slitting our throats while we sleep!"

"Oh, they can't do *that*," his wife assured him. The sound of shattering china interrupted her, but then she continued, "A bogle can't harm an innocent person in his own home—they can harass you, and they'll harm anyone who's lied or killed or betrayed a trust, anything like that, but they don't hurt innocents directly." She hesitated as something in the kitchen crunched. "At least, they aren't supposed to."

"*Listen* to that!" Mr. Fiorelli said. "It's got to *go*! Do you think the insurance is going to cover this?"

Mrs. Fiorelli looked at Mary, who shrugged.

"All right," Mrs. Fiorelli said, "how do we *get* it out?"

"It won't go of its own free will if we open the door?" her husband asked.

"I don't think so."

"Let's try." He marched back into the kitchen to the back door and swung it wide, then turned to face the bogle, which was crouched atop the refrigerator, watching him intently.

"Here, you," Mr. Fiorelli said, "you can go, now. You want to be free? Go ahead!"

"Ah, I'd none o' *that*!" the bogle replied. "'Tis a fine home I have right here!" It giggled, and threw a cracker at him.

Mr. Fiorelli stared at it, frustrated, then closed the door, turned, and marched back to the living room.

"Now what?" he growled.

"Maybe if we ignore it, it'll get bored and go away," Mrs. Fiorelli suggested. "Or at least shut up."

Her husband glowered. "You'd need earplugs to ignore that thing," he growled.

"I have some earplugs in my room," Mary volunteered. "For concerts."

She blinked, opened her mouth, and then closed it again.

"And I have an idea!" she said. "Wait right here!"

She ran upstairs to her room, and began rummaging through her dresser; then she snatched up the boom box she'd gotten for Christmas and a couple of tapes.

She ran back downstairs, the boom box bumping her thigh, and handed each of her parents a set of earplugs.

"Here," she said, "you're gonna *need* these!"

"Mary, what…" her mother began.

Mary explained, as she headed for her father's big stereo that she ordinarily wasn't supposed to touch.

"That thing came from rural Scotland, right?" She pressed the power button, and the displays lit up. "And it hasn't been out of that trunk in years? And they mostly live out in lonely, deserted places? Then I'll bet it's used to being the loudest thing around." She slipped a Led Zeppelin tape into the tape deck on the stereo. "Well, around here," she said, slipping in the earplugs, "it's an amateur!"

She hit PLAY, and turned the volume to 10.

The opening words of "Black Dog" roared from the speakers.

Mary couldn't hear anything from the kitchen any more, but she slid another tape into the boom box and cranked that all the way up, as well. Then she inched warily down the little hallway and peered into the kitchen.

The bogle was cowering in the sink, hands over its big pointed ears.

"Stop it!" it shrieked, its voice barely audible over the racket from the two stereos.

"No," Mary said. "You get out of our house!" She pointed toward the back door.

The thing leapt from the sink and scampered to the door; it fumbled with the knob, got it open, and stumbled outside.

Mary dashed over and locked the door; then she turned off the boom box.

And when she turned off the living room stereo as well and took out the earplugs, she thought that was the end of it.

It wasn't.

Hours later, when the kitchen had been cleaned up and the three of them were just finishing up a late supper, there came a timid knock at the kitchen door.

The Fiorellis all looked at one another; Mary rose, and cautiously peered out through the small barred pane.

"It's the bogle," she said. "It looks scared."

"Don't let it in!" her father ordered.

"I won't." She unlatched the door and opened it a crack, but kept a foot behind it.

"What do you want?" she demanded.

"Ah, lass, a little peace!" the bogle said, trembling. "The world's gone mad since I last roamed abroad! Great machines everywhere, roarin' and shriekin', and their stenches foulin' the air, chargin' doon the highways and flyin' overhead, and flashin' lights and shoutin' people and every sort o' noise imaginable brayin' and wailin' aboot..."

"It isn't any better in here," Mary said warningly.

"I know, lass—but could ye see your way clear to let me back in me trunk? I swear I'll go back, you can lock me in—'tis cramped, but 'tis better than this world o' yours!"

"I don't know..." She looked at her parents.

"Oh, all right," her mother said.

Mary swung the door open, and the bogle dashed inside, heading straight for the basement.

A minute later it was securely locked back in its trunk.

"Maybe we should ship it back to Scotland," Mary suggested, when she returned to the dinner table. "I feel a bit sorry for it."

"Maybe," her mother agreed.

"But on the other hand," Mary said, "I bet no one else around here has a bogle in the basement!"

(Dedicated to the memory of my grandfather,
John Watt, who was raised just outside Dundee.)

THE MAN FOR THE JOB

The wizard Gallopius frowned and said, "You know, I wonder sometimes how it is that all these peculiar bits of wizardry one hears about
in the legends wound up scattered about the countryside, stashed away in
caves and dungeons and the odd mausoleum, rather than put away safe
and secure in someone's personal vault. When *I* make some especially
puissant talisman, you can rest assured that I don't go hiding it under an
altar somewhere, or set some silly chimera guarding it. I keep it close at
hand, where I can get my hands on it in a hurry should the need arise."
He pulled a thick volume from a shelf, dislodging a cloud of dust.

"Then do you have something we can use?" the tallest of his five
visitors rumbled. "This dragon has to go, and my brothers and I..."

"And sister," the only woman among the five interrupted. "I'm part
of this too, Buk."

Buk looked at his sister, grimaced, and said, "Yes, well, this dragon
is making our lives miserable, and it's plain we can't get rid of it without
some magical assistance. Do you have anything here we can use?"

The wizard's frown deepened. "Well, not right here," he admitted.
"Our ancestors may have had strange notions about where to hide their
magical kickshaws, but there's no denying they knew more about how to
make them than anyone alive today. I can whip you up a first-rate aphro-
disiac or love philtre in a matter of hours, lay a curse of boils on all and
sundry, but weapons fit for fighting a sixty-foot fire-breathing dragon?
I'm afraid that's beyond me. Haven't a thing that would serve. A plague
of boils would just make it mad."

"But everyone in town said you could help us find what we need!"
another of the brothers said.

"And indeed I can," the wizard replied. "But I don't have it here, and
I can't make it myself. That was the entire point in what I was just saying—I do know of something that should serve your purposes, but I'm
afraid it's one of those legendary bits of bric-a-brac that someone tucked
away, for reasons I can't begin to imagine, in an eccentric location."

"A quest!" the shortest male among the five exclaimed. "By the Essence, a true quest! Glorious!"

"Oh, shut up, Akdar," said the man who had not yet spoken. "We have a dragon to slay—who has time for quests?"

"We don't appear to have much choice," said Buk. "What is this legendary thing, and where can we find it?"

"It's a helmet," the wizard said. He thumped the immense book onto a handy table and opened it to a particular page, displaying an elaborate illustration. "The Helmet of Justice's Balance, created by Biren the Obsessive in the reign of Oshwal the Third, some three hundred years ago. As you can see, it's a great ugly thing with silver wings sticking out like oversized ears—you'd have to be a fool to wear something like that into battle if it weren't enchanted."

His guests clustered around the table and studied the picture; the lone woman had to shoulder her way between two of her siblings to get a look.

"Enchanted how?" Buk asked.

"I couldn't say," the wizard said. "At least, not the details. The text is amazingly vague, even more so than usual, about just what spell is on the silly thing. It does say, though, that its wearer is so transformed as to pass unrecognized by his own kin, that even a man's own dog won't know him whilst he wears this headgear—I'd say that implies some sort of concealment spell, suitable for creeping up on this dragon of yours, but the nature of the transformation is never specified. And it goes on to say that the wearer cannot be harmed by flame or blade, and shall not tire before his foe, and I think the utility of *that* in confronting your dragon should be obvious." He picked up the book and slammed it shut, raising another cloud of dust.

"Is that all?" asked one of the men.

"That's all it *says*," the wizard answered. "But there's no telling whether that's the entire enchantment. These old wizards did the most astonishingly complex magic sometimes. If it does anything else, you'll just have to find out for yourselves."

The four men looked at one another, while the woman stared at the closed book.

"All right, if that's the best you can do for us, where is it?" Buk asked.

"Just the other end of the valley," the wizard said. "There's an abandoned shrine there, a temple of the Old Reformed Cult of the Withering Light, and the legend says the helmet is somewhere in the shrine, defended by three guardians."

"Three of them, four of us…"

"Five!" the woman snapped.

"Right, five," Buk corrected himself. "Three of them, five of us—we should be able to manage that, even if one of us is just a girl!"

"Woman," the woman said. "I'm twenty years old."

Gallopius smiled crookedly. "Well, actually, I didn't say the three guardians are individuals. The first is an enchanted hedge that grew up overnight and wrapped the entire temple in poisonous thorns."

The four men looked at one another again.

"The second guardian is a dozen warriors from the infamous Isle of Kurderak."

"A dozen?"

"Maybe we can sneak in," the woman suggested.

"Maybe *you* can," one of the others retorted. "Men don't sneak."

The woman looked at him for a moment, then said, "That's stupid even for you, Filmar. Men sneak when they need to."

"Never mind sneaking," Buk said. "What's the third?"

"The third guardian is a monster hound," Gallopius explained happily. "Supposedly summoned from some Nether Realm, with poisonous fangs and the ability to smell your very thoughts."

"I don't like the sound of that."

"It's a *quest*, Filmar," Akdar said. "It's not supposed to be easy!"

The wizard snorted. "You may be overestimating the difficulty," he said.

All five looked at him. "How?" Buk asked.

"I'll let you see for yourselves," the wizard said. "I'd suggest you be on about it—it's a good three miles, and it's already past noon."

Akdar laughed. "Three miles! A proper quest should cross a continent or two!"

"We don't *want* a proper quest," the woman replied. "We want the dragon to stop eating our sheep and our neighbors, and the sooner the better."

"Then let's do as the wizard says and get on with it," Buk said, turning toward the door. "Come on."

"That'll be three ducats for the consultation," Gallopius said quickly.

"Pay him, Filmar," Buk said.

Grumbling, Filmar obeyed.

An hour and a half later the party of five stood studying the former fane of the Old Reformed Cult of the Withering Light.

"He did say it had been three hundred years," one of the brothers said.

"Vines and hedges can live that long if they're properly cared for, Sidi," the woman said.

"Well, Arulla, I'd say this one wasn't properly cared for," Sidi replied.

That was obvious. While dried-out woody strands of vine still clung here and there to the temple ruins, and several stumps still thrust up from the bare dirt, all still sufficiently toxic to have somewhat deterred termites, rot, or other parasites, it was clear that the first guardian, the dreaded venomous hedge, was long dead.

"Why would anyone care for it?" Filmar asked. "Of course it's dead!"

"Then that just leaves two," Buk said. "Weapons ready, boys!" He matched his actions to his words, drawing the short sword he wore on his belt.

None of the others had swords; Filmar and Sidi carried spears, Akdar had a club in one hand and a dagger in the other, and Arulla had only a knife. Together, they advanced up the crumbling marble steps.

At the top Buk pushed at the door; it yielded not an inch. He threw his shoulder against it, and the ancient panels shattered; unable to catch himself he tumbled through the newly-made opening and landed in a cloud of dust and splinters.

He leapt quickly to his feet, sword ready, as the two spearmen rushed through the door to his aid.

They found no opposition. Instead Buk found himself standing amid dust and scattered bones as the others hurried in.

Light filtered in through the shattered door and holes rotted through the roof, and for a moment the five looked around, baffled, trying to make sense of what they saw.

Every vertical surface in the room, from the floor to as high as a tall man could reach, was covered with writing. It wasn't the careful work of temple artisans, but a rough scrawl, written in what appeared to be a mixture of charcoal and blood.

Wonderingly, Arulla stepped to the nearest wall, where the writing was largest and clearest. "It's kind of old-fashioned," she said.

"Probably three hundred years old," Buk. "Can you read it?"

Arulla nodded, and read aloud, "What sort of idiot wizard hires mercenaries and then seals them up in a temple so even he can't get in? How could anyone be stupid enough to lock us in here and not feed us? What did we do to deserve this?" She dropped down a few lines and read, "Biren is an imbecile. Biren has the brains of a hamster. Biren licks the private parts of dead weasels. Biren's mother..." She blushed, and stopped reading.

"I think we get the idea," Filmar said. He looked around at the bones, noticed that several bore toothmarks, and decided not to look any more. "Two guardians down."

"There's the door to the inner sanctum," Akdar said, pointing.

"Right," Buk said cheerfully, clearly heartened by the condition of the first two guardians. "I'll take a look." He crossed the antechamber and gave the inner door a good, hard kick.

It burst open, revealing another ruined chamber. Again, there were bones on the floor—but these were not scattered, and not remotely human, and a gigantic rusty chain was wrapped around them.

For a moment the five siblings stood and stared silently at the bones. Arulla was the first to look away, and to notice the deep gouges in the marble walls, gouges that matched the size of the skeletal claws.

She shivered. "I think I'm *very* glad I wasn't here three hundred years ago," she said.

Akdar started to say something disparaging her courage, then thought better of it and admitted, "Me, too."

"Where's the helmet?" Filmar demanded.

"Probably back in there somewhere," Arulla said, pointing toward the space behind the red marble altar that occupied the center of the room.

Buk clambered quickly across the altar, sword ready in his hand, and looked around. He frowned, then turned back to face his brothers.

"I don't see..." he began. Then something caught his eye, and he looked down.

"Oh," he said, "here it is." He reached down and picked up a gleaming silver helmet, very much like the illustration in Gallopius' book.

"Wait!" Akdar called, as Buk lifted the thing. "Don't put it on yet!"

Buk paused. "Why *not?*" he demanded.

"Because...well, we don't know anything about the transformation. It might be dangerous."

"Akdar, *somebody's* got to wear this thing if we're going to get any use out of it!"

"Oh, of course! I meant it might be dangerous to the *rest* of us if we're too close."

Buk frowned. He, Filmar, and Sidi looked at one another as Arulla stared at the helmet and Akdar at his oldest brother.

"We could wait in the antechamber," Arulla suggested.

"Good idea," Akdar said. "Come on, then—let Buk try it on in private!"

"This is silly," Filmar protested. "It's just a helmet!"

"It's a *magic* helmet," Akdar said. "That's the whole point, isn't it?"

"Oh, come on," Arulla said, as she headed for the ruined door. "Just do it, all right?"

"But I want to see!" Filmar insisted.

"You'll see next time," Akdar said. "If it's safe, I mean."

"Go on," Buk said.

Reluctantly, Sidi and Filmar joined their youngest two siblings in the outer chamber, and stood for a moment looking at the bloody graffiti.

Then a high-pitched scream came from the inner fane—a scream that was Buk's voice but somehow altered, and pitched higher than any sound that they had heard from Buk in the fifteen years since his voice first broke.

Filmar didn't hesitate; he dashed back into the inner sanctum, his spear ready.

The other three stood ready, listening intently, but not setting foot past the broken door.

"Oh, Death and Essence!" Filmar said. "Take it off!"

The other three looked at one another, puzzled.

"I think I hear whimpering," Sidi said.

"I *know* I hear whimpering," Arulla said. "What I don't know is who's doing it, or why."

Then the whimpering stopped, and for several seconds total silence reigned.

"Should we come in?" Akdar called.

"*No!*" Buk roared, his voice cracking but otherwise back to normal.

"Should...should I try it?" Filmar asked, his own voice shaky.

"What is going *on* in there?" Arulla demanded.

Then Filmar screamed, a high, thin squeal of terror that ended abruptly, to be followed by the sound of metal striking stone.

"Don't break it!" Buk called. "We *need* it!"

"No, we don't!" Filmar replied. "*I'm* not wearing that thing again!"

"I'm going in there," Akdar said, suiting his actions to his words.

Sidi and Arulla looked at one another.

"I'll wait," Sidi said.

Arulla shrugged. "Me, too," she replied.

They stood waiting as the other three whispered in the inner chamber. Then Akdar said loudly, "It does *what?*"

"Try it," Filmar answered.

A moment later Akdar squeaked, "By the Ancient Powers! Get it *off!*"

Then the three were whispering and mumbling, too low for Arulla or Sidi to hear. Arulla amused herself by reading some of the grafitti on the walls, admiring the author's command of invective.

"Should we ask Sidi?" Filmar said audibly.

"Or, much as I hate to suggest it, Arulla?" Akdar said.

"I don't see much point in trying Sidi," Buk said. "It'll do the same thing to him it did to the rest of us."

"But it *can't* do it to Arulla!" Akdar insisted.

Arulla looked up from the grafitti, puzzled, and met Sidi's gaze. Her brother shrugged. "*I* don't know what they're talking about," he said.

"Arulla?" Filmar called. "Could you come here, please?"

"Wait a minute," Sidi said, before Arulla could respond. "I think I'd like to know what's going on before you start dragging our sister into this."

"Nobody *dragged* me," Arulla replied angrily. She strode toward the inner sanctum, and Sidi hurried after her.

"All right," she demanded, "what is it that this magic helmet does that's so terrible?"

Her brothers ignored her as Filmar beckoned Sidi over. Arulla stood, hands on her hips, and listened as Filmar whispered to Sidi.

"...shriveled right up..." she heard.

Akdar nodded. "Like turning inside out," he said. "And..." He gestured at his chest instead of finishing the sentence.

"Do you want to try it?" Buk asked, holding out the helmet.

Sidi stared at the thing, then shook his head. "No, thank you," he said.

"But it can't hurt *Arulla*," Akdar said. "She's *already* a woman!"

Arulla had been just short of shouting a complaint about all the secrecy, and stopped abruptly, her mouth open.

Was *that* the mysterious transformation the helmet performed? It turned men into women? No wonder dogs wouldn't recognize their masters—men and women smelled different.

"Give me that," she said, stepping over and snatching the helmet from Buk's hand. Before her startled brothers could react she had set the thing on her head.

The transformation was very, very quick, but not instantaneous; she could feel her hips shrinking, her limbs thickening and lengthening. Her shoulders expanded, her chest enlarged and flattened, and the seams of her blouse ripped open. The drawstring of her skirt snapped as her waist added several inches—and the changes beneath that skirt were best left undescribed. Hair sprouted from her chin.

"Good heavens," she said, and her voice was deep and resonant. She looked down at herself, and felt suddenly unsteady—it was farther to the floor than it ought to be. She was four or five inches taller than she had been a moment before.

"She's almost as big as *you*, Buk!" Filmar said as he stared.

Arulla lifted her gaze and realized that Filmar was right—she could look Buk in the eye on the level, without tipping her head at all. She could look directly *over* Akdar's head.

But she felt huge and awkward and top-heavy.

"This will take some getting used to," she said, "and I'll want you to teach me to use that sword, Buk—but I think I can handle the dragon."

"By the Ancients, this is horrible," Akdar said.

"This is madness," Filmar said.

Buk grimaced silently.

Sidi smiled. "It works for me," he said.

A rulla did not wear the helmet for the long walk home; she was still unsteady when she tried to walk in male form, as her narrower hips refused to move the way she expected them to. Instead she carried it tucked under one arm.

Filmar and Akdar both offered vigorously to carry it for her, but she declined, and asked Buk and Sidi to help enforce her decision.

She knotted the broken drawstring of her skirt, but the torn seams in her blouse weren't so simple; she stamped an old bone from the temple floor into splinters and used those as makeshift pins to hold the seams closed.

When at last they neared their village half a dozen of their neighbors came out to greet them.

"Well?" old Herrel called. "Did you get help?"

The brothers looked at one another, and before they could settle on a response Arulla called, "We've hired a warrior with magical armor to deal with the dragon." She lifted the helmet. "I'm carrying this for him."

Sidi smiled. "His name's Rull," he said, before any of the others could contradict Arulla's story.

"So where is he?" Herrel demanded.

"He'll be along," Arulla said. "He said he wanted to look around a little first."

"You think he can handle the job?"

Buk looked sourly at Arulla. "I hope so," he said.

T he mysterious Rull was the subject of much speculation in the village. He did eventually turn up—no one saw him arrive, but the day after the five sibs returned Buk and "Rull" were out in the fields, practicing swordplay with a pair of sticks.

The other brothers wouldn't let anyone else get close, but observers who watched from afar were not impressed with Rull's performance.

"He looks clumsy as a drunken ox," Sheria said. "I don't think much of trusting *him* to kill the dragon!"

"We're counting on the magic armor," Filmar said uneasily.

"And I think Rull may have a few tricks up his sleeve," Sidi added.

"I certainly hope so," Filmar muttered.

Three days after Rull's arrival, the dragon emerged from its cave for another meal.

"But I'm not ready," Arulla protested, when the reports reached her. She had been scrubbing the stewpot. "I'm still clumsy as a kitten!"

"Clumsy as a boy who's just grown a foot," said Buk, who had brought the news. "I remember what it was like, and it's probably worse for you, since it's so much faster. But the dragon's here *now*, and we can't put it off. You'll be safe enough while you wear the helmet, and you'll just have to tire the beast out."

They had tested the helmet's powers, and had found that its wearer was indeed immune to harm from flame or blade—but a good solid punch still hurt just as much as ever.

"What if it steps on me?" Arulla asked.

"Don't let it," Buk replied.

Arulla glowered at him.

"Look, we never said it wouldn't be dangerous," Buk said. "You insisted on being included anyway. Now, are you going or not?"

"I'm going," Arulla said. "Just let me change." She tossed the stewpot on the hearth, where it rang loudly and rolled wildly across the stones. Then she rose and stamped off toward her tiny bedroom.

Buk had provided her with clothing—"Rull" was almost exactly the same size and build as the eldest brother, and Buk was wealthy enough to have three complete changes of everyday attire. No one in the village had any actual armor, of course, other than the magic helmet, but Arulla assumed she wouldn't need any.

A moment later "Rull" emerged, walking with the rolling gait of a sailor—she still hadn't adjusted completely to male hips. She had the helmet on her head and Buk's sword in her hand. She picked up Filmar's spear and marched out the door of the house, headed toward the upper field.

Buk followed hastily along. Arulla turned to look at him, and Buk explained, "I'm just planning to be there in case you need any advice or encouragement. It's your fight."

Arulla grimaced, and marched on.

The two siblings spotted the dragon from a goodly distance—after all, a sixty-foot dragon is fairly noticeable. They stopped to stare.

"It's big," Arulla said unhappily.

This was an understatement; the creature was gigantic, covered in gleaming green scales, with intimidating claws and teeth and even a stubby pair of horns. The one comfort in its appearance was the lack of wings—a flying dragon would have been too much.

"So are you," Buk said. "*And* you've got magic on your side."

Arulla nodded reluctantly, and when pushed began walking again.

They were still fifty yards away when the dragon turned to stare at them. Buk said, "I think you're on your own from here," and stopped in his tracks.

Arulla bit her lower lip and adjusted her grip on her brother's spear, then advanced further.

The dragon watched as Arulla inched forward, spear raised. Then it spoke, in a voice like an avalanche.

"You have found your death, warrior—and I my lunch."

Before Arulla could reply—or even decide whether or not she wanted to—the dragon spat a great gout of fire at her.

It washed over Arulla like so much warm mist, hardly even mussing her hair—though the wooden shaft of Filmar's spear was badly charred. Encouraged, Arulla took another step forward.

The dragon closed its mouth and stared intently at Arulla.

"Ah," it said. "Magic. I haven't seen much of that lately."

"Yes, foul worm!" Arulla bellowed, as she broke into a charge. "Magic that will spell your doom!" She closed the last few feet quickly, and rammed the spear into the dragon's belly.

The badly-burned shaft shattered, and the iron spearhead bounced harmlessly from the dragon's thick green scales.

The dragon looked down thoughtfully at the attacking warrior.

Arulla drew her sword and thrust it hard at the monster's heart.

The sword-point skidded across the green scales like a washcloth over baked-on cheese, leaving no mark.

The dragon lifted one foreleg and casually kicked Arulla aside, knocking the sword from her hand.

"Dragons have magic, too," it said. "Didn't you know? Can't keep a bellyful of fire with just your common sort of flesh and bone. I'm as armored as you are."

Arulla lay on her back on the grass for a moment, then reached up to make sure her helmet was still in place. It wouldn't do to turn back into a woman—an all-too-vulnerable woman—here. Once she was certain her gender identity was secure for the moment, she sat up.

"Whoever sold you your magic cheated you," the dragon said. "Didn't he tell you you need a magic sword to pierce a dragon's hide?

Nothing less will do. We're proof against all lesser weapons, and all poison and disease, and all the other mortal ills. If not for magic swords I do believe we'd be immortal."

Arulla decided that if she survived this she would do something terrible to Gallopius. She reached for her sword.

The dragon's forefoot snapped out and slapped down on top of the weapon.

"Listen, warrior," the dragon said, "I am a dragon and a father of dragons, and I have come here to live, and I intend to stay many more years. Your magic protects you, for the moment—I could probably find a way around it, but I would prefer not to bother. Therefore, if you wish, you may go now, and tell the villagers that you have failed, and they might as well accustom themselves to feeding me their sheep and children."

"I'm not going anywhere," Arulla said angrily. "I'm supposed to get rid of you, and that's what I intend to do."

"Your sword isn't magic."

Arulla just glared.

The dragon sighed a great puff of acrid smoke. "So what are you going to do?" it asked.

"I'm going to find a vulnerable spot," Arulla said. "Just as soon as you take your foot off my sword."

"I don't *have* a vulnerable spot," the dragon growled.

"So you say."

"Fine!" The immense green claw lifted, and Arulla snatched up the sword. "Go ahead and try. Whack at me all you like. And when you give up, we'll reach an agreement."

Arulla got to her feet, hesitated for a moment, then started hacking wildly at the dragon's leg. The sword bounced harmlessly from the impenetrable scales.

The monster rolled its eyes. "Great Essence, he can't use a sword any better than *that*?"

Arulla ignored it and kept chopping.

"You'll dull the edge," the dragon warned her. She ignored it. "You're going to ruin it!" the dragon insisted. "A good sword deserves better—show some respect!"

Arulla kept swinging wildly.

Behind her, far enough away that the dragon hadn't noticed him, Buk shook his head despairingly, then buried his face in his hands. Despite the lessons, the dragon clearly knew more about swordplay than Arulla did.

Arulla didn't notice. She was determined. She had come this far, and she wasn't about to give up.

She didn't need to limit herself to one spot, though; after a moment she moved her attention from the dragon's foreleg to its flank, with no greater success.

She worked her way along its body, foot by foot, flailing and hacking, without leaving a mark on the gleaming scales—but she could see, after awhile, that she was chipping the sword, just as the dragon had warned. She paused to catch her breath and think.

"Give up?" the dragon asked, curling its long neck to look at her.

"Never!" Arulla roared, startling herself with just how loud her voice was in this male body.

"Listen, warrior," the dragon said, "I have sheep to eat, but I don't want you following me around indefinitely. Surely we can come to some agreement."

"Like what?" Arulla asked suspiciously.

"A time limit, perhaps—if you find a vulnerable spot, or any other way to harm me, by nightfall, then I will go away never to return. If you do *not* harm me, then at nightfall *you* will go away and stop bothering me. Fair enough?"

"And if I don't agree?"

"Then I'll swat you away, stamp on your sword until it breaks, and try to find some way around that magical protection of yours."

Arulla certainly didn't want *that*. She frowned, then shrugged. "Agreed," she said. "Until nightfall." She began chopping again.

The dragon sighed. "I'm going to take a little nap," it said. "Wake me when you're ready to give up."

Arulla didn't bother to reply.

The dragon lowered itself to the ground, curled its neck around until its head was alongside its belly, curled its tail up around its head, and closed its eyes. A gout of flame and smoke erupted from its nostrils as it settled peacefully.

Arulla kept chopping. The helmet's spell kept her from tiring, allowing her to keep up a pace that would ordinarily have been utterly exhausting.

She worked her way the full length of the dragon's body, then climbed up on the monster's tail, thinking that perhaps there was some weakness the monster thought she couldn't reach. She studied the thing's head—the stubby useless horns, the scaly ridges above the eyes, the fine black stripes along the muzzle. She stabbed here and there, without doing any harm.

The dragon opened one eye and glared at her. "You *are* managing to be annoying," it said.

"I'll find a way to be more," she said. "Sword or spear or magic, I'll find *something*."

"You'll forgive me if I don't wish you good luck," the dragon said. Then it closed the eye again.

Arulla frowned. There *had* to be some way to hurt the creature! She clambered along the tail, poking at the scales here and there.

She had called the dragon a worm earlier, as was traditional, but looking at it it really wasn't one. It wasn't exactly a serpent or lizard, either. It was clearly reptilian, but its legs were jointed more like a cat's than a lizard's, and the way it curled itself up was catlike. A cat's most vulnerable spot was its belly, but she had already tried the dragon's belly without success.

She studied the creature, then jumped down from the tail and walked around it. When that revealed no obvious weaknesses, she got down on her belly and tried to peer underneath. Perhaps it had curled up in an attempt to protect some vulnerable spot.

She thrust the sword beneath the dragon's tail.

The beast's eyes opened, and it said, "Really, now, that's rather rude, don't you think?" It uncurled, its tail sweeping her aside and knocking her to the ground, then curled up again facing the opposite direction. While it was shifting position Arulla very briefly got a good look at its underside.

She didn't see any obvious weaknesses. She did see that it—or rather, *he*—was male.

Inspiration struck. She got slowly to her feet.

She did not start flailing away with the sword again. Instead she backed carefully away, then turned and ran to where Buk had watched the entire thing.

Her brother frowned at her as she approached.

"You're giving up?" he said angrily.

"No," she said. "I know how to defeat it. I need your help, though."

His frown turned to puzzlement. "What?"

She explained her scheme.

"I don't like it," he said when she had done.

"Do you have a better idea?"

"No," he admitted.

"Then come on."

A few moments later Buk and Arulla—not Rull, but Arulla in her natural form, still wearing Buk's now-baggy tunic—marched cautiously out onto the pasture where the dragon slept. The Helmet of Justice's Balance was in Arulla's arms; the chipped and ruined sword was in Buk's hand.

Arulla climbed quickly up on the dragon's tail. She moved as delicately as she could, horribly aware that she was no longer invulnerable to the dragon's flame. Without Buk's boots on the rough edges of the scales hurt her feet, but she ignored that as she reached over and placed the helmet securely on one of the two stubby horns.

A shudder ran through the dragon as Arulla turned and jumped to the ground. She ran for shelter as the dragon stirred and raised its head.

"What did you do?" the monster asked uneasily. Its voice was unchanged—but after all, it was a dragon, not a human being.

"I found a way to harm you," Buk said.

"I do feel strange," the dragon admitted.

"I think you'll find a portion of your anatomy has been removed," Buk said.

"A portion…" The dragon suddenly reared up and looked down at itself. Then it let out a bloodcurdling, earth-shaking shriek.

"Father of Dragons, you called yourself," Buk said. "I don't think you'll be fathering any more."

The dragon screamed again. "I'll kill you!" it roared, swinging its head toward Buk.

"I can undo it!" Buk gasped, holding an arm up protectively.

The dragon stopped in mid-lunge and swallowed a mouthful of flame. "You can?" it said.

Buk nodded hastily.

"Then do it!"

"First swear that you'll leave this area and never return."

"I swear by the Essence that if you make me whole again, I will gladly depart and never again set foot here."

"Good," Buk said, his voice shaking. "Set your head on the ground and close your eyes."

The dragon obeyed.

Buk began reciting nonsense and backing away slowly, while Arulla dashed out of the bushes, jumped up on the scaly ridge above the dragon's eye, and snatched the helmet from the horn. She slapped it quickly on her own head as the dragon quivered with the transformation. The beast's eyes started to open, then snapped tightly shut again.

Buk, seeing that, turned and ran.

Arulla jumped down and hurried to where Buk had stood a moment before, hoping the monster wouldn't notice that her boots had vanished and the helmet reappeared.

"There," she said. "All better. You can see for yourself."

The dragon opened its eyes and studied itself.

"How did you do that?" it demanded.

"None of your business," Arulla said. "Now, weren't you just leaving?"

The dragon eyed her, then shrugged for its entire length. "So I was," it agreed. "There are plenty of sheep in the world—I don't need yours." It turned away.

Arulla watched it go, and did not move from the spot until it was out of sight, over the shoulder of the hill.

Then she turned, and found Buk approaching from the bushes.

"Not bad," he admitted, as Arulla removed the helmet and shrank back to her normal form. "How did you know it would work?"

"I remembered you and the others back at the temple," Arulla said. "The transformation scared you all silly."

Buk grimaced. "That's different," he said. "We're men; it's a dragon. Why did you think it would react the same way?"

Arulla smiled sweetly.

"Because it was just as obnoxious as *you* are, brother dear," she said. Then she threw him the Helmet of Justice's Balance and began the long walk home, her hips swaying, comfortable in her own shape.

CHAPERONE

"It'll be easy," she'd said. "Just keep an eye on them, that's all. Make sure they don't spike the punch, that sort of thing. They're kids trying to act grown up—nobody's there to cause trouble."

He snorted at the memory. Seventeen-year-old kids didn't need to *try* to cause trouble. Seventeen-year-old kids *are* trouble. They were bad enough in the classroom, with all the structure and discipline in place; give them money and fancy clothes and a chance to grope each other in public and you were just *asking* for disaster.

But it was his turn. He'd been teaching at Pierpont for eight years now, and had never yet chaperoned a dance or prom; he'd always found excuses before.

This year the excuses had run out—every other male faculty member had taken a turn or two, and he hadn't; no one else wanted the job; and as Ms. Jonas had explained, at least one male chaperone was required in case real muscle was needed, and to make periodic sweeps through the men's room.

So here he was, wearing his best suit, on his way to stand guard over the Pierpont Senior Prom to try to keep the public lewdness, alcohol poisoning, and general depravity to a minimum. He pulled into the hotel parking lot, found a space, then marched through the lobby to the ballroom.

It was a pleasant enough ballroom, with plastic chandeliers lighting the dance floor and red-flocked wallpaper half-hidden by the official "decorations." A glittering banner reading "Congratulations Class of 2000!" hung on one wall. The caterers were moving back and forth along the buffet, but so far as he could see they weren't actually doing anything, just making sure everything was in place. The photographer had set up a plastic floral arch in one corner at the opposite end of the room, and was sitting there looking bored; in the other corner at that end the band was unpacking their equipment. He watched the musicians for moment, wondering just how bad they would be, but then Ms. Jonas came hurrying up and grabbed his arm.

"Ken! Good, you're here! We need you to go take a look around, make sure no one's hidden anything in the halls or men's room."

"Hidden anything?" He eyed her warily. "Like what?"

She blinked at him. "Like *liquor*, of course. Or anything, you know, illegal. Or handcuffs. Anything like that."

His eyebrows rose. "Handcuffs?"

She waved a hand dismissively. "That only happened once, and she wasn't hurt."

"You said you weren't expecting trouble!" he protested.

"I'm not *expecting* it," she said, exasperated. "I'm trying to *prevent* it. Right now, though, I'm busy here with the set-up, so would you be a dear and *please* take a look behind the fire extinguishers and in the men's room and so on?"

It was something to do other than stand around, so he agreed, still grumbling for form's sake.

He took his time about it, rambling through the entire hotel, checking every odd corner and every stall in every men's room—after all, if anyone objected to his absence, he could say he was doing as instructed. He found three cigarettes and half a can of beer in a potted plant at the entrance to the hotel pool, but nothing else at all suspicious.

By the time he returned to the ballroom the first kids had arrived and were milling about aimlessly—one couple was determinedly waiting for the photographer, who was nowhere to be seen, though his assistant was sitting by the arch looking worried. The band was tuning up, and so far didn't sound as bad as he had feared. Ms. Jonas had set up a receiving line at the entrance, greeting couples as they arrived and directing them to the souvenir keychains.

Ken watched a couple work their way in—Alex Pettigrew and Cherisse McAllister, he uncomfortable in a tux, she right at home in a stunning low-cut ice-blue dress. He knew them both from class, and was startled to see them together—he had known that Cherisse had broken up with her thug of a boyfriend, Ray Kowalski, but how had Alex ever managed to snag her for the prom? Ken had thought Alex was beneath Cherisse's notice, and besides, he'd been keeping company with Ginny Vogtman.

Kids were full of surprises.

Then someone tugged gently at his sleeve. "Mr. Harris? Ms. Jonas asked me to get you…"

A moment later Ken found himself in charge of distributing keychains displaying the school logo and the gold caption, "Beyond the Fields We Know."

That wasn't quite as trite a theme as one might expect from a prom, but then there had been a great deal of fuss about this being the last senior prom of the twentieth century, with traditionalists pitted against futurists in choosing a theme; this had been a compromise.

Ken rather liked it, but the keychains were still astonishingly ugly. He had been told his job was to make sure no one grabbed more than one, but he couldn't imagine why anyone would *want* more than one.

But he did as he was told.

The band started playing, opening with a fairly slow number he didn't recognize, presumably a recent hit; the first dancers wandered out onto the floor.

The kids looked good, he noticed—better than he had expected, and far better than their rather tacky surroundings. A few boys were still not up to the challenge of a tux, and a few girls had overestimated their skill with make-up or misjudged how best to display their figures in choosing their dresses, but most were amazingly elegant and quite adult in their appearance. Rudy Ballenger's hair was combed for the first time in Ken's memory; Yuriko Yagama actually had a bosom when not wearing a grubby sweatshirt.

It was all illusion, he knew; next week they'd be back to their old selves. For now, though, the students parading past him could pass for sophisticated young adults.

Then Alex Pettigrew and Ginny Vogtman stepped up to get their keychains, and Ken blinked. He turned and glanced over his shoulder at the growing crowd of dancers.

"Didn't you already get one?" Ken asked Alex.

The boy blinked slowly, just once. "No," he said. "That must have been someone else."

Ken was quite sure it hadn't been anyone else, that Alex had already come past with Cherisse McAllister, but when he saw the kid's blank expression he decided not to press it. He shrugged. "Must have been," he agreed.

He watched as the two of them headed for the buffet, then turned to look at the dancers.

Sure enough, there was Cherisse, dancing with Alex Pettigrew—or someone very much like him.

And Alex had noticed Ken's attention. He stumbled, then apologized to his partner and led her to a table. Once Cherisse was settled and looking only slightly disgruntled, Alex hurried over to Ken.

"Mr. Harris," he said, "I saw you looking at us. Is something wrong?"

"You tell me," Ken said. "Look at those two at the buffet first, though."

"You mean Ginny and her date?" Alex said, without bothering to look.

"Yeah. Do you have a twin we don't know about, Alex?"

"Sort of." He looked furtively around and lowered his voice. "Listen, Mr. Harris, can you keep a secret?"

"Depends what it is. I think you've gone far enough now that you better tell me anyway."

Alex hesitated, then said, "My Aunt Margaret's a witch."

"A witch?"

"Yeah. A real witch. She does magic."

Ken prided himself on being open-minded, and put aside for the moment the question of whether there really were witches. "And this has what to do with your mysterious double?" he asked.

"Aunt Margaret made him. He's a doppelganger, a copy."

Ken stared at Alex for a long moment before deciding the boy was serious.

"Why?" he asked.

Alex glanced uneasily over his shoulder at Cherisse, who was waiting impatiently. He leaned forward, almost whispering.

"I've had a crush on Cherisse since ninth grade," he said. "I mean, *look* at her! Who wouldn't?"

Ken refrained from saying that *he* wouldn't—Cherisse was too brassy for his tastes. "Go on," he said.

"I always figured I never had a chance, but when she broke up with Ray, I thought that this might be, you know, that window of opportunity, that one time you have to grab for the gold ring…"

"This isn't an essay question, Alex. You can cut the bull."

"Right. Anyway, I asked her to the prom, and she said no, but she was nice about it, so then I asked Ginny, because you know, she's been my friend for years, and then Cherisse called up and said she'd changed her mind, and I couldn't say no when I'd asked her, could I? And I didn't want to hurt Ginny's feelings, but I couldn't be in two places at once. So I went to Aunt Margaret for advice, and she said I *could* be in two places at once—that she could summon up this spirit and make it look like me. And here we are."

"So you're the real one, and you're with Cherisse, and Ginny gets the phony?"

Alex blushed. "Well, yeah," he said. "I guess it's kind of scummy, isn't it?"

"Kind of," Ken agreed.

"But Mr. Harris, I'm *stuck* now! And if they find out we'll *all* be miserable, so can you please help me keep it quiet?"

Ken sighed. He wondered whether this was any better than booze or handcuffs; at least it was *different*. "I'll try," he said.

"Thank you!" Alex grabbed Ken's hand and shook it, then turned and hurried back to Cherisse.

Ken watched for a moment as the band began a new, much louder and faster tune, then looked down the other end of the room, where Ginny and the other Alex were standing.

This was going to be interesting, seeing whether they could avoid each other. He wondered just who Alex's Aunt Margaret was, and how she had managed it—he had never heard of a modern-day witch who could do such a thing.

Then he turned his attention back to distributing souvenir keychains.

He looked up a moment later, glancing at the ballroom door to see whether any end to the stream of arrivals might be in sight, and blinked in surprise.

Alex Pettigrew was standing there, talking to Ms. Jonas.

Ken quickly turned and spotted Alex and Cherisse waiting in line for the photographer; he turned again, and saw Alex and Ginny making their way toward the dance floor. He took another look—and not only was Alex talking to Ms. Jonas, another Alex was in the hallway outside the ballroom door, talking to a couple of other boys.

"Excuse me," he said. He quickly motioned for Ms. Liaw the biology teacher to take over the keychains and headed for the photography line.

"Excuse me, Ms. McAllister," he said, pulling Alex out of line by one elbow, "but I need a word with your escort."

"What is it?" Alex said, going pale.

Ken didn't say anything; he just pointed, carefully keeping his hand where Cherisse couldn't see it.

Alex looked, and went from slightly pale to bone-white.

"I have to get Cherisse out of here," he said. "If she sees she'll *kill* me!"

"I doubt Ginny will be thrilled, either," Ken said drily.

"I can explain to Ginny," Alex said, "but *Cherisse*...!"

"Suit yourself," Ken said. "If I were you, though, I think I'd want a word with Aunt Margaret."

Alex swallowed as he stared at the door; Ken turned to see yet another Alex ambling in.

"At least those three came stag," Ken said. "You'd spend the rest of your life hiding from your dates otherwise."

"Mr. Harris," Alex said, "I have *got* to get Cherisse out of here! Could you call my Aunt Margaret? Please? And ask her what to do?" He rummaged in the pocket of his tux and pulled out a crumpled slip of paper. "Here's her number."

Ken hesitated. This wasn't really any of his business. He was supposed to be here to keep out booze and break up fights, not mess around with witchcraft gone wrong.

But on the other hand, those surplus Alexes might well start a few fights, and he was desperately curious to hear what Aunt Margaret would say. He took the paper.

"Thank you!" Alex gasped; then he turned back to Cherisse and said, "I need some fresh air—could we go outside for a moment?"

Ken saw her jaw drop. "But we're in *line*," she said. "We'll lose our place!"

Alex looked helplessly at her, then glanced at Ken. Ken shrugged. Then he turned toward the door.

Ms. Jonas was glaring at two of the Alexes. "I don't know what you think you're doing…" she began.

"*I* do," Ken said, coming up behind them and grabbing an Alex with each hand. "Come on, you two—the real Alex told me all about your little prank." He leaned over and told Ms. Jonas, "They don't even go to Pierpont. I'll take care of them." Then he hustled them out the door.

They put up no real resistance; in the lobby they passed two more Alexes.

"You!" Ken said. "Come with me."

The others ignored him, but he was able to herd the two he held out to the parking lot. There he released them and said, "I know who and what you are, but I'm not going to try to convince anyone of that; instead, I am going to maintain that you are pranksters with forged I.D. who have no right to attend this prom. Now, go away!"

"I need to find Ginny Vogtman," the right-hand Alex said, in a curiously flat voice.

"So do I," said the other.

"No, you don't," Ken said. "One of you is already with her, and that's plenty."

"We were summoned and bound, and instructed to accompany her here in the guise of Alex Pettigrew," the left-hand doppelganger said.

"That was a mistake. *One* of you was supposed to accompany her, not five."

"There are nine of us in all," the right-hand Alex said.

"Nine," Ken said. "*Nine?*"

"I do not think we should speak with you further," the left one said. "We must find Ginny Vogtman and see that she has a good time."

"If all nine of you find her," Ken said, "she *won't*."

Neither Alex replied, but their blank faces made it clear they weren't convinced, and Ken, uncomfortably aware that there were six more superfluous Alexes around, all presumably in pursuit of Ginny Vogtman, decided he could not waste any more time on these two.

"Go *away*," he said, shoving them. Then he turned back to the hotel entrance.

They followed him in, but he ignored them and hurried to the hotel desk.

"I need a phone with an outside line," he said. "It's an emergency."

A moment later he stood, receiver in hand, listening to the phone ring on the other end of the line and watching half a dozen copies of Alex Pettigrew arguing with the door guards, while a crowd of puzzled promgoers gathered around them, waiting for the blockage to be cleared.

"Hello?" A woman had picked up. She did not sound at all like the traditional cackling Hallowe'en witch.

"Hello; I'm Ken Harris, one of the teachers at Pierpont High. I'm trying to reach Alex Pettigrew's Aunt Margaret," Ken said.

"That's me," the voice on the other end replied. "Something's gone wrong, hasn't it?"

"You don't know?"

"Not *what* went wrong," she said. "But it didn't feel right."

Ken hesitated, then decided to be blunt. "Alex tells me you're a witch, and that you summoned up these nine copies of him that are causing trouble here."

"*Nine?*"

Ken noticed she didn't argue with any of the rest of the bizarre accusation. "Well, at least half a dozen, and one of them said nine."

"Oh, damn. I said 'spirits' when I meant 'spirit,' but I didn't think... *nine?*"

"Yes. And they're causing rather a stir here—they all insist on finding Ginny Vogtman. Now, could you please tell me how to get rid of them?"

"They'll all disappear at dawn—they're spirits of the night, and the sun will dissolve their material forms."

"*Dawn?*" Ken looked at his watch; it wasn't quite ten o'clock. "Isn't there any way to get rid of them sooner?"

"Let me think," Margaret said. "I told them to accompany Ginny Vogtman, to treat her well and see that she has a good time, not to harm her, not to start any fights or drink anything alcoholic...if you can force them to break one of those orders, that would break the spell and free that spirit."

"In other words, as long as they behave themselves, there's nothing I can do?"

"Nothing I can think of," Margaret said unhappily.

"Well, thank you," Ken said. He hung up abruptly as he realized he didn't know Margaret's last name and was past the point he could gracefully ask for it.

No fighting, no alcohol—if he could just get a little booze into them, that should do it. But they wouldn't voluntarily disobey orders; he'd need to get them to drink without them realizing what they were drinking until it was too late.

If the punch were spiked...

But he had orders from Ms. Jonas to make sure the punch was *not* spiked.

Well, this wouldn't be the first time he disobeyed the principal's orders. Now he just needed something to add to the punch. The hotel bar was closed and locked—Ms. Jonas had insisted on that. The nearest liquor store was miles away.

But there were a couple of hundred high school seniors here to party—*someone* would have booze.

And he could guess who. He hurried back to the ballroom, and pushed his way through the gathered hordes at the door, where he found his way blocked by a collection of Alex Pettigrews.

"Alex!" he said.

He counted seven heads that turned toward him—which meant one surplus Alex was already inside. That could be bad.

"We'll let you in, one at a time, in a few minutes," he said. "Ginny's inside. But we'll do this in an *orderly* fashion, according to the rules!"

They stared silently at him.

"First, you need to let everyone else through. When they're all inside, you get your turn. Not before."

The seven stepped aside, in a shuffling mass of tux-covered elbows and knees. The crew guarding the door stared at him in amazement, then hastily began admitting eager prom-goers.

Ken slipped inside himself and looked around.

Cherisse and the real Alex were still in line for the photographer—but only one more couple was ahead of them.

And at the far end of the room Ginny Vogtman, close to tears, was standing between two blank-faced Alexes a few steps from the punch-bowl. Ms. Roshwald was standing guard over the punchbowl itself, watching Ginny and her dates, but doing nothing to intervene—she obviously considered protecting the punch her first duty.

Ken scanned the rest of the crowd, and spotted his target—Ray Kowalski, chatting with two of his buddies while their three dates stood nearby, looking rather disgruntled. Ken strode over.

"All right, Ray," he said, "hand it over."

Ray blinked at him, startled. "Hand over what, Mr. Harris?" He glanced at his pals, who were stepping back, pretending they didn't know him.

"The bottle. Gin, right?"

"I don't know what you're talking…"

"Oh, come on, Ray. Hand it over now and I won't tell anyone—no cops, no call to your parents, you can go on as if nothing happened. I've got enough to do without ratting on you." He looked meaningfully at the other two. "If it's one of you who has it instead, and that's why Ray's playing innocent, speak up. This is your last chance to get off clean."

"I don't know anything about it, Mr. Harris," Sparky Boone said.

"Give it up *now* and I won't check your cars," Ken said.

The three boys exchanged glances, and Ray reluctantly produced a Perrier bottle from under his tux.

"It's vodka," he said. "Not gin."

"Good enough," Ken said, taking the bottle. "And I won't check your cars, but play it smart, okay? Don't do anything that'll draw the cops. And don't drive again afterward until you've sobered up."

"Yessir."

Ken turned away, the bottle in hand—as a chaperone he could carry a Perrier openly, without drawing suspicion. Behind him he heard Sparky say, "Hey, that was pretty cool of him. For a teacher."

Ken made his way to Ginny; he walked up to her and asked, "Are you all right?"

She stared at him helplessly, and gestured silently at the two copies of Alex that flanked her. Both of them stared blankly at Ken.

"Aren't you supposed to be seeing that she has a good time?" Ken asked.

"Of course," one of them said.

"She doesn't look happy to *me*," Ken said.

Both Alexes turned to stare at Ginny, who looked ready to burst into tears.

Ken tapped the nearer one on the shoulder. "You look thirsty," he said, holding out the Perrier bottle. "It might cheer her up if you took a swig of this."

The thing looked at Ken for a moment, then accepted the bottle. "Would this please you?" it asked.

Ginny looked to Ken for a sign, and Ken nodded vigorously.

"Yes," she said.

The Alex lifted the bottle and drank—and vanished with a sharp crack and a puff of bluish smoke. Ken dove forward to catch the bottle before it hit the ground, and managed to only spill a little.

"Damn firecracker startled me," he said loudly. "Who threw that?"

A score of surprised faces turned to stare, including Ms. Roshwald—but Ms. Roshwald stood by her post at the punchbowl.

"Come on, who was it?" Ken demanded.

His audience retreated, and he grabbed the remaining imitation Alex by the arm. "Was that you, Pettigrew?"

Ginny was staring at him, astonished—but she seemed slightly less upset. That was good. It was almost certain that at least one girl in attendance would wind up crying before the night was over, but Ken was in no hurry to see it happen.

"I did not throw a firecracker," the other Alex said.

"Then who did?"

"No one."

Ken pursed his lips thoughtfully. "I think it was you."

Alex didn't answer, and Ken moved on. "So, Alex," he said, offering the bottle, "would *you* like a drink?"

"No," Alex said. "It's not allowed."

Ken nodded; he had expected as much. These things weren't very bright, but they could learn from observation.

"You wait right here, then," he said. "Ms. Vogtman, you'll see that he doesn't slip out, won't you?"

"Of course," Ginny said, looking uneasily at the remaining Alex.

Ken released him, and took a few quick steps to Ms. Roshwald.

"Ellie," he said, "how long has that slavedriver had you posted here?"

"Oh, not that long," Ms. Roshwald protested. "Not more than an hour."

"I'll take a turn," Ken said. "You go take a break, then take a turn at the door, why don't you?"

"Thank you," she said. "I could use a break. Do you know, I was seeing double for a moment?" She looked at Ginny and Alex. "I thought I saw two of him. It cleared up when that firecracker went off, though."

"Funny how that can happen," Ken said. "You go ahead and get a little rest." He gave her a friendly little shove—and a moment later the punchbowl was his.

He clattered about with cups and the ladle to cover pouring the remaining vodka into the punchbowl.

He was committing one of the cardinal sins a chaperone could commit, but at this point he didn't care; he just wanted to get rid of the extra Alexes before they mobbed poor Ginny. And a pint or so of vodka diluted by a punchbowl that size wouldn't be enough to impair a healthy teenager, in any case.

When he had finished his maneuvers, including refilling the Perrier bottle with ginger ale from the supplies under the table, he straightened up, brushed himself off, and called, "Ginny!"

Ginny was already watching him; he beckoned.

She came, with Alex following close behind.

"Have some punch," Ken said, holding out a cup.

Ginny took it and sipped. Her eyes widened.

"And I think your boyfriend wants some," he said.

"Yes," Ginny said. "Have some, Alex."

Alex hesitated, and asked, "No one has spiked it?"

"There's been a teacher guarding it every minute," Ken said. "How could anyone spike it?"

Alex nodded, accepted a cup, and sipped.

This time Ken didn't catch the cup; it clattered on the floor, spilling its contents, but did not break.

"All right," Ken bellowed, striding forward, "who's throwing those firecrackers? Whoever it is, when I catch him—well, you may not all be graduating on schedule!"

No one confessed; after a moment of belligerent posing, Ken shrugged and turned back to Ginny.

"Mr. Harris," she said, "what's going on? Who were those two? *What* were they?"

This had obviously gone beyond the point at which deception was any use. "Have you ever met Alex's Aunt Margaret?" Ken asked.

Ginny's eyes widened. "The witch?"

Ken glowered; why had everyone known about this witch but him?

But that wasn't fair, he realized; Ginny was Alex's close friend. They'd hung out together for years. If anyone would know, she would.

"Yeah, her," Ken said. "Alex couldn't make it, so he asked his Aunt Margaret to conjure up someone to come in his place. Only she messed up and sent *nine* of them." He pointed at the door. "They're all out there, waiting, and they all have orders to find you and make sure you have a good time."

"*Nine* of them?" She glanced uneasily at the door.

"Well, seven, now—they can't drink alcohol. It breaks the spell. Those two who got in here are gone."

"So *you* spiked the punch?"

"*Someone* had to."

Ginny giggled nervously.

"Look," Ken said, "I'm going to let them in, one at a time. You feed each one a cup of punch, and then I'll send the next. You can keep the last one, if you like."

"Where's the real Alex?" she asked.

"Not coming," Ken said. "It's a long story, and I'll let him tell you himself on Monday."

Ginny frowned. "He isn't here? Is he okay?"

"He's fine. Let's get these imitations dealt with, okay?"

Ginny gulped and straightened up—which did interesting things to the bodice of her dress, but Ken tried not to notice that. She nodded.

"Good!" he said, as he headed for the door.

After reassuring Ms. Jonas that he knew what he was doing, he leaned out into the hallway and pointed to one of the waiting Alexes. "You," he said. "You can go in. Ginny's by the punchbowl."

The spirit-creature did not offer any thanks, nor smile, but headed directly in the indicated direction.

A moment later he heard a snap.

"Another firecracker," he said to Ms. Jonas. "I hope nobody blows off any fingers." Then he leaned out into the hallway. "Next!" he called.

It didn't take long to dispose of the rest—but after the first three the delay before the telltale crack grew longer each time. Somewhere around the fifth one the band stopped playing.

When he admitted the last one Ken followed it in and watched.

As he had expected, the false Alex made a beeline for Ginny—but then it paused, a few feet away from her, looking around warily. The things were stupid, but not *that* stupid—it must have realized, when it saw none of its companions, that it was walking into a trap.

It was also walking into full view of a good-sized crowd. Ginny stood alone by the punchbowl, but just about everyone else at that end of the room had collected into a circle around her, watching.

Ken frowned. He should have expected that. The cover story about firecrackers was all very well for the sound, but someone must have seen a false Alex vanish and pointed it out.

The final Alex walked into the circle and said, "Hello, Ginny."

"Hello, Alex," Ginny replied calmly.

"Where did the others go?" Alex asked.

"I sent them away," she said. "You're supposed to make sure I have a good time, and I don't like crowds, so I gave them some errands to run."

"I didn't see them go."

Ginny shrugged. She ladled out a cup of punch. "Join me in a drink?" she said.

Alex approached cautiously, accepted the cup she offered, then lifted it to his mouth—and sniffed it warily.

"I think it's been spiked," he said.

Ginny glared at him. "What if it has?" she said.

"I'm not supposed to drink alcohol."

"And what if I insist?"

Alex hesitated.

Ginny glowered at him, then said, "I am not in the mood for any more of this." She swung a fist, and knocked the cup up out of Alex's hand, spraying sweet red liquid all over his face. He opened his mouth to speak, and punch dripped in.

He popped and vanished, leaving a curl of smoke.

Ginny turned and spotted Ken. "Mr. Harris," she called, "are there any more?"

"Nope," Ken said cheerfully. "That was the last of 'em."

"Then what about *this* one?" demanded a voice from the crowd.

Ken and Ginny turned to see Cherisse shoving Alex forward into the cleared area.

"We came over to see what was happening," Cherisse said. "*Imagine my surprise!*"

"Alex," Ginny said. She stepped forward and grabbed Alex by the lapel. "Are you the *real* one?"

"Uh…"

"Give him some punch!" someone called from the gathered audience.

Ginny dragged Alex to the punchbowl. "Drink," she ordered.

Alex obeyed; his hand, as he filled the ladle, was not steady, but he managed to get half a cup of punch. He drank it down in a single gulp.

He did not vanish in a puff of smoke.

"I'm the real one," he said miserably. "Ginny, I…"

Ginny interrupted him. "You're the real Alex?"

He nodded.

"You got your Aunt Margaret to whip up those phonies so you could bring Cherisse instead of me?"

He nodded again.

"Then I've got another punch for you," she said, as she hauled off and punched him.

She was aiming for his nose, but he tilted his head back at the sight of her approaching fist, so the blow caught him square on the chin. His head snapped back and he fell back, slamming into the table and sending table and punchbowl crashing to the floor.

Ken smiled. Now he wouldn't need to worry about anyone else drinking the spiked punch.

"Clean up!" he called. "We need some clean-up here!"

No one paid any attention; instead the gathered observers burst into applause. "Yeah, Ginny!"

"Atta girl!"

"Good one!"

"You go, girl!"

Ginny stood, waiting, her hands on her hips, as Alex managed to disentangle himself and get slowly back to his feet. He looked at Ginny, then turned his head to look at Cherisse.

She was gone.

"I'm sorry," he said. He turned and began shuffling toward the door, dripping candy-apple-red as he walked.

"Where do you think you're going?" Ginny demanded.

"I'm not looking for Cherisse," Alex said. "She's probably just as mad as you are."

"So where *are* you going?"

"Home, I guess."

"Oh, no, you aren't! You invited me to this prom, and you are not about to stand me up now!"

That elicited another round of applause.

Just then a squad of volunteers arrived, armed with sponges and paper towels, and attacked the mess. That added a new dimension to the chaos, and for a moment Ken lost sight of Alex and Ginny.

Then the pair emerged from the crowd. Ginny had a death-grip on Alex's arm and was guiding him.

"I have been standing here by this stupid buffet dealing with those idiot replicas for *hours*," she said, "and I have had *enough* of that. Now we're going to go get our picture taken, and no, you may *not* change out of that tux, I want to remember you just as you are, and after that, when the band remembers they're supposed to be providing music, we are going to *dance*, Alex Pettigrew, and you damned well better lead!"

Alex blinked wordlessly as he was dragged past.

Ken watched them go, and smiled.

That was taken care of.

Now he had to get on with his regular duties, and make sure Ray didn't get another bottle of booze in, that nobody spiked the punchbowl once it was refilled…

After all, seventeen-year-old kids didn't need to *try* to cause trouble. Seventeen-year-old kids *are* trouble.

OUT OF THE WOODS

Jenny slammed on the brakes and prayed the car would stop in time; the man who had stumbled onto the road in front of her showed no sign of moving out of the way, he was just *standing* there.

The tires squealed, and the car slewed sideways and came to a stop—and the man wasn't there. Jenny kept her hands locked on the steering wheel as she turned her head and stared out the passenger-side window.

She saw only empty road, huge dark trees, and drifting wisps of mist.

Had she imagined it? These English roads were narrow and winding and made her nervous, and the thick surrounding woods were spooky, but she hadn't thought she was far enough gone to be hallucinating.

Getting out of London for at least a few days of her month in Britain had seemed like a good idea, but right now she wasn't at all sure it hadn't been a major mistake.

The rental car had stalled, and she decided against trying to start it right away; instead she turned off the ignition and got out, pocketing the key.

She looked around, at forest on either side, at the empty road curving out of sight in either direction.

And then a muddy shape rose up out of the roadside ditch, not a dozen feet away, and she almost screamed, but at the last moment managed to turn it into a gasp.

It was the man, the man she had almost run down—he must have flung himself into the ditch at the last instant.

"Are you all right?" she called, once she'd caught her breath.

"Aye," he said.

Jenny grimaced. Only in rural Britain would anyone who spoke English say "aye" instead of "yeah."

"I'm sorry I didn't see you sooner," she said. "Do you need a lift somewhere?" The rental car company wouldn't like it if she got their upholstery all muddy, but she was paying enough that they could afford to clean it, and she *had* almost run the fellow down—a lift seemed like the least she could do.

"How do you say, lady?" the man replied—or at least, that was her best guess at his words. It might almost have been "lad" instead of "lady," but she gave him the benefit of the doubt.

His accent was one she'd never heard before—British, certainly, but an unfamiliar variant; she couldn't even be sure it was English. For all she knew, it was Welsh, or Scottish, or even Australian or South African.

And apparently her American accent was giving him a little trouble, too.

"Do you want a ride?" she said, speaking slowly and loudly and, she hoped, clearly.

The man eyed the rental car, then looked Jenny over. "Aye," he said at last. "And my thanks to you, lady."

This time it was definitely "lady."

"Get in, then," she said. She climbed in on the driver's side—the right, that is, a fact she still wasn't entirely used to.

The man approached the passenger side hesitantly and stood, looking down at the door.

Impatiently, Jenny leaned over and opened it for him.

He made an odd little noise that she took for a sign of relief, then carefully climbed into the car and settled on the seat.

Jenny looked at him, puzzled; she hadn't really noticed when she first saw him in the road, or standing in the ditch covered with mud, but he was dressed oddly—his pants were more like baggy tights, with crude garters just above the knees, and he wore a sort of tunic instead of a shirt. His hair was unfashionably long, but he was clean-shaven—or rather, he had no beard; he was a few days past clean-shaven.

The overall effect was vaguely medieval.

"Are you an actor?" she asked. "Is there some local festival or something?"

"Nay," he said, "I'm no player, but an honest workman."

She started the engine, and he startled at the sound.

"Where are you headed?" she asked.

"Eh?"

"Where should I drop you?"

He simply looked baffled, and she gave up. She would just drop him at the first pub she came to and let the locals deal with him. She put the car in gear.

He grabbed at his seat—he hadn't put on his seatbelt, she saw.

She drove slowly and carefully—the fog still lingered, and night was falling, and one scare on these roads was quite enough.

Besides, she wanted to be able to stop quickly and jump out if the man started to act even weirder. Now that she was over her initial concern about sending him into the ditch, she was having second thoughts about giving him a ride at all—back home in the States she wouldn't have picked up a stranger, so why should she here? Sure, England had less violent crime, but there were still nuts here and there.

Maybe if she talked to him he'd reassure her—or maybe she'd *know* he was a dangerous loonie.

"So what were you doing in the woods?" she asked.

He hesitated, then said, "Feasting with Queen Mab."

Jenny had trouble at first understanding what he said, but the words did eventually register.

He *was* a loonie, she realized, though not necessarily a dangerous one. She wished she hadn't offered him a ride.

"Oh?" she said.

"Aye. I'd followed a fairy light, and found myself at the Queen's table, whereupon I was bid join the feast, which I did with a will. I passed many a long year there in pleasant company, and but today did I at last depart."

"Oh," Jenny said.

For a moment they drove on in silence; then Jenny asked, just to break that silence, "You said *years*?"

"Aye, I'd say so," the man said. "Surely, years it must have been, for the world to have changed as it has—your garb, your speech, and this carriage are all strange to me."

Jenny blinked, trying to decide whether this was as completely non-sensical as it sounded. "Just when did you follow the fairy into the for-est?" she asked, and immediately wished she hadn't—it sounded so stupid.

"'Twas May Eve, in the Year of Our Lord fifteen hundred and ninety-five."

For a moment Jenny didn't respond.

"That was four hundred years ago," she said eventually.

"*Four* hundred, you say?" The man's eyes widened in wonder. "Zounds, so long as that?"

"Yeah," Jenny said.

They were nearing a village—not much of one, but she thought it would do to get rid of her passenger. She slowed still further and began looking for a sign that would indicate a pub or inn.

"You doubt me," the man said. "Perchance you think me mad. No wonder on it, I'd think the same were I you."

That was the most reassuring thing he'd said yet; she threw him a quick glance.

"What's your name?" she asked.

"William Tinker."

"I'm Jenny Gifford. Look, is there anywhere in particular I can drop you? Anyone who'd know what to do with you? Do you have any money or anything?"

"I've no coin, nay. As for one who'd know to aid me—a priest, perhaps, who knows the ways of fairies?"

"I don't think modern priests know much about fairies," Jenny said, though she admitted to herself that British priests might well know more than the American ones she'd met.

William Tinker hesitated, then ventured, very cautiously, "A witch, perhaps? I'm a good Christian, and would not consort with such, but…"

"A witch." Jenny grimaced. A psychiatrist would probably be better.

But then she spotted the pub on the corner and pulled over to the curb.

"Here," she said, "go in there and ask if they know a of a witch. Tell them you've been visiting fairies in the wood for four hundred years."

That was perhaps a bit cruel—they'd mock him, most likely.

But then they'd probably send him to the National Health, and get him taken care of.

Tinker looked at the signboard, then pushed at the car door; it didn't open, and he looked helplessly for a handle or latch.

Jenny leaned over and opened the door for him.

He got out carefully, then bobbed to her in something that was almost, but not quite, a bow. "My thanks to you, good lady."

She felt guilty about dumping the poor loonie like this, and she was momentarily tempted to park the car and go into the pub with him, to make sure things didn't get rough—but it wasn't

her problem, and she wasn't a native here.

He'd be all right. This was a peaceful English village, not a bar in Detroit or L.A.—or even London.

And it just wasn't her problem.

She took her foot off the brake and pulled away.

Three days later, in her hotel room in Bayswater, she had the TV news on as background while she wrote a letter to her parents back in Cleveland. Something startled her, made her look up, though it took a second to realize what she had heard.

William Tinker, that was it—someone on the TV had said the name William Tinker.

And there he was, the same man she had picked up on that lonely road, with a woman on either side—an overweight matron on his left, a thinner, younger woman on his right, both in long dresses and wearing necklaces.

Tinker himself was dressed in modern clothing now—a simple shirt and slacks—but it was unmistakably the same man. His hair was still long, but looked considerably cleaner now.

"…naturally, so-called modern scientists are dismissing his story without even bothering to investigate," the older woman was saying, "but *some* of us recognize the possibility of wonders."

The camera cut to a blond host in a tweed jacket. "Then you believe that Mr. Tinker really *has* spent the last four hundred years at a faerie feast?"

Back to the woman.

"No, not literally—but we believe *something* extraordinary has happened in that forest. It may be that Mr. Tinker was affected by forces in the wood that reverted him to a past life, and that he was really only in there for hours and simply swapped identities, or it may be that he really did enter in 1595 and was somehow transported to our own time—my compatriots and I favor this latter explanation, since it would account for his clothing, and the fact that no one fitting his description has been reported missing."

"And you consider this more likely than an attempt at fraud, or a simple delusion?"

"Oh, very much so," the woman said. "What would be the *point* of such a fraud? And we have medical reports that will attest that Mr. Tinker appears quite sane, other than his belief that he spent four centuries in that forest. Furthermore, his teeth show no sign of modern dentistry, and the doctors say he's never been immunized against *anything*, or received any of the other lasting benefits of the National Health—he doesn't appear to have ever seen a doctor before. We've asked linguists from Balliol College at Oxford to tell us whether his speech is authentically Elizabethan, and so far, while we haven't heard their final opinion, none have found any specific inaccuracies."

"And have any historians questioned Mr. Tinker?"

"Not yet," the woman conceded. "After all, he only emerged from the wood three days ago."

"So you believe that in fact, Mr. Tinker *is* from the sixteenth century?"

"Yes, I do."

"Mr. Tinker, do you have anything to add to that?"

Jenny stared as Tinker said, in that strange accent of his, "I do truly believe that I am William Tinker, born in the Year of Our Lord fifteen hundred and sixty-seven, and that I came upon Queen Mab's table in the forest on the last day of April in fifteen hundred and ninety-five—but if you say I am mad, I'll not debate. I think I am not, and yet to pass four centuries with the

Good Folk and not age a day is surely a great wonder; were it proven me that 'twas all a dream, that would be no greater marvel. In truth, I wonder whether all I see about me, this world of a

twentieth century, is not but a dream."

"Mr. Tinker, you seem to be in remarkably good health for a man more than four hundred years old," the host said, with just a slight sardonic edge to his voice.

"Aye," Tinker said. "'Tis the magic of the wood, beyond question."

Jenny sat and watched as Tinker and his two companions—presumably the village witches from that town she'd abandoned him in—held their own against the host's growing sarcasm.

The younger witch hardly said anything, but the older argued at length for the existence of powers beyond modern understanding—not fairies, but spirits or powers that gave rise to tales of fairies, or if even that seemed too mystical, she was willing to consider them as energy fields created by the living things of the earth.

Was it so utterly impossible that someone could become caught in such an energy field?

"And these fields," the host asked, "preserved our Mr. Tinker for some four centuries? Would this sort of thing be responsible for the legends of the Fountain of Youth, then?"

"It very well might," the elder witch declared.

Meanwhile, Tinker himself seemed to be growing ever more uncomfortable, caught in the middle of this debate, and when at last the host announced that time had run out, poor Tinker was visibly relieved.

Jenny turned off the set and sat on the hotel bed, staring at the blank screen, for several minutes.

Maybe, she thought, he *wasn't* a loonie.

After that she began to watch the news regularly. She saw the reports from the experts, proclaiming Tinker to be either genuine or the best fake ever—neither linguist nor historian nor physician could find anything to contradict his claimed origin.

The real bombshell was when his clothes were carbon-dated and proclaimed authentic late-sixteenth-century.

It was after that that reports of would-be explorers getting out of hand at the forest began. Curiosity-seekers had gone poking about there ever since Tinker's first television appearance, but now entire mobs were sweeping through the woods, searching for "Queen Mab's table." The authorities were dismayed, to say the least.

It was a relief to Jenny when the forest was closed to the public; she hated the thought of all those people trampling through the underbrush, scattering candy wrappers and beer cans on the moss.

She watched the televised reports with a sort of dreadful fascination. Picketers were protesting the government's decision to restrict access—there was talk of secret conspiracies to keep the "fountain of youth" energy for the government elite.

And there were a few reports coming in, not very reliable ones, of people disappearing into the forest and not coming back out—presumably, they'd found the fairies.

She spent hours on end in her hotel, watching. She knew it was stupid, a waste of her remaining vacation time, that she should be out enjoying London, but she couldn't tear herself away.

She was staring unhappily at yet another interview when someone knocked on the door of her room.

Startled, she opened the door.

There were three men standing there. One of them held a microphone, another a video camera.

The third, somewhat disguised by a woolen cap and sunglasses, was William Tinker.

"Ms. Gifford?" the man with the microphone asked.

"Yes," she said, puzzled. "What's going on?"

"We understand that it was you who first found Bill Tinker after he emerged from the enchanted forest," the man with the microphone said—Jenny recognized him now; he was a newsman. She couldn't think of his name.

She glanced at Tinker, who looked apologetic.

"I wished to speak with you," he said, "and I knew not how you might be found. I agreed that I would give your name, that you might be interviewed, if I might accompany them and speak to you in private."

His accent wasn't quite so distinctive any more—he was beginning to adjust to his new surroundings, she supposed.

"I don't *want* to be interviewed," she said. "I'm not part of this."

"Then you weren't the one who found him?" the newscaster asked.

"Oh, sure I was," she admitted. "I almost ran him down, so I gave him a lift into town, that's all."

"And did he tell you he was four hundred years old?"

She glanced at Tinker uncomfortably. "He said he'd been in the forest since 1595," she said.

"And did you believe him?"

"No. I thought he was nuts. But he seemed harmless."

"But didn't you tell him, when you dropped him at the Plow, to ask where he could find a witch?"

"I said something like that," Jenny admitted, embarrassed. "I didn't think he'd want to see a doctor. Listen, I haven't agreed to an interview, and I'm not going to—not until I've talked to Mr. Tinker in private."

It took some further argument, but eventually Jenny was able to close the door of her hotel room with Tinker and herself on the inside, the newscaster and cameraman outside.

"Now, why did you want to find me?" she demanded.

"Softly, pray," Tinker said, holding up a hand. "Your pardon, I pray you, Mistress Gifford."

She glowered at him.

"Prithee, lady, I come to you most humbly to ask a service—will you even hear me, or have I angered you by bringing with me these relentless hounds with their cameras?"

He pronounced "camera" in very nearly the modern fashion, she noticed—it was presumably a new word for him.

"What kind of a service?" she asked quietly.

"Lady, I beg you," he said, "though I be an Englishman born and bred, and loyal to my Queen, whiche'er Elizabeth it may be—can you take me with you to America? I must escape my own land!"

She stared at him.

"Why?" she asked.

"Need you ask?" he said, gesturing at the closed door. "In mine own land I shall have no peace, 'tis plain."

"Can't you just hide somewhere?"

"Where? This land is so changed I know naught of it."

"You know that forest," she said, a trifle bitterly. "Can't you go back there, to Queen Mab's table, if you can't take the modern world?"

His hands flew up in an odd gesture, then he hushed her and glanced at the door again.

"They'd have that of me," he said. "They'd have me lead them thither, with their cameras and mikers and all."

"Well, why not?" Jenny demanded.

He stared at her, chewing his lower lip, and she stared angrily back.

"You'd have the truth?" he asked.

"Of course!"

"All the truth, then?"

She blinked. "Yes," she said, a bit less certainly.

"In truth, then—there is no Queen Mab in the forest, no Little Folk."

"What *is* there, then? What about the people disappearing in there? Is this all a hoax?" Jenny tried not to let her fury show—he *was* a fake!

"Nay, nay! I am all I say, trapped four centuries in the wood, and I swear it in God's name. But 'twas no fairies that held me, but a demon, a spirit sprung from the wood itself."

"Go on," she said.

"'Tis plain enough. I was held there 'gainst my will," he said. "I'd followed a fairy light, as I thought it, though now I know 'twas but a lure, and then was I caught and held by the spirit within the wood."

"Why?" she demanded. "What did it want you for?" A thought struck her. "And is it still there?"

"Oh, 'tis yet there, verily. And it hungers, I doubt me not."

"*Hungers?*" she almost screamed. "What about all those people going in there looking for your fairy queen?"

"I fear that some of them will ne'er emerge," he said, shamefaced. "Oh, 'tis sinful of me, and a disgrace I do not bear easily—but if you only knew..."

"So tell me."

He sighed. "I was not alone when it lured me in," he said. "Else I'd not have been such a fool as to follow. I was with a dozen of my townsmen, gathering wood for a May Day blaze, when we saw the light before us. Kit saw it erst, and called out, and old Stephen warned him to let it go, but Kit laughed. 'What have we to fear, then,' he asked, 'when we are twelve stout Englishmen?' And in our folly we gave chase, into the forest depths—and there our paths turned back upon us so that we traveled ever in circles, trapped therein. And a voice spoke to us that bade us calm ourselves, calm and rest, and at last we did—we lay ourselves down and in our exhaustion we slept.

"And when we awoke, our Christopher was naught but bones.

"We shouted, we fought among ourselves, we attempted flight, but it did no good. We saw the sunlight wane, then reappear, over and over, for time had become strange to us.

"And at last we slept again, and when we awoke old Stephen was as Christopher, nothing but bone.

"And so it went, and we perished, each in our turn, until only I survived, and I knew what my fate was to be when next I slept, and in my despair I fell down upon my knees and cried out to whatever had trapped us, whatever had spoken that first day, and I begged for my life, I bargained, I offered whatever I could if only it would free me, spare my life and let me go."

"And it did?" Jenny asked.

Tinker nodded. "Aye," he said, "but erst it spoke to me again, and told me that it would trade my life for seven others—if I swore, by God and the Virgin, to bring it seven other lives, then I could go free. May God forgive me, lady, I did so swear—and but moments later I was on the high road, where you found me."

"And you sent it seven people?"

"I know not how many I sent it!" he wailed.

Jenny stared at him.

"Look you, lady," he said, "I bethought me that if I spoke of Queen Mab in the village, and said fairy treasure was to be had in the wood, then a few hardy souls would venture forth, and I'd be quit, and at little cost to my conscience, for they'd take the risk upon themselves, would they not? And I'd put that village behind me and ne'er set foot there again, and 'twould be an end on it." He gestured helplessly. "How was I to know of television, or motorcars, or tour buses? To send *hundreds* thither, at risk of their lives, was ne'er my intent, and now all England is cursed of me—my face blazoned on paper at every corner, and on the telly glass in every home! Take me to America, I beg you, let me put this behind me!"

She stared at his pleading eyes for a moment.

"We have television in America, too," she said at last. "You'd be news there, too."

His expression collapsed into despair.

"And you have to do something to stop them," she said, struck with sudden horrific realization. "All those people going into that forest...I bet they're still sneaking in, even though it's officially closed. My God, *I* was tempted to take a look!"

"What can I do?" He spread his hands hopelessly. "A tale once spun has a life of its own."

"That's true," she said thoughtfully.

"And if I speak the truth now, they'll stretch my neck ere morn, for betraying all those fools to their doom."

England wasn't known for lynchings, but this was a special case. "That might be true, too," she said. She considered carefully.

She wondered, for a moment, why she didn't just throw Tinker to the wolves—after all, he *had* betrayed all those innocents. By his own admission, he had meant to send seven strangers to their deaths—but then, he had seen his own companions killed horribly one by one and known he was next...

He'd done wrong, but he knew it, he wanted to make what amends he could. What good would it do to destroy him?

But they couldn't let more people feed the thing in the forest, whatever it was. Jenny didn't believe in demons or fairies, but there must be *something* in there.

And then she saw the way out. If one lie had lured people in, maybe another could turn them back.

"Listen," she said, "you're going to go on TV again—on television—and tell everyone that Queen Mab's angry about all these intrusions on her privacy. Remind everyone that fairies are dangerous—that's something we tend to forget nowadays. Remind them that fairies steal human souls. *That* should discourage most people—and anyone who goes in anyway, it's *his* problem."

"Aye," Tinker agreed reluctantly, after a moment's thought. "That should serve, I warrant. But am I to spend my *life* in television?"

"Oh, no," Jenny said confidently. "Don't worry. You're just a fad. It'll all be over in a few weeks, and you can settle down somewhere—I bet there are colleges that would hire you for their history departments. You must know the sixteenth century better than anyone else alive."

"Aye, perhaps," he said. "You'll accompany me, then, to the television?"

She hesitated, but then said, "Sure." She gestured. "Go ahead and open the door, and we'll tell your camera crew the news."

Jenny insisted they do their interview right there. The first few questions were harmless, asking about how she happened to pick Tinker up.

But then the newscaster asked, "Do *you* believe there are fairies in the wood?"

She glanced at Tinker, there beside her.

"Oh, yes," she said, "and in fact, I believe I've heard their voices."

Startled, the newsman asked, "Oh?"

"When I picked Bill up on that road. Maybe *he* didn't hear them, but I did. They were saying they wanted to be left alone, that he'd abused their hospitality long enough and that any other humans who bothered them would regret it."

She glanced at Tinker, who smiled gratefully at her.

"Indeed, I heard something," he said. "I'd not caught the words, though…"

And together, they blithely made up a whole network of lies.

The broadcast went well—and for the rest of her stay in England, Jenny Gifford found herself something of a celebrity. She spent a good bit of time in Tinker's company, helping him adjust to modern life—an adjustment he made with amazing speed.

And she was only slightly jealous when he bedded that young witch, rather than herself—but really, she told herself, he was a bit old for her, wasn't he?

She giggled at the thought.

By the time she returned to the States Tinker's moment of fame was already passing, and her own with it. Within a week of her arrival home, the whole thing seemed like a dream.

But for the rest of her life, she still shuddered whenever she passed thick woods.

GHOST STORIES

"Oh, sure, Damon, the old Hanson place is really haunted, but you go there anyway," Jeremy said sarcastically. "You play with the ghosts, right?"

"There's just one ghost," Damon said. "His name's Ichabod Hanson, and yeah, we play checkers, or cards, and he tells me stories and stuff."

"Oh, right," Jeremy scoffed. "And my teacher is Madonna in disguise, she gave up music to teach sixth grade."

"You don't believe me?" Damon asked, with a peculiar smile.

"Of *course* not!" Jeremy replied.

"Well, come on then, and I'll show you."

Jeremy didn't like the look on Damon's face, and he didn't like the look of the Hanson house, but he couldn't refuse a challenge like that.

"Okay," he said. "When?"

"What's wrong with right now?" Damon asked.

Jeremy blinked in surprise, and looked around at the bright sunshine. "Does the ghost come out during the day?"

Damon shrugged. "Sure."

Jeremy couldn't see any way out. "Okay," he said.

The old Hanson place had been built more than a hundred years ago— Jeremy had heard his mother say so—and it looked as if it hadn't been painted or repaired in all that time. It was all weathered gray wood, with just a few shards of glass left in the narrow windows.

The two boys parked their bikes in the tall grass by the porch, and Damon led the way up the sagging steps. The boards creaked under their weight, and Jeremy tried to be as light as he could—the ancient planks felt as if they might break at any moment.

The front door stood open, and Damon stepped inside. "Hi, Mr. Hanson?" he called. Jeremy stood nervously on the porch peering in; Damon leaned back out and whispered, "Listen, let me do the talking. Don't you say *anything*. Okay?"

Jeremy, who was beginning to think this might be more serious than he liked, nodded nervously.

"Come on inside," Damon said.

Warily, Jeremy stepped in—and the door closed behind him, all by itself.

He moaned.

He'd always thought most horror movies were stupid because nobody would be dumb enough to just walk right into those traps where the monsters could get them, the way the people in the movies always did, but here he'd gone and walked right into a haunted house, and now the ghost was going to get him…

But Damon didn't look scared at all.

"Good day, young Damon," a strange voice said, and Jeremy jumped. "'Tis a pleasure to see ye. Who might this other lad be?"

"Hi, Mr. Hanson," Damon said cheerily. "This is Jeremy." He nudged Jeremy. "Say hello," he whispered.

Jeremy said, "Uh…hi," to the empty air.

"A good day to ye, Jeremy," the voice said, and this time Jeremy could see him, an old man at the top of the stairs, with the sunlight from an upstairs window coming right through him—a rather small man, with a bushy beard and curly hair worn fairly long; he wore an old-fashioned black coat with big buttons, and a dark vest, and white pants. He was coming down the stairs toward them.

Jeremy backed up against the door.

"My name, as I suppose Master Damon's told ye, is Ichabod Hanson," the ghost said. "And I'd offer to shake hands with ye, had I still a palm solid enough to grasp."

Jeremy glanced at Damon, but didn't say a word.

"Jeremy didn't believe I really knew a ghost," Damon said.

"I suppose 'tis a hard thing for some to believe," the ghost said, smiling through his transparent beard. "I'm none too sure I'd have credited it myself, when I was yet alive."

"Tell 'im how you wound up as a ghost," Damon suggested.

"Would you hear the tale, lad?"

Jeremy nodded, then stood staring at the ghost, listening.

"I was, y'see," the ghost said, "a sailor out of Boston, having gone to sea as a boy, a few years before the War Between the States, and a fine life I found it. I sailed the world around any number of times and saw every port from Halifax to Hong Kong, but a day came when it seemed to me that the time had come for me to settle down. So I built myself this house, and I found myself a wife, and I tried me best to live me a quiet life here on the land."

He sat down on the stairs, and motioned at the boys; Damon promptly settled on the floor, and Jeremy cautiously followed his lead.

"I found, though," the ghost continued, "that the life of a landlubber was not for me. I'd a hankerin' to see foreign shores and strange sights that was not to be denied." He sighed an intangible sigh. "So with a kiss and a farewell, I left me wife and me home and took ship for a run to Singapore."

He smiled with the memory. "'Twas a fine voyage, lads, but when I come home, I was weighed down with the guilt of how I'd treated me missus, and I swore to her that I'd settle down good and truly this time, and for another six months I did just that—but then an old shipmate offered me a first mate's berth on a tea packet…"

And so it had gone, he explained, one voyage after another, and his wife had progressed from understanding to unhappy to angry, and, he said, he should have known better, for Mistress Sarah Hanson was from a family that was well known to have witchery in it.

"And at last," he said, "when I was perhaps a trifle too old to be traveling about as freely as all that, I told her one fine day that I'd a chance to captain a schooner on a run down to Rio de Janeiro, and she said she'd had quite enough of all that. She wanted her man at home, and where I'd got away from her before despite her asking and pleading and begging, she'd decided to resort to something a little stronger. And she put a spell on me, that I'd remain at home here forevermore. And she didn't say until I died, neither—she said *forever*."

Jeremy glanced at Damon, and Damon smiled back.

"So I've been here ever since," Hanson said, "and all in all, I've not minded a bit, no, not even when I sickened and died. I'd thought that might be the end of it, but no, I stayed here just the same, and kept me widow company of an evening, telling her tales of my adventures in foreign ports—those tales that were fit for a lady, and some that weren't, and what's more, keepin' myself largely to the truth." He smiled at the memory. "And you know, lads," he said, "it seemed to me that I enjoyed the telling near as much as I'd enjoyed the doing—or perhaps a shade more. I'd no need to spend weeks between ports living in a crowded cabin smelling of bilgewater, getting from one place to another, as I had before."

All in all, he told the boys, he was grateful to his wife for the curse she'd put on him—save that it had been lonely when she died, as no one had cursed *her*.

He paused for a moment, letting the lonesome silence sink in, then said, "But other folk happened along in time, and I enjoyed their company, told them a tale or two—just as I have Damon here, and as I'd be glad to tell *you*, Jeremy, if you'd like."

Jeremy nodded. "Yes, please," he said.

So Ichabod Hanson told Damon and Jeremy about his first visit to the Caribbean, as a boy of thirteen on a freighter hauling sugar, and how they'd run afoul of a hurricane and limped home with but a single mast and the hull full of water, and Jeremy listened to that, and thought he would gladly have listened forever, had not Damon eventually interrupted.

"It's past dinnertime," he said, pointing to the setting sun. "We'd better get home."

"Oh," Jeremy said, startled; he'd had no idea they had been there so long. "Oh, wow." He had been sitting cross-legged on the floor; now he looked up at the ghost and said, "Wow, thanks, Mr. Hanson. It was a pleasure meeting you."

"Come back any time, lad; 'tis a pleasure to have so attentive an audience as yourselves."

"Yeah," Jeremy said, "I will. I mean, it's too bad about the curse, but it's neat to hear all this stuff, you know?"

"Ah, the spell's hardly a curse, in truth, for my existence here's no hardship on me."

"Isn't there any way you can get out of it? Did she really curse you *forever*?"

"Oh, well, she done as good as, lad. The way of it was, we were talking, and she said I was the travelingest man she'd ever seen, and she saw no way that she could let me go the least little bit, for I'd be off to the far side of the globe in a trice if she even let me out to go to the market. And I said that I was no more besotted with travel than many another, and she'd stretched the truth of it. And she said that she'd never seen a man who'd gone as far as I, and never would until a man walked on the moon, and until then, I'd be cursed to stay inside these walls. So y'see, lad, 'tis as good as forever—I'm bound here until a man walks on the moon, and the word of it reaches me, and how could that ever happen?"

Jeremy's mouth fell open. "But my Dad says..." he began.

Damon poked him, hard, in the ribs; Jeremy turned and saw a finger pressed to Damon's lips, and didn't finish the sentence.

"Come on," Damon said, "it's time to go." He took Jeremy by the sleeve, opened the front door, and dragged Jeremy out onto the porch.

A few minutes later, as they were hurrying back toward their homes, Jeremy said, "But men *have* walked on the moon, years ago! My Dad told me all about it! Why haven't you told him?"

"Because, you jerk," Damon said, "I haven't heard all his stories yet!"

Jeremy thought that over. It wasn't like Mr. Hanson was in any hurry to move on, and Jeremy had hardly heard *any* of his stories.

"Right," he said. "Can I come back tomorrow? I promise I won't tell him."

Damon smiled. "Sure," he said, "any time."

THE FROG WIZARD

The charts didn't show an island there, but the greenish smudge on the horizon certainly looked solid. Captain Kai was curious, and his schedule was not particularly tight, so he ordered the helmsman to make for whatever it was—cautiously, of course.

It *was* an island. The charts were wrong. This was not really very unusual in these seas, but it was interesting.

An uncharted island could have its uses; Captain Kai dropped anchor and sent a dozen of his men ashore in the ship's dory to explore the place, with a lieutenant named Kwan in charge.

This was not exactly Lieutenant Kwan's idea of a good way to spend an afternoon, but he knew better than to argue. He sat in the stern of the boat muttering vile imprecations into his beard as his men rowed ashore.

The shore itself was unremarkable—a broad expanse of sandy beach stretching off in both directions, and at the top of the slope a line of palm trees. Kwan sighed as he clambered out of the boat; he knew that his sailors would treat the whole thing as a vacation from their dreary life aboard ship, and would run about as wildly and heedlessly as if they were the Emperor's personal guests in the pleasure gardens at Haichin. One or two would probably get lost, at least one was bound to eat something poisonous, and about half could be expected to return to the ship with rashes, stings, bites, bumps, and bruises from the local plants and animals. A broken wrist from falling out of a tree would be no surprise at all, and would mean a tongue-lashing from Captain Kai for Lieutenant Kwan—a man with a broken wrist can't haul on ropes, and it was an officer's responsibility to keep his men fit for duty.

Life aboard ship might be dull, but it was safe.

Kwan was still double-checking the highwater mark and making certain that nothing could possibly wash the dory back out to sea even if the man posted to guard it ran off or fell asleep when one of the men shrieked.

"It's started already?" Kwan muttered. He turned.

His men were scattered across the beach and along the line of trees. The shriek had come from Lin, who was now standing beside a palm and waving desperately.

Kwan sighed and trotted up the slope, waving for the others to join him. To his surprise, most of them actually obeyed.

A moment later all but three of the party stood clustered about Lin. Wen had, as ordered, stayed with the dory, while two others had drifted off somewhere.

"What is it?" Kwan demanded.

Lin pointed back into undergrowth beyond the palms—into the jungle, Kwan told himself resignedly. The tangle of greenery qualified as jungle.

"A demon!" Lin said.

"Oh, pfui," Kwan said. "There *are* no demons in the waking world!" That was what the priests of his faith taught, and depending on his mood he either believed it to be true, or hoped that it was.

"It was tall, and thin, with white hair all over its face, and horrible pale skin," Lin insisted.

"It wasn't just a man—a white, perhaps?" Kwan suggested soothingly.

Lin paused, then admitted, "Well, I didn't get a very good look at it."

Kwan nodded, and then shouted into the jungle, in his best trade pidgin, "Hey, we come be friends, you come talk, yes?"

The face that popped out of a cluster of ferns startled even Kwan, who thought he was ready for anything. He saw how Lin could have mistaken it for a demon; an unkempt, untrimmed white beard bristled in every direction from a thin, lined face. Pale blue eyes peered from sunken sockets, and a broad bald spot glistened with sweat. Despite the constant tropical sunlight, the skin was pale and pasty.

"Who are you?" this apparition demanded, in reasonably clear Language.

"I'm Kwan, third lieutenant aboard *Glory of Summer Dawn*, and these are some of the crew. Is this your island?"

The white man blinked.

"You could say that, I suppose," he said. "You...ah, you aren't from Batrachia?"

"I never *heard* of Batrachia," Kwan said, truthfully.

"Or King Alfred?"

"Nor King Alfred." This was a slight exaggeration, as Kwan had once heard of a legendary ruler by that name in one of the white countries, but that King Alfred had been dead for a thousand years or so, and whichever country it was that claimed this ancient monarch—Kwan could never keep all those little countries straight—it certainly wasn't Batrachia.

"What are you doing here, then?" the stranger demanded.

"Well," Kwan said, "We were passing by, and saw the island, and noticed that it wasn't on our maps, so we came ashore to see what was here."

"All right," the white man replied, "You've seen what's here—*I* am. Now what?" His eyes were wary, and reminded Kwan of a tiger he had once seen in the menagerie at the emperor's summer palace.

"I don't know," Kwan admitted. "Is there anyone else here?"

The answer came immediately.

"No."

"Ah...do you *want* to be here?" Kwan asked. "I mean, were you shipwrecked?"

"No, I got myself here on purpose; I don't need any rescuing, thanks."

Kwan considered this, unsure whether it indicated derangement—he wondered just how long the poor creature had been living alone on this island. He ventured, "Perhaps you might want to come speak to our captain, though?"

The bearded ancient blinked again, and said, "Why, that's very generous of you. I think I'd enjoy that. I haven't had anyone to talk to in a very long time now."

"Well, then," Kwan said, "Come back to the ship with us."

The white man squinted at him. "You're sure this isn't a Batrachian trick?"

"Oh, I'm quite sure," Kwan said quickly. This white man, Kwan decided, was not entirely sane.

"All right, then. Lead the way." The stranger stepped out of the bushes, and Kwan was horrified at the ragged condition of his garments. He wore only tattered remnants of something that might once have been an elegant robe.

What, Kwan thought, would Captain Kai make of all this?

He found out several minutes later, back aboard the ship.

"A castaway!" the captain exclaimed, "How marvelous!"

"I'm no castaway," the stranger protested. "I was there on purpose. My boat's around the other side of the island—if it hasn't rotted away."

"Ah," Kai said. "Then why were you there?"

"I'd rather not say."

The captain nodded. "As you wish. You will join us, though, for tonight's dinner? Surely, you will grant us this favor! We can exchange tales, as is the custom among our people."

"Well, I...it..." The stranger hesitated, but then his reserve collapsed. He bowed, and said, "Of course. You do me honor, good sir!"

Kai bowed in return, and Lieutenant Kwan stood by, admiring his captain. An exchange of tales was hardly mandated by custom in a situation like this, but it would almost certainly reveal many useful things without any sort of unpleasant interrogation, even if the stranger did not intend to tell his own story. A culture's tales tell much about its people, what they value, and what they believe.

The captain then turned his guest over to Kwan once again, to be cleaned up and made presentable in time for the evening meal.

Kwan did his best.

When the sun was half-sunken, and its last rays painted the water the colors of blood and gold, the ship's officers gathered around the white-draped table in the great stern cabin. The stranger's beard had been brushed out and the edges trimmed, but its length had been left intact, in honor of its owner's plentiful years; his rags had been replaced with one of Lieutenant Ma's brocade tea robes, as none of Kwan's was long enough.

The ship's officers were also wearing finery—not necessarily their best, but formal garb, all the same. Taking their cue from their captain, they seated themselves in near-silence, and made only polite small talk while they ate the meal of shellfish and vegetables that the ship's cook had prepared.

When the last dish had been cleared away, Captain Kai cleared his throat, and began speaking, in a pleasant sing-song, reciting the Tale of the Three Great Fishes.

When he had finished, he nodded to First Lieutenant Shi-Lu, who proceeded to tell the story of his notorious Uncle Shi, who had almost been beheaded for introducing rice wine to the island of Hsin Kuo, but had saved himself by besting the emperor in a game of Caravanserai.

And so it proceeded around the table, as the officers told stories they had heard as children, or recited the classics of the empire's literature, or recounted incidents that had befallen them or members of their families.

At last it was the stranger's turn. He coughed, glanced around, and began, and told this tale.

Long ago, in Batrachia, there lived a wizard. He was not really very *much* of a wizard, as it happens. No matter what he did, no matter how hard he tried, no matter how much he studied, he could only work one piece of real magic. He was very good at sleight-of-hand, and at all manner of stunts that *look* like magic, but that's not quite the same thing, and he knew it. *Real* magic means miracle-working, not putting a pigeon up your sleeve, and this wizard only knew one sort of genuine magic. He'd learned it as an apprentice. When spells for turning lead into silver regularly failed, when his love-charms just gave people belly-aches, when a simple geas made a smelly mess all over his carpet without even making the intended victim feel guilty about it, this one feat came easily to him. He could do it instantly, just with a wave of his hand.

It wasn't a simple, ordinary spell, either, like candle-lighting or card-flipping—he couldn't light a candle for all the gold in a dragon's hoard, but somehow he had mastered, without meaning to, a truly spectacular piece of magic. Perhaps some perverse minor deity had been having a joke with him in allowing him the easy use of this major transformation.

He could turn people into frogs.

A simple gesture, and anyone he chose would shrink down, turn green and slimy, and hop away, eager to eat bugs, as much a frog as ever grew out of a tadpole. He could do any number of people at a time, too, for that matter—turn whole nations into frogs, if he chose to.

He didn't choose to, however, and with very good reason. Unfortunately, he couldn't turn the frogs back into people again, and after one or two unpleasant incidents before he realized the situation, he swore never to use the spell again. He was too soft-hearted, in the ordinary course of events, to leave even his worst enemy stuck as a frog.

He practiced the gesture in secrecy, just in case he ever needed it, but he never used it.

He still wanted everyone to know he was a wizard, though. There were a good many wizards in Batrachia at the time, and they were something of an elite, highly respected by the rest of the population, and deferred to in several ways. A wizard could always count on a fair price at the village market, and no smith would ever miss the promised delivery date on a wizard's order. After all, angering a wizard is dangerous. He might turn you into a frog. Everyone knew that, even though in truth, most wizards didn't know that particular spell.

That this one wizard *did* know it, and had mastered it so completely, without ever learning any more useful or benign magic, was a source of constant private irritation, but he had no choice but to live with it.

And since he *had* mastered this spell, and really *could*, if he chose, turn people into frogs, he played the role of a wizard to the hilt. He wore a fancy hat, carried a wizard's staff, and lived in a well-furnished cave. He studied old books—partly in hopes of learning more magic, but mostly to keep up his image. He kept strange pets, such as lizards and giant spiders—nothing supernatural, though, since he had no way of manufacturing, summoning, or controlling such creatures. He equipped himself with a full wizard's laboratory, crammed with all the usual arcane paraphernalia—skulls, stuffed bats, mysterious powders, all of that—even though he couldn't use a single bit of it.

In short, he did everything a powerful wizard did, except to perform magic.

Reasonably enough, everyone in the vicinity assumed he was a great and powerful wizard.

This was all very well, and in fact it was exactly what the wizard wanted. He led a quiet, comfortable life, and had the respect and affection of his neighbors. Really, he was quite content with the situation.

Unfortunately, it didn't last, because late one summer Batrachia was invaded.

The first the frog wizard knew of this was when a messenger knocked on the door of his cave one morning, carrying a summons from King Alfred.

The wizard answered the door, expecting to see one of his neighbors come looking for a bit of advice, or maybe some villager asking after a philtre of some sort, and instead found himself face to face with a royal herald in full regalia.

The wizard blinked, and the herald unrolled a scroll and began reading. The wizard stood there, feeling rather foolish, and listened.

The herald read, "Whereas, Our Realm has been attacked, without provocation, by certain Enemies, and

"Whereas, Our normal methods of defense do not appear to provide a complete assurance of Victory against this foul invader, and

"Whereas, supernatural methods needs must be employed against this Desecration of Our Borders, and

"Whereas, Our enlightened rule has provided all alike, commoner and noble, mortal and magician, with great benefits and fair treatment

"Therefore, We call upon all those with any skills in arcane practices, be they in wizardry, sorcery, or other practices, to recognize their obligation to the Crown, and

"Therefore, all practitioners of Magic are hereby summoned forthwith to the Castle Royal, by Command of His Majesty Alfredus Rex.

"Signed, and with Our Seal, this fourteenth day of the Ninth Month, in the fifth year of our Reign."

The wizard was very impressed by all this, which sounded quite majestic, and when the herald had finished reading the wizard asked him just exactly what it all meant.

"It means that you're to come with me to the castle, immediately," the herald explained.

The wizard considered that for a moment, and then asked, "Why?"

"You're a wizard, aren't you?" the herald asked.

The wizard agreed emphatically that yes, he was indeed a wizard.

"Well," the herald explained, "All wizards are being summoned to the castle to help fight off the invader."

The wizard was not at all sure he liked the sound of that, and he said so.

The herald insisted, and made some rather nasty threats about what the king might do to uncooperative magicians. The wizard gave in on the major points, but he also insisted a little, and was allowed time to pack a bag.

While he was packing, and on the long walk to the castle, he asked the herald more questions, and got more of an explanation of just what was going on.

It seems that the exact reason for the invasion was not entirely clear to the Batrachians, but it appeared to have something to do with an insult the Batrachian king, Alfred the First, had unintentionally directed at the Grand Duke of Darchmont. Although the insult was completely inadvertent, the Grand Duke had chosen to take umbrage—he had probably been looking for an excuse. He had led an army of some four thousand men into Batrachia, marching through the peaceful countryside, burning villages and trampling farms, and in general making life very unpleasant for the citizenry.

The year had already been a bad one for the Batrachians, as the wizard well knew. Some quirk of the weather had cursed the kingdom with a veritable plague of gnats and mosquitoes, the crops had been poor, several wells had gone dry at midsummer, and then a few weeks later heavy rains had caused flooding along the rivers.

After all this, most people were not really surprised by the attack. As everyone knows, bad luck often comes in streaks. Some people had wondered if they had offended some god or other, but most just put it down to chance.

Naturally, King Alfred was quite upset by the invasion. The kingdom had been at peace for years, and the small standing army was out of shape, out of practice—and out building levees against the floods.

Even in the best of times, the Batrachian army was probably no match for the Grand Duke's force, and as it stood, defeat had appeared certain. From King Alfred's point of view that was completely unacceptable; the Grand Duke had announced that his honor had been impugned by the King, and that only a direct personal duel to the death between the two monarchs would satisfy him. As the Duke was young, fit, and famous for his skill with a broadsword, while King Alfred was aging, fat, lazy, and inept, this was the same as stating that he intended to kill the king.

King Alfred had therefore decided to find some way to drive the Grand Duke back across the border without an army. Obviously, that would take magic.

Accordingly, King Alfred had sent messengers out, and posted proclamations, and did everything he could to locate and gather every wizard in Batrachia. When they had been located, he summoned one and all, however powerful or puny, to his castle.

And that, of course, included this frog wizard.

The wizard really did not want to be involved in a war, but he did not see any graceful way to back out, so he went along with the herald without any serious argument.

Soon enough they reached the royal castle, where the wizard was introduced around, checked off a long list of magicians who were expected, and then generally made welcome.

He promptly found a quiet corner and did his best to stay there, out of the way, while the messengers and heralds brought in wizard after wizard. The frog wizard recognized several of them, while others were total strangers—and they kept on coming, and coming, and coming.

Really, he had had no idea that there were so *many* wizards in Batrachia! They kept on arriving for the next two days.

The frog wizard generally stayed in his corner, trying hard to be inconspicuous, and succeeding, for the most part. He slept on a mat in a wizardly barracks that had been improvised in a gallery, and he ate the bread and cheese and ale that the castle servants distributed three times a day, but other than that he simply sat quietly and watched and waited.

On the third day the wizards stopped coming. Instead, the invaders appeared and surrounded the castle.

By this time, though, the castle was full of wizards, dozens of wizards, wizards of every description, marching about and boasting of their prowess.

The Grand Duke's army arrived about midday and found the drawbridge up and the battlements manned—they had no way of knowing that the defenders were the castle servants, rather than soldiers. They spread out and settled in for a proper siege, setting up tents and pavilions, bringing up a battering ram, and so forth.

Meanwhile, inside the castle, the wizards were milling about, unsure just what was expected of them.

Around sunset, King Alfred appeared, in his best royal robes and wearing his crown, and announced to the gathered magicians that they were to use whatever magic they had at their disposal to destroy the besieging forces.

"When?" someone called.

"Right now," the king replied. He waved a dismissal, and retreated to his apartments.

The wizards looked at each other, shrugged, and began making magic.

The noted sorcerer Rudhira the Red brewed up lightning in a kitchen cauldron, balls of crackling blue-white lightning that hissed and spattered sparks across the floor.

Kiria the Blue etched a pentagram on the throne room floor with blue chalk, and set about raising a few cooperative demons.

Skellen the Fat began chanting a long, complicated spell intended to draw the floodwaters up from the river and wash the invaders away in a great wave.

Simon the Foul collected assorted leavings from the kitchen midden and began assembling and animating homunculi, nasty little man-shaped creatures the size of your hand that would sneak out of the castle and torment the enemy with poisoned hatpins and whispered curses.

All the various others set about their various fearsome sorceries, while the poor little frog wizard just sat there in his corner, looking scared and nervous.

Amid all that terrible magic, it certainly looked as if the Grand Duke's army were doomed.

But then things began to go wrong.

Skellen's great wave swept up from the river just as Rudhira's lightnings spilled out of the castle, and the two collided with a great hissing roar; the water put out the fire, while the fire boiled the water away into steam, steam that drifted harmlessly up into the night sky.

Kiria's demons sprang from the pentagram, hungry and ready for the sacrifice they had been promised. The invocation had directed them to devour those who did not belong in the area, and they obeyed that—but instead of the enemy soldiers they snatched up Simon's homunculi and gobbled them down like squirming candy. Homunculi don't belong in our world at all, and to a demon that's far more obvious than a human's nationality—demons aren't very bright.

Their hunger satisfied, the demons then vanished, and could not be conjured again until the next full moon.

Nor were these the only disasters as the wizards, accustomed to working in solitude, got in each other's way. Man-eating plants bloomed by moonlight and consumed wizards rather than soldiers; spells of sudden death became entangled with spells designed to send the invaders dancing helplessly and harmlessly away, and wizards died in jigs and gavottes; fearful illusions overlapped each other in grotesque juxtapositions that caused more laughter than fear among the besiegers.

Wizards were sent flying to the moon. Wizards were swallowed by the earth. Spells backfired, misfired, and crossfired, and the castle filled with smoke and strange light, while unearthly howls echoed from the stone walls.

Some of the spells worked properly—but not very many.

By dawn, the castle was still surrounded by about three thousand Darchmontane soldiers, and the wizards were all gone, banished or slain by spells gone wrong.

All, that is, except the frog wizard, who had stayed crouched in his corner, never even considering any attempt at magic.

As the sun rose, and the smoke cleared away, and the last eerie echoes faded, the castle's inhabitants crept out of hiding. The king, still in his regalia, emerged from his chamber and looked over the aftermath. His gaze swept across smeared pentagrams, spilled potions, and scattered scraps of wizards' robes, and fell at last on the frog wizard, curled up in the corner.

"You!" he called, "Come here!"

Reluctantly, the frog wizard got to his feet and came. He bowed deeply, and then knelt before the king.

"You're one of the wizards, aren't you?" King Alfred demanded.

The frog wizard nodded.

"You're really a wizard?"

"Yes, your Majesty," the frog wizard replied.

"You can work real magic?" the king persisted.

"Yes, your Majesty," the frog wizard said.

"Then *do* something about those soldiers out there!" King Alfred demanded.

"But, your Majesty…" the frog wizard began.

"*Do* something, wizard!" the king shouted, leaning over until he was yelling right in the wizard's face.

The frog wizard had never liked being shouted at; it made it hard for him to think.

"*Do* something about those soldiers!" the king insisted, pointing out a nearby window.

Without really meaning to, the frog wizard *did* something. He worked his one and only spell, directed at the soldiers outside, and all three thousand of them were abruptly transformed into bullfrogs—very large, hungry bullfrogs.

At first nobody realized what had happened, and the king continued to shout for several minutes before somebody tugged at his sleeve and pointed out that the invaders were gone, and had been replaced by a horde of amphibians that were now hopping about in mad confusion.

The king stared out the window, and, forgetful of the royal dignity, most of the other people in the room crowded around him and peered out over his shoulders.

Sure enough, the invading army was gone.

King Alfred turned to the wizard and demanded, "Did you do that?"

The wizard, too miserable to speak at the thought of what he had done to all those men, merely nodded.

"Is it permanent?" the king asked.

The wizard nodded again.

"You're sure?"

"I'm afraid so, your Majesty," the wizard replied.

The king's face broke into a broad grin; he whooped with joy, and his crown fell from his head.

He caught it and tossed it in the air, then danced about with joy in a manner not at all consonant with proper castle protocol, but quite understandable from a human point of view. After all, he had just been saved from certain death.

The wizard was nowhere near as happy, but he managed a weak smile in response to the king's obvious delight. And after all, he hadn't killed anyone, and for all he knew frogs could live long and happy lives, and soldiers faced death regularly as an occupational hazard. He tried to convince himself that it was all for the best.

And in fact, it did seem to be all for the best, at least from the Batrachian point of view. The war was clearly over, and had ended in an unmistakable Batrachian victory.

The castle servants were sent out to investigate and to collect the spoils, and by sunset that day the royal armory was jammed to overflowing with captured weapons. The frogs had been chased away, scattering in all directions, and the entire army's supply train had thus been abandoned, completely intact, to the victors.

The king and his councillors had spent the day alternately thinking up insulting terms to impose on the Grand Duke, if it should develop that he had not been among those transformed, and planning for a massive celebration of this miraculous deliverance.

The frog wizard sat in his corner, listening to all this, with no very clear idea what he was supposed to do.

Finally, around mid-afternoon, as he was getting very hungry, he got up the nerve to approach the king and ask what was expected of him.

"Should I go home now?" he inquired.

"No, of course not!" the king replied. "You're my honored guest, at least until after the celebration!"

Servants were called, and the wizard was given a hearty meal and a room for the night, but he still didn't really know what to do with himself. All his books and belongings were still back in his cave, after all. He spent much of the time sitting on his bed thinking about all those poor frogs, or staring out the castle windows, or aimlessly wandering the castle corridors.

This went on for the three days it took to organize the victory celebration.

At the feast, the frog wizard was dragged out in front of the rowdy, half-drunk mob of peasants and petty nobles, and was declared the kingdom's Royal Sorcerer. He was given the tallest tower in the castle for his own exclusive use, and servants were sent to his cave to fetch back all his belongings.

Everyone told the wizard that he was a hero. He tried very hard to feel like a hero, and to act like a hero, but he couldn't quite manage it. Failing that, he at least tried not to dampen anybody else's enthusiasm, and he had rather more success at this limited goal.

Indeed, everything in Batrachia seemed just fine for a time; the invading army was gone, and there were enough frogs to eat up all the extra flies and mosquitoes around the castle. The floods receded, the army returned to its usual duties, and life went on.

After awhile, though, unusual things began to happen.

Frogs began to turn up in odd places.

The weather was starting to turn colder, and ordinarily all the frogs would be burrowing down into pond-beds for the winter, but this year, instead, frogs were slipping into people's houses to stay warm. Peasants would come home from a day in the fields and find a couple of huge bullfrogs sitting on the hearth—big, determined bullfrogs that did not flee when chased with a fireplace poker, but merely ducked in a corner and waited for the poker-wielding peasant to give up and go away.

Frogs even began slipping into the castle.

And not only were these frogs getting in where they weren't wanted, but having consumed all the available insects, they were getting into the food, as well. Finding a frog on one's plate, licking at a pork chop or a leg of mutton, could ruin a man's appetite, and sent many a woman running for the poker.

Worst of all, the frogs seemed to recall enough of their human origins to have a rather warped sense of humor. Several people reported finding frogs in their beds and bathtubs, grinning lewdly—until now, nobody had realized that frogs *could* grin lewdly, but everyone agreed that that was exactly what the transformed Darchmontanes did.

Even royalty was not spared. Queen Gertrude scandalized the castle by running out into the corridor shrieking and totally nude after discovering a frog crouched between her legs in the bath, grinning up at her and licking about lasciviously.

The last straw was when the king himself, while dispensing high justice in the throne room, realized that something was wrong. Everyone seemed to be staring at the top of his head.

Puzzled, he reached up and found a frog, perched atop his crown and leering over the gold and jewels at the gathered courtiers.

Furious, he flung the crown to the floor and charged from the room, his councillors at his heels. Shouting imprecations, he marched up the stairs to the castle's highest tower, where he barged into the wizard's chamber without knocking and demanded, "*Do* something about these damned frogs!"

The wizard, startled, looked up from the book he was reading, blinked, and said, "What?"

King Alfred turned an interesting shade of purple as he stood in the center of the wizard's chamber, speechless with fury, trying to think of something suitably scathing to say.

At last he burst out, "These damned frogs are all your fault! *You* turned those soldiers into frogs! You couldn't sweep them away with a whirlwind, or make the earth swallow them up, or turn them into something harmless like rocks or daisies, no, *you* had to turn them into *frogs*! And now we've got frogs coming out of our *ears*, frogs everywhere!"

At that moment, the frog that had been on the crown stuck its head out of the back of the king's collar, where it had fallen when the crown was snatched off, and croaked loudly.

The king could take no more; he began shrieking wordlessly at the wizard as his councillors watched in horror from the doorway.

The wizard simply sat on his bed, the book on his lap and a baffled expression on his face, trying to figure out what he was supposed to do.

At last, the king had to pause for breath, and the wizard asked mildly, "What do you want me to do, your Majesty?"

"Do your damned *magic*, wizard! Do *something*!" the king said, as he marched forward and reached out to grab the wizard by the throat.

The wizard shrank back on the bed, but to no avail; King Alfred was a big man, with long, strong arms. He closed his hands around the wizard's neck and shouted, "*Do* something!"

The wizard had never liked being shouted at, and he discovered he liked being grabbed by the throat even less. It made thinking very difficult indeed.

Without thinking, he *did* something. His hand came up in a magical gesture, and he *did* it.

He turned the King into a frog.

The councillors still stared from the doorway as their sovereign shrank down inside his robes, turned green, and hopped out of his collar as a bullfrog.

This was no ordinary, placid frog, either. This was a *very angry* frog.

It let out a loud croak.

The other frog, the one that had been sitting at the back of the king's collar, croaked as well, and seemed to smirk.

The wizard looked at the two frogs, at the half-dozen courtiers jammed into his doorway, at the book on his lap, and then back at the two frogs sitting on the king's empty robes.

This, he saw, had gotten totally out of hand.

The wizard didn't think it would be a good idea to stay around. In fact, he thought that a quick departure would be a very good idea indeed. He closed the book and put it aside, then got to his feet and raised a hand threateningly.

"Step aside," he said, "Or I'll do the same to you!"

The king's councillors immediately stepped back, squeezing against both sides of the narrow hallway as the wizard marched past them and down the stairs.

Once he was out of sight he began running, because he knew that the councillors would not stay cowed for long. Sooner or later they would come after him, and the wizard did not want to know whether he really *would* turn more people into frogs if threatened with capture. He hoped he would not, but he wasn't sure.

He was safely across the drawbridge and out of the castle before he saw any signs of pursuit. Some simple sleight-of-hand sent most of the hunters off in the wrong direction, and he was able to slip safely away through the forest.

He made his way down to the sea, eventually, where he took ship aboard a sloop headed south. At a small island port he left his ship and stole a small lateen-rigged fishing boat, and sailed until he reached a small, uncharted island that he had heard spoken of, where he lived in peace thereafter.

With little else to do, he practiced his spell constantly, until he could do it perfectly without thinking about it at all—but of course, with no one there to trouble him, he never needed it.

Which is just as well, as he had no wish to have any more transformations on his conscience.

"…And that's the tale," the stranger told the officers of *Glory of Summer Dawn*.

Kwan and the others laughed politely, not believing a word of it. Captain Kai nodded his acceptance of the story, and then waved for a tray of after-dinner sweets.

Just then the ship lurched as a wave tugged it against its anchor chain. The cabin servant, a younger man not yet fully accustomed to the sea, stumbled; he fell against the stranger, and the entire tray of confections spilled into the old man's beard, leaving it awash in cream and honey and fruited syrups.

The stranger leapt to his feet, a hand raised in a peculiar gesture. Kwan looked up, startled, and saw the confusion in the white man's eyes—he had acted without thinking, from reflex, surprising even himself, Kwan was certain.

When Kwan looked down, the servant was gone, and a large frog blinked up at him from the cabin's carpet.

Kwan stared for a long moment; beside him, the white man let out a long, low sigh.

Across the table, Captain Kai whispered, "And he can defeat whole armies thus! What a weapon this could be, in the Emperor's service!"

"I knew it," the old man said, in the most miserable voice Kwan had ever heard. "Even here. I'll never be safe as long as I..."

Kwan looked up as the words stopped, just in time to see the old man gesture again—at himself.

Then there were two fat frogs on the carpet.

Kwan and the Captain stared at one another.

"I think," Kai told his lieutenant after a long silence, "that if we can't provide the Emperor with a mighty wizard to transform his foes, at least we might enrich his menagerie by an amphibian or two."

Kwan nodded. "And," he said, "it will give the Emperor's own magicians something to do—to attempt the restoration of these two unfortunates."

Thus it was that two ordinary frogs came to be the most pampered creatures in all the Emperor's collection—two, because the sailors had lost track, before reaching port, of which frog was which. Both seemed quite content with their lot.

And that was why, for years thereafter, every new magician to arrive at the imperial court was required to spend a day in fruitless experimentation at the frog pond.

HORSING AROUND

It isn't every day you meet a witch at the 7-Eleven. Jason thought it was a gag—right up until she tried to turn him into a horse.

He and Gus had been arguing about what seventh grade was going to be like, and whether the teachers were all geeks the way Gus' older sister Susannah said they were. They had been so busy arguing, in fact, that Jason had pushed through the door of the 7-Eleven without looking where he was going, and almost walked right into the witch.

She was standing at the magazine rack by the door, browsing through stuff like COSMOPOLITAN and VOGUE. She was dressed in a ratty floor-length black gown that would need cleaning to qualify as "filthy." Her greasy, waist-length black hair was unbelievably tangled, and her pointed black hat was so tall that she'd have to duck to get through the door. Her nose was spectacularly long and crooked.

"Hey," Jason said when he'd stopped just short of her and gotten a good look, "isn't it a little early for Hallowe'en?"

"Ha ha," she said, looking him in the eye. She turned back to the magazines.

Ordinarily Jason would have dropped it right there, but Gus said, "Wow, Jase, killer dialogue you've got there."

That was a challenge.

"So, guess you read those magazines for beauty tips?" Jason said. "*Witch* ones?"

The witch stared at him silently.

Jason desperately wanted to come up with something really clever, but with those dark eyes looking right at him his brain seemed to stop working. "Hey, Horseface," he began, planning a remark about using a currycomb instead of a hairbrush.

He couldn't think how to finish it, and for a moment he and the witch just stared at each other.

"If anyone around here is behaving like part of a horse's anatomy," the witch said, "I'd say it's you."

Jason swallowed, and tried to think of a comeback.

"Seems to me you might as well look the part," the witch said. She raised her hands and began mumbling something that sounded so weird it made the hairs on the back of Jason's neck stand up.

Before she could finish, Gus rammed into her side in a sudden body-check. "Oops, slipped," he said, as she stumbled over against the magazine rack.

The man behind the counter looked up from the six-pack of soda and bag of corn chips he'd been ringing up. "Hey, you boys get out of here and stop bothering my customers!" he shouted.

"Come on," Gus said, pulling at Jason's sleeve.

Jason came, stumbling back out through the door. He suddenly felt really strange.

"I think she tried to put a spell on me," he said once they were outside in the parking lot, only realizing how stupid it sounded after the words were out.

"Is that what it was?" Gus said, and punched Jason on the arm. "Heck, I thought she was getting ready for one of those kung fu moves or something, that's why I bumped her."

"Yeah—well, thanks," Jason said. His legs felt peculiar, full of twinges and twitches, a little like they did sometimes after a really long run. And his shoes were pinching.

"You okay, Jase?" Gus asked.

"No," Jason said. He kicked off his shoes; now his pants seemed too tight around the ankles.

"Maybe you better sit down," Gus suggested. He looked around for somewhere to sit.

Jason shook his head as he leaned on the hood of a pick-up. His legs didn't want to bend right; sitting down was not what he needed. In fact, without knowing why, he was standing on his toes.

His legs felt as if they were splitting right down the middle. He looked down at his stocking feet and almost screamed.

They were changing shape. And they *were* splitting down the middle, the front and back separating.

His socks tore a moment later; then the legs of his jeans began to split.

"Wow," Gus said, staring. "Like the Incredible Hulk, on TV!"

"She *did* cast a spell!" Jason shouted. He looked at his toes merging into hooves and said, "I'm turning into a horse!"

"Your face is still okay," Gus said. He was trying to stay calm, but Jason could see from his face how scared he was.

And if Gus was scared just *watching*...

Then Gus' words registered, and Jason realized that in fact he didn't feel any changes in his face—or for that matter, anywhere above his waist.

Below his waist, though, was another matter. He unbuckled his belt before the squeezing turned into actual pain.

His jeans were ruined; both legs were split. The side-seams were gone all the way to the waistband. He straightened up and looked down.

He couldn't even see his back legs from this angle. He turned and looked over his shoulder.

There he was, covered with reddish-brown hair; he twitched something that itched, a part of him that hadn't been there a moment before, and saw a newly-acquired dark brown tail, just the color of his hair, flick up.

From the waist down, he had turned into a horse.

More importantly, though, he realized he was standing there in the parking lot with no pants on, just the ragged remains of a pair of jeans dangling from his waist.

"I'm turning into a *horse!*" Jason shouted.

"I don't think so," Gus said. "I think you've stopped. Maybe I interrupted her before she finished the spell."

"So I'm going to stay *half* a horse?" Somehow, Jason didn't find this significantly better.

"You're a whaddayacallit, Jase—a centaur. That's not so bad. I mean, at least you can still talk and everything."

"But my pants… Gus, what am I going to *do?*" Jason looked around for someplace to hide, but there wasn't anywhere a centaur would fit.

Gus considered carefully, and Jason watched him hopefully. Gus grimaced in concentration; then at last he spoke.

"I don't know, Jase."

"Fat lot of help *you* are!" Jason snapped. He looked around, almost panicky. "I better apologize to her—I mean, I guess I said some rotten stuff. I don't know what got into me. Maybe she'll turn me back."

"Good idea," Gus agreed.

Together, they walked up to the door of the 7-Eleven, and Gus pulled it open. Jason started to enter the store, and discovered that he was now taller than before, as well as having more legs—he had to duck slightly to clear the doorframe.

"Hey," the clerk shouted, "You can't bring a horse in here!"

"I'm *not* a horse!" Jason shouted back, "I'm a…a centaur!"

The clerk glared, chewing his lip, then called, "Well, you still can't come in here! You aren't decent! And you're barefoot!" He pointed to a sign that read, NO SHIRT, NO SHOES, NO SERVICE.

"But…" Jason began.

"Out!" the clerk shouted.

Jason reluctantly backed out.

"Don't worry, Jase, I'll find her," Gus said. He stepped inside, leaving Jason to stand in the parking lot, worrying, and horribly aware of people staring at him.

In fact, by the time Gus reappeared Jason had collected a small crowd. None of them dared come too close, and no one spoke to him, but they all stared at him, and he could hear them talking among themselves.

"It's some kind of trick," someone said, as he watched Jason.

"Like the fake unicorn in the circus," a woman agreed.

Jason didn't know what to say to that, so he didn't say anything. He just stood, shuffling his hooves uneasily, until Gus emerged.

"She's not there, Jase," Gus said.

"Where'd she *go*, then? She didn't come out this way!"

Gus shrugged. "For all I know, she vanished in a puff of smoke. She's not in there, though. I went through every single aisle."

"But *now* what do I do?" Jason wailed.

"I dunno," Gus said.

"Who's going to turn me back?"

Gus shrugged again. "Maybe it'll wear off," he said.

Jason snatched at that idea. "Yeah!" he said. "I bet it will. I bet I'll wake up tomorrow same as ever. I'll probably turn back to a pumpkin at midnight, like in Cinderella."

"So what're you going to do for today, then?" Gus asked, with a glance at the crowd.

Jason said, "I better get home." He reached down for his shoes, but discovered that he couldn't reach them—even with his forelegs bent, his arms didn't reach the ground.

Gus saw the problem and handed Jason the sneakers. Jason took them without a word, tied the shoes together by the laces, and hung them around his neck—though he wasn't quite sure what use his shoes were ever going to be to him again if the spell *didn't* wear off.

He began walking dejectedly toward home. The crowd started to follow, but Jason turned and shouted, "Go away! Show's over!"

For a moment no one moved; then, muttering, the crowd dispersed, slowly and reluctantly, until only Gus walked at Jason's side.

"Jase, there could be possibilities in this centaur stuff," Gus said.

"Shut up," Jason answered. He was not interested, not unless Gus had some way to turn him back to normal.

"No, really," Gus insisted, "I bet you can run like anything, now! And you could give people rides…"

"I'm not even sure how I'm *walking*," Jason pointed out. "If I stop and think about it I'll probably trip over my own feet. I'm not about to try running."

"Oh, but…"

"Just shut up, okay, Gus?"

Jason walked on in morose silence, listening to the unfamiliar rattle of his hooves on the sidewalk. The sidewalk was awfully far away, too—he hadn't really noticed the change while it was happening, but ever since he had almost hit his head on that doorway he had known that he was considerably taller now than he had been that morning. Judging himself against Gus, he estimated that he was now a good six and a half feet tall, maybe more.

Which might have been pretty cool, if the bottom half hadn't been horse—and naked.

"I can't believe I'm walking down the street without my pants," he said. "It's like one of those awful dreams, where you go to school in your pajamas."

"I bet," Gus agreed.

Jason suddenly perked up. "I bet that's it," he said. "This is all a bad dream, right? I'm just dreaming?" He pinched his arm, the way people did in books and movies.

It hurt. And nothing changed.

"I don't think it's a dream, Jase," Gus said. "I mean, if it is, I'm having it, too."

"I guess it isn't," Jason said.

At last they reached Jason's house, and together the two walked up the driveway to the kitchen door.

The roof of the carport seemed uncomfortably close overhead, Jason thought. He knew it hadn't moved; he was just taller.

He opened the door and stepped in—and stepped in the rest of the way; it took a moment to get all four feet inside. His hooves thumped loudly on the linoleum.

"Wow, Jase," Gus said, "What's your mother gonna say?"

"I don't know," Jason said unhappily.

"Is that you, Jason?" his mother's voice called from the living room.

Jason looked at Gus. Gus shrugged.

"Jason?" his mother called. He heard her footsteps, and for a moment he wanted to hide—but she would have to find out sooner or later. He couldn't hide forever.

And besides, the whole thing still didn't seem completely real. Maybe when his mother saw him he'd be normal again, and it would all be over.

Then she stepped into the kitchen and saw him.

Jason had heard and read about such things for years, but he had never actually seen anyone faint before.

Centaurs don't kneel well, Jason discovered, and they aren't very good at sitting, either; he was more comfortable standing than in any other position. That wasn't really a big surprise, since he knew horses sleep standing up, but it meant that he towered over his mother when Gus brought her around.

She almost fainted again.

At last she recovered enough to order, "Out of my kitchen!"

"But, Mom…!" Jason protested.

"Out!"

Reluctantly, Jason backed out—there wasn't room for him to turn around without knocking anything over. He hit the back of his head on the doorframe, and stood in the carport rubbing it as Gus stepped out of the house with Jason's mother.

"Hi, Mom," Jason said.

"Jason, what *happened*?" she demanded.

"Well, there was a witch at the 7-Eleven…"

His mother listened silently to the whole story, then said, "If you weren't standing there in front of me I wouldn't believe a word of it. Witches and centaurs? And you've ruined your jeans. And I've told you to be polite to strangers!"

"I know," Jason said unhappily.

"And you can't come in the house like that."

Jason remembered how tight a fit it had been in the kitchen. "I guess not," he agreed. "But where'll I sleep? What'll I eat?"

His mother didn't have a quick answer to that.

Eventually, however, they cleared out the backyard shed for him, and put in a layer of blankets that he could lie down on if he wanted.

As for food, his mother brought it out to him. He had been afraid he might have to eat grass, but he found that he could eat most ordinary foods with no problem—with one exception.

He couldn't eat meat.

It still tasted fine, but when it reached his stomach he got horrible cramps. His digestion wasn't quite human any more, and the horse part was herbivorous.

Well, he could live with that—and he hoped it wasn't permanent. He'd never thought about being a vegetarian, but lots of people managed it.

By the time his father got home Jason was fairly well settled in his shed, and the situation was almost beginning to seem normal—though he missed watching TV and playing video games.

His father didn't see it as normal at all.

He didn't faint; instead he stopped dead in his tracks and stared.

Jason told the story again. It took longer for his father to accept it than it had for his mother, but at last it sank in.

"We'll have to find her," he said at last.

"How?" Jason asked. He didn't need to ask who.

"I don't know," his father admitted.

The weather that evening was warm and pleasant, so the family ate a picnic dinner in the backyard, Jason's parents seated at one side of the table while Jason stood at the other. Jason had to skip the chicken, but ate heartily of everything else.

In fact, he ate far more than usual, and he'd never been a finicky eater.

"There's a lot more to feed," his father pointed out. He added thoughtfully, "This could be expensive."

"Maybe it'll wear off," Jason suggested.

After dinner, they found they had unexpected company—Gus, who had gone home for his own supper, was back, with both his sisters.

"See?" Gus said, "I *told* you!"

The two girls stared, goggle-eyed, and Jason felt himself blushing. He had almost forgotten that he wasn't wearing pants, but now he was more aware of it than ever.

"Wow," said Susannah, Gus' older sister.

"Can I have a ride?" asked Ashley, the younger sister.

"I'm not a horse," Jason protested.

"But you're a centaur," Susannah said.

"Oh, *please*?" Ashley pleaded.

Reluctantly, Jason agreed.

It felt very strange to carry first Ashley and then Susannah around on his back; neither of them seemed to weigh much of anything, as his strange new body was much stronger than his old one. Gus helped the girls on and off, but expressed no interest in taking a turn himself.

The evening passed in a blur of walking and trotting about the yard, with one girl or the other on his back, clinging to his back or shoulders—he had no saddle or stirrups, nor any mane to hold on to.

At last Gus and his sisters departed, and Jason's family went inside, leaving Jason to settle down in his shed. He took a final look around the yard, then closed the door and went to sleep—standing up, because that was the only position he could get comfortable in. He hoped he would wake up entirely himself again, whether standing up or lying down.

Alas, the next morning he was still half-equine.

After breakfast his father reported no listings in the Yellow Pages under "witches," "enchanters," "sorcerers," "wizards," or "centaurs." The half-dozen entries under "magicians" all sounded like sleight-of-hand stage acts or party performers, but Jason's dad began calling them all in hopes of finding one who was more than that.

Gus' sisters returned that afternoon with some friends. By the end of the day word of Jason's condition had spread throughout the neighborhood and several surrounding streets, and a photographer from the town newspaper had turned up to take pictures.

By then Jason was confused and tired, and his feet hurt, but he was beginning to enjoy his sudden celebrity.

The next day his parents questioned everyone at the 7-Eleven, but found no one who could lead them to the witch; back home, Jason had begun charging a dollar apiece for a trot around the block, and was tucking a good bit of money away in his shirt pocket.

He let Susannah and Ashley ride free, though.

By the end of the week Jason and his parents had run out of ideas for locating the witch—or for that matter, *any* witch or miracle-worker. An attempted exorcism by a cooperative priest (most had refused to consider the idea) had done nothing at all; nor had the few strange rituals performed by various self-proclaimed magicians helped.

"I'm sure she'll turn up eventually," Jason's father said.

Jason wasn't so sure.

On the other hand, he was now a genuine celebrity, charging a dollar just to get into the back yard for a close look at him, and five dollars for a ride.

The crowds were not really much fun, and most of his friends stayed away, rather than be jostled.

"What's it *like?*" people would ask, and Jason could only shrug and say, "I don't know."

It was all very strange and confusing.

And Monday, Jason remembered as he settled to sleep on Saturday night, was the first day of the new school year.

"I'll have to wear shoes," he reminded his mother the next day.

"Well, we could call a farrier..." she said hesitantly.

"I am *not* going to have anything nailed to my toes!" Jason answered.

"Horses don't seem to mind."

"I'm not a horse! And what if I change back?"

"I suppose you're right," she agreed. "Maybe I can make something."

"What about pants?" Jason asked.

"I don't see how," she said. "I mean, if they insist, I'll try, but let's try it without first, all right, Jason?" She glanced involuntarily at his chestnut flank.

Jason sighed. "All right." Getting used to walking around in public without pants had been the hardest part of this whole experience, but he had to admit, when he thought about it, that he would look really stupid wearing anything below the waist—except maybe a blanket. He refused to even consider a saddle.

The shoes his mother came up with were more like bags with drawstrings than like ordinary shoes, but they worked reasonably well.

Jason was incredibly nervous as he walked to school—obviously, he couldn't ride the bus. The first day of junior high, and here he was, half human, half horse—as if starting at a new school wasn't bad enough!

He collected a crowd as he walked, and by the time he reached the school fifty or sixty people were following him, chattering in amazement.

The principal was standing by the front door, greeting the students as they arrived. When Jason trotted up he stared, then shouted, "Hey! You can't come in here!"

"But I'm a student," Jason protested. "I'm registered! Look, I'm in Ms. Hecate's homeroom!" He pointed to the class list posted by the door. "And I'm wearing a shirt and shoes."

The principal hesitated, glanced at the class list, looked back at Jason, then smiled.

"Ms. Hecate?" he said.

Jason nodded.

"All right, then," the principal said. "But try not to cause any trouble."

"Yes, sir." Jason clopped past—the bottoms were wearing out of his shoes already, and his hooves were loud on the tile floor.

He wondered whether Susannah was right, and the teachers were geeks. He wondered how this Ms. Hecate would react to having a centaur in her class.

He was *tired* of being a centaur; he really wished he hadn't mouthed off to that witch.

If he ever found her and got turned back, he promised himself, he wouldn't horse around like that again.

He made his way down the school corridor, jostling through the crowd of students, until he reached Room 8. He ducked his head, stepped inside—and froze.

There at the teacher's desk stood a woman—Ms. Hecate, presumably.

She was dressed in a ratty floor-length black gown that would need cleaning to qualify as "filthy." Her greasy, waist-length black hair was unbelievably tangled, and her pointed black hat was absurdly tall. Her nose was spectacularly long and crooked.

She smiled at him. "You must be Jason," she said. "I believe we've met before."

Jason swallowed. "Yes, ma'am," he squeaked. He wondered what she was going to do—was she still mad at him about the insults? Was she going to finish the job of turning him into a horse?

She considered him thoughtfully for a moment, then said, "For today, I'd like you to just stand at the back, if you don't mind."

Jason nodded.

Then Ms. Hecate added, "But tomorrow, bring a pair of pants, and your shoes, and we'll get you into a regular seat."

Jason smiled with relief. "Yes, ma'am," he said.

Well, he thought, at least *one* teacher wasn't a geek. It was going to be an interesting year.

SPIRIT DUMP

"There's this place I know," he said, perching himself on the corner of the desk, "Out past the Bannersburg landfill, near where the sheriff dumped all the confiscated booze from those moonshiners last year, that I visit when I need cheering up."

She looked up him, startled, and then grimaced. "It's that obvious?"

"Yup." He smiled.

She sighed.

His smile vanished. "Or if you'd rather just talk about it…"

She shook her head. "No," she said, "I tried that, with Angie—you know her, my apartment-mate, don't you? Well, anyway, I talked to her, and it didn't do any good."

"So what is it that's bothering you, anyway, if you don't mind my asking?"

"That's the thing—maybe that's why talking didn't work. I don't *know* what it is. I just feel like my life… I don't know, like it's not going anywhere, or maybe it's… Oh, hell."

He nodded. "Well, this place I mentioned is a lot cheaper than a shrink, and it's safer than drugs; care to give it a shot?"

"Where did you say?"

"Near Bannersburg. It's about half a mile past the landfill."

"What, is it a great view, or something? That's getting up in the hills, right?"

"Kind of. The view—well, there's a view, but it's not just that. It's hard to explain; it just seems like a place where you can dump your problems and worries and forget them."

She eyed him suspiciously. "And I suppose you were figuring you could drive me up there, to this place in the middle of nowhere, just the two of us for a look at this romantic scenery?"

He put a hand on his chest, fingers spread. "*Me?*" he said, "Would I try something like that?"

"Yes." She nodded emphatically.

He laughed. "True—and if that's what would cheer you up, Suze, I'd be glad to oblige. But honestly, it wasn't what I had in mind. Look, I can give you directions and you can drive up by yourself, or we can bring along a chaperone, or make a party of it."

"Really?" She studied his face, and saw nothing hidden there, no trace of sarcasm or spite or even lechery.

"Why are you telling me this, Paul?" she asked.

He shrugged. "Just trying to help out a fellow human being."

"That's it?"

He smiled crookedly. "Well, maybe I do have an ulterior motive— but I'm not going to tell you what it is until *after* you've seen the place."

She stared up at him for a moment, then said, "All right, you're on. But we'll bring Angie."

A ngie looked out the car window and pronounced, "Yuck."

Paul laughed. "That's the landfill," he said.

"That's a dump," Angie said. "I don't care what they call it, it's a dump. They were dumps when I was a kid, and changing the name doesn't change the fact that they're still dumps."

"They plow 'em under now, though," Paul pointed out. "It's more sanitary. The stuff doesn't just sit there collecting vermin."

"Whatever, it's still a dump, and it's ugly."

"Never said it wasn't." He glanced at Suze, and his expression dimmed; she wasn't laughing. She was staring dully out the window on the other side, watching the passing trees.

"There's nothing wrong with dumps," he said. "Gotta put all the trash somewhere, don't you?"

Angie snorted. "Dumps make me sick," she said. "When I was a kid, my uncle Bert used to hang around the town dump—he'd shoot rats there, they paid him a bounty, maybe a quarter each, which was hardly worth the bullet. He thought it was fun, though, and he'd pick through all the stuff and sometimes he'd bring home some of it. Old magazines, and sometimes books, and machinery parts—he used to fix my mother's washing machine, and I don't think he ever in his life paid for parts. And people throw away the damnedest things."

"Doesn't sound so bad," Paul said.

"Yeah, it was—everything he brought in stank. *He* stank. And he was filthy, always. I can still see him standing there, holding up a bunch of mangled rats by their tails…"

"Well, there probably aren't any rats in the landfill back there, any- way," Paul said. "That's why they bury it all now, so rats won't get in there."

"'Course, that means nobody can pick through it, either," Angie pointed out. "Uncle Bert would lose out both ways—if he hadn't drunk himself to death ten years ago."

Paul shrugged. "I guess he would," he agreed. He shook his head. "And people throw away the damnedest things."

A moment later they turned off the main road—which wasn't exactly a highway to begin with—onto a narrow strip of dirt. Angie started away from the window as they passed within inches of the tree branches on either side.

"Shit," she said. "You sure you know where you're going?"

"I'm sure," Paul told her.

About a quarter mile from the road the car suddenly emerged into sunlight; Paul brought it to a stop and killed the engine. "Everybody out," he announced, "We're here."

Angie leapt out and looked around; Suze didn't move until Paul came around the car and opened her door.

She looked up at him, then reluctantly climbed out.

The three of them stood in a strip of grassy meadow atop a small ridge. Behind them were the woods, all secondary growth and brambly underbrush; ahead of them the land dropped off abruptly, a steep slope of bare earth and tuffets, perhaps fifteen or twenty feet high. Grass and wildflowers filled the gap between trees and drop, which varied from about a dozen feet in width to as much as forty.

At the foot of the slope the scrub forest gradually resumed, starting with grass and weeds, graduating through thorns and briars to bushes, a few browning evergreens, and finally to crowded, unhealthy maple and ash.

Suze looked around, appalled.

"*This* is your great scenic spot?" she demanded.

Angie said, "Looks more like Uncle Bert's old hang-out, only without the trash. They'd throw it all down the slope and let it pile up at the bottom."

"Hey, I said it wasn't the view that mattered—though I'd like to point out that you can see Sugarloaf if you look over that way." He pointed to the distant mountain, a blue lump on the horizon.

"So what is it, then?" Suze asked.

"Come here, and I'll show you," Paul told her, marching up to the very brink and beckoning her forward.

Slowly, reluctantly, she approached.

"Come on," he said, "I'm not going to push you over or anything."

Both women came up to stand beside him.

"Now," he said, "Look down the slope and tell me what you see."

Obediently, the two peered over the edge.

"Nuthin'," Angie told him.

Suze blinked.

"Not even a beer can, right?" Paul asked.

"I don't know," Suze said. "It's... I don't see anything, but it *feels* like there's something down there."

Paul nodded.

"Okay, Suze," he said, "I want you to take all that anger and depression and whatever it is that's got your spirit so weighed down lately, and I want you to gather it all up into a big lump and throw it down there."

She turned to stare at him. "What?"

"Like a visualization exercise," he said. "Like in meditation, or biofeedback, or something. Just concentrate on it, think of it as if it were a real, tangible thing, and throw it down there."

Suze hesitated.

"Oh, go ahead," Angie said. "Can't hurt to try."

"All right."

She concentrated. She thought of the gloom as a big grey something that had hung down over her, and suddenly she could *see* it, she could see this dark, foul thing, half cloud, half slime, that was covering her, and she reached up with both hands and heaved it up, revolted by the feel of it, heaved it up and flung it out over the brink. It fell, streaming grayish gunk that settled after it in a noisome, clinging cloud.

And suddenly she felt better than she had in weeks.

She blinked, and realized that the day was warm and sunny, that even though the trees down there were thin, their leaves were green and bright, the sunlight golden on the ground. The wildflowers on the ridgetop were cheerful, like a scattering of children's drawings. A monarch butterfly was vividly orange as it fluttered from one blossom to the next.

"Wow," she said.

Angie looked at her, startled.

Paul grinned. "Worked, huh?"

"How did you do that?" Suze demanded—but she wasn't angry; she felt too good to be angry. She was just curious.

"*I* didn't do anything," Paul told her. "*You* did."

"Come on," Suze insisted, grinning.

"No, really! Or really, it's this *place* that did it. Take a look over the side, there—carefully."

A bit doubtful, Suze approached the edge as closely as she dared and looked down.

"What am I supposed to see?" she asked.

Angie, beside her, said, "I don't see a damn thing but rocks and dirt."

"Suze," Paul said, "try to see that bad mood you threw down there."

"I won't get it back, will I?" she asked, with just the faintest trace of apprehension.

"No, no, of course not!"

She glanced at him, then stared back down the slope, trying to recall what that gray squirming mess had looked like...

And there it was.

And there was a great deal more.

She saw, faintly but definitely, gray and black and sick brown and bilious green and hot red, and gray and more gray. The slope was covered with the stuff, with oozing blobs and barbed chunks and a hundred other hazy, intangible shapes.

"Oh my god," she breathed.

"People throw away the damnedest things, don't they?" Paul asked her, grinning.

"What?" Angie shouted. "What is it? What's down there?"

"What *is* all that stuff, Paul?" Suze asked.

"Well," he said, pointing, "that spiky reddish thing is that bout of bad temper I had last summer and just couldn't get rid of. The dark oily thing there is from when my mother was thinking about suicide—I brought her out here. But most of them I don't know; they were here before I ever saw the place."

Angie was staring at him, he realized. She probably thought it was a joke, he told himself.

"I learned about it from my grandfather," Paul explained. "And he claimed to have heard about it from an old Indian who said this was the place where men could come and leave whatever evil spirits were troubling them. Granddad called it the spirit dump."

"I never believed in any of that stuff," Suze said, still staring down the slope.

Paul shrugged. "I don't know if it's evil spirits, or if it's something in the air here, or magnetic fields, or maybe it's all hallucinations; I just knew that it worked for me, and that it seemed to work for my mother, and Granddad said it worked for him. And I wanted to see if it would work for everybody, or if maybe it was just my family—or just my imagination. And when you'd been in a funk for the past week I figured it was a chance to find out."

"What are you *looking* at, Suze?" Angie demanded. "Ain't nothin' down there!"

Suze shuddered. "All that stuff..." she murmured. She stepped back from the edge.

"Let's get back in the car," she said. "I'll tell you about it later."

* * * *

Paul sat at his desk, tapping a pencil on the blotter as he watched Suze talking brightly to Roger and Amy. He frowned.

He hadn't told her to keep the spirit dump secret; he hadn't thought it was necessary. He didn't suppose it could really hurt if more people found out about it; after all, from the amount of stuff accumulated there already, plenty of people had known about it over the years.

Still, it bothered him. Suze was practically advertising the place, like a missionary seeking converts. Roger and Amy were just the latest in a long series.

But then, why shouldn't she proselytize? What could happen? Was he afraid that the magic would get used up somehow?

Maybe that was it.

Or maybe he was just being selfish; he had this wonderful cure-all, and he was being asked to share it, and he wanted it all for himself.

Maybe that was it. He tapped harder.

When the pencil broke he went back to his paperwork.

B y the end of the second week his agitation had reached such a level that it was interfering with his work, with his driving, with every-thing.

Obviously, the thing to do was to drive out to the spirit dump and chuck his worry over the cliff. That would prove that the place still worked, for one thing.

So, Saturday morning, he headed out past the Bannersburg landfill.

There were fresh tire tracks at the turn-off, several of them. He real-ized he had a headache.

Along the narrow access road a tree-branch snapped off against his window, the broken end dragging across the side of his car, and his head began pounding.

And when he reached the strip of meadow and found a Chrysler mini-van half-blocking his path, so that he had to steer carefully between its rear bumper and the trees in order to get out into the clearing, the headache was unbearable. Enraged, he climbed out and shouted.

Faces turned toward him, half a dozen faces—people he didn't even know. He marched out toward them.

"Hey, Paul," someone called.

Paul followed the voice and spotted Roger. "What are you doing here?" he demanded.

Roger grinned at him and shrugged. "Suze told us about this place," he said, "so we thought we'd check it out."

Paul stared at him for a moment, then stamped on up to the edge of the cliff and peered over, forcing himself to not just look, but to *see*.

The mass of spiritual debris lay upon the barren slope, stretching a hundred yards in either direction, but with the largest concentration directly below him. And there were dozens of new additions since his last visit—most of them small, most of them thin and gray and relatively harmless-looking, but still, *dozens*. More, he thought, than had been added in all the years he had been coming here.

"What have you been throwing down there?" he bellowed.

"Nothing much," someone answered.

"A hangover," someone else said, evoking laughter from two or three others. Paul saw that it was one of the strangers, a big, overweight man with ragged black hair. He was holding an open can of beer.

"A *hangover*? For Christ's sake, a hangover goes away by itself!"

"Yeah, well, I'd rather have it doing it down there than in me," the fat man retorted.

"And how do you know it will? Maybe it'll just sit down there and fester!" Paul shouted.

"So what?"

"So d'you want this to *fill up*? What happens then?"

The fat man shrugged.

"Damn it, you get down there and get that hangover back!" Paul ordered.

The fat man snorted. "You're crazy," he said.

"Get down there!"

"Make me."

Paul charged.

The fat man sidestepped and swung an arm to fend off his attacker; Paul, half-blind with fury and the pain of his headache, stumbled directly into the blow.

At first he didn't know what had happened; he knew he was falling, that the grass had gone out from underneath his feet, but he thought he would land on his back on the meadow.

Then he realized that it was taking too long, and an instant later he slammed backward into the bare dirt and rolled, involuntarily.

He tried to catch himself, but all he managed to do was to turn his roll into a slide; he still wound up at the bottom of the slope.

At the bottom of the slope, and *underneath* the contents of the dump.

Despair washed over him, thick gray drowning despair, as he lay on his back, trying to gather his senses. He stared up at a sky gone the color of mud and a sun gone dim and brown, and the futility of it all filled him, pressed down on him. Simply to breathe took an effort, and it was horribly tempting to just stop, to let his breath out and forget to take another…

He reached up and pushed the thing off him, and the sun was bright again, the sky blue. His head still hurt, and one foot stung oddly, but the suffocating hopelessness was gone.

Whoever had thrown *that* down here, he thought, had done the right thing.

He looked around. He was sitting on the bare dirt, near the bottom of the slope, and all around him were the vague, indistinct shapes and colors of the dump's contents. Above, at the top of the slope, Roger and half a dozen strangers were staring worriedly down at him.

It didn't look like a particularly difficult climb—except that it went right through the center of the dump.

Frowning, he looked around. Could he go down the slope the rest of the way, and around?

No; the dump extended well past him, down to the trees, almost as great a distance as that to the meadow atop the ridge. And the walk around either end would be a good, long one, from the look of it.

So he would just have to climb straight up the slope.

"Are you all right?" Roger called.

"I'm okay," Paul called back.

"Can you get back up?"

"Sure," he said. He got to his feet—or tried to.

There was something clinging to one leg, something sharp and rusty brown, something that stung, that seemed to twang every nerve and tendon in his ankle. He winced, reached down, and plucked it off.

It burned his hand, and he flung it quickly aside.

Then he started climbing.

He knew, from his very first step, that he was going to be wading through decades, maybe centuries of accumulated psychic detritus; he tried to brace himself for it, but he really didn't know how. Nothing he had ever done had prepared him for something like this.

A green like rotting cheese roiled up his leg, and a rush of envy swept over him. *Roger* was safe up there, the smug bastard...

He tore the envy away and took another step, and a rush of guilt flooded him—how could he think ill of Roger, who hadn't meant any harm?

He hesitated with that one, and tried an experiment. He reached down and tore off a few fragments—just little ones, like sickly, gray-black cotton balls.

He hadn't been sure it was possible, but in fact it was easy; easier, he thought, than it should have been. He was sure he was doing something wrong here, that this was immoral somehow, but he forced himself.

He collected about a dozen pieces, then wadded them up and stuffed them in his pocket.

He knew he shouldn't be doing it, it was a really terrible idea…

Then his hand came out of his pocket and he smiled; the idea no longer troubled him at all.

"What are you doing there, Paul?" Roger called.

Paul had just tried to squeeze between two very large, nasty-looking things, and in doing so had run his leg right onto a hot red spike of anger. He snapped his head up and glared at Roger.

"What the hell does it *look* like I'm doing?" he bellowed. "Fat lot of help you are!"

He shook his leg free of the bad temper and took another step.

This was really very boring. Tiresome. Maybe he should just settle down somewhere and rest until it got more interesting. Climbing up the slope wasn't any fun…

He waded on, through depression, ennui, anger, envy, guilt, shame, greed—and some surprises.

Lust, for one. That, he thought, was probably a relic of a more strait-laced era. It was all he could do to keep his hands out of his pants until he had scrambled up past it.

And pride. Sinful pride, a huge, seething mass of it. He wondered if whoever dumped it had kept any; the sheer quantity was amazing.

Maybe it had grown, since being dumped. Could it *do* that?

Any number of questions piled into his mind, and he realized he'd stepped on a lump of curiosity. He kicked it aside, and lost his balance. He put out an arm to catch himself.

And mindless panic swept over him, abject terror. He froze.

He was near the top, but suddenly he was scared to go any farther.

"Paul?"

He looked up, and Roger's face was there, hanging above him like some looming horror about to pounce. The dirt was soft and crumbling beneath him; at any moment, he knew he would plummet back down the slope, he would break his neck against one of those trees at the bottom, he'd slash himself on the thorns and lie there bleeding and crippled, and Roger would just laugh, Roger had planned it all, the whole thing, he'd put Suze up to it, her depression wasn't real at all.

They were all in it.

He started to take a step back down the slope, away from his enemy up there, that monster that had pretended to be a friend, that had lured him into this trap.

Monster—that was it. Roger wasn't human at all. He was some kind of demon. He'd planned it all, he'd probably created the spirit dump in the first place just to trap people. He lured his prey out here with his phony cures, then trapped them in the dump where he could torture them, where he could suck out their souls, where he could blind them with thorns and let flies drink the blood and...

If he stepped back, that might be what the fiend wanted. There could be barbed metal spikes there, spring-loaded spears that would thrust up into his belly, his groin. They'd missed him the first time, but now the Roger-thing was trying to drive him back to where the traps, the other monsters, were waiting. Little things with teeth and claws and shining bright eyes—he could almost see them, behind him, on either side, everywhere.

He didn't dare move.

But he didn't dare stay where he was, either. He began trembling, not merely with fear, but as he struggled with himself over what to do.

He knew he could never defeat the monsters—not just the Roger-thing, but all the others that must be lurking up there out of sight, that had been hiding in among the trees. But maybe he could at least try, maybe somebody would hear his screams as he tried to escape and they brought him down, fangs and claws and sharp steel blades gleaming.

He lunged forward, and the fear lost its grip. He sprawled on the slope, his hand reaching the grass at the top of the cliff, his face falling smack into the hangover that someone had thrown down just moments earlier. The world spun, his head throbbed, Roger's shuffling footsteps were like huge grating sandpaper sounds, like fingernails on a blackboard, but at least he wasn't terrified any more.

Just nauseated.

Then someone had hold of his arm, and he was being pulled up, and he reluctantly managed to get his feet under him and clamber up the last few feet onto the meadow. The hangover came with him, and he blinked owlishly at his rescuers. The light hurt his eyes.

"Are you all right?" someone asked. He winced.

"Don't shout," he whispered.

Someone giggled. "I think he got my hangover," he said.

Paul nodded, then winced again as the movement made his headache worse. When the others released his arms he sank down to sit cross-legged on the grass, where he gradually managed to pry the hangover, bit by bit, out of his head and gut.

When he finally flung it back over the side it was as if the sun had burst through stormclouds, and he took a deep, gasping breath in relief.

Then he sat for a moment, gathering his thoughts, as the others all huddled about him. He stuck a hand in his pocket and pulled out a little wad of guilt.

He felt bad about what he was about to do—but he told himself that was just the guilt, he didn't let it stop him.

"Give me a hand," he said, reaching out.

Two people took his hands, one on each side, to help him up; when he was upright he made sure to leave a little bit of guilt with each of them.

A little guilt never hurt anybody.

"Roger," he said, after quickly dipping his hand back in his pocket, "thanks for pulling me up." He reached out to shake hands.

Roger, a bit reluctantly, shook, and took a little guilt away with him.

Two others were clapped on the back.

The last of the group he didn't bother with; the poor woman looked guilty enough already. And he still had a fair-sized lump in his pocket that would come in handy when he talked to Suze on Monday and asked her to stop broadcasting about the place. He wasn't sure how he would store it that long, but he was sure he could manage it.

"Bet you're glad to be out of there," someone said. "I'm really sorry if we caused you trouble."

"It's nothing," Paul said. "Really."

"Yeah, well," Roger said, "*I* wouldn't want to go down there! We could see your face—it looked awful."

"It wasn't so bad," Paul insisted.

"I'll bet you wouldn't want to do it again!"

"Oh, I don't know," Paul said, looking back, remembering lust, and pride, and the wad of guilt, and thinking of Angie's good old Uncle Bert. "People throw away the damnedest things."

ARMS AND THE WOMAN

"It's not as if we didn't know this one was coming," Uril said loudly as he stumbled over a rock that protruded from the mud. "The books are very clear, and the astrologers confirmed the date."

"We should have done something sooner," Staun grumbled. "If we'd been sent out a little sooner we wouldn't have to rush like this. We could have gotten there before it started raining, and we wouldn't have to hurry. Why did the Council leave it until the last minute?"

"Because they're a bunch of squabbling old fools," Captain Lethis said as he pushed aside a dripping branch that hung low over the overgrown road. "We were supposed to be here days ago, but they wasted time arguing about who should go, and how many, chosen how, and who should pay for it all, and a dozen other details, until all of sudden they realized that the prophesied date was almost upon us."

"If the Undead Lord gets loose because of their delays, I swear I'll cut a few of their throats," Staun said.

"And if he does I won't lift a hand to stop you," Lethis agreed. "But let's not let it come to that, shall we?" He turned and beckoned to the stragglers, bellowing, "Come on, you!"

The other soldiers, with much cursing and grumbling, picked up the pace a little; behind them came a ragged little crowd of others, tagging along.

Officially the Council had chosen ten men for this errand, but altogether, including friends, helpers, family, and assorted camp-followers, there were almost thirty people slogging through the Forbidden Marsh in the pouring rain, making their way toward the ruins of Haridal Keep. There had been almost fifty when they left the Citadel two days before.

Near the rear of the party, a young woman named Siria was listening to the complaints and thinking that the score who had abandoned the quest were the sensible ones. After all, if this worked the way it was supposed to, there probably wouldn't be much to see or do; the legends said that whoever wore the magical armor that the wizard Karista had given King Derebeth sixteen hundred years ago would be immune to the black sorcery of the Undead Lord, and could therefore easily strike the monster down before his resurrection was complete, sending him back to the grave for another four hundred years.

If it was really that quick, Siria doubted she would have a chance to ingratiate herself with anyone—she could be charming, given time, but she might not have that time.

And she really didn't have anything to offer other than charm. These past two years since her father's death she had used up everything else—not that there had been much to begin with. She was too small to keep up the land her father had worked, not strong enough to work it, and the lord had sent her away, giving the land to a husky young man more suited to farming.

Since then she had wandered hither and yon, looking for a place, and had found none. What she *had* found was that soldiers were often generous with a pretty girl, especially when they had just done something strenuous and dangerous and were feeling proud of themselves.

She hoped that this particular job would qualify, that the soldiers would find errands for her along the way, and when the Undead Lord was properly dispatched that they would invite her to join their celebration.

It shouldn't be dangerous. The stories and written records from before the Extermination, left by the wizards who had dominated the world back then, were fairly clear about what needed to be done.

The earliest report of the Undead Lord dated back sixteen centuries, to a time when the world was awash in chaos and powerful magic—nothing like the quiet present day. That first time King Derebeth had disposed of the Undead Lord after a long, fierce struggle, and everyone had thought that was the end of it—but four hundred years later, when certain stars aligned properly, the creature had reappeared. After some messy delays the legendary Kurlus of Amoritan had retrieved Derebeth's armor, not to mention the sacred Sword of Light, and dealt with the problem.

Eight hundred years ago the local wizards had been ready—even though magic was already in decline astrology was in full flower by then, and they had known the exact time when the Undead Lord would rise again. They were waiting, with a mercenary warrior by the name of Porl already wearing the armor and wielding the sword, and the Undead Lord had scarcely begun to materialize before being dispersed. The whole thing was over in a few minutes, according to the reports.

Four hundred years ago there had been some doubt about whether the Undead Lord would put in another appearance, and matters had been complicated by the Third Lodrian War, but a party of soldiers had been waiting. A Lieutenant Rusran had worn the armor and dealt the required blow.

Again, it just took a few moments.

So there wouldn't be much to see unless something went wrong and the Undead Lord was able to restore himself fully to life—and in that case, anyone in the area stood a good chance of winding up dead or ensorcelled. Siria did not care for that possibility—but she didn't expect it to arise. Captain Lethis and his men would see to that. They were the best that the Council had had on hand, and would surely handle this nasty business quickly and efficiently. They had all handled pre-Extermination relics before.

While she had supposedly come along to run errands beforehand, Siria was mostly looking forward to a time when the Undead Lord was safely gone. Once Captain Lethis and his men had the job done, no matter how easy it proved to be, they'd be feeling good, and might be generous with a woman who helped them feel better. The Council paid its soldiers well—especially when left-over magic was involved. The world was still cluttered with this sort of remnant of the bad old days before the Extermination, and the Council did not stint those brave souls who helped dispose of these menaces. Lethis and his men would have fat purses when this was done, even though sending the Undead Lord off to another four hundred years in limbo did not appear especially difficult or dangerous.

Of course, there might be unknown dangers. Siria had heard that the accounts of the previous manifestations were not as detailed as the Council might have wished—there was a mention in the record of the Undead Lord's third appearance that the wizards had had some brief difficulty in finding a suitable candidate before choosing Porl, but there was no explanation of what the selection criteria had been. The report from the Lodrian Wars mentioned in passing that Rusran was given the job at the last minute when his commanding officer, a Captain Orilik, proved unable to do it, but again, there was no explanation of why Orilik wasn't up to the task.

And of course, since the Extermination there were no wizards or sorcerers to ask for more details—they were all long gone. Only their written records and the scattered bits of magic remained.

This lack of clear, detailed information had worried the Council somewhat, and that was why they were sending ten of their finest, rather than two or three volunteers; it wouldn't do to have no one in the party fit to wear the armor.

Lightning flashed, followed all too closely by a sudden clap of thunder; a moment later the rain turned from a drizzle to a torrent.

"Oh, enough!" a woman to Siria's right exclaimed. "If they want me, they can find me back in Splittree." She turned around and began slogging in the other direction.

As if that were a signal a handful of the party turned back, as well—but the ten soldiers kept on marching forward, and Siria stayed with them, as did a dozen others. After all, Siria had no place to go back in Splittree, no family waiting for her anywhere, and she was already soaked to the skin.

Uril, the big bushy-bearded pikeman from the Stoneford Marches, paused and looked back at the shrinking of their retinue. Siria smiled at him, and he smiled back.

That was promising—when this was done maybe he would spend some money on her, buy her a good dinner back in Splittree perhaps. She had been thinking that the group turning back were probably the smart ones, that she was a fool to stay, but Uril's smile prompted her to reconsider. Uril would soon have money to spend, and she would not be particularly demanding; he might keep her around for quite some time, which would certainly be preferable to approaching strangers in inns and taverns.

And she was surely already as drenched as she could get…

That was when she slipped and fell face-first in the mud.

Before she even realized properly what had happened Uril had her arm and was lifting her back to her feet.

"Thank you," she mumbled, looking down at the huge brown smear down the front of her frock and hoping there was no damage that wouldn't wash out.

"You're quite welcome," Uril said. "You'll want to be a little more careful up ahead—it's just as slippery and a good bit steeper."

Siria muttered something, she didn't know exactly what, and turned away, ostensibly to brush the mud from her frock, but really to hide her blush. Here she had wanted to impress Uril as someone charming, someone who would be good company, and then, right in front of him…

Well, there was nothing to be done about it now.

Uril turned away and marched on through the marsh, and a moment later Siria followed, ignoring the snickers of the others. She kept to herself after that, apart from the rest of the group; she had no desire to turn those snickers into open laughter by letting them see her take another tumble.

Half an hour later the trees thinned enough to give them a clear view of Haridal Keep, former home to assorted necromancers and monsters. Captain Lethis and his men marched on, undaunted, but some of the others stopped and whispered.

Siria couldn't hear what they were saying, but she could imagine. Haridal Keep, even after sixteen hundred years, was impressively forbidding. The castle had been built atop a huge mass of bare stone that thrust up from the earth, and some of the walls had not been built atop the outcropping, but carved directly from it. The towers had long since crumbled, and the battlements were broken and uneven, but most of the walls still stood straight and strong.

"I think I'll wait here," a plump woman declared loudly. "It'll all be over by sundown, won't it?"

A chorus of discussion arose, reached a quick crescendo, then died away as most of the party began to settle down under the trees, spreading canvas from branch to branch to keep off the rain.

Siria hesitated—it would be good to get under shelter—but then slogged on, following the ten chosen soldiers. Staying with the others, constantly displaying her soiled frock, would be too embarrassing.

Besides, she was curious to see the inside of Haridal Keep, and what the famous magical armor and sword looked like, and whether the Undead Lord would actually appear.

It was only when the party reached the long crumbling stair up to the castle gate that she realized that she was the only one besides the soldiers who had come this far. She hesitated before setting foot on the steps. Maybe she shouldn't be here. She didn't really belong with these professional heroes when they were going about their job.

"Come on," Uril called, waving to her from a dozen steps up.

"Captain Lethis won't mind?" Siria asked.

"Why would he? Come on and get out of the rain—assuming there's any roof left in this drafty old ruin!"

Quickly, Siria scampered up the steps.

If nothing else, this got her feet out of the clinging, slippery mud that had made the journey so miserable. That alone made it worth the effort.

The main gate was a heap of broken stone; the soldiers simply marched over it, but Siria, with her much shorter legs, had to clamber awkwardly. Uril glanced back at her and hesitated, as if he might come to her aid, but she determinedly didn't meet his gaze as she picked her way through the mess.

Past the gate was an empty stone courtyard, and then a gap in the yard-thick wall that had once divided the courtyard from the great hall. That gap had once had an archway and door in it, but they were long gone, the arch crumbled, the stones above it fallen away leaving an opening that was as broad as a farmer's wagon at the base, and that widened to three times that at the top.

There was no roof, no shelter from the rain, in the great hall. Siria brushed wet hair from her eyes to see Captain Lethis standing there, consulting a document, with the other nine men gathered about him.

"The entrance to the crypt was behind the high table," Lethis said.

"That would be *that* way." He pointed to one end of the room, but how he made his choice Siria could not guess. She followed along as the men marched across the ruined hall and began poking through the rubble that filled one end.

"Here," Staun said, as he uncovered a black opening.

"Right," Lethis said. "We'll need a light."

"Light it once you're inside, out of the rain," Uril suggested.

"Good idea," Staun agreed, and Lethis nodded. Then they began climbing down into that lightless pit, one by one. Siria heard a splash, and quiet cursing, and muttered comments, as the ten men vanished into the hole.

She hesitated. That opening did not look inviting at all—but she had come this far, and what was the point of standing in the rain?

And then a faint orange glow appeared in the blackness as someone got a light going, and she realized from how brightly it shone that the daylight, not very strong to begin with, was fading—the afternoon must be almost over, the sun nearing the horizon. She would be waiting in the dark soon no matter where she was; she might as well go on.

Cautiously, she climbed over the stones and lowered herself into the hole.

Strong hands reached up and grabbed her waist, and she yelped with fright before realizing that it was Uril, helping her down.

A moment later she was standing in a tunnel with the soldiers, a tunnel where the low spots in the uneven floor were flooded to various depths. Three of the men held lanterns that thinned, but did not fully disperse, the surrounding gloom.

"This way," Captain Lethis said, pointing. As he started walking, and the others fell into step behind him, he asked, "Did anyone get a look at the sun before we came down here?"

"Couldn't see it through the clouds," Staun grumbled. "I *told* you we waited too long."

The captain did not bother replying; instead he broke into a trot down the passage.

The others followed him through what seemed to Siria a senseless maze of passages and tunnels, dark corridors of rough stone with broken floors and barrel-vaulted ceilings. She had to run to keep up.

At least, she thought as she stumbled around the fourth or fifth corner, she was out of the rain.

And then they were in the chamber they sought, and she almost fell down the half-dozen steps that led into it.

The soldiers were already arranging themselves around the contents of the chamber—a black stone sarcophagus that gleamed as if freshly polished, and beside it a dusty, sagging wooden chest.

Staun prodded the chest with the toe of his boot, and one side caved in.

"Rotted through," he said.

"It's four hundred years old," Uril pointed out. "That's from the Third Lodrian War."

"Get it open," Lethis ordered. "If it's not the armor and sword, it probably says where they are."

"You think the Undead Lord is in this?" Fellan asked, pointing at the sarcophagus.

"If he's not, then we're in trouble, because I don't know where else he could be," Lethis replied, as Staun knelt and tugged at the lid of the chest.

The lock pulled free of crumbling wood and the chest opened, revealing a long, narrow oilcloth bundle, a rolled and tied parchment, and a tangle of rotting wool threads and dully-gleaming metal. Lethis promptly snatched up the parchment, while Staun prodded gingerly at the mess of wool and metal.

"This is it," Lethis said, as he unrolled the parchment and read it. "Someone had terrible handwriting, and it's in Old Mardish, but it definitely mentions King Derebeth, and that's the word for armor." He turned to one of the other soldiers. "Grulli, you know some Old Mardish, don't you?"

"A little," Grulli said, accepting the parchment. He squinted at it and held it closer to a lantern as he read, then nodded. "It says the Undead Lord will rise today, and must be stopped with the Sword of Light wielded by a person wearing the armor of King Derebeth." He lowered the parchment and gestured at the box. "That's the sword and armor, and the Undead Lord will appear in the sarcophagus."

Staun lifted out the bundle of metal and unfolded it, tearing away the dessicated remnants of the wool to reveal a mail shirt of bizarre and ancient design that somehow, despite centuries of neglect, showed not a speck of rust or corrosion.

Other than the odd pattern of links and the lack of aging, it was a very ordinary mail shirt, with no magical aura that Siria could see. She hoped whatever spell was on it still worked.

"Captain, it's up to you to choose who wears it," Staun said. He looked at the shirt. "I don't think it will fit me."

The others gathered around and stared at the mail shirt; Siria, who had been watching from the bottom step rather than setting foot in the crypt itself, came forward as well, peering around the soldiers for a closer look at the miraculous garment.

"It does look a little small," Uril said.

"No one ever said Derebeth was a big man," Lethis said. "I suppose ancient heroes came in all sizes."

"Captain," Uril said nervously, "maybe ancient heroes came in all sizes, but *we* don't. We're all big men. I don't think *any* of us can get that thing on."

Lethis looked suddenly worried. "Maybe it will magically expand on the right person," he said. "Staun, try it on."

Staun obeyed, pulling the mail over his head, but his hamlike hands would not fit in the sleeves, and the tunic would not fit over his broad shoulders. He lifted the metal shirt off again and passed it to Grulli.

While Grulli struggled with the garment, Staun unwrapped the Sword of Light from the oilcloth bundle. Siria stared in awe at the gleaming, ivory-hilted weapon; it shone in the dim glow of the lanterns as if it were in direct sunlight, sparkling like freshly-polished silver. This weapon clearly *was* magic; it had all the glamour the mail lacked.

"There's no problem with the sword, anyway," Staun remarked, as he hefted it.

Grulli had no more success with the mail shirt than Staun had; he passed it on to Uril.

After Uril came Lethis, then Mokor, then Fellan, and so on. By the time the eighth of the ten was struggling unsuccessfully to don the shirt everyone in the room had become aware of an odd whistling sound.

"It's coming from the tomb," Uril said, stepping back.

"We have the Sword of Light," Staun said. "Why don't we try to dispose of the Undead Lord with that, even without the armor?"

"It doesn't look as if we have much of a choice," Lethis said, as Orpac gave up and passed the armor on to Kael—who was the largest of them all, and the armor had shown no signs of any unnatural expansion.

"At least now we know why Porl and Rusran got the job," Uril said. "They must have been runts."

Siria, unnoticed by the men, grimaced at that. As a "runt" herself, she suddenly felt a new empathy for those heroes of old.

"Captain, maybe if we open the coffin and I go at whatever's inside with the sword…" Staun suggested.

"Do it," Lethis agreed, as Kael handed the shirt to Worna, the last of the ten carefully-chosen warriors. Staun stepped up to the side of the sarcophagus with the sword in his right hand, and reached for the lid with his left.

"Captain, I don't know…" Uril began.

"Do you have a *better* idea?" Lethis demanded.

"Maybe," Uril said. He pointed at Siria, who was trying hard to stay well out of the way. "It might fit *her*."

The whistling sound was growing louder and deeper, and suddenly the lid lifted from the black sarcophagus, rising unsupported into the air. The whistling turned into the roar of a great wind, and the three lanterns flickered and dimmed. To Siria it seemed not so much as if the light faded as if darkness poured in from somewhere, like oily smoke.

"Worna," Lethis ordered, "throw her the shirt."

Worna struggled to get his right arm out of the shirt so he could obey.

Staun thrust the Sword of Light into the darkness beneath the sarcophagus lid—then screamed, and snatched it back. Siria stared in horror—something black, like an animate liquid, was crawling up Staun's arm, wrapping itself around his wrist and elbow.

Staun's grip loosened, and the Sword of Light fell from his hand, to bounce on the edge of the sarcophagus and land ringing on the stone floor.

The sarcophagus lid fell away to the other side and landed with a deep, thick thump that shook the stone floor.

"Oh, blast," Lethis said. "All right…"

And then he stopped and stood motionless and silent.

Staun, too, was now frozen, and Uril, and Fellan.

And Worna finally had the mail shirt off.

"You, wench!" he called. "Here!" And he balled the shirt up and flung it at Siria.

She ducked, letting it hit the wall behind her. She turned, snatched it up, and by the time she turned back a shape was forming in the air above the open coffin—a shape that was black and vaguely manlike, but not quite human. The only distinct feature that was visible as yet was a pair of red eyes that seemed to glow as they scanned across the men in the room.

"Oh, Holy Mother," Siria gasped, clutching the mail shirt to her chest.

At that the red gaze suddenly swung in her direction, and she lifted up the shirt to cover her face.

Even through the protective mail, she could feel the thing's displeasure.

She began bunching up the mail, struggling to get the shirt over her head.

"I can't believe this," she said to no one. "We're all as good as dead—*I'm* no hero! I'm just a poor orphan girl. Even if I get this thing on, all I can do is run for help, and by the time anyone gets back here…"

She didn't complete the thought.

She pulled the shirt on—it fit fairly well, in fact. Her arms slid easily into the sleeves, and her head popped through the neck.

And she almost wished it hadn't. All the ten men, the Council's ten best warriors, were turning toward her now, their expressions dazed and flat. The shape in the air was thickening, becoming more solid.

"You can't hurt me!" Siria said, but her voice trembled.

Staun bent down and picked up the Sword of Light, but he did not use it against the Undead Lord; he didn't even look at the black thing. Instead he hefted it and took a step toward Siria.

She swallowed. Maybe the Undead Lord *could* hurt her—he couldn't harm her directly while she wore the armor, but the Sword of Light could probably hack right through the mail.

And even if it couldn't cut the magic armor, it could cut her exposed throat, or split her skull.

"Staun," she said, "drop the sword! *Please!*"

"Woman," Staun said, in a strained and unnatural voice, "you are all that stands between the Undead Lord and his freedom."

Siria swallowed again.

It was true, she knew. The Council had left it until too late and had sent the wrong men, and the Undead Lord was materializing—had materialized, really. In a few moments he would be completely revived, and it would probably take a war to stop him—if anything in these wizardless post-Extermination times *could* stop him!

Staun took another step toward her, and another—and to either side others were joining him, forming a line, trapping Siria against one wall of the chamber.

She had no weapon, no way to fight them—and even if she could, what good would that do against the Undead Lord?

But if she just stood here, Staun would kill her, and the Undead Lord would be free. She looked up, over Staun's shoulder at the thing hanging there, at the red eyes that watched her every move.

She was no warrior—but she had fought a few, in her own way. She had never been on a battlefield, but more than once she had been face to face with drunken soldiers who wanted their way with her.

She had been defending herself from rape then, not death, but the methods she had used then were all she had.

Staun stepped forward, sword rising to strike—and she slid suddenly down the wall until she was sitting on the floor, her legs thrust out before her, knees bent.

Startled, Staun checked his thrust and pulled the sword back. Puzzled, he lowered his gaze.

He was moving very slowly and stupidly, Siria saw. That was surely, she thought, because he was doing what the Undead Lord wanted, rather than what *he* wanted.

She flung herself forward, between Staun's legs; before he could react she had rolled over onto her back and taken aim.

"I'm sorry, Staun," she said. Then she kicked as hard as she could, with her leg fully extended.

Her foot hit soft tissue, and Staun's breath came out in an astonished and agonized whoosh. He crumpled forward, dropping the Sword of Light.

Siria whirled and grabbed for the Sword, snatched it away and pulled herself out from beneath poor Staun's crumpling form.

The others were turning, trying to surround her, but they, too, were slow and stupid, as if wading heavy-laden through deep water. She rolled clear, still clutching the sword, then leapt to her feet and ran toward the sarcophagus.

The Undead Lord glowered down at her, and a voice spoke from nowhere, inside her head.

You will not defeat me, it said. *Not again! I will not be...*

Then she plunged the Sword of Light into the black shape above the sarcophagus.

It exploded; black vapor swept over her, snatching her breath away, and she fell backward, gasping. She landed sitting on the floor, legs splayed, left hand behind her hip—but her right hand still held the Sword of Light, and she still wore King Derebeth's armor. She did not lose consciousness, or collapse further; instead she sat, dazed, for a moment, while the vapor dissipated and the menace of the Undead Lord passed away for another four centuries.

And then it was all over, and she had a bruise on her right hip and had skinned several knuckles. Her foot hurt, and her eyes stung. Somewhere behind her Staun was rolling on the floor, moaning.

"Well," Captain Lethis said at her left shoulder, "I suppose we had better get the lid back on that thing, then pack up the sword and mail for next time."

"And *this* time," Uril said, "I think we had better make sure everyone knows just what a skinny little fellow King Derebeth was!"

Siria looked up at Uril, but could not yet find her breath to speak.

"You were very brave, young lady," Lethis said. "And clever, too."

"You probably saved our lives," Fellan added.

Still looking at Uril, Siria managed to say, "Then perhaps someone could buy me a dinner when we get back to Splittree."

"Well, it won't be Staun," Orpac said. "I don't think he'll want anything to do with *any* women for awhile, and I'm *sure* he won't want *you* around!"

"I'm sorry," Siria said, turning to look over her shoulder. Staun was now sitting with his back against the wall, still breathing raggedly.

"Don't be," Uril said. "As Fellan said, you saved us all."

Siria looked up at him again. "Then you'll buy me that dinner?"

Uril laughed. "You can buy your *own*," he said.

Siria shook her head. "No, I can't," she began.

"Yes, you can," Uril said. "Once we get back to the Citadel, anyway. You've just earned yourself full pay for this errand—hadn't you realized?"

Startled, Siria looked at Lethis, who was helping Grulli and Worna lift the stone lid of the sarcophagus back into place.

"Of course," Lethis said. "And you'll be offered a place at the Citadel. It's the usual reward for disposing of dangerous magic. The Council prefers to keep anyone who can handle themselves that well where they can watch them."

Siria's mouth opened, but no sound emerged.

That meant no more begging. No more cozying up to men she didn't like in order to scrounge a meal.

Her mouth closed; then she said, "But that's at the Citadel."

Uril laughed again. "Fine," he said. "Then *I'll* buy you dinner in Splittree. And maybe we'll talk a little, get to know each other. Here you've saved my life and I don't even know your name!"

"Siria," Siria said, with the broadest smile she had allowed herself in ages. "And I think I'd like that.

MITTENS AND HOTFOOT

The day was bright and warm, and Mittens couldn't believe his humans would actually expect him to stay indoors. When the door opened to let the big human out that morning, Mittens slipped past his feet and hid in the bushes.

The big one didn't notice; he traipsed down the front walk utterly oblivious to the kitten crouching behind the azaleas, got in his car, and drove away.

Mittens was free!

He waited until the car was out of sight, then trotted out of the bushes and looked around.

Grass, flowers, trees—the whole wide wonderful world lay spread out before him!

Where to go, what to do?

He ran out onto the grass, wrestled with one blade, chewed on another, noticed his tail and gave a quick chase, then spotted a butterfly.

That was a worthy opponent! Mittens forgot about his tail and set out in pursuit of the fluttering insect.

It was a grand and glorious hunt, the butterfly flitting from place to place apparently unaware of Mitten's leaps and lunges, blithely ignoring the claws and fangs that passed within inches of its delicate wings.

The chase wound across the front lawn, around the side of the house, then down through the vegetable garden, between the strakes of a picket fence into the yard next door, and into the neighbor's back-yard flower garden.

Then, just as Mittens was closing in for the kill—or so Mittens told himself, at any rate—a jet of fire came from nowhere and fried the butterfly to a crisp.

Astonished, Mittens stopped almost in mid-leap and froze, back arched, paws braced.

Where had *that* come from? What had happened to the fluttery thing?

Leaves rustled, and a head emerged from a clump of tiger lilies—a little green, scaly head with smoking nostrils.

Mittens backed away, tail in the air.

A long, thin neck followed the head, and a long, thin body supported by four short legs, and finally a long, thin tail that dragged on the ground. The entire creature, though, was only a little over a foot long, and no taller than Mittens himself.

Mittens stared, wide-eyed, back arched. He'd never seen such a thing.

Of course, being only twelve weeks old, he hadn't seen much.

The two animals stared at one another; then the baby dragon turned away.

Mittens couldn't resist; he pounced.

Almost immediately, he decided that was a bad idea; the dragon writhed about, and spat an angry flame at inoffensive air. The kitten leaped away sideways, back arched again, tail puffed up.

The dragon didn't pursue him; it just untangled itself, then turned to watch Mittens with those golden lizard-eyes.

Mittens didn't like that. Mittens considered for a moment, then decided that whatever this thing was, it was best left alone. He turned and scampered away.

For the next hour Mittens had a wonderful time, running about the garden, chasing butterflies and other interesting creatures; he forgot all about that nasty lizard thing.

At last, tired and happy, Mittens decided it was time to go inside and take a nap. He clambered up the back steps to the kitchen door.

It was closed, of course. Somehow, Mittens had never thought about that—if he needed a human's help to get *out*, then he needed help to get *in*, too!

He mewed piteously; maybe a human would hear him and let him in. He mewed again, as loudly as he could.

The door didn't budge.

This was bad. Mittens wanted to curl up on his own little red cushion. He wanted to get inside where his food and water dishes were. Yards and gardens were fine for play, but the *important* stuff was in the house. It was getting hot out here, and the sun was too bright, and he didn't like it any more.

He mewed again.

The door didn't move. No one came. He couldn't hear anything moving inside the house.

Well, Mittens wasn't stupid, by kitten standards; he hopped down the steps and circled the house, trying every door and window he could reach.

All were closed tight.

How could this be? Hadn't the humans *noticed* that he was outside? Hadn't they realized he would want to come in? Where *were* they, asleep? Or had they all gone out without his noticing it?

Stupid, inconsiderate humans!

He tried clawing at the back door, but his tiny claws couldn't do much more than scratch the paint. He meowed as loud as he could—all to no avail.

He couldn't get in by himself; he needed help.

And if the humans weren't around, he'd have to find some other kind of help.

Bill Abbott waved farewell to his carpool and turned toward his house. Then he stopped, startled.

His next-door neighbor, a rather odd fellow named Cawley, was poking through the Abbotts' azaleas, muttering.

"Lose something?" Abbott asked.

Cawley looked up, startled. "As a matter of fact, I did," he said. "A pet. She must have got out somehow, I'm not sure how."

Abbott hadn't known Cawley kept any pets. "What sort of pet?" he asked. "A cat?"

"No, a...a sort of lizard," Cawley said. "Her name is Hotfoot."

"Odd name for a lizard," Abbott remarked. "What is she, an iguana?"

Cawley hesitated. "No," he said, "no, actually, she's a baby dragon."

Abbott blinked. "You mean, like a Komodo dragon? From Asia?"

"European," Cawley said. "If you see her, let me know, would you?"

"Of course," Abbott said. He walked on past Cawley and the azaleas, found his key, and let himself into the house.

He smelled smoke.

Janet or the kids had probably burned breakfast or something, but Abbott was a bit worried all the same. He peered into the living room.

There was Mittens, curled up asleep on his little green cushion. Nothing was burning.

Abbott hurried down the hall to the kitchen.

There he found the source of the smell—and as he looked at it, he remembered what Cawley had said, and remembered that Mittens' cushion was *red*, not green.

He walked slowly back to the living room and looked again.

Sure enough, Mittens and Hotfoot were curled up together on Mittens' bed, both sound asleep. A thin wisp of smoke trailed up from Hotfoot's snout.

Abbott stared, then sat down abruptly on the nearest chair.

He shook his head.

He wanted to be a good neighbor, and all that, and he didn't like to cause anyone trouble; live and let live was his motto. All the same, he was going to have to talk to Cawley about this. When Hotfoot made that foot-wide hole through the back door she might have burned down the house.

He wondered what the local zoning regulations said about keeping dragons.

JUST PERFECT

The envelope had no stamp or return address. The lack of an address wasn't unusual—it was amazing how many would-be writers didn't bother with details like that—but the absence of a stamp was odd.

The envelope was still flawlessly clean and smooth, too.

It must have been hand-delivered, he decided. Either the author was local, or somebody was trying stunts to get attention.

The address, he noticed with a start, was hand-written, in the most beautiful handwriting he had ever seen. He stared at it for a moment, mesmerized. Then he shrugged, picked up the letter opener, and slit the flap.

He pulled out the manuscript and put it aside for a moment while he read the cover letter.

"The time has come," the letter said, "To let My people know a little more of My nature. Among all the false prophecies and fraudulent scriptures, however, even the ineffable Truth might be lost. Accordingly, I have chosen to use the form of a short story, and to speak in My Own words, rather than relying on scribes and prophets. Furthermore, I have chosen your magazine to bear My Word."

Another goofball trying to be cute, the editor thought, frowning.

"I am not another goofball trying to be cute, in your phrase," the letter continued. The editor blinked, and read on. "Nor am I a religious nut espousing any bizarre faith or mistaken belief. I do not prate here of any great secrets of the universe. Instead, as all good fiction must, I simply tell a story, and through it reveal certain truths of the human—and divine—condition. I do not expect you to believe me, but I do ask that you give the story a fair trial."

The signature was illegible; it might have been four Hebrew letters.

"Screwball authors," the editor muttered.

He put aside the letter, picked up the manuscript, and began reading.

At the end of the first paragraph his eyes widened. At the end of the second a surprised bark of laughter escaped him. By the time he reached the foot of the first page he was giggling hysterically, but unable to tear his gaze from the words in front of him.

By page four he was sobbing uncontrollably.

By page seven he was smiling through his tears, smiling so hard that his cheeks hurt.

When he reached the conclusion, on page ten, he simply sat for a long moment in silent awe.

The story was perfect.

Literally, undeniably, absolutely perfect.

The author was an absolute genius. Despite the silly gimmicky cover letter. Publishing this thing would be a real coup—it was a sure award-winner, guaranteed a slot in every "best of the year" anthology. And it looked like a first sale, which meant he'd get credit for discovering this guy—whoever he was. There wasn't any by-line—obviously a real beginner.

A beginner with absolutely incredible talent.

He sat back and basked in the story's afterglow, and in warm thoughts of all the good things that would come of publishing it.

The phone rang; annoyed at the disruption of his mood, he picked up the receiver and demanded, "Yes?"

The voice on the other end was calm.

"Your story? You mean you're the one who wrote this?" the editor asked.

He listened, then replied, "Well, yes, it's excellent—simply amazing, in fact. We'll pay you our top rate of eight cents a word..."

"Of course we'll handle reprint rights if you want—I'm sure that it'll be picked up several places."

"I don't see an address on here; where can we get hold of you?"

"Anywhere? You mean, just...just pray?"

"Yes, of course I believe in You." And in fact, the editor realized, he was beginning to, for the first time since childhood. "Where should we send the check?"

"*Any* charity? Why, thank You."

As he listened to the calm, fatherly voice the editor looked at the manuscript, thinking.

The story was perfect—so incredibly good, so powerful, so moving, so complete, so *right*, that any other story would be a let-down afterward.

It was *perfect*.

And given its Author, how could it be anything else?

The editor cleared his throat. "Uh, there's just one thing, uh, sir," he said. "I mean, it's a great story, really stunning—of *course* it is, since You wrote it—but You *do* understand we'll want to make a few little editorial changes..."

TRIXIE

The black kitten swiveled her head back and forth, her golden eyes wide, wary, and staring, as she was carried down the block and up the front walk of No. 1224. When Annie raised her arm to ring the doorbell the kitten panicked and tried to scramble up her blouse to her shoulder, only to be grabbed firmly and held where she was on Annie's chest.

"There, there, sweetie," Annie said soothingly, as she petted the frightened creature. "You'll be fine."

The door opened and the kitten turned her head to stare at an unfamiliar face, a round but heavily lined face beneath fine, frizzy white hair.

"Hello, Sally," Annie said. "May we come in?"

"Of course!" Sally said. "You'll have to introduce me to your friend."

Annie stepped into a living room that smelled of lavender and chicken soup. "She doesn't have a name yet," she explained, setting the kitten on the sofa. "I brought her for you—I thought you could use some company, living here alone."

"For me?" Sally looked down at the kitten. "Oh, you shouldn't have! I'm not so alone as all that—I have help. And, well, I'm not a young woman. I'm ninety-two…bending down to clean a box…"

"Oh, I'll do that," Annie interrupted. "I'd be glad to. I'll come over every Sunday to take care of it—more often, if you like. It must be so hard for you to take care of this place! And you do it so well—it's spotless! I wish *my* house were half so tidy."

"Oh, really, it's not hard to keep up; you'd be surprised who helps out."

"That nephew of yours?"

Sally snorted. "Albert? Not likely! No, I have other friends who take care of some of the housework."

"I'd love to meet them."

Sally frowned. "Well, maybe someday."

"But they're not here all the time—couldn't you use some company?"

Sally looked at the kitten. "I'm not sure how my helpers would like it."

"Are they allergic to cats?"

"They might be; I'm really not sure."

The kitten ignored the human conversation; she had gotten over her fright sufficiently to take a look around. She crept forward and peered over the edge of the cushion at the floor, thought about jumping, then reconsidered. Instead she turned and ran to one end, bounced off the arm of the couch, then scampered to the back of the cushion and thrust a paw into the opening there.

"She *is* an adorable little thing, though, isn't she?" Sally said, as she watched her feline guest's actions.

"I knew you'd like her. If she ever gets to be too much trouble I'll take her back, but really, I'd feel better if I knew you weren't completely alone here."

Sally gave in. "All right," she said. She reached out to pet the kitten.

The kitten allowed a few quick strokes, then decided she'd had enough and rolled over, out from beneath Sally's unsteady hand, down behind the couch cushion.

That was not quite what she had intended; she scrabbled along, then burst up into the open air a foot or so away from where she had disappeared.

"Oh, she's a tricksy little thing!" Sally exclaimed.

And from then on the kitten's name was Trixie.

Annie brought over Trixie's litterbox and a supply of cat food, and the matter was settled—Trixie would live with Sally Schultz henceforth.

Trixie spent the rest of the afternoon happily exploring her new home, discovering which furniture she could fit under and which she could not, finding the kitchen with its wonderful smells and her litterbox's new location in the laundry room, and running wildly back and forth for no reason other than kittenhood.

When she had had enough running she discovered Sally's lap and settled there for a time, purring as Sally gently petted her. When Sally's hand grew tired, Trixie bounded off to explore behind the sofa.

Supper was followed by another session on Sally's lap, this time with the TV on; the supper dishes were left, unwashed, in the sink.

And then, finally, Sally stood and announced, "I'm going to bed, Trixie; you'll have the house to yourself for awhile. Take good care of it for me!"

She turned off the TV and the light and shuffled into her bedroom, but this time, when Trixie tried to follow, Sally closed the door, shutting her out.

"I'm sorry," she said through the closed door, "but I'm not up to having a kitten bouncing on me while I'm trying to sleep. Maybe when you're a bit older, and we know each other better."

Trixie didn't understand a word, but she heard and accepted the apologetic tone. She didn't meow at the door or otherwise protest; instead she rambled off around the house, looking for prey.

She stalked down the darkened hallway, smelling the air and watching the shadows. A faint whiff of something caught her attention—not a mouse or bird, something sweet. She made her way silently to the kitchen doorway—even kittens can be silent when they want to.

Something was moving in the kitchen—she could hear rattling and thumping. It wasn't loud enough for humans, but it wasn't catlike, either. She crept in and looked around.

There was something moving on the kitchen table, and something on the counter; water was running and the dishes were rattling in the sink. Everywhere was a gingery, unfamiliar scent.

Trixie leapt to the seat of a chair, and then onto the table, and found herself face to face with something she had never seen before.

It was roughly her own size, but shaped like a human. Its skin and clothing were entirely gingerbread-brown, from the tip of its pointed hat to its curly-toed shoes; its face was long and narrow, with a pointed chin, and pointed ears thrust up on either side of its cap. It held a great wad of cloth in one hand, and had evidently been polishing the table when it heard Trixie's approach.

It squeaked at the sight of her, and the rattling from the sink ceased abruptly. From the corner of her eye Trixie could see more of these creatures on the counter and the edge of the sink, all of them turning to stare at her.

Trixie considered the situation for a moment.

One of the creatures would be a little large for prey to begin with; half a dozen of them were definitely more than any sensible kitten would tackle. The fact that they weren't running away made it plain that *they* didn't consider themselves prey, either.

They were too small to be considered humans, and therefore she could not expect food, petting, or pampering from them. She didn't think they could even open the bedroom door for her, so she could crawl into bed with Sally.

They might be playmates; Trixie had had playmates when she was younger, before being separated from her two littermates. She meowed questioningly.

The creature before her squeaked again, then shrugged, made a shooing gesture, knelt down, and began polishing the table.

That wasn't any fun. Trixie ambled over and batted at the polishing cloth with one paw, claws sheathed.

The creature chittered angrily and snatched the cloth away. Trixie leapt after it.

The creature dropped the cloth and glared angrily at Trixie, then whistled.

Trixie paid no attention at first as she batted the oily cloth around the slippery tabletop; then she felt a sudden grip on her tail and looked up to find herself surrounded by the little brown people.

One of them snatched away the cloth, and when she tried to pursue it another yanked at her tail. She turned, spitting, and swiped, claws out.

The brown things didn't back down or give back the cloth; instead they moved in in a coordinated effort. One grabbed each of her four legs, one ducked under her chin and lifted her head, and one kept a grip on her tail. Then, together, they carried her to the edge of the table and dropped her, no more roughly than necessary given her squirming, to the floor.

She angrily jumped back to the chair and prepared to jump back on the table, only to find herself confronted by a solid barrier of the creatures.

Trixie knew the proper cat thing to do in a case like this; she sat down and began washing herself, pretending she had never had any intention of jumping onto the table.

After that she generally ignored the brown creatures. She watched them occasionally as they washed and dried and put away the dishes, dusted the furniture, and swept the floor, but did not interfere with them.

And at the first light of dawn they all scurried away and vanished—Trixie didn't see where they went, which annoyed her, and she resolved to do better next time.

An hour or so later Sally emerged from her room, and a new day began with a generous breakfast, followed by curling up on Sally's lap in front of the TV.

The days thereafter followed a similar pattern—by day Sally and Trixie kept one another company, and at night while Sally slept Trixie and the little brown creatures ignored each other while the creatures cleaned the house. Over time Trixie grew from a kitten into a cat; Sally slept longer and moved about less. Annie visited often, remarking sometimes on how tidy Trixie was in using her box—which wasn't really true; the brown creatures cleaned up spills, though they didn't change the litter. Sally's nephew Albert stopped by occasionally, and tried to talk Sally into moving into a nursing home. There were phone calls and other visitors, as well, and the comforting flicker and mumble of the TV.

One day each year Annie brought over a little cake for Sally's birthday. Trixie was there for the ninety-third and ninety-fourth.

And then one morning Sally didn't come out of her bedroom to give

Trixie breakfast. Trixie waited and waited, but Sally never emerged. Trixie began meowing, and when that didn't work and the hunger became serious she began yowling. She reached up and batted at the bedroom doorknob, but couldn't budge it.

The phone rang, interrupting a yowl, and Trixie ran to the device, ready to demand attention when Sally came to pick up the receiver, but even then, Sally didn't appear. The phone rang and rang, but finally stopped.

A few minutes later it rang again, and was again ignored.

And then, perhaps half an hour later, the doorbell rang—again, without effect.

Albert's voice called, "Aunt Sally? Are you all right?"

Trixie meowed loudly.

A key rattled in the lock, and Albert stepped in. Trixie meowed anxiously and ran beside and around him as he called, "Aunt Sally?" and made his way to the bedroom door. His big human hand easily turned the knob Trixie had been unable to move. The instant the opening was wide enough Trixie dashed inside and jumped on the bed.

Sally was still there—but cold and lifeless.

"Oh, hell," Albert said. He turned and hurried to the phone in the living room.

Trixie meowed at Sally for a moment, then gave up and went out to the living room to meow at Albert.

No one paid any attention. No one fed her or petted her.

And then strangers came, and talked to Albert, and looked at Sally, and took her away, and still no one paid any attention to Trixie, until at last Albert and Trixie were alone in the house, and Trixie meowed so insistently for attention, practically climbing his leg, that Albert finally noticed her.

"What am I going to do with *you*?" he asked.

Trixie meowed once more and led the way to the kitchen, to her bowl.

Albert sighed and got out food, and sat at the table watching as Trixie ate.

"I suppose it's off to the pound for you," he muttered. "*I* don't want a cat, certainly!" He looked idly around the kitchen. "At least you haven't made a mess of the place the way I thought you would. It's amazing that Aunt Sally kept this house up so well at her age."

Trixie was too busy eating to pay much attention.

She was just finishing, licking her paws, and Albert was sitting at Sally's desk looking through the drawers, when the doorbell rang. Albert closed the drawers and rose, and Trixie trotted out to see who had come.

It was Annie, her expression worried. "Albert?" she said. "What happened? I just got home from work, and Ms. Rose next door told me there was something going on here…"

Albert stood silently, helpless to answer; Annie saw his face and asked, "Where's Sally?"

"She's gone," Albert said.

Annie sat down heavily on the sofa. "*Gone* gone?"

"She was ninety-four," Albert said.

"I know, but…"

Trixie had long ago given up on Albert, but Annie knew how to pet a cat, and right now Trixie desperately wanted some proper attention. She jumped into Annie's lap, interrupting whatever Annie had been saying.

Annie's breath came out in a startled rush, but she recovered quickly and began stroking Trixie, scratching behind her ears and smoothing her fur.

Trixie settled down and began purring.

For a moment no one spoke; Albert settled uneasily onto a chair and sat facing Annie with his hands on his knees.

"What's going to happen to Trixie?" Annie asked at last.

Albert hesitated. "Well, I don't know," he said. "If I don't find someone who wants her I guess she'll go to the pound…"

"No!" Annie said, startling Trixie out of purring. "No, I'll take her. I don't have a cat right now; I'd be glad to keep her."

"I hoped you would," Albert said, relieved.

And that was settled. Twenty minutes later Trixie found herself being carried up the street to No. 1216, reversing the trip she had taken two years earlier.

Once she was delivered Annie returned to the other house to fetch Trixie's food and litterbox, while Trixie began to find her way around her new home.

Annie's house was both familiar and different. The rooms were in the same places and the same sizes as in Sally's house, but the furniture was entirely different—and it wasn't anywhere near as clean. Trixie wrinkled her nose in disgust as she explored her new home. Where Sally's house had smelled of fresh food and flowers, Annie's smelled of mildew and neglect.

This, Trixie thought, would never do. She looked up at Annie as the human passed by with the litterbox and meowed reproachfully.

"What is it, Trixie?" Annie asked. "Do you miss Sally?" She knelt, put the box aside, and petted Trixie. "So do I. But she's gone, and we'll just have to get used to it."

Trixie meowed again, but Annie did not respond properly by getting out a broom or duster; instead she just went on stroking Trixie's fur and talking about Sally.

After awhile Trixie noticed with distaste that Annie had stopped talking, and water was dripping from her eyes. She pulled free of Annie's petting hand and went to wash herself in private—and to think.

Annie was all very well; Trixie had liked Sally, after a cat's fashion, but she understood that Sally was gone, and while that was unfortunate there wasn't much she could do about it, and Annie was an acceptable substitute.

This new house, though, was so dusty Trixie found herself sneezing every time she poked her head under the furniture, and it simply didn't smell right at all. It wouldn't do. Any cat who stayed here would have to spend all her time just licking dust from her fur.

Annie didn't seem to understand that, and presumably, since she had lived here for some time, she didn't care.

Trixie couldn't very well clean the house herself; even if she had hands, it would be beneath her dignity as a cat. But *somebody* had to clean the place.

Of course, Sally hadn't cleaned her own house; she had had the brown creatures to do it. Why didn't Annie have any?

Trixie looked around and decided that Annie *needed* some brown creatures—and after all, with Sally gone, they wouldn't have anything to do at the other house any more.

The question was, how could she get them from *there* to *here*?

The direct approach seemed in order; Trixie went to the back door and meowed.

Annie emerged from the laundry room and saw her.

"Oh, no, Trixie," she said. "You live *here* now. And I'm not going to let you outside—it's too dangerous. You could catch something; I don't know if Sally ever got you all your shots."

Trixie meowed.

"*No*," Annie said emphatically.

Trixie knew what "no" meant. It meant that the human saying it was not going to cooperate.

Well, she thought, we'll just *see* about that. Then she sat down and began grooming herself, to lull any suspicions Annie might have.

Just then the doorbell rang; Annie hurried to answer it, and found Albert standing on the stoop. Trixie followed at Annie's heel, watching and awaiting her moment, and when Albert started to step inside she dashed for the opening.

Before anyone could stop her she was outside. Annie shrieked, but couldn't push her way past the startled Albert quickly enough to grab

Trixie before the fleeing cat ducked behind a bush, out of sight.

A moment later Annie and Albert were standing on the front lawn, looking up the street toward Sally's house, calling, "Here, Trixie!"

"I don't see it anywhere," Albert said.

"Well, but she *must* have wanted to go back home," Annie said. "Where *else* would she go?" She looked about, mystified.

Behind the bush Trixie crouched down, her black fur invisible in the shadows. There wasn't any point in going back down the street yet; the brown creatures wouldn't come out until the middle of the night.

Annie and Albert walked down the street, calling and searching; Trixie watched them go.

Some time later they came wandering slowly back. Albert said, "I'm sure the cat will turn up again. When it gets hungry it'll find you. Or maybe it'll be waiting on Aunt Sally's steps tomorrow when I go back."

"I hope so," Annie said, unconvinced. She climbed the two steps to her front door and stood there, arms crossed over her chest, as she looked around the neighborhood for some sign of Trixie's whereabouts.

Albert waved goodbye and left, and at last Annie shrugged, shivered in the cooling evening air, and went back inside.

Trixie snoozed cheerfully behind the bush.

Hours later she awoke, yawned, stretched, and ambled out of concealment.

The street was dark and deserted. No cars rumbled on the pavement; most of the windows were unlit. This was just what Trixie wanted; the brown things would probably be hard at work. She strolled easily down the block.

In front of Sally's house she paused, considering.

She was outside. The brown creatures were inside. This could be a problem. Cats couldn't open doors.

She had seen the brown things open cabinet doors often enough, though, and sometimes the pantry or the laundry room door—they had never opened the bedroom door, but Trixie thought they *could* have, if they wanted. If they could do all that, they could presumably let Trixie into the house.

The question was, would they?

Trixie thought they would. After all, they liked everything to be in its proper place, and Trixie's proper place had always been inside that house. If she could just get their attention…

She ambled around the side of the house, and bounded up to the kitchen windowsill—fortunately, the screen was not in place. There she peered in through the glass.

The brown creatures were there—and apparently puzzled by the lack of dirty dishes, as two of them were sitting on the edge of the sink, looking about unhappily.

Trixie meowed, loudly, and thumped her tail against the glass.

The brown creatures started and looked up at her. Then they began to make their odd little noises at each other.

Trixie meowed again, and patted the glass with one paw.

One of the brown creatures climbed up on the sash and pried at the latch, while no fewer than four of the others gathered on the inside sill, staring out at Trixie.

That was perfect. Trixie had thought out exactly what she had to do, and it appeared she would have her chance.

The latch snapped open, and the brown creature jumped down from the sash; then all five bent down and began heaving. The window slid open slowly; Trixie waited. Then, when the opening was wide enough, she pounced.

The brown creatures scattered, squealing, but not quickly enough. She had caught one of them in her forepaws. Now she snatched at it with her mouth, and got her jaws around its neck.

Then, as gently as she could, as gently as if she were handling her own kitten, she picked the shrieking creature up, turned around, and leaped back out the window to the ground.

There she began trotting up the block toward Annie's house, holding her head up as high as she could, with the brown thing squirming in her hold.

Behind her the other creatures chattered and squealed, then followed her, one by one, leaping out the window and chasing her across the close-trimmed lawns.

At last she reached Annie's house, climbed awkwardly up the two steps to the front door, and waited, still securely holding her captive.

The brown creatures gathered around her, chattering. Trixie waited, making it as obvious as she could that she expected them to open the door for her.

Eventually, as Trixie's jaws began to tire, two of the creatures stepped forward. One hoisted the other up onto his shoulders, and the top creature stretched up until he could reach the doorknob. He grabbed it and pulled himself up, then climbed on top and seated himself on the knob, where he looked thoughtfully at the lock in front of him. He pulled a tool from his pocket, squinted into the keyhole, and set to work.

A moment later he squealed in triumph and pocketed the tool. Then he stood up, braced his feet against the knob and his hands against the doorjamb, and pushed.

The knob turned, and a moment later the door was open.

Trixie trotted inside, into the center of the living room. There she sat down and waited until all the brown creatures had collected around her.

Then she released her captive. It fell to the floor and moaned quietly, then sat up, dazed but unhurt, as Trixie jumped aside.

The others surged forward and hugged their freed companion, squeaking at one another. Then they stopped and looked around.

They looked at dust bunnies and cobwebs and cookie crumbs, at forgotten saucers and used tissues and lost coins, and in unison they said, long and low, "Oooooh!"

And then they set to work, as Trixie curled up, purring, on the couch.

The next morning Annie found Trixie asleep on the living room sofa. She stopped dead in her tracks and stared at the cat.

"How'd you get in?" she demanded. She crossed to the front door and found it closed, but unlocked. She frowned, and turned back to Trixie.

"See how upset I was about you?" she said. "I forgot to lock this last night! A burglar could have come in and killed us both."

Then she stopped and looked at the door again. It was quite solidly closed—but Trixie was inside.

Had a burglar gotten in, and let Trixie in by accident? Annie looked around to see if anything was missing.

The TV was where it should be, and the stereo…but *something* didn't look right. She stared for a moment, trying to see what it was.

Then, finally, it struck her. Everything was *clean*.

Annie had never heard of burglars who dusted.

"Did *you* do that?" she asked Trixie. Then she shook her head. That was silly. Cats couldn't clean house.

"It must've been elves," she said. "Or brownies."

Trixie began purring. Annie understood, and she didn't seem to mind. Living here would be all right, then. She hopped off the couch and rubbed against Annie's leg.

"You want breakfast?" Annie asked. "Is that it?"

Trixie had just been expressing her pleasure at how things were working out, but food was always welcome; she ran ahead, and met Annie at the kitchen door, meowing for her food.

Annie took a single step into the kitchen and stopped dead. In the living room the cleaning had been fairly subtle; here it was staggeringly obvious. Dishes had been washed, dried, and put away; years of soap-scum had been cleaned from the sink and faucets, and the old chrome gleamed brightly.

"It *is* brownies," she said, and this time she meant it. She looked down at Trixie. "Or Albert—did he find you somewhere, and bring you back, and clean everything to surprise me?"

Trixie looked up at her in utter disgust at such an absurd suggestion, then meowed.

"Oh, you want your food," Annie said. She filled Trixie's bowl quickly, and set it down. Then she looked around again.

"It's as clean as Sally's," she said. "I never understood how she kept it…"

She stopped dead in mid-sentence. Her hand flew to her open mouth.

"Sally's helpers," she said. "*She* had brownies helping her!" Her eyes widened. She looked down at Trixie again. "*That's* why you ran off! You were bringing them here!" She stared at the shining-clean sink. "Are they going to stay?"

Trixie began purring again. Annie smiled.

"Trixie," she said, "you *are* a tricksy one!"

IN RE: NEPHELEGERETES

"The son of a bitch just up and *left* me!" the blonde wailed; Benny Perelman resisted the temptation to cover his ears. Her voice wasn't bad, but the volume was more than his tiny office could handle, and her accent was the worst of everything California had to offer, blending midwestern twang, Hispanic lilt, and that distinctive Valley Girl rhythm. "He didn't even *pretend* it was anything else," she said. "It has been a delight,' he says, 'nay, a myriad delights, but it's time I returned to my wife…'" Her expression shifted abruptly to astonished fury. "I didn't even know the bastard still *had* a wife!"

Benny tried to smile sympathetically, but the resulting expression was closer to a wince. Unless there were something more to the story, this dumb broad's dreams of collecting palimony for her six-week fling with someone else's husband were on a par with Benny's own hopes of winning a few million in Vegas, the chief difference being that Benny *knew* he was never really going to hit the big jackpot.

There might be a chance at an out-of-court settlement, though—or less politely, a little blackmail—if the male in question was rich enough, and sufficiently desirous of keeping his reputation unsullied.

"So what's this guy's name?" he asked.

"Zeus Nephelegeretes," she replied, somehow managing to produce the entire sesquipedalian surname without stumbling. Benny supposed she'd practiced it—he could imagine the poor bimbo standing in front of the mirror with a white dress, trying out "Mrs. Nephelegeretes" for size.

At least Benny thought it had to be a real name—*nobody* would have come up with a fake like that! That would make finding the guy easier.

She was looking at him expectantly, as if waiting for a comment. "Greek, huh?" Benny asked.

Her expression changed to utter disdain. "Well, *duh!*" she said.

"Is he rich?" Benny asked, dispensing with subtlety.

"He's *Zeus*, for heaven's sake!"

Benny decided not to admit his ignorance of just who this Nephelegeretes character was; he didn't want to look stupid in front of a potential client, and he could always look the name up later.

But it sounded like the guy *was* rich.

"So tell me about it, Ms…uh…" He had already forgotten the name she had given him; he hadn't expected the interview to get even this far.

"Darwin," she said. "Bambi Darwin. I told you."

"Of course, Ms. Darwin. So how did you and, um, Zeus…" Benny wasn't about to attempt that last name after only hearing it once. "How did you meet?"

"I just stepped out my door one morning and there he was, waiting for me in the driveway," she said. "Not that I knew it was him, or anything; all I saw was a Harley. I thought someone must have left it by mistake, you know? Though I don't see how they could have…"

"Wait a minute," Benny interrupted. "He was on a motorcycle? If he was still there, why'd you think someone had left…"

"He wasn't *on* a motorcycle," Bambi interrupted right back. "He *was* a motorcycle. A big, beautiful Harley-Davidson, standing there in my driveway, all gleaming chrome and black leather…" She sighed.

Benny blinked. "I don't get you," he said. "Was he on the Harley or not?"

Bambi stared at him.

"You really *don't* get it, do you?" she said. "He's *Zeus*. Olympian Zeus. King of the gods. That Zeus."

Puzzled, Benny said, "You said his name was Neffle-something."

"Nephelegeretes. It means 'cloud-gathering.' That's what Homer called him."

"Homer who? Simpson?"

"Homer the blind poet who wrote the *Iliad*. Jesus, how'd you ever get through law school?"

That was a new one on Benny; he stared at Bambi Darwin, the starlet with peroxide hair and spectacular bosom, the absolute epitome of the California blonde, who was calling *him* dumb.

She stared back for a moment, then sighed.

"Okay, look," she said. "You ever study Greek myths in school? Maybe saw *Clash of the Titans*, that Ray Harryhausen flick?"

"Sure," Benny said.

"So, you remember Zeus, the king of the gods? Big guy, threw lightning bolts like javelins, had the hots for anything with tits?"

Benny vaguely remembered some guy sitting around on clouds in "Clash of the Titans." "Sure," he said. "Who played him? This Neffle guy?"

Bambi looked ready to strangle him.

"*No*," she said, biting off short whatever word had been about to follow the negative. "I mean the *god himself.*"

Benny stared at her. It was April, but three weeks past the first, and she looked completely serious. He protested, "But those guys lived thousands of years ago! Besides, they were just myths!"

"Gods are *immortal*, you bo... Mr. Perelman. A couple of thousand years is nothing to them. Believe me, I *know*."

Benny continued to stare at her, and the truth gradually penetrated.

Ms. Bambi Darwin genuinely thought she had been boffing a god.

This led him immediately to the conclusion that Ms. Bambi Darwin was crazy as a bedbug.

"Anyway," Bambi said, settling back, "if you remember the stories, Zeus used to turn himself into stuff in order to get the women he wanted. He turned into a swan to seduce Leda, and a shower of gold for Danae. For me, he turned into a Harley-Davidson." She shrugged. "I've gotta admit it worked. It's the fastest way anyone's ever found to get between *my* legs."

Benny winced. "If we ever get to court, don't even *think* of repeating that," he said.

She sat up angrily. "Hey, do I look..." She stopped, and the anger vanished. A bit sheepish, she said, "Well, yeah, I suppose I do look it, but just take my word for it, Mr. Perelman, I am *not* stupid."

Just nuts, Benny thought. He nodded. "Of course not," he said.

"So anyway," she continued, "there was the Harley sitting in my driveway, and there wasn't anyone else in sight, so I went over to take a look at it, and, you know, I just sort of wanted to try it out. So I climbed on, and I swear I didn't touch the key, which was right there in the ignition but I did *not* touch it, and it started up, and next thing I knew I was halfway to Redondo Beach, and I figured what the hell, I'd just take a look at the ocean then head back. So I got down to the beach, to the state park, and stopped the bike and sort of settled in, looking out at the Pacific, all sparkling in the morning light—it was beautiful, you know? And the Harley was all hot, and the vibration, and everything... Anyway, I leaned forward over the handlebars—and wham, there I am sitting astride Mr. Cloud-Gatherer, with my hands in his hair and his face in my cleavage, and...well, right there on the beach—I mean, he was *so* hot. It was pretty clear how he got all those women in the stories." She blushed slightly, and Benny was charmed; he hadn't seen a woman blush in years.

She'd presumably screwed *someone* for all those weeks, even if it wasn't the King of the Gods; maybe he could get her some sort of settlement just out of sympathy.

"So afterward I wasn't about to say no to anything, you know?" she continued. "Except he didn't want me to tell anyone about him, and

I couldn't help saying something to my mother—I tell her everything. But other than that I went along with whatever he wanted. He moved in to my place in Gardena, and I thought we had a pretty good thing going, and then this morning wham, he says goodbye and walks out, and I was pretty upset, but then I remembered something I'd read about where demigods come from, so I stopped by the drugstore for a home pregnancy test, just in case. I was taking precautions, you know, but the stories…well, damn it, the stories were right!" Her eyes began to cloud up. She swallowed, and said, "My mother warned me. I was on the Pill, but hey, gods are, y'know, *divinely* potent. I knew right away I wanted to sue the bastard, and I have friends who recommended you, so I called you, and here I am."

"Child support?" Benny brightened. That had *much* better odds than palimony. "Or are you going to get rid of it?"

"I don't think I *dare* get rid of it," she said.

"Um," Benny said, remembering her delusion. He supposed aborting a god's kid wouldn't go over very well. Then he brightened. "Well, we can say you have religious reasons for keeping the child."

Bambi smiled weakly—the first time she had smiled since arriving in his office. "You got it," she said.

It was Benny's turn to frown deeply as something occurred to him. He thought he had a case here, if the broad really was pregnant—he could probably turn her obvious derangement into a few extra grand in every payment—but first he had to find the defendant.

"So…if he walked out on you, and the two of you only saw each other at your place in Gardena and on the beach, how're we going to find him? I tend to think process servers aren't exactly welcome on Mount Olympus."

She grimaced. "Yeah," she said. "I know. But he's got a few temples still, in Greece and Italy, and he gave me a fax number…" She fumbled in her purse, then handed Benny a slip of paper.

Benny took it. "Olympus has a fax number?"

"Hey, *everybody* has a fax number these days," Bambi said. "Why shouldn't they?"

Benny couldn't answer that. He looked at the paper, and saw that it was an overseas number; he didn't recognize the country code.

"Worth a shot," he said. "We can't subpoena him, but maybe once he knows there's a kid coming, he'll agree to a meeting…"

He agreed. The return fax was in a bold Roman font, floridly worded, professing great affection for Ms. Bambina Munoz-Darwin and acknowledging—hell, Benny though, *boasting* of—the paternity of her unborn son.

"Of course it's a boy," Bambi muttered. "Damned old-world sexist pig."

The fax also agreed to a meeting, with the understanding that all cooperation was entirely dependent upon no mention of Ms. Munoz-Darwin's condition or recent involvement being made in any wedding chapel or other temple of Hera anywhere on Earth, nor any further faxes being sent.

"Well, I'll be damned," Benny said, as he read the document through for the second time. "*He* thinks he's Zeus, too."

B enny had to admit that the guy looked the part of a god—tall, majestic, magnificently broad-shouldered, his face calm and unlined. He wore his white hair and beard long, and arrayed in ringlets; the contrast with his smooth, youthful complexion was striking.

He was dressed in an impeccable grey suit, and filled the conference room doorway quite convincingly, almost hiding another figure who stood just behind him—a shadowy figure, almost as tall. The white-haired man announced, "My brother has chosen to accompany me. I trust you have no objection."

"Of course not," Benny said. "We have nothing to hide." He gestured at the waiting chairs. "Come in and make yourselves comfortable."

The two men entered and seated themselves, Zeus striding boldly, his dark brother moving silently, almost stealthily. Benny stared at the brother, but seemed unable to see him properly; he got an impression of someone large, dark, and forbidding...

Uncomfortable, he tore his gaze away and looked around the table. "Well, we're all here," he said.

Then he noticed that Bambi wasn't listening. She was staring at the dark figure.

Benny frowned and turned to Zeus. "I'm sorry, I didn't get your brother's name...?"

"Hades," Zeus said. "I had thought you would recognize him."

"Hades?" Benny looked at the dark figure and paled slightly under his tan. Whoever and whatever that guy was, Benny didn't want anything to do with him.

"If you're trying to intimidate us it isn't going to work," Bambi snapped. "I'm not scared of *him*."

Her voice didn't sound entirely steady, and Benny glanced at her.

She was still staring at Hades. From her expression, she really *wasn't* scared.

That didn't mean she wasn't reacting, though.

Benny suppressed a groan; he leaned over and muttered, "Hey, pay attention. We have business to conduct." Then he leaned closer and whispered, "What *is* it with you? You have a thing for gods? That guy gives me the creeps! And if you act like a round-heeled slut it isn't gonna make my job any easier!" He glanced at the two gods—somehow, here in the room with them, he was having much less difficulty in believing they were indeed gods—and wondered whether Zeus had brought Hades along deliberately, knowing Bambi would find him attractive.

Tall, dark, and handsome, yeah, but still, Benny wondered, what did Bambi see in *him*?

"Sorry," Bambi said, turning away from that ominous figure. "Guess maybe I *do* have a fascination with the divine." She giggled nervously and stole a quick glance at Hades. "Or maybe a deathwish."

"Well, whatever it is, it can wait," Benny said. Then he turned to Zeus and spoke up.

"In your fax you acknowledged impregnating my client," he said. "May I ask what your intentions are toward the child and mother-to-be?"

"I have no intentions," Zeus replied. "The child is mine, and will be a mighty hero. When he is grown he may come to me as a son comes to a father, to be recognized and accorded the treatment he deserves."

"Hm." Benny cleared his throat. "I'm afraid that isn't sufficient. Under the laws of this state you have an obligation to provide for the feeding, clothing, shelter, and education of your offspring. If you are un-able to do in person—as I understand to be the case here, since you're married—then you must make support payments to the mother until the child is grown."

"Payments? I do not traffic in earthly wealth." Zeus, already domi-nating the room, seemed to swell. "I am not bound by Man's laws, nor do I recognize this state of which you speak."

"You damn well *better* recognize the State of California!" Bambi said, suddenly angry. "This isn't your precious Greece! This is *my* place, my family's homeland, where *our* rules apply and you old gods don't count for anything special!"

"California?" Zeus glanced at Hades, who shrugged. "I have kept up with the times in many ways, but these western lands are still strange to me. The legendary isle named for the Amazon queen Califia—is that what you claim this place to be?"

"You're in Orange County, in the State of California, yes," Benny said.

"I had not troubled myself to learn the local names," Zeus remarked.

"Interesting. Califía was deified, was she not?"

"I haven't…" Benny began.

Bambi interrupted him. "You *bet* Califía was deified—you're not the only god around here, Zeus!" As Benny tried unsuccessfully to quiet her, she shouted, "Maybe you'd *better* trouble yourself a little more in the future. You think you can just go where you want and do as you please, and not pay any attention to the consequences? Well, think again! I'm not just any bimbo, Mr. Lightning Bolt, I'm a true Californian and proud of it—a daughter of Califía!"

"And I am King of the Gods, the lord of Olympus," Zeus said in reply—not shouting, but firmly, in a voice that brooked no dispute. "I *will* do as I please. And I accept the consequences of my actions. You say the laws of your people require me to support my son; it is a just law. I will see that he is provided for. I cannot make payments in your currency, however. I have no earthly wealth."

"Uh huh," Benny said. "And just how will you provide for him, then?"

"That is what we are here to resolve." He turned to Bambi. "Beloved treasure," he said, "what would you have of me? I give you my blessing; good fortune shall be yours. What more do you ask?"

"I've got all the blessing I need from my mother," Bambi grumbled, her arms folded across her chest. "What I *want* is someone who'll help me raise the kid—but *you*, you're going back to your wife!"

"I must," Zeus said. "Hera is not to be dismissed, not even by me. And for your own safety she must never know of our liaison; she would take vengeance upon you, and upon the child, for she has not the power to strike against me directly."

"So I get to raise a demigod by myself. A single mother in a tract house in Gardena, no support payments, gotta get daycare whenever I'm working…"

"Perhaps other arrangements can be made," Zeus said thoughtfully, with a glance at his brother.

"Like what?" Bunny demanded, before Benny could intervene. "You going to take us back to Olympus with you?"

"No; Hera would find you. But perhaps there's another possibility." He gestured at Hades.

Benny and Bambi both turned to stare at the dark brother.

"Him?" Bambi said. "What, *he's* going to come live in Gardena and play babysitter?"

"No. But for half the year you could live with him, in his own shadowy home, as his honored guest, your every need attended."

"*Half* the year?" Benny asked.

Zeus nodded. "In the summers, when his own wife is away visiting her mother in the daylight lands. In the winter Queen Persephone is at home, and were she to know of this arrangement she might well let a word slip—if not to Hera herself, then to Demeter, or some other."

"And you don't think your brother himself might blab?" Bambi asked.

"As you may have observed," Zeus said drily, "he does not speak o'ermuch. That was why I trusted him to accompany me here, as advisor."

"So you didn't already have this planned out?" Benny asked suspiciously.

"Do not question me too closely, mortal," Zeus said mildly.

"How do we even know he agrees?" Bambi asked.

"*I agree*," Hades said, in a voice that sent chills down Benny's spine—but which apparently touched Bambi somewhere else, as her mouth came open slightly, her breath quickened, and her eyes grew big and dark.

"So do I," she whispered. Then she shook herself. "But my mother's gonna hate it," she said. "She *hates* it if I go out of state, even for a minute."

"Don't agree to anything yet," Benny warned Bambi. "We're still talking." He thought, but did not say aloud, that the suggested arrangement didn't cover his fee, and he wasn't about to consider *anything* settled until that was taken care of.

But the rest was simply details.

Hades was waiting by the ferryboat as Bambi hurried down the ramp dragging an immense suitcase. Benny was a few steps up the slope, making sure that everything went off as arranged; he took the suitcase and accompanied her to the boat.

She was just beginning to bulge a little around the middle, but was still gorgeous; her golden hair stood out like a beacon in this rather gloomy place.

"Your mother's not seeing you off?" he asked, as he handed the suitcase to Hades.

"No," Bambi said. "She's too upset. I'm sorry about that; you'll have to live with whatever she does about it."

Benny had yet to meet Bambi's oft-mentioned mother, and had no intention of changing that any time soon, so he thought he could bear up under her displeasure—especially since he had, indeed, negotiated himself a good fee, in the form of certain divine assurances of good fortune.

"I'm sure she'll be fine," he said.

"Well, I've warned you," Bambi said doubtfully, as she took Hades' hand and stepped onto the ferry.

"Sure," Benny said. "What's your mother's name, so I'll know if she calls?"

Bambi stared at him open-mouthed. "Didn't I tell you? I'm *sure* I did, when I got so mad at the meeting!"

"I don't remember it," Benny admitted.

"My mother's name is Califia," Bambi said as Hades pushed the boat off.

Benny blinked.

"See you in six months!" Bambi said with a wave, as the ferry vanished into the shadows.

"Six months!" Benny called after her. "Have a good time!"

Then he turned away and walked slowly up the ramp, out of the dim netherworld into a California May…

Where it was already starting to snow.

IN FOR A POUND

The moment she was absolutely sure they were out of earshot of anyone else, she hissed at him, "Are you *nuts?*"

He smiled at her as he held open the car door. "I don't think so," he replied.

"But *running for mayor?*" She stood beside the car, not willing to interrupt the discussion even long enough to take her seat.

"Why not?" he asked, still smiling that toothy smile of his. "Seriously, Jen, do you see anyone better suited to the job? I'm an upstanding member of the community, I've had a good education, I have a career in public service…"

"Dave, you *know* why not!" She pointed at the sky. "You're going to have a *demonstration* of 'why not' in another hour or so!"

His politician's smile vanished, and he looked at her with an expression that just reeked of sincere concern—an expression she was quite sure he had practiced for hours in front of the mirror. "And why should that disqualify me from serving as mayor? Surely you realize it's just an occasional inconvenience. So I'll be unavailable a couple of nights each month…"

"*Inconvenience?*" She stared at him, astonished. "Dave, you're a *werewolf*, remember? You inherited a genuine gypsy curse. That's a bit more than an inconvenience!"

"Why?" he asked mildly.

Her jaw dropped.

"Really, Jen—it's not as if I'm running for president. It's just mayor of Eltonburg. So I'll want to spend a couple of nights a month in private; so what?" He patted her on the arm, urging her into the car.

Stunned, she sat. She watched through the windshield as he walked around and climbed in the driver's side.

"Dave," she said, "suppose there's a City Council meeting on a full moon? Suppose there's a disaster—a blizzard, say—on the night of a full moon?"

He shrugged. "I'll be ill, or unavoidably detained. These things happen; people will understand. It hasn't been a problem for me before."

"Before you were just a police lieutenant, not the mayor!"

"Detective lieutenant," he corrected her—he was touchy about the distinction between the two sides of Eltonburg's police department, enforcement and investigation. He started the car and looked over his shoulder to be sure the street was clear.

"Whatever. Don't you think that even in Eltonburg, some reporter might stumble across the truth? Old Bill Beasley isn't going to give up his job without a fight, despite the indictments—he's going to have his people checking up on you all through the campaign, just looking for some little flaw. What if he notices you're never around at the full moon? How are you going to explain that? Suppose he says you spend a couple of nights a month at the strip clubs down on Route 8—how are you going to prove you *don't*?"

Dave frowned as he swung the car around the corner onto Main Street. "He couldn't prove I *do*."

"He wouldn't *have* to prove it—what are you going to say instead? That you grow fur and go running through the streets on those nights?"

"Well, why not?" Dave asked. "I've never hurt anyone. Sure, I'm not quite myself when I'm a wolf, but I'm no ravening monster. Even real wolves aren't, and I never *completely* forget who I am. I've chased a few cats, sure, but I never bit or clawed anyone—not even the cats. Not even that damned spitting Persian down on Third Street."

"So you'd just admit the truth? And you think people will vote for a werewolf? You know how old-fashioned some of the people in this town are—and they're Mayor Beasley's biggest supporters. You don't see Beasley standing up in front of the congregation at Calvary Baptist and getting them worked up about the spawn of Satan?"

"I'm not the spawn of Satan…"

"Tell Reverend Henry that!"

He settled into an angry quiet for the remainder of the drive home.

When they were out of the car but still in the garage he burst out, "Damn it, Jenny, I *am* running for mayor, because *somebody* has to to get that crook Beasley and his weaselly flunkies out of office! Yes, I'm a werewolf, and it *is* a drawback, and an inconvenience, and we don't want anyone to find out, but I don't think it's going to come out—maybe Beasley will find out I'm never around at the full moon and will try to make something out of it, but who'll believe him? I'll just say it's private business, all in the family, and you'll back me up, and my mother will, and the voters'll believe us. Why shouldn't they?"

"Because they're human, and they want to believe the worst of any politician they hear about." She sighed. "But if you want to risk it, I won't stop you. You're right, you'd be the best mayor Eltonburg's ever had, and *someone* has to run against Beasley. But I don't *like* it, Dave!"

"No one's asking you to like it," he muttered. He twitched and stumbled as he reached for the door to the house.

Jenny knew the signs. "Get those clothes off," she ordered. "We don't want them torn. That suit cost $600."

He sighed. "Right," he said, pulling off his tie. "I guess I cut it closer than I meant to." He slipped off his jacket and handed it to her.

His fingers were already shrinking by the time he started on his shirt-buttons, the nails thickening into claws. Jenny hurried to help.

Undressing him was a lot more fun the other twenty-odd nights of the month, she thought—he'd be returning the favor, and when the clothes were off he wouldn't drop down on all fours and run off howling.

He might howl a little, or drop to all fours, but he wouldn't run off. And he wouldn't be furry and wagging a tail.

By the time his pants were entirely off he was more wolf than man, and a moment later he was *all* wolf. He trotted to the overhead door and glanced back at Jenny expectantly.

"Oh, all right," she said. She pushed the button, and the door lifted. She stopped it once it was high enough for him to slip out.

"Don't be all night, okay?" she called. "I'd like to get to sleep at a reasonable hour."

He didn't answer; instead he ran off, tongue lolling, down the street.

She sighed, pushed the button to close the door, then stooped and scooped up his clothes. It would serve him right if she *didn't* wait up, and he turned back on the front porch.

Of course, then the neighbors might see him out there naked, which would be hard to live down—and his mayoral hopes would be completely dashed. She trudged into the house and up the stairs, the bundle of clothes in her hand.

An hour later she was in the kitchen, treating herself to a glass of wine, when she heard the growl of a truck's engine and glanced out the front window.

She froze, and set the wineglass down carefully. Then she rounded the corner to the foyer and stepped out the front door onto the porch.

The Animal Control van was cruising slowly down the street; as she watched it stopped under a streetlight, and a man in a gray uniform jumped out, holding a pole with a loop on the end.

A second man came around the front of the van. "There he is!" he called, pointing at the Rosenthals' bushes.

Her heart sank. Dave had been careless, and had been spotted.

She tried to think what she could do. If she claimed he was her dog... well, they had discussed this. He had no collar, no registration, no vaccination tag, and the Animal Control people would insist, quite reasonably, that she take her dog in and get him a license and get his shots taken care of.

Except he couldn't come in for a rabies shot unless the full moon was in the sky, and the vets weren't generally open then.

The two men were rushing for the bushes, one to either side, trapping their prey between them. She saw a flash of gray fur, and the two men dove, pole sweeping around, and then the three were all in a heap on the Rosenthals' lawn, and a moment later the two men were dragging a snarling, struggling wolf toward the van.

"Hey!" she called, stepping down from the porch—she'd find a way around the problem with the shots; maybe she could claim religious grounds for not having it done. "Hey, that's my dog!"

The two men ignored her as they heaved Dave into the cage in the back of the van and slammed it shut. She hurried toward them.

Once the cage was locked, one of them turned to face her.

"That's my dog," she said, pointing.

"He hasn't got a tag," the uniformed man said.

"We hadn't got around to it yet."

"Well, you can't let him run loose with no tag, lady. Eltonburg's got a twenty-four-hour leash law."

"I know, I know, I'm sorry—we've just been so busy…"

"The law's the law, lady. You want him back, you can come down to the pound and claim him, first thing in the morning. And bring your checkbook."

"In the *morning*?" A vision of Dave waking up naked in a cage at the pound appeared before her. "Can't I have him back now? I…I don't feel *safe* without him watching the house!"

The man shook his head. "Sorry, lady. We got rules—we find a dog running loose with no I.D., we take it to the pound. No exceptions. Look, it's just one night."

"But…" She stared at Dave, who stared back at her with frightened yellow wolf-eyes.

The other man slammed the van door. "No exceptions," he said.

The first man said, a bit more kindly, "Look, lady, we used to cut folks some slack on this, but we just got tired of people who let their dogs run around wild, and promised every time oh yeah, we'll be down first thing tomorrow and get a license, we'll put a collar on him right away…and then nothing, and two or three days later we'd pick up the same dog chasing someone's cat up a tree, or digging in someone's lawn, still with no tag. So now we have to be tough about it—some people ruined it for the rest of us, y'know?"

"I know, but…"

"I'm sorry, lady." He turned away.

She watched helplessly as the two men climbed into their vehicle and drove away.

This was a nightmare. They were taking her husband away! And tomorrow morning, when the moon set, he'd turn back to himself there in the dog pound, stark naked, and they'd find him there, and it would be in all the papers, and they'd assume it was a prank, or that he'd been drunk, and any chance he might actually be elected mayor would be gone…

And besides that, it would just be so *embarrassing!*

She couldn't let that happen. She had to get him out of the pound *tonight.*

But how? She supposed there must be someone there at night, but it would just be a guard, and she wouldn't be able to claim Dave—the night watchman, or whoever was there, would just tell her to come back in the morning.

She'd have to *force* them to free Dave.

And how was she going to do *that?* Walk in there with Dave's service weapon and order them to free her dog?

She blinked as she stood on the lawn, watching the Animal Control van round the corner onto Armistead Avenue.

Why *not* just walk in with the gun and demand her dog?

Well, for one thing, they would recognize her, and the night watchman probably had a gun of his own.

But she could get around that…

She stood, thinking hard, for a moment, then turned and went inside.

A few hours later, somewhere between 2:00 and 3:00 in the morning, she cruised down the deserted streets and parked the car in an empty lot two blocks from the pound; she didn't want anyone getting her license number. Then she got out and opened the trunk. She was trembling; it took three tries before she could get the key in the lock.

It opened at last, though, and she reached in and pulled out Dave's bulletproof vest.

She'd never worn it before, and it was too big for her, but she got it on and tied it in place, the kevlar panels pressing uncomfortably on her breasts—it was meant for a man, not a woman, and she was big-chested.

Then she pulled on the old black raincoat, to further hide her figure—she was already wearing black jeans and a black T-shirt, to make it as difficult as possible to see any distinctive details about her. Her feet were in old deck shoes with black stockings pulled up over them, to blur any markings or footprints.

Then came the motorcycle helmet with the dark visor, hiding her face and hair completely—and making it hard to see; it was like wearing sunglasses at night.

It *was* wearing sunglasses at night, really—the tinted visor was meant to serve the same purpose, as well as keeping bugs out of a motorcyclist's teeth.

And then came the scary part, as she lifted Dave's pump-action twelve-gauge out of the trunk.

She had fired the gun exactly three times. The first time she had started at the bang when it went off, but the other two she had been ready for it. She had still completely missed the target Dave had set up for her, and the next day her shoulder had been sore from the recoil, but she had fired it.

Her hands trembling again, she loaded five rounds of birdshot into the magazine. That wouldn't kill anyone, she was pretty sure, but it should be enough to hurt and to scare away anyone who got in her way.

Thus equipped, she marched toward the pound.

There were lights on—not very many, but at least two. That was a good sign; she needed there to be someone in there she could frighten into opening Dave's cage. She reached the main entrance without serious incident, despite being almost blind with the helmet's visor down; she had to lift it to peek now and again. Once she reached the entry she held the shotgun in one hand, and pounded on the door with the other.

Nothing happened; she pounded again.

She was starting to think about what she would do if the night watchman refused to answer when a surly voice called, "Who the hell is it at this hour?"

"It's an emergency," Jenny called. "I need to use your phone."

"Oh, Christ…" The door started to swing open.

Jenny thrust the barrel of the shotgun into the crack, then pushed herself after it, stepping into the building.

She found herself in a narrow hallway, on a scuffed linoleum floor between green concrete walls, lit by bare bulbs in wire cages overhead. Backing away from her was a young man in a dirty T-shirt and torn jeans.

The lights at least let her see through the confounded visor. "Put up your…" she began; then she stopped as she realized he already had both hands raised high.

"Oh god oh god oh god," he said, stumbling backward down the hall. "Listen, there's no money here, I swear there isn't, if there were I'd have stolen it myself."

"I don't want money," Jenny growled, trying to lower her alto voice to a tenor—she had hopes that her disguise hid her sex as well as her face.

"What, did Uncle Bill do something again? Listen, I swear, I didn't have anything to do…"

"Shut up," Jenny growled, aiming the shotgun at the man's nose.

The man—a kid, really—shut up and froze where he was.

Uncle Bill?

"Who are you?" Jenny demanded. "Who's Uncle Bill?"

"I'm Rafe Hayes," the kid said. "Uncle Bill's the mayor. My mom's brother."

"Mayor Beasley is your uncle?" She stared for a moment; yes, there was a resemblance. "He got you this job?"

Rafe nodded eagerly. "You don't want to hurt me," he said. "My uncle would get really pissed."

"I don't care what your uncle wants!" Jenny roared—aware as she did that her bellow was not up to Dave's standards; she didn't have a man's lung capacity or a cop's experience in yelling. "I'm here for my… for the animals." It had occurred to her at the last instant that revealing she was after a particular "dog" might not be wise. She didn't want to attract everyone's attention to that one specific canine, especially not when she'd told the animal control crew that Dave was her dog.

"Oh!" The kid looked suddenly relieved. "You're an animal rights activist? Which group?"

"Uh…Free Our Furry Friends," Jenny improvised hastily.

"I haven't heard of that one…"

"We're new."

"So, like, do you have a specific agenda? Have you got a truck here, or something, to take 'em away?"

"That's not your problem. You just open the doors I tell you to open and keep your mouth shut and your hands where I can see 'em." She jabbed with the gun; Rafe's hands, which had started to descend, rushed back up toward the ceiling.

"Okay," he said, staring at the gun.

"Good. Now, where are the cages?"

Rafe led the way down the corridor and through a door into the depths of the pound. Jenny found herself surrounded by dogs of all sizes and varieties, most of them asleep, a few stirring at this unexpected intrusion. A Great Dane whined at her, and a Pomeranian yapped.

She didn't see Dave.

"Where are the newest ones?" she asked. "The ones they brought in tonight?"

"Oh, they're in the other room," Rafe said. "We don't put 'em in here until the vet's okayed them."

"Show me," she growled. An Alsatian growled in response. "Shut up," Jenny told the dog. Then she gestured with the gun.

Rafe led the way to the holding area; here half the cages were empty, several held cats—and crammed into one of them was a big gray wolf, wide awake and watching them silently.

"Let that one out first," Jenny said, pointing. "That cage is too small for him; it's inhumane."

"Yessir," Rafe said. He fetched a ring of keys from a peg by the door and unlocked Dave's cage. Dave bounded out the instant the door opened, then hesitated, looking at Jenny and Rafe and Jenny's gun.

"Good dog," Jenny said. "You're free now." She waved at the room's open door, and Dave trotted out into the passageway, out of sight.

Now Jenny found herself facing a dilemma; to maintain her cover story of being an animal rights activist she needed to let more animals go—but she didn't particularly *want* a bunch of strays roaming the area.

She hoped they wouldn't do any real harm.

"Let out the others," she said.

Rafe hurried to unlock the cages, releasing the half-dozen cats—and while he was doing that, Jenny stepped back out into the hallway and closed the door.

Dave was waiting there; he looked up at her expectantly. Obviously, he thought she had a plan.

She didn't; she was making this up as she went along. She needed some way to get out of here without making a mess of it all. She wasn't a detective like Dave, with lots of police training…

Police. She looked at him, and then smiled.

"Is that a siren?" she shouted. "Damn it, did you call the cops?"

"No, I swear…!" Rafe called back. A cat yowled and hissed, and Rafe muttered something Jenny couldn't make out.

"You stay in there until I tell you to come out, you…you untrustworthy person, you!"

Lame, Jenny, she told herself. Really lame. "You untrustworthy person"? She giggled. "Come on, Dave," she said. "The car's that way."

Together, woman and wolf ran for the door.

They were almost there when Rafe burst out of the room with a pistol in his hand and fired at her.

The first shot went wild, chipping concrete from the wall, but the sharp bang startled Jenny; she stumbled, but caught herself without falling.

The second shot hit her square in the back and felt like she'd been kicked.

"Ow," she said, as she turned around and raised the shotgun.

Dave had already spun around and was charging down the hallway;

Rafe fired again, this time at the animal plunging toward him.

"No!" Jenny shouted, raising the shotgun—but she couldn't shoot; she might hit Dave.

And Dave didn't seem to be hurt. Rafe fired again, at point-blank range, and then Dave's teeth closed on his wrist. Jenny heard something crunch horribly, and the pistol fell to the floor. Then Rafe went over backward, the wolf on top of him...

"No!" Jenny shouted. "Da... Don't! Get off him!" She raised the shotgun again and pointed it directly at her own husband.

The wolf turned and glared at her, those big yellow eyes almost glowing. For a moment they stared at each other—and Jenny realized she was staring along the barrel of the shotgun, the sights aimed directly at Dave.

She lowered the gun, and Dave leapt off Rafe and ran for the door.

Jenny hesitated until she heard Rafe groan—he was alive and conscious, so she didn't think he could be *that* badly hurt. She turned and yanked open the door; Dave bounded out, with Jenny close behind.

A moment later they were in the car, Dave in the back and Jenny driving. She pulled out of the lot with tires squealing.

They made it home safely, and Jenny staggered inside. She dropped the shotgun, peeled off her black raincoat and her kevlar armor, tossed aside the motorcycle helmet, and then leaned against a wall, panting. Utterly exhausted, she let herself slide down until she was sitting on the floor.

Dave came to her, tongue lolling from his mouth, and put his head in her lap. She petted him once before falling asleep, sprawled there in the foyer.

She was awakened by the transformation; dawn's light was streaming into the house, and the head in her lap had changed from a wolf's to a man's. Dave's eyes, human once again, looked up at her.

"That little bastard shot you!" he said.

"I had your bulletproof vest on," she said. "He shot *you*, and you weren't wearing anything!"

He still wasn't, she noticed admiringly. Her husband was unquestionably a fine-looking man—when he was a man at all.

"Just fur," he said. "I guess the stories are true, though—you need silver bullets to kill a werewolf."

"I would rather never have tested that," she said, stroking his hair.

"Would you really have shot me if I'd done what I wanted to and ripped his throat out?" Dave asked.

"I don't know," Jenny admitted. "And I *really* don't want to test *that* one!"

"Same here," he said. "But I'm glad you aimed—helped me get my temper back under control. I mean, the little bastard *shot* you!"

"I'm fine," Jenny insisted.

Dave sat up. "Let me see your back," he said.

She was too tired to argue; she turned and let Dave pull up her shirt.

"Nasty bruise," he said. "Skin's not broken."

"Told you," she muttered.

"Yeah, you did," he agreed. "And you told me I was crazy to run for mayor, and you were right about that, too." He shook his head. "I probably broke that kid's wrist tonight, and I might've killed him. And... and if the silver bullet part is true, then maybe the contagious bite is true, too, and he'll be out there running around on all fours next month, same as me. That's *bad*, and we'll have to do something about it. This whole werewolf thing—I was kidding myself, Jen. It's not just an inconvenience. It'd never work, me being mayor."

She twisted around to face him. "You're not going to run?" she asked.

"No, I'm not," he said.

She remembered Rafe Hayes talking about his uncle, Bill Beasley. She remembered Rafe making threats and promises and firing that gun wildly. She remembered a dozen other things about Bill Beasley and his family, and she considered what might have to be done to ensure that Rafe Hayes didn't become a public menace at the next full moon.

"Then *I* will," she said.

SOMETHING TO GRIN ABOUT

When the doorbell rang Melody dropped the phone, tossed the stack of bills on the table, and ran to answer it, expecting to see Todd there in the hallway with some new argument. She'd had the last word before he stormed out—she already regretted that, and he wasn't likely to let it stand. Sooner or later he'd be back to shout at her some more.

But it wasn't Todd; it was a uniformed deliveryman, not UPS or FedEx or any she'd seen before, but some courier service with a fancy, unreadable red and blue logo that was blazoned across the man's breast pocket and the back of his clipboard. On the floor by the deliveryman's feet was a large plastic box.

"Melody Duke?" he asked. Before Melody could reply, he held out the clipboard. "Line 8," he said.

She signed, and while she did he lifted the plastic box by a handle on the top and set it inside her door. When she was done she handed the clipboard back and looked down at the box.

"Where's it from?" she asked, but he had already turned away and gotten halfway down the stairs.

She shrugged, started to bend down for a look at the tag wired to the handle, then remembered the phone. She gasped, ran back to the kitchen, snatched up the receiver, and said, "Mother?"

The line was dead; her mother had hung up.

"Oh, *poop*," she said. Not that the discussion had been going anywhere; her mother still didn't like Todd and still didn't think she was safe living here, and Melody had been through all that with her parents any number of times without any minds changing.

She glared at the phone for a moment, then hung it up. Then she realized she had left the apartment door standing open with the mysterious package just inside, and despite what she told her parents this was not *really* a completely safe neighborhood, especially with Todd gone for the moment…

She dashed back to the living room, hauled the plastic crate inside, and slammed the door. For good measure she threw the deadbolt, then flopped down crosslegged on the floor to look over her new acquisition, whatever it was.

The tag on the handle had her name and address in the TO: portion; the FROM: read, "Abigail Duke, 7 Little Moreton Lane, Chester CH6, ENGLAND."

Her British grandmother.

Her grandmother who had just gone into the nursing home.

Her grandmother who owned a cat Melody had promised to look after, a promise that Melody, eight thousand miles away, had not until this moment taken seriously. Now, however, she looked at the plastic crate and realized that yes, this was a pet carrier.

"Ohmigod," she said. She turned the crate around, and yes, there was the door, with rows of little airholes punched in it. She bent down and peered through the holes.

The crate was empty.

Melody blinked, and sat up.

Had her grandmother's cat *escaped* somehow? How could it have? The door was still latched. Had someone stolen it? She'd heard about people who stole cats and sold them to testing laboratories. Or had Grandma Duke maybe gotten confused and sent the crate empty? She'd always been a little dotty, as Melody's father put it, and now she was so old…

Melody had only met her grandmother three or four times, but the old lady had never seemed *that* dotty.

Of course, Todd would never stand for a cat around the place, so it would be just as well if there *was* no cat, but maybe the cat had just found some corner to hide in. Maybe if she took a closer look…

Melody untwisted the wire from around the latch and popped the door open—and out stepped the cat.

It was a very *large* cat, with splendid stripes and a long graceful tail that swayed elegantly as it strolled daintily away from the pet carrier. It was rather plump, but not actually *fat*. Dark tufts projected from the tip of either ear, and it moved in utter silence, its broad and well-furred paws soundless on the well-worn carpet. When it was well clear of its prison it turned, settled to the floor, wrapped its tail about itself, and grinned up at Melody.

She blinked at it in surprise. She'd never seen a cat grin before, and how in the world could a cat that size have hidden from her in that carrier? She looked from the cat to the carrier, then back again, and the cat simply grinned at her.

It was unquestionably a magnificent animal, but still…

"I can't keep a *cat!*" she said, to no one in particular.

The cat tipped its head and looked at her. "Whyever not?" it asked.

Melody blinked again. The cat's expression had been so easy to read, she told herself, that she almost thought she'd heard it speak.

"It's not allowed," she said, not sure why she was saying this aloud. "My lease says no pets. And anyway, Todd's allergic to cats and he hates animals. And my mother would complain about how much it would cost to *feed* a cat. She thinks I'm wasting my money trying to live here instead of staying home with her, and if I were feeding a cat..."

"And how is it your mother's business?"

"Well, that's what *I* keep saying," Melody agreed. "It's my money, and I can spend it any way I like, can't I?"

"I don't know," said the cat. "Can you? You certainly *may*, for all of me, but I wouldn't be sure you *can*."

It was at that point that Melody realized she was holding an actual conversation with a cat.

"You can *talk*!" she said.

"So can you." The cat had a pleasant voice, either a tenor or a low alto, Melody couldn't decide which, with the same lovely British accent as her grandmother.

Which made sense, in a way, if you admitted a cat could talk in the first place. She stared at the cat for a moment, and it grinned placidly back.

"I must be mad," she said at last.

"Oh, we're all mad here," the cat replied.

"I know that line," Melody said, staring at the cat. "I know *all* of this...a talking, grinning cat? A Cheshire-Cat?"

The cat licked the tip of its tail thoughtfully, then remarked, "Your grandmother *does* live in Chester, after all; what *other* sort of cat ought she to have?"

"You can disappear," Melody said accusingly. "That's why the box looked empty!"

The cat did not deign to reply to that.

"This is crazy," Melody said. "That was in a story, it wasn't true. I *must* be mad!"

"Oh," the cat said, "is *nothing* one reads in stories true, then? How curious."

"I didn't mean *that*," Melody said. She stared at the cat.

It wasn't disappearing. It did talk, and it did grin, though.

"This is crazy," Melody said again.

The cat did not bother to reply to that.

"Listen, I really can't keep you here!" Melody said. "The landlord won't stand for it. No pets, it says so in the lease. It's right there in... what are you doing?"

The cat's tail had gotten shorter, she was sure of it—and as she watched, more of it vanished, followed by the animal's hindquarters, and then the rest of it, until nothing was left but the grin.

Melody was not a calm person. She had been known to lose her composure over a misplaced can of soup or a crooked shower curtain. Ordinary catastrophes such as a missed train or broken heel could reduce her to hysterics. Todd's tantrums and invective had brought on tears for *months* before she had gotten used to them. Even so, watching a cat disappear inch by inch, until nothing remained but the grin, when a cat had no business grinning in the first place, was beyond question the single most unsettling thing she had ever seen in her life. It was all she could do to keep from screaming, and a small, strangled squeak did escape, despite her best efforts.

The cat's head reappeared.

"I don't think your landlord would notice me, should I prefer that he not do so," the cat said.

"I guess not," she said weakly.

"I don't suppose you'd have such a thing as a piece of liver about?" the cat asked. "I spent a very long time in that box. I'm hungry." As he spoke, the rest of him abruptly reappeared.

Melody stared at the cat for a moment, then resigned herself to it— the Cheshire-Cat was real, it was here, it was hungry, and it was her responsibility, at least for the moment. "I'll see," she said.

She stumbled to the kitchen and opened the refrigerator, and then, for no reason she was aware of, glanced up.

The Cheshire cat was sitting on top of the refrigerator, curled up with its head on its forepaws, watching her.

Melody screamed.

The cat blinked lazily and continued to stare at her as she caught her breath and, hand on her heart, tried to calm down; then it grinned.

"Did I startle you?" it asked.

"You scared me half to death!" she said. "I left you back in the living room!"

The cat didn't reply to that, but instead looked down and asked, "Is there any liver?"

"No," Melody said as she rummaged through the refrigerator's drawers and compartments. "There's some hamburger—would that do?"

"That would certainly be better than nothing," the cat said. It vanished.

Melody stared at the spot where it had sat for a moment, then turned and cautiously looked around.

The cat was standing on the counter, just under the phone, the tip of its tail brushing the receiver.

That seemed as good a place to feed it as any, Melody decided; she pulled out the styrofoam tray with its left-over lump of ground beef, peeled off the plastic wrap, and put it on the counter.

"Thank you," the cat said. Then it began eating.

By the time Melody had closed the refrigerator and turned back, the hamburger was gone.

"Is there any more?" the cat asked wistfully.

"No," Melody said, very definitely. "No, there isn't. And you can't stay here. Even if you *can* hide from the landlord. My mother would nag me about wasting money, and Todd would be sneezing all the time—if he came in at all! If I kept a cat he might not come back!"

"Who's Todd?"

"My boyfriend. Sort of. I mean, he is, but we fight a lot, or sometimes, when he gets mad about something or I get mad, so he keeps leaving me, but he doesn't really, I mean we don't really break up, because then he always comes back, sooner or later, after he's over being mad or if he gets mad at his new girlfriend, if he has one, which he did twice, the rat, and I apologize and promise not to do whatever it was again, if I can figure out what it was I did. And I make him dinner and we'll be back together until he gets mad again."

The cat stared at her for a moment, then said, "Would you care to reconstruct that statement so that it makes sense, or shall I simply accept the intelligible portions as they stand and ignore the rest?"

"Oh, shut up. I don't know why I'm talking to a *cat*, anyway."

"Perhaps because *I'm* speaking to *you*," the cat suggested.

"Which you have no business doing! Cats can't talk!"

"I can. And I'm quite certain I'm a cat."

"Well, you're not *my* cat. You can't stay here!"

"And where am I to go, then? Your grandmother sent me here because she believed you had promised to take care of me when she could no longer do so; it wasn't *my* idea."

Melody frowned, and looked about helplessly. She could hardly take her grandmother's cat to the pound; she would have to find it a new home.

"Maybe one of my friends could take you," she said.

The cat considered that.

"I'll ask around," she said.

"And for now?"

"You can stay for now, I guess," Melody reluctantly conceded.

"In that case, might I trouble you for some more food? Fish, perhaps, if there's no liver to be had?"

Melody shuddered. "I hate seafood," she said. "Look, I'll go down to the market and buy some cat food, okay? Liver flavor, if they have it."

"Being a cat, I can't honestly say I would be grateful, but I would very much enjoy being properly fed."

"All right, then," Melody said.

When she returned to the living room Melody noticed the now-empty cat carrier, and took a moment to tuck it away out of sight in the coat closet before she prepared to go out. She didn't want Todd seeing it when he came back; he hated pets. He might hit her again; he hadn't lately, but if he found out she had a cat he might.

As she got on her jacket and collected her purse she had the distinct feeling that she had lost her debate with the cat—but that was hardly new; she lost arguments with Todd and with her mother all the time, and she'd probably have lost arguments with her boss and her co-workers at the shop if she'd ever had the nerve to argue with any of them in the first place.

Losing to a cat seemed somehow a bit worse, though, and in retaliation she slammed the door on her way out, which did not trouble the cat at all. It watched her go, then washed itself and settled to sleep on the kitchen counter.

It was awakened a moment later by a loud ring from the telephone. Annoyed, the cat uncurled and glared up at the device.

It rang again.

The cat got to its feet, stretched up a paw, and knocked the receiver from its hook. It fell rattling to the counter, then lay still, the receiver directly in front of the cat.

"Hello?" a voice said. "Melody?"

"I'm afraid Melody isn't here," the cat said into the mouthpiece.

For a moment there was silence, and the cat considered resuming its nap; then the voice said, "Who am I talking to? That's not Todd's voice. Who are you?"

"I'm Melody's new boarder," the cat replied. "Most people just call me Cat."

"Boarder? You mean a roommate? Melody didn't tell me!"

"I've just arrived," the cat said.

"Oh! Well, I...well, that's wonderful. I'm Melody's mother, and I've been telling her for *months* that it wasn't safe living there alone, that it was too expensive...are you splitting the rent?"

"I expect to do my share, Mrs. Duke," the cat answered.

"And...well, what about Todd? I know Melody denied it, but I thought he was living with her, and there isn't *room* for three, is there? *Todd* never paid any rent, of course—I think that's why he kept coming back."

"I haven't met Todd, Mrs. Duke. I believe he's left."

"For good, I hope. I know I shouldn't say such things, but really, Melody can do better, I'm sure, if she'd once get rid of him!"

"I wouldn't know. I do know Todd isn't here, and I am."

"Well, that's wonderful. You have such a lovely accent—is it English?"

"I'm from England, yes. From Cheshire."

"What an interesting coincidence—my mother-in-law lives in Cheshire!"

"Yes, I believe Melody mentioned that."

"You said your name is Catherine?"

"Just Cat will suit me fine, Mrs. Duke."

"Melody isn't there?"

"She stepped out to the market just now."

"Oh. Well, when she gets back, you tell her that I called, okay?"

"I'll do that, Mrs. Duke."

"All right, then. Good-bye!"

"Good-bye." The cat reached up with one paw and pressed down the hook.

Unfortunately, it had no way to hang the receiver back up—that was more than mere paws could handle. The result was a dial tone that was not particularly to the cat's liking, even before it changed to the phone-left-off-the-hook warning. The cat eyed the noisy receiver with distaste. It decided a nap was no longer practical; it hopped down from the counter and ambled into the living room.

The doorbell rang. The cat stopped, midway across the living room, and glared at it.

"Melody?" a male voice called.

At this new intrusion on its privacy the cat wondered whether perhaps this place was insufficiently peaceful to be a suitable residence—but it was, as yet, unfamiliar with any better alternative in the area. With a flick of its tail, it vanished.

A key scraped in the lock, and the apartment door opened; a young man stepped in.

"Melody? It's me—I came back for my stuff!"

The cat watched, unseen.

"Come on, bitch, I know you're here!" the young man shouted.

The cat considered that. It did not much like this loud, ill-mannered person. Furthermore, if this was Todd, he was an obstacle to the cat's remaining comfortably settled here. Something would have to be done about that. Ordinarily, the cat preferred to simply watch humans going about their foolish little lives, but in this case intervention seemed appropriate.

"Is that anything to call her?" the cat asked.

The young man—Todd, the cat supposed him to be—looked about, but was unable to locate a source for the words he had just heard, and concluded that he had just imagined them, or perhaps overheard something from another apartment.

"Damn," he said. He marched in, leaving the door standing wide open, and peered into the kitchen.

No Melody.

He tried the bedroom—also vacant. The bathroom was dark and empty.

He returned to the bedroom and began collecting his belongings from the nightstand and dresser into a laundry bag—and incidentally pocketing a few dollars Melody had left in the bedside drawer.

"Is that money yours?" the cat asked; its head had appeared, floating in mid-air just behind Todd's ear.

He whirled, but the cat's head had vanished again.

"So you're a thief, as well as an exploitive scoundrel?" the cat asked from the other side.

"The bitch owes me!" Todd protested.

"Oh? For what? For putting up with months of abuse? For apologizing when you demand it? For cooking your supper and paying your rent?"

"What is this?" Todd demanded. "Is this place haunted or something? Is this someone's idea of a joke?"

"I suppose it would be too much to suggest this is the voice of your conscience," the cat said musingly.

"I don't have a goddamn conscience, Jiminy Cricket," Todd said sneeringly. "Who *are* you?"

Then he sneezed messily.

"Damn," he said, as he groped for the box of tissues on the dresser.

The cat chose that moment to rematerialize, back on the floor just behind Todd's right leg. It stretched out one large, well-furred paw, extended its claws as far as it could, and then dug them firmly through Todd's sweatsock into his ankle.

"Aaaaugh!" he screamed into the tissue he had been using to wipe his nose.

The cat retracted its claws and vanished.

"What the..." Todd's sentence was interrupted by another sneeze. As he bent over, the cat applied a pawful of claws to Todd's left ankle.

The noise Todd produced in response was a fascinating combination of scream, sneeze, cough, and choke. He staggered back and sat down heavily on the bed, both fists clenched, a soggy tissue dangling from one of them.

"*Who did that?*" he demanded, looking about wildly.

The cat, of course, had vanished again; now its head reappeared behind Todd's right shoulder and spoke.

"I did it," the cat said. "And I'll do more of the same as long as you're here, or if you ever set foot in this apartment again."

"Fine!" Todd said, flinging down the tissue. "That's just goddamn fine, whoever you are! The bitch isn't worth it. Hey, Melody, you hear me? You ain't worth it. I can find another girl who'll treat me better!" He looked down at his ankles and saw blood seeping through his socks.

"Oh, Jesus, I'm bleeding," he said. "Damn it, look at that! Look what you did! Jesus!" He dabbed at the blood and only succeeded in spreading it further. He snatched a handful of tissues from the box and stuffed them into his socks as makeshift dressings, and was interrupted several times by sneezes as he did so.

"Doesn't she ever dust in here?" he grumbled. "What the hell am I sneezing at?"

The cat considered the sight of Todd, sitting on the edge of the bed and bent down to stuff tissues in his socks, and was unable to resist.

Todd felt a sudden weight on his back, and the mysterious needles that had gouged his ankles suddenly scraped across the back of his neck.

"*All right!*" he said, jumping up. He whirled, but saw no sign of his attacker. "All right, I'm going! Jesus, give me a minute!"

"No," the cat said.

"Oh, crap," Todd said, grabbing a final clump of tissues with one hand and his nose with the other as he fought back a fresh attack of sneezing. He snatched up his laundry bag and fled, hobbling.

The cat watched him go.

When Todd was out of sight, and his footsteps had faded to inaudibility, the cat pushed the apartment door closed.

The phone was still making its annoying buzzing noise, but the bedroom was reasonably quiet; the cat jumped up on the bed, curled up, and went to sleep.

Several minutes later Melody returned, and discovered, as she fumbled for her key, that the door was unlocked. Worried, she opened it.

"Todd?" she called.

No one answered. She stepped in and looked around.

Nothing was out of place, so far as she could see. The phone was buzzing, though; she went to the kitchen, put her bag of groceries on the counter, and hung the receiver up.

She didn't remember leaving it off the hook. "Todd?" she called.

"He isn't here," the cat replied. "He was, though. He collected a few things, and then left."

"He did?" Melody frowned. Todd almost always left a few things behind; that was one reason she always expected him to come back eventually.

"And your mother called," the cat said.

"She did? How do you know?"

"I knocked the phone off the hook," the cat admitted.

"Oh, she's probably furious!" Melody snatched at the receiver and dialed.

A moment later, as Melody was making frantic apologies, her mother said, "Oh, that's all right—but why didn't you *tell* me about that lovely Cat?"

"Cat?" Melody said, horrified.

"Your new roommate! She sounds wonderful; I'll have to meet her sometime."

Melody glanced at the cat, which stood in the kitchen door, grinning at her. "Roommate," she said weakly. "Right."

Five minutes later Melody hung up the phone and glared at the cat.

"I don't know how you did that," she said.

"Your mother doesn't seem to object to my presence here," the cat remarked.

"No, she doesn't," Melody agreed. "You said Todd was here?"

"Well, a young man who had a key was here."

"That was Todd. Did he see you?"

"No, I don't believe he did."

"Well, *that's* something, anyway."

"Did you buy food for me?"

"Oh, yeah." Melody fished a can of cat food out of the bag of groceries and slapped it into the electric can opener.

She watched thoughtfully as the cat ate.

"All right," she said at last, as it licked its paws after finishing, "you can stay until Todd comes back. But the minute he's back, out you go."

The cat curled up and began to purr. "That," it said, "will suit me just fine."

BEST PRESENT EVER!

Arnie Bellingham, age seven, looked at the big package sadly. He made no move toward opening it.

He had asked for it, but he had hoped Santa would somehow know he didn't really want it. Alas, it seemed Santa's magic wasn't that thorough—or perhaps Arnie had done something to annoy Santa, and this was his punishment. He didn't *think* he had been naughty, but the big man's standards were a little vague.

"Aren't you going to open it?" his mother asked.

Arnie looked up and tried to smile. "I think I'll wait until I can take it outside," he said.

"Well, okay," she said, "but after all the fuss you made about wanting it, I thought you'd at least want to take it out of the box."

"I will," Arnie assured her. "I'm…I'm *savoring* it."

She smiled, and leaned over against Arnie's Dad, nuzzling his ear. Arnie seized his opportunity, picked up the big box, and headed back to his room. Once there he set the box on his bed and stared at it.

He really didn't want a Super Mega Soaker—but Jayden Abbott, three houses up the street, did, and Jayden had been far too naughty to expect Santa to cooperate. Jayden's parents had told him flat out that they knew he was on the naughty list, and had been pretty blunt that *they* weren't about to give him any weapons, either, not even toy ones—they did seem to have some issues with their son's behavior, even though Arnie was pretty sure they didn't comprehend the true extent of Jayden's evil. When Arnie had hinted to them that Jayden had been bullying him, the Abbotts had talked about Jayden getting carried away sometimes, Jayden didn't always know his own strength, and he and Arnie would just have to work it out between themselves. They had told Jayden to behave himself, and Jayden had been apologetic and remorseful—until the instant his mother was out of sight, whereupon he had smiled hatefully at Arnie and warned him not to try *that* again, if he didn't want more of his toys broken or stolen.

His own folks had been even less help. When Arnie had told them Jayden stole his stuff, they had punished him for lying to cover up losing things without even *asking* any of the Abbotts about it. Mrs. Abbott would at least look, and if Jayden hadn't had a chance to hide whatever it was yet, Arnie got it back. Temporarily.

But Jayden never got punished, and the thefts and breakage and threats continued. Arnie couldn't even avoid Jayden; since they were the only two boys near their age in the neighborhood, their mothers *insisted* they play together. Mrs. Abbott said Arnie was a good influence on her boy, and Arnie's Mom was always worried about Arnie spending too much time alone, so they were thrown together whether they liked it or not. Which suited Jayden just fine. It meant he had someone to hit, and a source of goodies to swipe.

Arnie had learned not to ask for anything expensive for his birthday or Christmas, since Jayden would just steal it or break it, so his folks had been surprised when he asked Santa for the biggest water gun available. They never seemed to guess it was because Jayden had grabbed him from behind on Thanksgiving, when the grown-ups were all inside getting their dinners ready, and had twisted his arm almost up to his neck, and had *ordered* him to ask for it if he didn't want to get the snot beat out of him. Jayden and Arnie both knew that Arnie would never get to use it—not unless being Jayden's target counted. The best Arnie could hope for was that Jayden would fill it with water, instead of something more inventive and disgusting, before turning it on him.

Now it was Christmas morning, and the Super Mega Soaker was here, using up all Arnie's credit with Santa for the year. He sighed as he stared at the box.

The box moved.

Arnie blinked, and stared harder. Had he imagined that? He took a step closer.

The box wobbled.

It shouldn't do that, Arnie was pretty sure. He had been planning to deliver it to Jayden unopened, so that Jayden couldn't blame him if there was anything busted or missing, but now he was having second thoughts. He put a hand on the box to steady it, and felt it jerk again.

"Okay," he said to no one. "*That's* not right."

"Hello?" a squeaky voice said, from somewhere inside the box. "Is someone out there?"

Arnie felt a sudden sinking dread. Santa had messed up, and put the wrong toy in the box. This was some talking teddy bear or something, not a Super Mega Soaker at all. If Jayden didn't get his water gun, Arnie might find himself losing a few baby teeth earlier than he wanted. He grabbed the scissors off his desk and attacked the box. A moment later he pried up a flap and started to look inside.

A tiny hand reached up out of the box, and the squeaky voice said, "About time!"

Arnie stepped back, and stared as an elf climbed out of the box.

Arnie hadn't even been sure that elves really existed. Sure, he knew Santa was supposed to have a bunch of elves working for him, making toys, but Arnie wasn't stupid; he had noticed that Santa's presents arrived looking exactly like the ones in the toy stores, so he had figured that Santa bought them all from regular factories, and the elves and the workshop at the North Pole were just a story. He had thought there might be a warehouse up in Canada or Alaska somewhere, but not a workshop at the North Pole.

But the green-clad, pointy-eared thing staring at him out of the Super Mega Soaker box was unquestionably an elf, and not a talking teddy bear.

"Hey," it said. "Where am I?"

"You're in my room," Arnie replied.

The elf looked around, taking in the Transformers bedspread and the shelves of junk. "Yeah," it said. "I can see that. But where's your room?"

"In my house," Arnie said. Then, realizing what the elf probably meant, he added, "1205 East Palmcroft Drive, Tempe, Arizona."

"Arizona?" The elf scratched his ear. "That's one of the United States, right?"

"Uh…yeah," Arnie said.

"That's all right, then," the elf said. He looked out the window. "Pretty sunny for December, isn't it?"

Arnie looked out the window as well. He shrugged. "About the same as always," he said.

The elf jumped out of the box, the bells on the curled toes of his shoes jingling, and scampered over to the window. He shaded his eyes as he looked out.

"Where's the *snow*?" he said.

"Snow?" Arnie was baffled. "It doesn't snow here."

It was the elf's turn to look baffled. "What?"

"It doesn't snow here," Arnie repeated. "Anyway, who are you, and what are you doing here? Why were you in that box?"

"I'm Dimble," the elf said, holding out a hand, which Arnie cautiously shook. "I escaped! They always told me there was no way out, that we were all trapped there for life, but I did it—I got out, and here I am!"

"Escaped from *where*?" Arnie asked, confused.

"From Santa's workshop, of course!" Dimble looked out the window again. "It *really* doesn't snow here? I'd heard there were places like that, but I thought they were a myth! If it doesn't snow, how does Santa land his sleigh?"

"I don't know," Arnie said. "I never thought about it." He hesitated, then asked, "What do you mean, escaped?"

"I got away! I'm free!"

That didn't make any sense to Arnie. "Was Santa keeping you prisoner or something?"

"Well, *duh*!" Dimble said. "Have you ever seen an elf anywhere else but the North Pole?"

"No," Arnie admitted.

"You think that's because we all *want* to stay in that frozen wasteland? Uh uh. It's because the only way in or out is in Santa's sleigh, unless you want to walk across about a thousand miles of ice and snow."

That didn't sound right at *all*. "But I thought Santa was a good guy!" Arnie protested.

"That's what they *want* you to think," Dimble said, tapping a finger on his head. "That's what they tell all of us. They say it isn't safe anywhere else, that elves were almost extinct until Santa brought our ancestors to the Pole, but I don't buy it. He just wants a supply of cheap labor, so he set up his workshop in the middle of nowhere and tells us scare stories about the rest of the world."

"You really think so?" Arnie asked.

"I'm *sure* of it!"

"But *you* got out."

"Sure, by hiding in that box," Dimble said, pointing at the empty carton. "Santa delivered me here right on schedule. But none of the others had the brains and nerve to try it."

"Wow," Arnie said.

"Yeah. I got tired of copying all the toys kids asked for, so I buried that Super Mega Soaker in a snowdrift behind the brewery, and got my buddy Kibz to seal me in the box and make sure it went on the sleigh, and here I am!"

That reminded Arnie of something. "The Super Mega Soaker?"

"Yeah."

"It's in a snowdrift at the *North Pole*?"

"Yeah." Dimble saw the horrified expression on Arnie's face, and said, "Is that a problem? I know you asked for one, kid, but I can make it up to you somehow—I'm pretty good with my hands."

"It wasn't for me," Arnie said, swallowing. "It was for Jayden, up the street. He's going to beat me up if I don't give it to him."

Dimble looked shocked. "He *what*?"

"He'll beat me up."

It was the elf's turn to look horrified. "But...but...nice kids don't *do* that!"

"He's *not* a nice kid," Arnie said. "He's a naughty one. That's why he had *me* ask for the Super Mega Soaker—Santa never brings him *anything*."

"But...but that's not *right*," Dimble said. "Good kids are supposed to get their presents to keep. Naughty kids aren't supposed to take them!"

Arnie grimaced. "Tell Jayden that."

"I will!" Dimble exclaimed. "You just wait and see, I will!" Then he hesitated. "Um...how old is this Jayden?"

"Eight," Arnie said. "And he's big for his age."

"Hey, I can take an eight year old!" Dimble said, puffing out his chest. "Just you wait and see."

Arnie looked at the elf, which stood scarcely a foot and a half tall including his green cap, and tried not to show his disbelief. Maybe Dimble knew kung fu or something, he thought.

"You show me this bully," Dimble said, "and I'll give him the thrashing he deserves!"

"Okay," Arnie said. "I'll take you over to his house this afternoon." Maybe that would take care of the problem of the missing water gun—Arnie could show Jayden the empty box and tell him there'd been a screw-up, and the elf would back up his story, even if he couldn't beat Jayden up.

Or maybe the elf really *could* beat up Jayden. Elves were magical, weren't they? Dimble had somehow survived the trip from the North Pole with no food, water, or air-holes; maybe he was stronger than he looked.

Nonetheless, Arnie was wary, a few hours later, as he approached Jayden's house, cutting across the back yards as usual. Dimble was back in the box, which was tucked under Arnie's arm. Jayden liked to surprise his visitors. He had once surprised Arnie with a whiffle bat to the head, and when Arnie protested Jayden had shrugged and said, "Hey, it's just plastic. Be glad I didn't have a wood one."

Arnie rounded the final fence cautiously, and there was Jayden, throwing a kickball up and catching it. He spotted Arnie, and said, "*There* you are!" as he flung the ball straight at Arnie's face. "What took so long? Did you get it?"

Arnie ducked, and the ball bounced off the plank fence, ricocheting harmlessly off to the side. Neither boy paid any attention to it as Jayden focused his attention on the box under Arnie's arm.

"You *did* get it!" he said. "Bring it here!"

"There's a problem," Arnie said, but then Jayden was grabbing the box and pulling it free, and Arnie decided he didn't need to say anything. Jayden would find out for himself, soon enough.

Jayden dropped the box to the ground, fell to his knees, and tore open the cardboard flaps—and a foot and a half of angry elf jumped up and socked him in the nose.

"Hey!" Jayden said, and Arnie expected him to grab at his nose— Arnie knew that that's what *he* would have done. Jayden, though, was made of sterner stuff, and instead he grabbed at Dimble's throat, closing both hands around the elf's neck.

The elf's eyes widened in surprise, and he thrust a tiny fist at Jayden's chin. It glanced off as the boy jerked his head aside.

"You wanna fight?" Jayden said. "Okay, let's fight, then!" He stood up, his hands still locked around Dimble's neck.

Dimble flailed wildly, kicking both feet at Jayden's belly, both hands jabbing at his face. Jayden did nothing to avoid these blows, beyond blinking whenever one came near his eyes.

Arnie watched, not saying a word. It was quite clear that Dimble did *not* know kung fu, or have any sort of magical fighting prowess.

Jayden let the elf pound futilely for a moment, then turned, took two long steps, and slammed the elf against the fence.

"Owww!" Dimble squealed.

Jayden swung again, and a third time, and Dimble went limp. Arnie gasped. Jayden held his captive up and looked at it.

"Holy jeez," he said. "It's an elf!"

"Yeah," Arnie said.

"Cool! Where'd you get it?"

"It was in the box instead of the gun," Arnie said.

"No foolin'? Wow." Jayden stared at the dangling creature. "That might be even better than a soaker!"

Arnie made a noise that he hoped Jayden would take as agreement.

"Here, you take it," Jayden said, handing Dimble to Arnie. "I gotta show my mom, but she says never to bring animals in the house."

"I don't think an elf is—" Arnie began, as he took the limp elf from his tormentor.

"You hold on, okay? If you let it get away I'll knock the crap outta you."

Before Arnie could reply, Jayden had turned and was running toward the house, bellowing, "Hey, Mom! You gotta see this!"

Arnie stood, and watched him go. Then he looked down at Dimble, and saw one eye open.

"Is he gone?" the elf whispered.

"Yeah," Arnie said. "But he's coming right back."

"Then let me get the heck out of here!"

"I thought you were going to thrash him."

Dimble blushed. "I guess I misjudged a little," he said.

"A little," Arnie agreed.

"Come on, kid, let me go! Nobody's supposed to know elves are still around. I can't let him keep me prisoner—if I was gonna do that, I might as well have stayed home!"

"What'll you do, though? Where will you go?"

Dimble let out a shuddering sigh. "I don't know," he said. "I guess I'll head north."

"Back to the North Pole?"

"Eventually, maybe. Come on, kid, don't let him take me!"

"He'll beat me up if I let you go."

"No, he…I…oh, heck, kid, I'm sorry, but please…"

Arnie sighed deeply. He dropped Dimble to the lawn. "Merry Christmas," he said.

"Thanks, kid—you *are* on the nice list!" Dimble tipped his hat, and then scurried away. He moved much faster than Arnie would have expected, and was long gone by the time Jayden and his mother appeared.

"Come on, Mom!" Jayden said, pulling at his mother's hand. "You gotta see the elf!"

"I'm coming. Hello, Arnie."

"Hello, Mrs. Abbott," Arnie replied.

"Where is it, Arn?" Jayden demanded.

"Where's what?" Arnie asked. Jayden wouldn't hit him with his mother right here, he knew that. As for later, Jayden was already going to kick his butt for letting Dimble go; lying about it probably wouldn't make it any worse.

Jayden stared at him. "What are you, retarded? Where's the *elf?*"

Arnie was committed now. "What elf?" he asked.

"Don't be stupid," Jayden said. "The elf. The one that was here! The one I beat up!"

"I don't know what you're talking about."

Jayden stared at him, then turned to his mother. "It was here, Mom, I swear! A real elf, with a funny hat and jingle bells on its feet!"

"Jayden, elves aren't real," Mrs. Abbott said. She sounded worried. "You're old enough to know that."

"But I saw it, Mom! One of Santa's elves! It tried to hit me, so I picked it up and knocked it around, and I gave it to Arnie to hold, and he let it get away!"

"There are no elves, Jayden. Santa isn't real. We told you that." She glanced at Arnie, her expression momentarily even more worried.

She probably thought she shouldn't have said that in front of him, but it didn't bother Arnie; he'd heard grown-ups say Santa wasn't real before. He figured it was just more weird adult stuff, like all that politics talk, or the kissing thing.

"But I saw it!" Jayden insisted. "I held it in my hands! I hit it against the fence!"

She turned back to her son, her expression still worried, but now angry as well. "You did what?"

"I hit it against the fence. It was kicking me!"

She turned to Arnie. "Did you see this?"

"No, ma'am."

"Did he have an animal of some kind that he was abusing?"

"I don't know, ma'am. I didn't see one."

"Did you see an elf?"

"No, ma'am. Of course not. Elves are just baby stories."

Jayden's mouth fell open as he stared at Arnie. "You *liar*!" he said.

Arnie didn't say anything; he just tried to look innocent.

Mrs. Abbott grabbed Jayden by the arm. "I've had enough of this," she said. "We've put up with you being rude and destructive too long, because boys will be boys and we thought you'd outgrow it, but now even your *fantasies* are about hitting things! I don't care what your father says, Jayden, you are going to see a therapist, and you are going to stop telling stupid lies, and you are going to start behaving like a civilized human being. It's Christmas, and here you are making up stories about hurting *Santa's elves*!" She looked at Arnie. "Arnie, go home, please. I'm afraid Jayden is not going to play with you today."

"Okay, Mrs. Abbott."

"I think Jayden may be going to a new school soon, too."

"I'm sorry to hear that," Arnie lied.

"Run on home."

"Yes, ma'am." Arnie turned, picked up his empty box, and headed home. As he walked, he heard Jayden screaming wild protests about elves and stolen water guns and Santa cheating.

He saw no sign of Dimble. He hoped the elf was okay.

As he arrived in his own yard his mother was standing by the back door. "Oh, *there* you are!" she said. She saw the open box in his hand. "How's the squirt gun?"

"Fine," Arnie said. "I let Jayden borrow it."

She frowned. "I'm not sure that was a good idea," she said. "Oh, I found this in the wrapping." She held out a booklet.

Arnie took it, and saw it was the instructions for the Super Mega Soaker. It was sticky on the back—apparently it had been stuck to the outside of the box. "Thanks, Mom," he said. He opened it, mildly curious about the toy he hadn't gotten.

There was handwriting in it, in green ink. Startled, Arnie glanced up at his mother, but she was already walking back into the house. If she had written a note in it, Arnie thought she would have stayed around to watch him read it. He looked down at the instructions.

"Arnie—" the note said, in unfamiliar, old-fashioned handwriting that was surprisingly easy to read. "You didn't really want the Super Mega Soaker anyway, did you? And Dimble needed a chance to see the world. Hope it works out. Don't worry, I'll find Dimble and pick him up before he gets into too much trouble. Merry Christmas!" It was signed, "Santa."

Arnie stared at it, and almost tripped as he walked into the kitchen door.

"So did you like your present?" his mother asked from where she stood by the sink.

Arnie looked up at her, and broke into the biggest grin he'd worn since the Abbotts moved in up the street. He looked at the empty box, at the instructions, and at the box again.

"I loved it!" he said. "Best present ever!"